T✳H✳E BONE YARD

INTRODUCTION BY
DEAN R. KOONTZ

Stories by
F. PAUL WILSON
SHERI S. TEPPER
RAY GARTON

PUBLISHED IN HARDCOVER
AS *NIGHT VISIONS 6*

BERKLEY BOOKS, NEW YORK

The publishers would like to express their gratitude to the following people. Thank you: Dawn Austin, Kathy Jo Camacho, Stan and Phyllis Mikol, Wayne Sommers, Dr. Stan Gurnick PhD, Kurt Scharrer, Bertha Curl, Ken Morris, Gary Fronk, Linda Solar, Greg Manchess, Luis Trevino, Raymond and Teresa and Mark Stadalsky, Howard Morhaim, Chet Williamson, Stan Wiater, Chelsea Quinn Yarbro, Dennis Etchison, Tom Pas, Tony Hodes, Ken and Lynda Fotos, and Ann Cameron Williams.

And of course, special thanks go to the most important people to this book. Without them this collection would not exist: F. Paul Wilson, Sheri S. Tepper, Ray Garton, and Dean R. Koontz.

Originally published in hardcover as
Night Visions 6.

This Berkley book contains the complete text of the original hardcover edition. It has been completely reset in a typeface designed for easy reading and was printed from new film.

THE BONE YARD

A Berkley Book / published by arrangement with
Dark Harvest Press

PRINTING HISTORY
Dark Harvest edition published 1988
Berkley edition / May 1991

ISBN: 0-425-12726-5

A BERKLEY BOOK® TM 757,375
Berkley Books are published by The Berkley Publishing Group,
200 Madison Avenue, New York, New York 10016.
The name ''Berkley'' and the ''B'' logo
are trademarks belonging to Berkley Publishing Corporation.

PRINTED IN THE UNITED STATES OF AMERICA

10 9 8 7 6 5 4 3 2 1

Introduction

Every introduction for a book like this is expected to begin with an overview of the horror field.

That is how I will begin.

Every introduction for a book like this is expected to tell you something about the contributors and say good things about them.

Happily, I can—and will—do that. I will say a few things about the whole *Night Visions* enterprise, as well.

Every introduction for a book like this is expected to be little more than boosterism, proclaiming the unalloyed wonderfulness of the entire genre.

I'm going to disappoint you on that one.

If we treasure dark fantasy as entertainment and art, we have to be honest when we write about the current state of the field. A lack of honesty in such matters only contributes to the corruption of the genre by encouraging sloppy thinking and writing.

1

• • •

The genre.

Jack (not his real name) was a major figure in the publishing industry, not involved in the horror genre but at least passingly familiar with it, and he went to *The Exorcist* when it was first released in theaters. He told me that he wanted to see if the film—and the book from which it was derived—seemed to presage a new direction in popular entertainment, which was what people were telling him. (And did it ever!) Popular entertainment was his business, and he had to study trends. A confirmed atheist, he was not expecting to be scared by a story that relied so heavily on superstitious mumbo-jumbo. If anything, he expected to be highly amused.

According to his wife, by the time the end-credits rolled up and he left the theater, he was pale and deeply disturbed. He refused to talk about the film, a distinct departure from his habit of analyzing every movie he saw and gleefully demolishing the bad ones. He was an intelligent man, quick-witted, acerbic; listening to him critique either a good or terrible movie was always entertaining. This time he had nothing to say. Two days later, when he had finished reading the novel, he was silent about that too. "I don't think I can talk about it," he said to me, "at least not sensibly. I find it too disturbing, and I don't *like* the way it disturbs me, so I'm just going to put it out of mind."

He was not a lapsed Catholic whose buried guilt the film had resurrected. In fact he was not even from a Christian family. Nor had the movie stirred up guilt over his abandonment of Judaism, for his parents had not kept that ancient faith or inculcated it in him; having never been in the embrace of Judaism in the first place, he could not have abandoned it. He had been a lifelong nonbeliever, secure in his atheism—and yet *The Exorcist*, relying on religious mythology and archetypes for its effects, full of the mumbo-jumbo that he ridiculed and despised, had not only frightened him but left him emotionally and intellectually shaken.

Good horror stories have a power equal to or exceeding that of all other types of fiction, and at times their effect can be more profound than stories in other genres.

The Exorcist isn't even particularly well written. It's filled with clumsy syntax and is often grammatically weak. William Peter Blatty's imagery is frequently flat, his metaphors sometimes less than appropriate. He does have several unique narrative devices that work splendidly, and he has an unerring sense of narrative pace and structure, but his strengths do not outweigh his weaknesses as a stylist. Nevertheless *The Exorcist* is a good book, a superior book, and it deserves to be the bestselling horror novel of all time—which it is, by a factor of three or four.

Blatty's weaknesses of style are more than balanced by his tremendous conviction. His novel is not just a spook show. Blatty wants to do more than scare you. He wants to move you. He wants to make you think. He wants to help you reaffirm your faith, if you have any, or make you doubt the wisdom of faithlessness. Many of the scenes in his book are complex, functioning on multiple thematic levels, and no scene is entirely devoid of a greater meaning that transcends plot.

As I write this, seventeen years after the publication of Blatty's book, the horror genre is in the middle of a growth cycle. More new books than ever are being published in the field. Major houses are launching horror lines, after the upstart TOR Books showed them that the concept was viable. We are unquestionably in a boom.

And we are overwhelmed by trash.

Sturgeon's Law—which states that ninety percent of *everything* is crap—needs to be revised to be applicable to the horror field these days; the percentage has to be raised. Attempting to read nineteen out of any twenty horror novels, a well-educated person will despair, for so many writers seem never to have learned the basic rules of grammer and syntax. Most books and stories have nothing to say; they speak neither to the mind nor heart; they are clockwork mechanisms laboring mightily to bring forth, on schedule, not a cuckoo bird but a vague shiver of ersatz fear.

In the days when comparatively little horror was published,

prior to Ira Levin's excellent *Rosemary's Baby* in 1967, the reader could find more of quality than he can now, when the bookstore shelves sag under the weight of volumes in the genre. The roots of modern horror fiction can be traced to the work of exceptional writers who knew how to spin magic into sentences and whose work was unfailingly literate: H.P. Lovecraft, Frank Belknap Long, Fritz Leiber, Joseph Payne Brennan, Ray Bradbury, Richard Matheson, Theodore Sturgeon . . . When Levin and Blatty proved that horror could be sold to a broad audience beyond the small group of diehard fans, the genre seemed poised for a long golden era.

But something went wrong.

Oh, yes, we've enjoyed some superior work in the seventeen years since *The Exorcist*. Stephen King's *The Shining* and *The Dead Zone*, come to mind. Dan Simmon's excellent *Song of Kali*, Patrick Suskind's *Perfume*, and a couple of dozen other books and a double score of shorter pieces by a number of writers spring to mind. But even if I used the precious space here to list them all, it would be a strikingly short compilation of first-rate work given the time span and the thousands of titles published therein. And we see less prime stuff these last few years than just a decade ago.

I am not the only one to have noticed this sad state of the field. The subject frequently comes up in conversations with other concerned writers. At the 1988 American Booksellers Association convention, Charles Brown, editor-publisher of *Locus*, was first to brace me about the "deplorable state of modern horror," and before the weekend was done, half a dozen other people in publishing raised the same issue with me, unprompted. They seemed to feel that my year as the first president of Horror Writers of America might have given me some special insight.

It didn't. What it gave me was heartburn.

But I have been thinking about the state of our microcosm, and several observations are unavoidable.

Too many writers have turned away from their responsibilities as storytellers and craftsmen and artists, and instead of honing their talent and skills through hard work and polish,

have tried to hold the reader by repeatedly shocking him, lay-
ering on the gore and violence with the misguided notion that
vividly portrayed evisceration can substitute for storytelling,
that splatter can compensate for lousy writing. Their only theme
seems to be nihilism, which is singularly unattractive to the
majority of readers, and which is boring to any reader who
thinks. Nihilism, after all, is the intellectual conceit of the
perpetual adolescent, no more interesting to the mature mind
than Fruit Loops are to the mature palate.

One reasonably well-known writer, one who stands near the
center of this current trend, has written and spoken often about
what he sees as the "virtue" of pushing into new realms of
perversity and repulsion. He argues that those who see this
path as an artistic and moral dead end are essentially brothers-
under-the-skin of narrow-minded born-again Christians! That
is intellectual McCarthyism. Furthermore he has written that
if one condems horror fiction that sets out *only* to repulse and
scare, such condemnation is akin to dismissing comedy because
it seeks only to induce laughter, or love poetry because it deals
only with love. But those comparisons are, of course, specious.
Good comedy plays upon our fears and hopes and dreams,
turning a mirror on us, reflecting our emotional and intellectual
matrices in all their glorious complication. Can anyone see a
Woody Allen comedy or a Steve Martin standup routine or an
old Chaplin film—and be oblivious of the fact that they are
comprised of threads of love, hate, joy, fear, hope, despair,
and every other human emotion, and that they hope to do *more*
than just evoke laughter? Can anyone read the love poetry of
Shelley, Keats, Byron, Browning, and other great poets, and
really believe that the work is *only* about love? If that is the
level of intellectual activity among those who propound the
superiority of splatter fiction, no wonder so much of that
subgenre is dreadful.

Don't get me wrong. I am not opposed to violence and gore
in fiction. Previously, when expressing my distaste for this
Grand Guignol school of horror, I've been accused of being a
fuddy duddy who doesn't believe in spilling blood on the page.
Such an accusation can only be made by those who have never

read my books. *Whispers* contains a few scenes of brutality exceeding anything I've read in splatter fiction, and even *Watchers* is not without its descent into "wet terror." Violence and its biological consequences are a legitimate part of all fiction, not just horror, but it is ultimately pointless to write about them to the virtual exclusion of other aspects of life and human interaction, and it is a sign of moral and intellectual bankruptcy to rely on them as the primary means of sustaining a reader's interest in a story. If nothing else, it's just plain *lazy*.

At the other end of the spectrum, there are those who insist that only quiet horror—*very* quiet horror—is worthwhile. In their stories, the violence is nearly always offstage. Paragraphs are spent evoking fear through long descriptions of the whisper of the wind, the queer shape and movement of a shadow, or the shudder of a leaf. Or, in the case of some minimalists, nothing at all is described in detail—not wind or shadows or shuddering leaves or even *characters*—and the prose seeks to evoke fear by the use of spare images and skeletal storylines that, by their very coldness and hollowness, stir thoughts of death and loneliness and despair. The quiet-horror writers tend to write better prose, line by line, than those who wade gleefully hip-deep in blood and perversion. But to my way of thinking, while quiet horror is preferable to blood-bath stories, it is too frequently carried to extremes in the writer's attempt to escape association with "popular" fiction, and the result is horror without human association, horror without meaning; it's as boring and empty as mindless splatter tales.

Both extremes usually fail as fiction because they do not deal with the splendid *gaudiness* of human life, with the rich brew of emotions that are a part of everyone's existence every day. They condense experience, as fiction should, but then they filter it through one type of graying cloth or another, straining out the more interesting colors, producing monotone novels and stories.

The worst problem with current horror fiction, aside from the woefully weak prose style of some of its writers, is that most of its creators fall into one or the other of these camps, and too few work in the middle ground. After countless experiments, after the waxing and waning of hundreds of schools of writing since the time of Dickens, anyone familiar with the broader world of English-language fiction can see that virtually all of the important and lasting works have been those exploring human experience from an all-inclusive point of view, concentrating on every aspect of human existence, limiting themselves in no way, focusing on joy as well as terror, on love as well as hatred, on sentiment as well as cynicism.

In spite of its flaws, *The Exorcist* is a good book because it includes both quiet and noisy horror, scenes both subtle and coarse. It succeeds because it is not only about pain and death and darkness but about self-sacrifice and love and light; the public responded to the novel not primarily because young Regan's head turns around 360° or because she vomits all over people, but because Father Karras gives up his own immortal soul to save a child *who is essentially a stranger to him*. "Take me," he tells the demon in the girl, and it's him that the demon has wanted all along. How appealing. And how true of what is best in us. But splatter writers would be appalled by the sentiment, and those writing quiet horror would no doubt find the priest's commitment too gaudy.

Blatty's novel is also better than much of what followed it because of its aforementioned conviction, which is often lacking in both splatter and quiet horror. Too many writers of both schools tell us stories of possessed children or demon-haunted places, dwelling in great detail on the nature of Evil, with a capital E—but do not themselves believe in the existence of Good as a living force in the universe. Their demons, therefore, don't ring true, and their Evil is as convincing as that of the figures in a carnival funhouse, for if Good as a living force does not exist, neither does Evil as a living force, since all of our mythology requires the existence of the former before the latter can even come into existence. That leaves the author dealing with good and evil in the lower case, whether he knows it or not. Blatty is a Catholic. His conviction comes through; his willingness to include his faith in the novel, in a time when faith is out of fashion among writers and critics, puts the Evil in his novel in perspective and makes for a well-rounded story that *convinces* and that has something worthwhile to say about life, regardless of whether the reader is a believer, an agnostic, or an atheist.

Of course, it is not necessary for the horror writer to be a person of faith in order to write fiction of real depth, though he might be well-advised to shy from *supernatural* horror if he is, in fact, an atheist; he will bring no truth to the work and, instead of creating worthwhile fiction from his rationalist worldview, will be doing little more than grinding out hack work about things that in his heart he views as the delusions of the immature. Whether a writer is a believer or an atheist, he can write first-rate, well-rounded horror fiction only by stepping out of the limitations of a single school, by being as unafraid of sentiment—and even sentimentality—as he is unafraid of gore and violence.

Why are horror writers so much more polarized than those in most other genres? Why do they fall into such opposed camps, with so few in the middle ground?

I believe it is because so many of them regularly attend fan conventions—and learn the wrong lessons there. Those get-togethers are pleasant, and the people at them are interesting and fun to be with. But some of the hardcore fans who go to conventions tend to have narrow tastes; and they encourage writers to produce for their tastes. Some are passionate about quiet horror. Some are passionate about splatter fiction. Writers in both camps make the mistake of believing that hardcore convention-goers are representative of the larger book-buying public. They are not. They are good people, all right, but they're not representative. Writers in either camp can be flattered dangerously, even creatively warped, by the attention they get at the conventions. The true audience, the mass audience that makes careers in the long run and ultimately determines what books and stories will last, is more catholic in its taste, open to a broader range of thought and experience. The lasting works of horror will be those that reach that broad audience, that speak not to narrow views of the human condition but to open minds. Dickens was hugely popular in his day and did not write to the prejudices of a small group; Dostoevsky was a writer adored by the masses because he did not speak only half the truth but all of it; Robert Louis Stevenson, Twain, Balzac, Poe . . . virtually *all* the writers who have out-lasted their time have explored the human condition from the point of view of neither the nihilist nor the Pollyanna. They used every narrative technique, were open to joy as well as terror, faith as well as doubt, and wrote for the masses in all their gaudy, wonderful, dreadful, exciting diversity.

Because many horror writers were conventioneers and heavy readers of fanzines before becoming established authors, they are familiar with criticism only of the fan type, which has its purposes but which is not ever deep or telling. Thus, when many writers turn to writing criticism of their own, they produce shallow analyses. Like the fan critics, they seldom look at the grammar, syntax, aptness of metaphor, thematic structure, validity of characterization, verisimilitude of background, or tightness of plot. They either like it or dislike it. And their judgment is based not on the work's intrinsic virtues or lack of same, but on how well it conforms to their own prejudices. For example, only in horror will you find a plethora of critics exhaustively discussing the ''subtext'' of a work that has no *visible* thematic purpose whatsoever. Beyond this field, a critic would be well aware that if a work is not about something in a very visible way, if it is not exploring an issue or issues on the surface for all to see, if its characters don't talk about complex ideas and deal with complex ideas as part of the story, if it appears to be only a tale, then it is only a tale. Subtexts cannot exist in a creative vacuum; a book cannot be a metaphor for Vietnam if, on the surface, it is only about monsters, blood, sex, drugs, and rock and roll. Good writers aren't *coy* about a message when they have one to impart; they don't conceal it for the private delectation of a cognescenti of prose-dissection specialists; they for God's sake *write* about it up front. Because of the poor quality of criticism within the field—as I write this, even the genre's few professional magazines offer book columns that are fannish in essence and without deep insight and observation—new writers often use bad writing as paradigms because they see it praised, not realizing that the praise was lavished on the work because of its slavish conformation to the expectations of hardcore-fan sensibilities. Sometimes it seems that each generation of writers becomes more committed than the one before it to the constriction of the genre's creative parameters; worse, in their roles as writers and critics, many of those working in horror/dark fantasy seem to have been lobotomized by excessive convention-going and by reading this kind of fiction to the exclusion of all else, until they seem virtually incapable of *seeing* the broader world, until they are so creatively and intellectually inbred that they have no valid standards by which to judge accurately their own work and that of others.

One critic and writer in the field professes to believe that there are only two things worth writing about: eros and thantos, love and death (or fear). This is an idea he apparently picked up from an academic—an obviously third-rate academic. To believe that all of human experience can be boiled down to two themes, to *truly* believe this and not merely to cling to it as a convenient justification for a failure to write complexly, an author must be intellectually and emotionally blind to the actual diversity of human feeling and motivation. To state further, as this critic does, that horror is as successful as any fiction when it delivers on half of those possible themes, when it deals strictly with death (fear), is to do a grave disservice to the genre by operating as an apologist for its writers' tendency to play safe by massaging the prejudices and fulfilling the blinkered expectations of its hardcore audience. Thinking of this dismal quality informs those racksful of unreadable books that crowd the marketplace, whether they proudly proclaim themselves to be just fun trash or masquerade as literature. With such standards, we would have to accept that the basest pornography, though limiting itself solely to the excitation of lust, is equal in literary merit to any work in the horror genre or in any other, that any hack who lathered the pages of his book with enough blood and feces to disgust us and evoke our fear of death was the equal to the best writers in our field.

The genre cannot thrive by feeding on such lies.

If we treasure this field, we must speak the truth about it at every stage of its development. At the moment the truth is that we are in a dark age, in spite of the apparent boom. The truth is, if we separate into cliques and encourage one another in the development of narrow schools of fiction, if we praise illiterate work for the sake of friendship, if we place more importance on networking at conventions for the advancement of our careers than we place on the painful act of creativity in the solitude of our dens and offices, we are contributing to a prolonged adolescence of the genre and perhaps to its ultimate dissolution as a viable literary force.

Night Visions.
This series of anthologies, of which the volume you now hold is the sixth, was conceived as a vehicle to provide writers with greater freedom to explore horror and dark fantasy fiction at shorter than novel length and without the restrictions of most other markets. Each contributor is allowed approximately 30,000 words, which he can use in any way he wishes. The opportunity exists to experiment, to seek new themes and narrative approaches, to surprise readers with work that is somewhat different from one's usual material—or to confirm one's usual approach with stories that are the carefully reduced essence of one's style—and to write novelettes and novellas, which are not easy to sell to most magazines.

The success or failure of *Night Visions* therefore rests solely with the contributors, for regardless of whether some of the volumes in the series carry editorial credits, there is little or no actual editorial work done in the classical Maxwell-Perkins sense. Here, the writers generally are left to glorify or hang themselves. This is risky business. Those who consent to contribute are braver than they might realize!

Happily, Dark Harvest has turned this risky business into a commercially successful enterprise, which pretty much assures its continuation for the foreseeable future. The series offers a unique forum, and the field owes the publisher a nod of gratitude for the risk it has taken.

• • •

The contributors.

When the preliminary ballots were counted for the first-ever Bram Stoker Awards, which are given for superior achievement by the Horror Writers of America, F. Paul Wilson had two works in the short-story category: "Dat-Tay-Vao" and "Traps." The framers of the Bram Stoker Awards Rules and Procedures had not anticipated such a development. They had not provided a mechanism by which a double-nominated writer could remove one of his works from a category to avoid competing with himself and thus reducing his chances of receiving the honor. Such a mechanism now exists; it was labeled the F. Paul Wilson Rule, and it was instituted, unfortunately, too late to benefit the man whose name it bears. In defense of those who devised the rules, it's astonishing that a single writer should be twice nominated in a category for which there were literally hundreds of eligible stories. As a tribute to Paul Wilson, from his peers, it is remarkable, even if he can't put it on his mantel and admire it!

Paul, a deceptively mild-mannered and pleasant-looking man, has developed a reputation as one of the genre's more darkly imaginative authors. His bestselling novel, *The Keep*, was an ambitious attempt to tell a story of the supernatural in the context of the very real evil of Nazism in World War Two. Blending history with an element of the fantastic, while exploring the story more in the form of a mainstream thriller than in horror-genre terms, he created something fresh, which since has been often imitated by other writers but never equalled. Freshness informs *The Tomb*, as well, and his unusual new novel *Black Wind*. He is currently at work on three interconnected novels more directly in the horror genre than was *Black Wind*, and will have a story collection in the stores soon.

In *The Bone Yard*, Paul offers three novelettes. In "Feelings," we meet a medical malpractice attorney, Howard Weinstein, whose great success in his field is predicated largely upon his shortcomings as a human being—specifically, upon his lack of empathy. Without empathy, he also lacks perspective; without perspective he lacks a conscience. Howard's fate is both chilling and darkly humorous.

"Tenants" deals with a symbiotic relationship conducted on a high wire. George Haskins shares his home with strange tenants who serve and protect him in some ways; but their contributions to the quality of his life are predicated on his fulfillment of his responsibilities to them, and for his own peace of mind, he cannot think much about what might happen if he failed to be a good landlord. The villain of this piece, Gilroy Conners, meets a fate as dark and almost as eerily humorous—killers who also write greeting-card verse?—as that of Howard Weinstein in "Feelings."

"Faces" is about a frightening but also pathetic mutant who more easily elicits dread and pity than a laugh. Except . . . well, even while Paul reports the monster's grisly depredations, there's something very blackly amusing about the name the press gives to the creature, about the creature's megalomaniacally narrow view of the world, and about the cosmic degree of tragedy that, by the end, permeates the tale.

This seasoning of quiet dark humor, spicing the horror, isn't something many writers would risk. But let me assure you, if Paul Wilson was a standup comic instead of a writer, the audience in Vegas would laugh—but they'd be white-faced and trembling too.

Sheri S. Tepper lives on the Haystack Ranch in Colorado, about fifty miles from Denver, and without intending to cast any aspersions on Denver or Colorado, one can safely say that she makes her home in the middle of nowhere. If we can believe fiction, it is in such lonely country that the ravenous aliens always land, looking for human brains to snack on, and there, too, ancient demons—of Indian origin or otherwise—live in the earth, biding their time until unwary people free them by one unthinking act or another.

For the most part, however, the open spaces and solitude do not inspire Sheri to write tales of horror. The greater body of her work is in fantasy and science fiction. Though she launched her writing career in midlife—*The Revenants*, her first novel, was begun when she was 21 but not published until she was 53—she is the author of many well-received novels, including

The Awakeners (published in two volumes as *Northshore* and *Southshore*) and *Maryann, the Magus, and the Manticore*. Her *The Gate to Women's Country*, published by Doubleday-Foundation, is about a futuristic society divided by sex; it manages to explore seriously the relationship of the sexes in the context of a well-rounded story, without the use of stereotypes, falling into none of the traps that swallow most such books, forsaking bitter feminism for a successful humanistic approach.

In *The Bone Yard*, Sheri uses her 30,000 words in a single novella that combines her love of fantasy and gardening to singular effect. Curiously, her protagonist in "The Gardener" suffers from the same flaw that brings down the antagonist in Paul Wilson's "Feelings": a lack of empathy. Tower Willis, would-be famous landscape designer, is capable of the cruelest acts, without a moment of guilt, because he does not have the ability to perceive how his selfishness and thoughtlessness hurt other people. In part, Sheri is saying that one must have a vivid imagination and must regularly exercise if it one is going to have empathy for others and be a well-rounded person, for to grasp the effect of one's acts on others requires the ability to imagine their most profound reactions. Tower Willis is so unimaginative that he cannot see the doom into which he is descending, though all around him are aware of it, and though the reader sees it all too clearly. His encounter with the fantastic might not teach him compassion, but it certainly teaches him the cost of having none.

Ray Garton is a young writer who lives in northern California, and in spite of the sunny land in which he makes his home, his work is generally darker than that of the other authors in this volume. His early novels, *Seductions and Darklings*, gained him attention, and his *Live Girls*, a clever and chilling variation on the vampire theme, was on the final ballot for the first Bram Stoker Awards program that was organized by the Horror Writers of America. *Crucifax Autumn* was recently published by Dark Harvest (in paperback by Pocket Books as *Crucifax*, a less evocative title than the author's original). He is currently at work on *Dark Channel* for Avon, which he says

is a "New Age yuppie horror novel." In spite of the fact that
Ray can be an amusing guy in conversation, anyone familiar
with his past work would not be inclined to think that *Dark
Channel* will be as lighthearted as that capsule summary of it.

In *The Bone Yard*, Ray uses his allotted wordage to give us
one novella. "Monsters" is about religious fanaticism and the
effects of guilt, especially *unearned* guilt, on the human psyche
and on human relationships. The lead character, once a Seventh-day Adventist, is tormented by other members of that faith
who have not deviated from the One True Path and who dis-
approve not only of his deviation but of his subsequent choice
of a life's work—horror writing. Ray is on record as a former
Adventist himself, and he's got a supply of stories about the
persecution he endured upon making the same decisions as his
protagonist in "Monsters." Interestingly, the most obsessive
of the fanatics in this story are capable of brutality because,
regardless of the sincerity of their religious convictions, they
are unable to empathize with the point of view and feelings of
anyone not of their group; they are afflicted with the same
disease as Howard Weinstein in Paul Wilson's "Feelings" and
Tower Willis in Sheri Tepper's "The Gardener." And though
Wilson, Tepper, and Garton did not consult one another about
their plans for this volume, though any linkages among their
choice of themes are purely accidental, they have nearly—and
curiously—provided *The Bone Yard* with a unifying theme.

The readers.
As discussed earlier, the three contributors to this volume
stand or fall entirely on their own words. No editor's hand has
improved—or detracted from—their work in this book. Writing is a daring occupation in the best of circumstances, but
here it requires more courage than usual.

My opinions of these stories are of no consequence, therefore
largely have not been offered in any depth. The opinions of
those who later review this book are of no consequences either,
for ultimately the judgments of critics amount to nothing.
Charles Dickens was reviled by most critics but loved by the

masses, and we know who won *that* one. The same is true of Dostoevsky and virtually all other writers who outlasted their eras. Great popularity is not the sole determinant of value—else we'd have to give Jackie Collins a Nobel Prize!—but it does seem to be one essential requirement; no story can have real insight into life, real power, without being accessible to—and speaking intimately to—the masses, for it is in the accretion of individual experience into cultural and sociological coral reefs that patterns of truth can be seen. The only important literary judge is time, and time in this case is synonymous with readers, generation after generation of readers, who keep works alive because those works are immensely readable, entertaining, full of meaning, and speak to both the mind and heart.

And here is why I've written such a much longer introduction than I was paid to produce: to argue that if we care about this genre, we must be honest among ourselves and must work not with one eye on the needs of the marketplace, not with an awareness of what the hardcore fans want, not with the hope of pleasing other authors and winning the awards their organizations bestow in too great a plenitude, not with the hope of gaining entrée to the "right" circles among our fellow writers, and not with the desire to please the critics, but with the energy and enthusiasm and broad vision that appeals to all readers, everywhere. We must use every working day—and especially the unique opportunities that books like *Night Visions* provide us—to explore every aspect of the human condition, not just blood and bile and death, but also joy and love and hope and faith, for only when we produce well-written fiction with high standards and with a full emotional range—and only when it has a meaning more profound than nihilism—will we have a chance of rising above the current dark age, speaking to readers with an empathetic voice, and thereby winning time's judgment for ourselves and the genre.

F. Paul
Wilson

Feelings

"Five million dollars, Mr. Weinstein? *Five million?* Where did you come up with such an outrageous figure?"

Howard Weinstein studied his prey across the table in his office conference room. Until today, Dr. Walter Johnson had been little more than a name on a subpoena and interrogatories. His C.V. put his age at fifty-one but he looked a tired old sixty as he sat next to the natty attorney the insurance company had assigned him. His face was lined, haggard, and pale, his movements slow, his voice soft, weak, his shoulders slumped inside a grey suit that looked too big for him. Maybe the strain of the malpractice suit was getting to him. Good. That might spur him to push his insurance company for an early settlement.

"Five *million?*" Dr. Johnson repeated.

Howard hesitated. *I'm* the one who's supposed to be asking the questions, he thought. This is my show. But he had asked his last question and so the deposition was essentially over. He wanted to say, *It's my favorite number,* but this was a legal proceeding and Lydia's fingers were poised over her steno machine's keyboard, awaiting his reply. So he looked Dr. Walter Johnson straight in his watery blue eyes and said,

"That's the compensation my client deserves for the permanent injuries he suffered at your hands due to your gross negligence. He will suffer lifelong impairment—"

"I saved his life!"

"That is hardly clear, Dr. Johnson. It's up to a jury to decide."

"When you sue me within my coverage," Dr. Johnson said, staring at his folded hands where they rested on the table before him, "I can say to myself, 'He's doing business.' But five million dollars? My malpractice coverage doesn't go that high. That will ruin me. That will take everything I own—my house, all the investments I've made over the years, all the money I've put away for my children and future grandchildren—and still leave me millions in debt. You're not just threatening me, you're threatening my family." He looked up at Howard. "Do you have a family, Mr. Weinstein?"

"Is that a threat, Dr. Johnson?" Howard knew the doctor was making no threat, but he reacted instinctively to keep the defendant off balance. He had no children and had divorced his wife three years ago. And anyway, he wouldn't have cared if the doc had been threatening her.

"Oh, no. I was simply wondering if you might have any conception of what this sort of threat does to someone and to his family. My homelife is a shambles. I've had constant stomach aches for months, I'm losing weight, my daughters are worried about me, my wife is a wreck. Do you have any idea what kind of misery you cause?"

"I am more concerned with the misery you caused my client, Dr. Johnson."

The doctor looked him square in the eyes. Howard felt as if the older man's gaze were penetrating to the back of his skull.

"I don't think you feel anything for anyone, Mr. Weinstein. You need a real lesson in empathy. Do you even know what empathy is?"

"I have empathy for my clients, Dr. Johnson."

"I sincerely doubt that. I think the only empathy you know is for your bank account."

"Okay, that's it," Howard said, nodding to Lydia at the steno machine as he closed his case folder and rose from his seat. He had let this go on too long already. "The deposition's over. Thank you for your cooperation, Dr. Johnson. We'll see you in court."

He ushered out the defendant and his attorney, then stepped over to where Lydia was packing up her gear. "Let me see the end of that tape," he said.

"Howie—!"

Ignoring her mild protest, he opened the tape compartment and pulled out the long strip of steno paper. As he scanned through it, looking for where when Dr. Johnson had begun running off at the mouth, Lydia said:

"You're really not going to ruin him, are you? You're really not going to take everything he owns?" She was thin, dark-haired, attractive in a brittle sort of way.

Howard laughed. "Nah! Too much trouble. It's S.O.P.: Ask for an exorbitant amount, then settle for somewhere near the limit of his coverage. Taking all his assets—which I could probably get if we go to court—and going through a long liquidation process would be a big hassle. Best thing to do is to get that big check from the insurance company, take my forty percent, then move on to the next pigeon."

"Is that all he is? A pigeon?"

"Waiting to be plucked."

He knew there was something wrong with the metaphor there, but he didn't bother to figure out what. He had found the spot he had been searching for on the tape. He marked it with a pen.

"Stop the transcription here."

"Why?"

"It's where the doc made his closing sob story about threatening his family and—"

"—your empathy for your bank account?" She smiled up at him.

"Yeah. I don't want that part in the deposition."

Her smile took a mischievous twist. "I sort of liked that part."

"Ditch it."

"I can't do that."

"Sure you can, Sis."

Her smile was gone now. "I won't. It's illegal."

In a sudden surge of anger, Howard ripped the offending section from the tape and tore it into tiny pieces. He never would have dared this with any other licensed court stenographer, but Lydia was his sister, and big brothers could take certain liberties with little sisters. Which was the main reason he used her. Her name had been Chambers since her wedding four years ago, so no one was the wiser.

He tossed the remains in the air and they fluttered to the floor in a confetti flurry.

Lydia's lips trembled. "I hate you! You're just like Dad!"

"Don't say that!"

"It's true! You're just a 'Daddy Shoog' with a law degree!"

"Shut *up!*" Howard quickly closed the door to the outer office. "I told you never to mention him around here!"

He prayed none of the secretaries had heard. One of them might get to thinking and might make the connection. She might find out that Lenny Winter, the Fifties d-j known as "Daddy Shoog," was really Leonard Weinstein, Howard's father. And then it wouldn't be long before it was all over Manhattan: Howard Weinstein was the son of that fat balding guy doing the twist and shilling his "One Mo' Once Golden Oldies" albums like Ginsu knives (*"But wait! There's more!"*) on late night tv commercials.

God! He'd never be able to maintain credibility at another deposition, let alone conduct a court case.

He had made every effort to avoid even a faint resemblance to his father: He'd grown a thick, black moustache, he took care of his hair, combing in a style his father had never used when he had a full head of it, and he kept his body trim and hard. No one would ever guess he was the son of Daddy Shoog.

Had to hand it to the old jerk, though. He was really cleaning up on those doo-wop retreads, especially since he was forgoing the inconvenience of paying royalties to the original artists.

"Too bad you inherited Dad's ethics instead of his personality. The only reason I come around is because I'm family. You've got no friends. Your wife dumped you, you've—"

"*Your* marriage didn't last too long either, Miss Holier Than Thou."

"True, but I'm the one who ended it, not Hal. You got dumped."

"Elise didn't dump me! I dumped *her!*"

And did a damn fine job of it, too. Left her without a pot to pee in. God, had he been glad to be rid of her! Three endless years of her nagging, "You're never home! I feel like a widow!" Blah-blah-blah. He'd taught her the folly of suing a lawyer for divorce.

"So what have you got, Howie? You've got your big law practice and that's it!"

"And that's plenty!" She pulled this shit on him every time they argued. Really liked to twist the knife. "I'm just thirty-two and already I'm a legend in this town! A fucking *legend!*"

"And what are you doing after lunch, Mr. Legend? Going down to St. Vincent's to scrape up another client?"

"Hey! My clients are shitbums. You think I don't know that? I know it. *Damn*, do I know it! But they've been injured and they've got a legal right to maximum recovery under the law! It's my duty—"

"Save it for the jury or the newspapers, Howie," Lydia said. Her voice sounded tired, disgusted. She picked up her steno gear and headed for the door. "You and Dad—you make me ashamed."

And then she was gone.

Howard left the files on the desk and went into his private office. He ran a hand through his thick dark hair as he gazed out at Manhattan's midtown spires. What was wrong with Lydia? Didn't she understand? The malpractice field was a gold mine. There were million-dollar clients out there who hadn't the vaguest inkling what they were worth. And if he didn't find them, somebody else would.

He'd come a long way. Started out in general practice, then sniffed the possibilities in liability law. Advertising on tv had brought him a horde of new clients, but all of them combined hadn't equaled the take from his first medical malpractice settlement. He had known then that malpractice was the only way to go.

Especially when you had a method.

It was simple, really. All it took was a few well-compensated contacts in the city's hospitals to let him know when a certain type of patient was being discharged. One of Howard's assistants—Howard used to go himself but he was above that now— would arrange to be there when the potential client left the hospital. He'd take him to lunch and subtly make his pitch.

You couldn't be *too* subtle, though. The prospective client was usually a neurosurgical patient, preferably an indigent sleazo who had shown up in the hospital emergency room with his head bashed in from a mugging or a fight over a bottle or a fix, or who'd fallen down a stairway or stumbled in front of a car during a stupor. Didn't matter what the cause as long as he'd wound up in the ER in bad enough shape for the neurosurgeon on call to be dragged in to put his skull and its contents back in order again.

"But you're not right since the surgery, are you?"

That was the magic question. The answer was almost invariably negative. Of course, the prospect hadn't been "right" *before* the surgery, either, but that was hard to prove. Nigh on *impossible* to prove. And even if the potential said he felt pretty good, he usually could find some major complaint when pressed, especially after it was explained to him that a permanent post-surgical deficit could be worth somewhere in the neighborhood of seven figures to him if things went his way.

Yeah, they were druggies and winos and all-purpose sleazos and it was an ordeal to be in conference with one of them for more than just a few minutes, but they were Howard's ticket to the Good Life. They were the perfect malpractice clients. He *loved* to stick them in front of a jury. Their shambling gaits, vacant stares, and disordered thought patterns wrung the hearts of even the most objective jurors. And since they were transients with no steady jobs, friends, or acquaintances, the defense could never prove convincingly that they had been just as shambling, vacant, and disordered before the surgery.

In most cases, the malpractice insurer took one look at the client and reached for his checkbook: It was settlement time.

Yeah, life was sweet when you knew the bushes with the best berries.

Lydia was still fuming when she reached the garage downstairs. She handed in her ticket and found herself waiting next to Dr. Johnson. He nodded to her.

"Can't they find your car?" she said for lack of something better.

He shrugged. "Seems that way. Goes with the rest of the day, I guess." He looked tired, haggard, defeated. He smiled suddenly, obviously forcing it. "How'd I do up there?"

Lydia sensed his desperate need for some hope, some encouragement.

"You did very well, I thought. Especially at the end." She couldn't bring herself to tell him that his final remarks were shredded on the floor of the conference room.

"Do you think I have a snowball's chance in hell of coming out of this with the shirt on my back?"

Lydia couldn't help it. She had to say something to ease this poor man's mind. She put her hand on his arm.

"I see lots of these cases. I'm sure they'll settle within your coverage limits."

He turned to her. "Settle? I'm not going to settle anything!"

His intensity surprised her. "Why not?"

"Because if I agree to settle, it's as much as an admission that I've done something wrong! And I haven't!"

"But you never know what a jury will do, Dr. Johnson."

"So I've been told, over and over and over by the insurance company. 'Settle—settle—settle!' They're scared to death of juries. Better to pay off the bloodsucking lawyer and his client than risk the decision of a jury. Sure! Fine for them! They're only thinking about the bottom line. But I did everything right in this case! I released his subdural hematoma and tied off the leaking artery inside his skull. That man would have died without me! And now he's suing me!''

"I'm sorry," Lydia said. It sounded lame to her but it was all she could say. She felt somehow partly responsible for Dr. Johnson's misery. After all, Howie was her brother.

"Maybe I should have done what a lot of my fellow neurosurgeons do: Refuse to take emergency room calls. That way you don't leave yourself open to the shyster sharks prowling around for a quick fortune. Maybe I should have gone into general practice with my brother back in our home town. A foggy little place on the coast . . .''

He rubbed a hand across his eyes. "Looks pretty hopeless, doesn't it. If I go to court, I could lose everything I've worked for during my entire career, and jeopardize my family's whole way of life. If I settle, I'm admitting I'm wrong when I know I'm right.'' His jaw tightened. "It's that damned greedy bastard lawyer.''

Although Lydia knew the doctor was right, the words still stung. Howard might be a lot of things, but he was still her brother.

"Things have got to change," Dr. Johnson said. "This kind of abuse is getting way out of hand. There's got to be a change in the laws to control these . . . these Hell's Angels in three-piece suits!''

"Don't hold your breath waiting for tort reform," Lydia said. "Ninety-nine percent of state legislators are lawyers, and they're all members of law firms that do a thriving business on liability claims. You don't really think they're going to take some of the bread and butter off their own tables, do you? Talk about conflict of interest!''

Dr. Johnson's expression became bleaker. "Then there's no hope of relief from the Howard Weinsteins of the world, is there? No way to give him a lesson in empathy, in knowing what kind of pain he causes in other people.''

Dr. Johnson's car pulled up then, a maroon Jaguar XJ.

"I don't know how to teach him that lesson," he said. "My brother might, but I certainly don't.'' He sighed heavily. "I honestly don't know what I'm going to do.''

"Keep fighting," Lydia told him as she watched him walk around the car and tip the attendant.

He looked at her over the hood of the Jaguar. There was a distant, resigned look in his eyes that made her afraid for him.

"Easy for you to say," he said, then got in and drove off.

Lydia stood there in the garage and watched him go, knowing in some intangible way that she would never see Dr. Walter Johnson again.

"He's dead! God, Howie, he's dead!"

Howard looked up at Lydia's pale, strained features as she leaned over his desk. He thought, *Oh, no! It's Dad! It'll be in the papers! Everyone will know!*

"Who?" he managed to say.

"Dr. Johnson! The guy you deposed last week in the malpractice case! He killed himself!"

Relief flooded through him. "He killed himself? Did he think that would let him off the hook! The jerk! We'll just take his estate to court!"

"Howard! He was depressed over this suit. You drove him over the edge!"

"I did nothing of the sort! What did he do? Shoot himself?"

Lydia's face got whiter. "No. He . . . he chopped his hand off. He bled to death."

Howard's mind suddenly went into high gear.

"Wait a minute. Wait. A. Minute! This is great! *Great!* It shows tremendous guilt over his negligence! He cut off the appendage that damaged his patient! No, wait! *Wait!* The act of suicide, especially in such a bizarre manner, points to a deranged mind. This means I can bring the hospital executive committee into the suit for allowing an obviously impaired physician to remain on the staff of their hospital. Maybe include the hospital's entire department of surgery, too! Oh, this is big! *Big!* Thank you, Lydia! You've just made my day! My *year!*"

She stood there with her mouth hanging open, looking stupid. "I don't believe you."

"What? What don't you believe? What?" What the hell was wrong with her, anyway?

"Isn't there a limit, Howard? Isn't there a place where you see a line and say to yourself, 'I can't cross over here. I'll cause too much pain on the other side.' "

He smiled at her. "Of course there is, Sis. And as soon as I find it, I'll let you know."

She didn't smile at the joke. Her face was hard, her eyes icy. "I think Dr. Johnson asked a good question last week. Do you have feelings, Howie? Do you ever feel anything for anybody but yourself?"

"Get off the soapbox, Sis."

"Gladly," she said. "Off the soapbox and out of your slimy presence." She turned toward the door, then back again. "Oh, by the way, I think you should know about Dr. Johnson's hand. You know, the one he cut off? They can't find it."

Howard fluttered his hands in the air. "Oooh! I'm scared! Maybe it will come crawling after me in my sleep tonight!"

She spun and slammed out the door. Howard immediately got on the intercom to his receptionist. "Chrissie? Get hold of Brian Jassie down at the coroner's office."

Missing hand? That sounded awful weird. He wanted the straight dope on it. And Brian Jassie could get it for him.

Brian had all the details by 4:00 P.M.

"This is what we got so far," he told Howard over the phone. "It's a strange one, I tell you."

"Just tell me what happened, Brian."

"Okay. Here's how they think it went down. About ten o'clock last night, at his Fifth Avenue office, this Dr. Johnson ties a tight tourniquet just above his right wrist with neat little pads to put extra pressure over the main arteries, and whacks off his hand. Records show he was a southpaw. There's evidence that he used local anesthesia. Well, he must have, right? I mean, sawing through your own wrist—"

"Brian!"

"Okay, okay. After the hand is off, there seems to be an interval of about half an hour during which we have no idea what he does, maybe some ritual or something, then he sits down, lowers his stump into a bucket, and loosens the tourniquet. Exsanguinates in a couple of minutes. Very neat, very considerate. No mess for anybody to clean up.''

A *real nut case*, Howard thought. ''Why do you say he was involved in some ritual?''

''Just a guess. There were candles all around the room and the histology department says the hand was off for around thirty minutes before he died.''

''Then you have the hand.''

''Uh, no, we don't.''

Howard felt a little knot form in his stomach. ''You're kidding.''

'' 'Fraid not. The forensic team looked everywhere in the office and around the building. No hand.''

So Lydia hadn't been pulling his chain. The hand really was missing. Well, that would only reinforce his contention that Dr. Johnson was mentally unbalanced and shouldn't have been allowed to practice. Yes, he would definitely bring the hospital executive committee into the suit.

Still, he wondered about that missing hand. He sat there smoothing his moustache and wondering where it could be.

The package arrived the next day.

Chrissie brought it to his desk unopened. It had come by Federal Express and was marked ''Personal And Confidential.'' Howard had her stand by as he opened it, figuring it would have to be shoved into somebody's file—most of the ''Personal And Confidential'' mail he received was anything but.

Chrissie began to scream when the hand fell out onto his desk. She kept on screaming all the way down the hall to the reception area. Howard stared at the hand. It lay palm up on his desk blotter, a deathly, bled-out white except at the ragged, beefy red wrist stump. The skin was moist, glistening in the fluorescent glare. He could see the creases that ran along the palm and across the finger joints, could even see fingerprint whorls. A faintly sour smell rose from it.

This had to be a joke, Lydia's way of trying to shake him up. Well, it wasn't going to work. This thing had to be a fake. He'd seen those amazingly lifelike platters of sushi and bowls of sukiyaki in the windows of Japanese restaurants. What was it they called the stuff? *Mihon*. That was it. This was the same thing: expertly sculpted and colored plastic. A gruesome piece of anatomical *mihon*.

Howard touched it with his index finger and felt a faint pins-and-needles sensation run up his arm and all over his skin. It lasted about the time between eye blinks and then it was gone. But by then he had realized from the texture of the skin and the give of the flesh underneath that this wasn't *mihon*. This was the real thing!

He leapt out of his chair and stood there trembling, repeatedly wiping his finger on his suit coat as he shouted to Chrissie to call the police.

Howard was late getting out of the office that day. The endless questions from the detectives and the forensic people had put him far behind schedule. Then to top everything off, his last call of the day had been from Brian at the coroner's office. According to Brian, the forensic experts downtown said that the hand had definitely belonged to the late great Dr. Walter Johnson.

So now he was shook up, grossed out, and just plain tired. Irritable, too. He snapped at the Rican garage attendant—Jose or Gomez or whatever the hell his name was—to move his ass and get the car up front pronto.

His red Porsche 914 squealed down the ramp and screeched to a halt in front of him. As he passed the attendant and handed him a fifty-cent tip—half the usual—he could almost feel the man's animosity toward him.

No, wait . . . it was more than *almost*. It was as if he were actually experiencing the car jockey's anger and envy. It wormed into his system and for a moment Howard too was angry and envious. But at whom? Himself?

And just as suddenly as it came it was gone. He was once again just tired, irritable, and anxious to get himself out to the Island and home where he could have himself a stiff drink and relax.

Traffic wasn't bad. That was one advantage of leaving late.

He cruised the LIE to Glen Cove Road, then headed north. He stopped at the MacDonald's drive-thru just this side of the sign that declared the southern limit of "The Incorporated Village of Monroe." He ordered up a Big Mac and fries. As he handed his money to the pimple-faced redheaded girl in the window, a wave of euphoria rolled over him. He felt slightly giddy. He looked up at the girl in her blue uniform and noticed her fixed grin and glazed eyes.

She's stoned! he thought. *And damned if I don't feel stoned, too!*

He took his bagged order from her and gunned away. The feeling faded almost immediately. But not his puzzlement. First the lot attendant and now the kid at Mickey-D's. What was going on here?

He pulled into his spot in the Soundview Condominiums lot and entered his townhouse. It was a three-storied job with a good view of Monroe Harbor. He'd done some legal work on the land sale and so had been able to get in on a pre-construction purchase. The price: one hundred and sixty-nine large. They were going for twice that now.

Yeah, if you knew the right people and had the wherewithal to take advantage of situations when they presented themselves, your net worth could only go one way: Up.

Howard pulled a Bud from the fridge and opened up the styrofoam Big Mac container. As he ate, he stared out over the still waters of the Long Island Sound at the lights along the Connecticut shore on the far side. Much as he tried not to, he couldn't help thinking about that severed hand in the mail today. Which led his thoughts around to Dr. Johnson. What was it he had said about empathy last week?

I don't think you feel anything for anyone, Mr. Weinstein. You need a real lesson in empathy.

Something like that. And then a week later he had sat down in his office and cut off his hand, and then had somehow got it into a Federal Express overnight envelope and sent it to Howard. *Personal And Confidential.* And then he had let himself die.

. . . a lesson in empathy . . .

Then the hand had arrived and Howard had touched it, felt that tingle, and now he seemed to be able to sense what others were feeling.

... *empathy* ...

Yeah, right. And any moment now, he'd hear Rod Serling's voice fill the room.

He finished the beer and went for another.

But let's not be too quick to laugh everything off, he told himself as he nibbled on some fries. Law school had taught him how to organize his thoughts and present cogent arguments. So far, there was a good case for his being the victim of some sort of curse. That would have been laughable yesterday, but this morning there had been a real live—no, strike that, make that *dead*—a dead human hand lying on his desk. A hand that had once belonged to a defendant in a very juicy malpractice case. A man who had said that Howard Weinstein needed a lesson in how other people felt.

And now Howard Weinstein had encountered two instances in which he had experienced another person's feelings.

Or thought he had.

That was the question. Had Dr. Johnson done a number on Howard's head? Had he planted some sort of suggestion in his subconscious and then reinforced it by sending him a severed hand?

Or was this the real thing? A dead man's curse?

Howard decided to take a scientific approach. The only way to prove a hypothesis was to test it in the field. He tossed off the second beer. Time to hit the town.

As he gathered up the MacDonald's debris, he noticed a dull ache all along his right arm. He rubbed it but that didn't help. He wondered how he could have strained it. Maybe it was a result of jerking away after touching that hand this morning. No, he didn't remember any pain then. He shrugged it off, pulled on a sweater, and stepped out into the spring night.

The air was cool and tangy with salt from the Sound. Too beautiful a night to squeeze back into the Porsche, so he decided to walk the few blocks west down to the waterfront nightspots.

He had only gone a few steps when he noticed that the ache in his arm was gone.

Canterbury's was the first place he came to along the newly renovated waterfront. He stopped in here occasionally with some of his local clients. Not a bad place for lunch, but after five it turned into a meat market. If AIDS had put a damper on the swinging singles scene, you couldn't tell it here. The space around Canterbury's oval bar was smoky, noisy, and packed with yuppie types.

Howard squeezed up to the bar and suddenly felt his knees get rubbery. He leaned against the mahogany edge and glanced at the fellow rubbing elbows with him to his right. He was downing a straight shot of something and chasing it with a few generous chugs of draft beer. There were four other shot glasses on the bar in front of him, all empty.

Howard lurched away toward the booths at the rear of the room and felt better immediately.

God, it's happening! It's true.

As he moved through the crowd, he was assaulted with a complex mixture of lust, boredom, fatigue, and inebriation. It was a relief to reach the relative sanctuary of the last booth in the rear. The emotions and feelings of the room became background noise, a sensory muzak.

But they were still there. On the way from the city it had seemed he needed physical contact—from the garage attendant, the girl at Mickey D's—to get the sensory input. Now the feelings seemed to waft through the air.

Howard shut his eyes and rubbed his hands over his temples. This couldn't be happening, couldn't be real. This was the stuff of *Twilight Zone* and *Outer Limits* and *Tales from the Darkside*. This sort of thing did not happen to Howard Weinstein in little old Monroe, Long Island.

But he could not deny his own experience. He had felt drunk before noticing that the guy next to him was doing boilermakers.

Or had he?

Maybe he had unconsciously noticed the guy with the ball

and the beer as he had stepped up to the bar and his mind had done the rest.

It was all so confusing. How could he know for sure?

"Can I get you something, Mr. Weinstein?"

Howard looked up. A well-stacked blonde stood over him with a tray under her arm and her order pad ready. She was thirtyish with too much make-up and too-blonde hair, but on the whole not someone he'd kick out of bed. She was dressed in the standard Canterbury cocktail waitress uniform of short skirt, black stockings, and low cut Elizabethan barmaid blouse, and she was smiling.

"How do you know my name?"

"Why shouldn't I? You're one of the more important men in Monroe, aren't you?"

She was interested in him. Howard couldn't read her thoughts, but he sensed her excited response to his presence. She was probably attracted to money and power and apparently he represented a modicum of both to her. There was a trace of sexual arousal and an undercurrent of anxiety as well.

Anxiety over what? That he'd give her the cold shoulder? He tried to see if he could affect that.

"Nice to be recognized," he said, "especially by such an attractive woman" . . . he craned his neck to see the name tag centered on her cleavage . . . "Molly."

The anxiety all but vanished and the sexual arousal rose two notches.

Bingo!

He ordered a Chivas and soda. He was ready for her when she returned with the drink.

"Looks like you'll be working late tonight, huh?"

He could feel her excitement swell. "Not necessarily. It's still the off season so it's not really crazy yet. When the tables are kinda slow like tonight I can usually get off early if I ask."

"Why don't you ask. I've got no plans for the evening. Maybe we could think of something to do together."

Her sexual arousal zoomed.

"Sounds good to me," she said with a smile and a wink.

Howard leaned back and sipped his scotch as he watched the gentle sway of her retreating butt.

So *easy!* Like having all the answers to a test before you sat down to take it.

This was a *curse?*

What a night!

Howard walked along the waterfront through the morning mist. He was still a little weak-kneed. He'd had loads of women over the years, plenty of one-night stands, even an all-nighter with a couple of pros. But never, *never* anything like what he had experienced last night.

As soon as they had got to Molly's apartment and begun the foreplay, he had found himself tapped into her feelings. He could sense her excitement, her pleasure—he was more than just aware of it, he was actually experiencing it himself. He could tell when he was going too fast or not fast enough. He found he could toy with her, tantalize her, bring her to peaks but keep her from going over the top. Finally he brought her to an Everest and leaped off with her. Her climax fused into his and the results were shattering. She was left gasping but he was utterly speechless.

And that had only been the first time.

Molly had finally fallen asleep telling him he was the greatest lover in the world, really meaning it. Howard had drifted off with her, thinking it wouldn't be bad if that message got around to all the attractive single women in town. Not bad at all.

He had awakened early and Molly had wanted him to stay but he had begged off. He was catching a new emotion from her: She was starting to get lovey-dovey feelings for him—or at least thought she was. And why not? Decent looks, money, power, and a great lover to boot.

What's not to love?

Those feelings tripped off sirens and red lights for Howard. Uh-uh. No love. Just good times and fun and stay loose. Love meant trouble. Women started thinking of marriage then.

He felt her hurt and disappointment as he left, trailing vague promises of getting together again real soon. But he couldn't go home just yet. He was too excited, too exhilarated. This was great! This was fantastic! The possibilities were endless. He walked on, exploring them in his mind.

A siren broke into his thoughts. He looked around and found he was in front of Monroe Community Hospital. An ambulance was racing up the road. As it neared, he felt a growing pressure in his chest. His breath clogged in his throat as the pain became a great lead weight, crushing his sternum. Then, as the ambulance passed and pulled into the approach to the emergency entrance, the pain receded.

Whoever was in that ambulance was having a heart attack. Howard was sure of it. He watched as the ambulance attendants carried someone into the emergency room on a stretcher. Heart attack. No doubt about it. Just one more bit of proof on the side of this so-called curse Dr. Johnson had laid on him. And it would be so easy to confirm. Just go up to the reception desk and ask: *Did the ambulance get here with my uncle yet? The man with the chest pain?*

He started across the lawn toward the four-story brick structure. As he neared it however, he began to feel nauseous and weak. His head pounded, his abdomen burned, ached, cramped, and just plain hurt. Every joint, every bone in his body hurt. He began to wheeze, his vision blurred. It all got worse with each step closer to the hospital but he forced himself on until he reached the emergency entrance and opened the door.

. . .pain . . .fear . . .pain . . .hope . . .pain . . .grief . . .pain . . .rage . . .pain . . .despair . . .pain . . .joy . . .pain . . .pain . . .pain . . .pain . . .

Like a physical assault from a Mongolian horde, like a massive torrent from a sundered damn, like ground zero at Hiroshima, the mental and physical agony flooded over Howard, sending him reeling and stumbling back across the driveway to the grass where he crumbled to his knees and crawled as fast as he could away from the hospital. Anyone watching him would have assumed he was drunk but he didn't care. He had to get away from that building.

He felt almost himself again by the time he reached the sidewalk. He sat on the curb, weak and nauseous, swearing he would never go near another hospital again.

It seemed there were drawbacks to this little power of his after all. But nothing he couldn't handle, nothing he couldn't overcome. The advantages were too enormous!

He had to talk this out with somebody. Brainstorm it. But with whom? Suddenly, he smiled.

Lydia lived in the garden apartments on the downtown fringe, a short walk from here.

Of course!

Howard had looked like he was on drugs when Lydia opened the door to her apartment. She had been in the middle of a nice little dream of being married with two kids and no money problems when the pounding on the door had awakened her. Her brother's face had loomed large in the fish-eye peephole so she had opened up and let him in.

That proved to be a mistake. Howie was absolutely manic. While she made coffee he stalked around her tiny kitchen waving his arms and talking a mile a minute. Watching him, she thought he might be on speed; listening to him, she thought he might be on acid.

But Howie didn't do drugs.

Which meant he had gone crazy.

"Do you see what this means, Sis? Do you *see!* The possibilities are endless! Can you imagine what this will let me do at a deposition? If my questions are getting into a sensitive area, I'll *know*! I'll sense the defendant's fear, his anxiety, and I'll keep hitting those sore spots, pushing those secret buttons until he comes across with what I want. And even if he doesn't, I'll know where to look for the dirt. Same's true with cross-examinations in the court room. I'll know when I've hit a nerve. And speaking of court rooms, I thought of something that's even better—even *better!*" He stopped and pointed a finger at her. "Juries! Jury selection!"

Lydia stirred the boiling water into the instant coffee—decaf, for sure. She didn't want to hype him up even the tiniest bit more. "Right, Howie," she said softly. "That's a good point."

"Can you imagine how I'll be able to stack the jury box? I mean, I'll *know* how each juror feels about the case because I'll ask them point blank. I'll say, 'Mrs. So-and-so, how do you feel about the medical profession in general?' If I get some sort of warm glow from her, she's out, no matter what she says. But if I get anger or envy or plain old spitefulness, she's in. I can pack a jury with doctor-haters on all my malpractice cases!" He giggled. "The settlements will be *astronomical!*"

"Whatever makes you happy, Howie," Lydia said. "Now why don't you sit down and drink your coffee and take it easy." She had heard about Dr. Johnson's hand winding up on his desk yesterday. The shock must have got to him. "You can lie down on my bed if you want to."

He was staring at her.

"You think I'm nuts, don't you?"

"No, Howie. I just think you're feeling the strain of—"

"Right now I'm feeling what you're feeling. Which is a lot of disbelief, a little anxiety, a little fatigue, and a little compassion. Very little compassion."

"You don't need a crystal ball or a voodoo-hoodoo curse to figure that one out."

"And you've got a low backache, too. Right?"

Lydia felt a chill. Her low back did hurt. Her period was due tomorrow and her back always ached the day before.

"Half the world's got backaches, Howie."

"You've got to believe me, Lydia. There's got to be a way I can—" His eyes lit. "Wait a minute. I've got an idea." He began yanking the kitchen drawers open until he got to the utensils. He pulled out a paring knife and handed it to her.

"What's this for?" she said.

"I want you to poke yourself here and there on your body with the point—"

"Howie, are you nuts?"

"Not hard enough to break the skin; just enough to cause a little pain." He took the pen from the message pad by the phone and pointed to the kitchen door. "I'll be on the other side of the door there and I'll mark the spots and number them on myself with this pen."

"This is crazy!"

"I've got to convince you, Lydia. You're the only one in this world I trust."

Damn him! It had been like this all their lives. He always knew what to say to get her to go along.

"Okay."

He got on the other side of the swinging door. Lydia put her back to it and poked the knife point at the center of her left palm. It hurt, but certainly nothing she couldn't bear.

"That's one," said Howie from the other side of the door.

Lydia turned her hand over and jabbed the back of her hand.

"That's two," Howie said.

Lucky guesses, Lydia told herself uneasily. For variety, she poked the point gently against her cheek.

"Very funny," Howie said, "but I'm not writing on my face."

The words so startled her that the knife slipped from her grasp. As she grabbed for it, the blade sliced into her index finger.

"Hey!" Howie said, pushing through the door. "You weren't supposed to cut yourself!"

"It was an acc—" And then she realized. "My God, you knew!" She sucked her bleeding finger. *He knew!*

"Of course I knew. As a matter of fact, for an instant in there I actually *saw* the cut on my finger. Look here. Even drew it for you. See?"

Lydia did see: A half-inch crescent was drawn in ink across the pad of Howie's right index finger, perfectly matching the bloody one on her own.

Suddenly Lydia was weak. She lowered herself into a chair. "My God, Howie, it's really true, isn't it?"

"Sure is." He stood over her, beaming. "And I'm going to milk it dry." He turned and started toward the door.

"Where are you going?"

"Back to the condo. I need some sleep, and I've got a lot

of thinking to do. Don't make any plans for dinner tonight. I'm treating. Lobster and champagne at Memison's.''

"Aren't we generous.''

"Make reservations for two.''

And then he was gone. Lydia sat there trying to accept the fact that something that simply didn't happen in real life was happening in hers.

On the way home, Howard kept well away from the hospital. As he walked he realized that the courtroom was small potatoes, just a springboard into politics. *United States Senator Howard Weinstein*. He liked the sound of that. He'd know who to trust and who to boot. And after he'd built up his power base, maybe he'd go for the White House.

Hey, why the hell not?

He was tempted to stop by his father's place out on Shore Drive and see what he was up to. He hadn't heard from the old man in a couple of weeks. Might be interesting to see how Dad really felt about him. And then again, it might not.

He went straight home.

His right arm started bothering him at the front door. The ache was worse than he remembered from last night. Just to test a theory, he walked back outside again. The pain disappeared by the time he got to the parking lot. It reoccurred when he returned to the condo.

Which meant that someone nearby had a bad case of bursitis or something. So why the hell didn't the jerk do something about it?

Howard was too tired to worry about that now. He downed a couple of shots of scotch to calm his nerves and crawled under the covers. As he closed his eyes and tried to ignore the throb in his arm, he realized that he felt a little sad. Why? Or did the emotion even originate with him? Maybe somebody else nearby was unhappy or depressed about something. Was he getting more sensitive or what? This could get confusing.

He pushed it all away and wrapped himself in dreams of dazzling courtroom prowess and political glory.

● ● ●

The pain awoke him at four in the afternoon. The aching throb in his right arm was worse than ever. He wondered if it had anything to do with touching the hand. Maybe Dr. Johnson was getting even with him after all.

That was not a pleasant thought.

But then why would the pain stop as soon as he left the condo? He couldn't figure this out.

He phoned Lydia. "How about an early dinner, Sis?"

"How early?"

"As early as possible."

"I made reservations for 7:30."

"We'll change them."

"Is something wrong, Howie?" There was a hint of real concern in her voice.

He told her about the pain in his arm. "I've got to get out of here. That's the only time it stops."

"Okay: Meet you there at 5:30."

That was when the peasants ate, but the pain wouldn't allow Howard to be snooty. He took a quick shower and hurried outside before his hair had dried. Blessed relief from the pain came at the far end of the parking lot.

"I'll take that one," Howard said, pointing out a big-tailed two-pounder in Memison's live lobster tank.

"Excellent choice, sir," the waiter said, then turned to Lydia. "And you, Miss?"

"I'll have the fish dinner, please."

Howard was surprised. He sensed a skittish reluctance in her. "No lobster? I thought you loved lobster!"

She was staring at the tank. "I do. But standing here and pointing out the one I'm going to eat . . . somehow it's not the same. Makes me feel like some sort of executioner."

Howard couldn't help laughing. "I swear to God you're from Mars, Sis. From *Mars!*"

When they returned to the table, Howard refilled their tall, slim champagne glasses from the bottle in the bucket. He watched a fly buzz angrily against the window that ran alongside their table. Outside at the marina, the boats rocked gently at their moorings. He savored the peace.

"You're awful quiet, Howie," Lydia said after a moment.

"Am I?"

"Compared to this morning, you're a sphinx."

Howard didn't know what to tell her, how to say it. Maybe the best thing to do was to lay it all out. Maybe she could help him sort it out.

"I think I'm having second thoughts about this special 'empathy' I've developed," he said finally. "Maybe it really is a curse. I seem to be getting increasingly sensitive. I mean, as I walked over here I got rushes of feelings from everyone I passed. There was this little kid crying on the corner. He had lost his mom and I found myself—*me*—utterly terrified. I couldn't move, I was so scared. Thank God his mother found him just then or I don't know what I'd have done. And when she whacked him on the backside for running off, I felt it. It hurt! The kid was the worst, but I was picking up all sorts of conflicting emotions. It was almost a relief to get in here. Good thing we're so early and it's almost deserted."

"Why'd you have our table moved? To get away from that fat guy?"

Howard nodded. "Yeah. He must have stuffed himself from the buffet. I thought my stomach was going to burst. I couldn't enjoy my dinner feeling like that. And if he's going to have a gallbladder attack, I don't want to be near him."

The fly's buzzing continued. It was beginning to annoy him.

"Howard," Lydia said, looking at him intently. She only called him Howard when she was mad or really serious about something. "Can this really be happening?"

"Don't you think I've asked myself that a thousand times since last night? But yes, it's real, and it's happening to me."

He signaled their waiter as he passed. "Could you do something about that fly?"

"Of course."

The waiter returned in a moment with a fly swatter. He swung it as Howard was pouring more champagne.

Pain like Howard had never known in his life flashed through his entire body as his ears roared and his vision went stark white. It was gone in an instant, over as soon as it had begun.

"My God, Howard, what's the matter!"

Lydia was staring at him, wide-eyed and ashen-faced. He glanced around. So were the other people in the place. He felt their disapproval, their annoyance. The waiter began sopping up the champagne he had spilled when he had dropped the bottle.

"Wh-what happened?"

"You screamed and spasmed like you were having a seizure! Howard, what's wrong with you?"

"When he swatted that fly," he said, nodding his head in the direction of the retreating waiter, "I . . . I think I felt it."

Her disbelief stung him. "Oh, Howard—"

"It's true, Sis. It hurt so much for that one tiny second there I thought I was going to die."

"But a fly, Howard? A *fly?*" She stared at him. "What's wrong?"

Suddenly he was very hot. Terribly hot. His skin felt like it was on fire. He looked down at his bare arms and watched the skin turn red, rise up in blisters, burst open. He felt as if he were being boiled alive.

. . . boiled . . .

His lobster! The kitchen was only a few feet away. They'd be cooking it now—dropping it live into a pot of boiling water!

Screaming with the pain, he leaped up from the table and ran for the door.

Outside . . . coolness. He leaned against the outer wall of Memison's, gasping and sweating, oblivious to the stares of the passers-by but too well aware of their curiosity.

"Howard, are you going crazy?" It was Lydia. She had followed him out.

"Didn't you see me? I was burning up in there!" He looked down at his arms. The skin was perfect, unblemished.

"All I saw was my brother acting like a crazy man!"

He felt her concern, her fear for him, and her embarrassment because of him.

"When they started boiling my lobster, they started boiling *me!* I could feel myself being boiled alive!"

"Howard, this has got to stop!"

"Damn right it does." He pushed himself off the wall and began walking down the street, back toward his condo. "I've got some thinking to do. See you."

Lydia was having her first cup of coffee when Howard called the next morning.

"Can I come over, Sis?" His voice was hoarse, strained. "I've got to get out of here."

"Sure, Howie. Is it the arm again?"

"Yeah! Feels like it's being crushed!"

Crushed. That rang a bell somewhere in the back of her mind. "Come right over. I'll leave the door unlocked. If I'm not here, make yourself at home. I'll be back soon. I've got an errand to run."

She hung up, pulled on jeans and a blouse, and hurried down to the Monroe Public Library. A *crushed arm* . . . she remembered something about that, something to do with the Soundview Condos.

It took her awhile, but she finally tracked it down in a microfilm spool of the Monroe *Express* from two years ago last summer . . .

Howard looked like hell. He looked distracted. He wasn't paying attention.

"Listen to me, Howard! It happened two years ago! They were pouring the basement slab in your section of condos. As the cement truck was backing up, a construction worker slipped in some mud and the truck's rear wheels rolled right over his arm. Crushed it so bad even Columbia Presbyterian couldn't save it."

He looked at her dully. "So?"

"So don't you see? You're not just tuned in to the feelings and sensations of people and even lobsters and bugs around you. You're picking up the *residuals* of old pains and hurts."

"Is that why it's so noisy in here?"

"Noisy?"

"Yeah. Emotional noise. This place is crowded, I mean *jammed* with emotions, some faint, some strong, some up, some down, some really mean ones. So confusing."

Lydia remembered that these garden apartments had been put up shortly after the war—World War II. If Howard could actually feel forty-plus years of emotion—

"I wish they'd go away and let me sleep. I'd give anything for just a moment's peace."

Lydia went to the medicine cabinet in the bathroom and found the bottle of Valium her doctor had prescribed for her when she was divorcing Harry. She shook two of the yellow tablets into her palm and gave them to Howard with a cup of water.

"Take these and go lie down on my bed. They'll help you sleep."

He did as he was told and shuffled off to the next room, moving like a zombie. Lydia's heart went out to him. She called a friend and begged her to take the steno job she had lined up for this afternoon, then settled down to watch over her big brother.

He slept fitfully through the day. Around dark she took a shower to ease her tension-knotted muscles. It helped some. Wrapped in her terrycloth robe, she returned to the kitchen and found him standing there looking worse than ever.

"I can't stand it!" he said in a voice that sounded as if it were going to break into a million jagged pieces. "It's making me crazy. It's even in my dreams! All those feelings! *I'm going nuts!*"

His wild eyes frightened her. "Just calm down, Howie. I'll make you something to eat and then we can—"

"I've gotta get outta here! I can't take it any longer!"

He started for the door. Lydia tried to stop him.

"Howard—'"

He pushed her aside. "Got to get *out!*"

By the time she threw on enough clothing to follow him, he was nowhere to be seen.

• • •

The night was alive with fear and joy and lust and pain and pleasure and love, emotionally and physically strobing Howard with heat and light. He needed relief, he needed quiet, he needed peace.

And there, up ahead, he saw it . . . a cool and dark place . . . almost empty of emotions, of feeling of any sort.

He headed for it.

She got the call the next morning.

"Are you Lydia Chambers, sister of Howard Weinstein?" said an official sounding voice.

Oh, God!

"Yes."

"Would you come down to the Crosby Marina, please, m'am?"

"Oh, no! He's not—"

"He's okay," the voice said quickly. "Physically, at least."

Lt. Donaldson drove her out to the buoy in a Marine Police outboard. Howard sat in a rowboat tied to the bobbing red channel marker in the center of Monroe Harbor.

"Seems he stole the boat last night," said the lieutenant, who had curly blond hair and looked to be in his mid-thirties. "But he seems to have gone off the deep end. He won't untie from the buoy and he starts screaming and swinging an oar at anyone who comes near. He asked for you."

He cut the engine and let the outboard drift toward Howard and the rowboat.

"Tell them to leave me alone, Sis!" Howard said when they got to within a couple of dozen feet of him.

He looked wild—unshaven, his clothes smudged and wrinkled, his hair standing up at crazy angles. And in his eyes, a dangerous, cornered look.

He looks insane, she thought.

"Come ashore, Howard," she said, trying to exude friendliness and calm confidence. "Come home now."

"I can't, Sis! You can explain it to them. Make them understand. This is the only place where it's quiet, where I can find peace. Oh, I know the fish are eating and being eaten below, but it's sporadic and it's far away and I can handle that. I just can't be in town anymore!''

Lt. Donaldson whispered out of the side of his mouth. "He's been talking crazy like that since we found him out here this morning."

Lydia wondered what she could tell the lieutenant: That her brother wasn't crazy, that he was suffering from a curse? Start talking like that and they'd be measuring her for a straight-jacket, too.

"You can't stay out here, Howard."

"I have to. There's a gull's nest in the buoy and the little birds were hungry this morning and it made me hungry, too. But then the mother came and fed them and now their bellies are full and they're content" . . . he began to sob . . . "and so am I and I just want to stay here near them where it's quiet and peaceful."

She heard the lieutenant growl. "All right. That does it!"

He stood up and signaled to shore. Another larger boat roared out from the marina. There were men in white jackets aboard, and they were carrying something that looked like a net.

"He'll be asleep for awhile yet, Mrs. Chambers," said Dr. Gold. "We had to inject him with a pretty stiff dose of Thorazine to quiet him down."

It had been horrifying to watch them throw a net over her own brother and haul him into the bigger boat like a giant fish, but there had been no other way. Howard would have died out on the water if they had left him there.

She had spent most of the morning signing papers and answering countless questions on Howard's medical and emotional history, family history, current stresses and strains. She had told Dr. Gold everything, including Howard's receiving the hand in the mail two day ago. *God, was it only two days ago?* Everything . . . except the part about feeling the pain and emotions of other people . . . and animals and even insects. She couldn't bring herself to risk trying to explain that to Dr. Gold. He might think she was sharing her brother's psychosis.

"When can he leave?" she asked.

"Not for twenty-eight days at least. That's how long he's committed. Don't worry too much. This appears to be an acute psychosis precipitated by that grisly incident with the severed hand. We'll start his psychotherapy immediately, find an appropriate medication, and do what we can to get him on his psychological feet again as soon as possible. I think he'll do just fine."

Lydia wasn't too sure of that, but all she could do was hope. At least the Monroe Neuropsychiatric Institute was brand new. It had opened only last winter. She had heard about it, but since she never came to this part of town, she hadn't seen it until now. It seemed pleasant enough. And since most of the patients here were probably sedated to some degree, their emotions wouldn't be too strong. Maybe Howard had a chance here.

Dr. Gold walked her to the door.

"In a way it's sort of ironic that your brother should wind up here."

"Why is that?"

"Well, he's one of the limited partners that developed this little hospital. All of the limited partners got a certified historic rehabilitation tax credit for investing, one of the few goodies remaining after tax overhaul."

"Rehabilitation?" A warning bell sounded in a far corner of her mind. "You mean it isn't a new building?"

"Oh, my goodness, no. We've cleaned it up to look spanking new, but in reality it's a hundred and fifty years old."

"A hundred and fifty—"

"Yes. It was abandoned for such a long time. I understand it was being used for dog fights before we took it over. Even used it as a place to train young fighting pit bulls. Trained them with kittens. A sick, sick—" He stared at her. "Are you all right?"

"Dog fights?" Oh, God, what would that do to Howard? Wouldn't the residual from something like that send him right up the wall?

"I'm sorry if I upset you."

"I'm okay," she said, steeling herself to ask the next question. "What was the building originally?"

"Originally? Why I thought everybody knew that, but I guess you're too young to remember. Up until the late 1960s it was the Monroe Slaughterhouse. One of the busiest in the—"

He stopped as the sound came down the hall—a long, hoarse, agonized scream that echoed off the freshly painted walls and tore into Lydia's soul.

Howard was awake.

Faces

Bite her face off.

No pain. Her dead already. Kill her quick like others. Not want make pain. Not her fault.

The boyfriend groan but not move. Face way on ground now. Got from behind. Got quick. Never see. He can live.

Girl look me after the boyfriend go down. Gasp first. When see face start scream. Two claws not cut short rip her throat before sound get loud.

Her sick-scared look just like all others. Hate that look. Hate it terrible.

Sorry, girl. Not your fault.

Chew her face skin. Chew all. Chew hard and swallow. Warm wet redness make sickish but chew and chew. Must eat face. Must get all down. Keep down.

Leave the eyes.

The boyfriend groan again. Move arm. Must leave quick. Take last look blood and teeth and stare-eyes that once pretty girlface.

Sorry, girl. Not your fault.

Got go. Get way hurry. First take money. Girl money. Take the boyfriend wallet, also too. Always take money. Need money.

Go now. Not too far. Climb wall of near building. Find dark spot where can see and not be seen. Where can wait. Soon the Detective Harrison arrive.

In downbelow can see the boyfriend roll over. Get to knees. Sway. See him look the girlfriend.

The boyfriend scream terrible. Bad to hear. Make so sad. Make cry.

Kevin Harrison heard Jacobi's voice on the other end of the line and wanted to be sick.

"Don't say it," he groaned.

"Sorry," said Jacobi. "It's another one."

"Where?"

"West Forty-ninth, right near—"

"I'll find it." All he had to do was look for the flashing red lights. "I'm on my way. Shouldn't take me too long to get in from Monroe at this hour."

"We've got all night, lieutenant." Unsaid but well understood was an admonishing, *You're the one who wants to live on Long Island.*

Beside him in the bed, Martha spoke from deep in her pillow as he hung up.

"Not another one?"

"Yeah."

"Oh, God! When is it going to stop?"

"When I catch the guy."

Her hand touched his arm, gently. "I know all this responsibility's not easy. I'm here when you need me."

"I know." He leaned over and kissed her. "Thanks."

He left the warm bed and skipped the shower. No time for that. A fresh shirt, yesterday's rumpled suit, a tie shoved into his pocket, and he was off into the winter night.

With his secure little ranch house falling away behind him, Harrison felt naked and vulnerable out here in the dark. As he headed south on Glen Cove Road toward the LIE, he realized that Martha and the kids were all that were holding him together these days. His family had become an island of sanity and stability in a world gone mad.

Everything else was in flux. For reasons he still could not comprehend, he had volunteered to head up the search for this killer. Now his whole future in the department had come to hinge on his success in finding him.

The papers had named the maniac "the Facelift Killer." As apt a name as the tabloids could want. But Harrison resented it. The moniker was callous, trivializing the mutilations perpetrated on the victims. But it had caught on with the public and they were stuck with it, especially with all the ink the story was getting.

Six killings, one a week for six weeks in a row, and eight million people in a panic. Then, for almost two weeks, the city had gone without a new slaying.

Until tonight.

Harrison's stomach pitched and rolled at the thought of having to look at one of those corpses again.

"That's enough," Harrison said, averting his eyes from the faceless thing.

The raw, gouged, bloody flesh, the exposed muscle and bone were bad enough, but it was the eyes—those naked, lidless, staring eyes were the worst.

"This makes seven," Jacobi said at his side. Squat, dark, jowly, the sergeant was chewing a big wad of gum, noisily, aggressively, as if he had a grudge against it.

"I can count. Anything new?"

"Nah. Same m.o. as ever—throat slashed, money stolen, face gnawed off."

Harrison shuddered. He had come in as Special Investigator after the third Facelift killing. He had inspected the first three via coroner's photos. Those had been awful. But nothing could match the effect of the real thing up close and still warm and oozing. This was the fourth fresh victim he had seen. There was no getting used to this kind of mutilation, no matter how

many he saw. Jacobi put on a good show, but Harrison sensed
the revulsion under the sergeant's armor.

And yet . . .

Beneath all the horror, Harrison sensed something. There
was anger here, sick anger and hatred of spectacular propor-
tions. But beyond that, something else, an indefinable something that had drawn him to this case. Whatever it was, that
something called to him, and still held him captive.

If he could identify it, maybe he could solve this case and
wrap it up. And save his ass.

If he did solve it, it would be all his own. Because he wasn't
getting much help from Jacobi, and even less from his assigned
staff. He knew what they all thought—that he had taken the
job as a glory grab, a shortcut to the top. Sure, they wanted
to see this thing wrapped up, too, but they weren't shedding
any tears over the shit he was taking in the press and on tv and
from City Hall.

Their attitude was clear: *If you want the spotlight, Harrison,
you gotta take the heat that goes with it.*

They were right, of course. He could have been working on
a quieter case, like where all the winos were disappearing to.
He'd chosen this instead. But he wasn't after the spotlight,
dammit! It was this case—something about this case!

He suddenly realized that there was no one around him.
The body had been carted off, Jacobi had wandered back to
his car. He had been left standing alone at the far end of the
alley.

And yet not alone.

Someone was watching him. He could feel it. The realization
sent a little chill—one completely unrelated to the cold February wind—trickling down his back. A quick glance around
showed no on paying him the slightest bit of attention. He
looked up.

There!

Somewhere in the darkness above, someone was watching
him. Probably from the roof. He could sense the piercing scru-
tiny and it made him a little weak. That was no ghoulish
neighborhood voyeur, up there. That was the Facelift Killer.

He had to get to Jacobi, have him seal off the building. But he couldn't act spooked. He had to act calm, casual.

See the Detective Harrison's eyes. See from way up in the dark. Tall-thin. Hair brown. Nice eyes. Soft brown eyes. Not hard like many-many eyes. Look here. Even from here see eyes make wide. Him know it me.

Watch the Detective Harrison turn slow. Walk slow. Tell inside him want to run. Must leave here. Leave quick.

Bend low. Run cross roof. Jump to next. And next. Again til most block away. Then down wall. Wrap scarf round head. Hide bad-face. Hunch inside big-big coat. Walk through lighted spots.

Hate light. Hate crowds. Theatres here. Movies and plays. Like them. Some night sneak in and see. See one with man in mask. Hang from wall behind big drapes. Make cry.

Wish there mask for me.

Follow street long way to river. See many lights across river. Far past there is place where grew. Never want go back to there. Never.

Catch back of truck. Ride home.

Home. Bright bulb hang ceiling. Not care. The Old Jessi waiting. The Jessi friend. Only friend. The Jessi's eyes not see. Ever. When the Jessi look me, her face not wear sick-scared look. Hate that look.

Come in kitchen window. The Jessi's face wrinkle-black. Smile when hear me come. TV on. Always on. The Jessi can not watch. Say it company for her.

"You're so late tonight."

"Hard work. Get moneys tonight."

Feel sick. Want cry. Hate kill. Wish stop.

"That's nice. Are you going to put it in the drawer?"

"Doing now."

Empty wallets. Put moneys in slots. Ones first slot. Fives next slot. Then tens and twenties. So the Jessi can pay when boy bring foods. Sometimes eat stolen foods. Mostly the Jessi call for foods.

The Old Jessi hardly walk. Good. Do not want her go out.

Bad peoples round here. Many. Hurt one who not see. One bad man try hurt Jessi once. Push through door. Thought only the blind Old Jessi live here.

Lucky the Jessi not alone that day.

Not lucky bad man. Hit the Jessi. Laugh hard. Then look me. Get sick-scared look. Hate that look. Kill him quick. Put in tub. Bleed there. Bad man friend come soon after. Kill him also too. Late at night take both dead bad men out. Go through window. Carry down wall. Throw in river.

No bad men come again. Ever.

"I've been waiting all night for my bath. Do you think you can help me a little?"

Always help. But the Old Jessi always ask. The Jessi very polite.

Sponge the Old Jessi back in tub. Rinse her hair. Think of the Detective Harrison. His kind eyes. Must talk him. Want stop this. Stop now. Maybe will understand. Will. Can feel

Seven grisly murders in eight weeks.

Kevin Harrison studied a photo of the latest victim, taken before she was mutilated. A nice eight by ten glossy furnished by her agent. A real beauty. A dancer with Broadway dreams.

He tossed the photo aside and pulled the stack of files toward him. The remnants of six lives in this pile. Somewhere within had to be an answer, the thread that linked each of them to the Facelift Killer.

But what if there was no common link? What if all the killings were at random, linked only by the fact that they were beautiful? Seven deaths, all over the city. All with their faces gnawed off. *Gnawed*.

He flipped through the victims one by one and studied their photos. He had begun to feel he knew each one of them personally:

Mary Detrick, 20, a junior at N.Y.U., killed in Washington Square Park on January 5. She was the first.

Mia Chandler, 25, a secretary at Merrill Lynch, killed January 13 in Battery Park.

Ellen Beasley, 22, a photographer's assistant, killed in an alley in Chelsea on January 22.

Hazel Hauge, 30, artist agent, killed in her Soho loft on January 27.

Elizabeth Paine, 28, housewife, killed on February 2 while jogging late in Central Park.

Joan Perrin, 25, a model from Brooklyn, pulled from her car while stopped at a light on the Upper East Side on February 8.

He picked up the eight by ten again. And the last: Liza Lee, 21, Dancer. Lived across the river in Jersey City. Ducked into an alley for a toot with her boyfriend tonight and never came out.

Three blondes, three brunettes, one redhead. Some stacked, some on the flat side. All caucs except for Perrin. All lookers. But besides that, how in the world could these women be linked? They came from all over town, and they met their respective ends all over town. What could—

"Well, you sure hit the bullseye about that roof!" Jacobi said as he burst into the office.

Harrison straightened in his chair. "What did you find?"

"Blood."

"Whose?"

"The victim's."

"No prints? No hairs? No fibers?"

"We're working on it. But how'd you figure to check the roof top?"

"Lucky guess."

Harrison didn't want to provide Jacobi with more grist for the departmental gossip mill by mentioning his feeling of being watched from up there.

But the killer *had* been watching, hadn't he?

"Any prelims from pathology?"

Jacobi shrugged and stuffed three sticks of gum into his mouth. Then he tried to talk.

"Same as ever. Money gone, throat ripped open by a pair of sharp pointed instruments, not knives, the bite marks on the face are the usual: the teeth that made them aren't human, but the saliva is.''

The ''non-human'' teeth part—more teeth, bigger and sharper than found in any human mouth—had baffled them all from the start. Early on someone remembered a horror novel or movie where the killer used some weird sort of false teeth to bite his victims. That had sent them off on a wild goose chase to all the dental labs looking for records of bizarre bite prostheses. No dice. No one had seen or even heard of teeth that could gnaw off a person's face.

Harrison shuddered. What could explain wounds like that? What were they dealing with here?

The irritating pops, snaps, and cracks of Jacobi's gum filled the office.

''I liked you better when you smoked.''

Jacobi's reply was cut off by the phone. The sergeant picked it up.

''Detective Harrison's office!'' he said, listened a moment, then, with his hand over the mouthpiece, passed the receiver to Harrison. ''Some fairy wantsh to shpeak to you,'' he said with an evil grin.

''Fairy?''

''Hey,'' he said, getting up and walking toward the door. ''I don't mind. I'm a liberal kinda guy, y'know?''

Harrison shook his head with disgust. Jacobi was getting less likeable every day.

''Hello. Harrison here.''

''Shorry dishturb you, Detective Harrishon.''

The voice was soft, pitched somewhere between a man's and a woman's, and sounded as if the speaker had half a mouthful of saliva. Harrison had never heard anything like it. Who could be—?

And then it struck him: It was three a.m. Only a handful of people knew he was here.

''Do I know you?''

''No. Watch you tonight. You almosht shee me in dark.''

That same chill from earlier tonight ran down Harrison's back again.

"Are . . . are you who I think you are?"

There was a pause, then one soft word, more sobbed than spoken:

"Yesh."

If the reply had been cocky, something along the line of *And just who do you think I am?*, Harrison would have looked for much more in the way of corroboration. But that single word, and the soul-deep heartbreak that propelled it, banished all doubt.

My God! He looked around frantically. No one in sight. Where the fuck was Jacobi now when he needed him? This was the Facelift Killer! He needed a trace!

Got to keep him on the line!

"I have to ask you something to be sure you are who you say you are."

"Yesh?"

"Do you take anything from the victims—I mean, besides their faces?"

"Money. Take money."

This is him! The department had withheld the money part from the papers. Only the real Facelift Killer could know!

"Can I ask you something else?"

"Yesh."

Harrison was asking this one for himself.

"What do you do with the faces?"

He had to know. The question drove him crazy at night. He dreamed about those faces. Did the killer tack them on the wall, or press them in a book, or freeze them, or did he wear them around the house like that Leatherface character from that chainsaw movie?

On the other end of the line he sensed sudden agitation and panic: "No! Can not shay! Can *not!*"

"Okay, okay. Take it easy."

"You will help shtop?"

"Oh, yes! Oh, God, yes, I'll help you stop!" He prayed his genuine heartfelt desire to end this was coming through. "I'll help you any way I can!"

There was a long pause, then:

"You hate? Hate me?"

Harrison didn't trust himself to answer that right away. He searched his feelings quickly, but carefully.

"No," he said finally. "I think you have done some awful, horrible things but, strangely enough, I don't hate you."

And that was true. Why didn't he hate this murdering maniac? Oh, he wanted to stop him more than anything in the world, and wouldn't hesitate to shoot him dead if the situation required it, but there was no personal hatred for the Facelift Killer.

What is it in you that speaks to me? he wondered.

"Shank you," said the voice, couched once more in a sob.

And then the killer hung up.

Harrison shouted into the dead phone, banged it on his desk, but the line was dead.

"What the hell's the matter with you?" Jacobi said from the office door.

"That so-called 'fairy' on the phone was the Facelift Killer, you idiot! We could have had a trace if you'd stuck around!"

"Bullshit!"

"He knew about taking the money!"

"So why'd he talk like that? That's a dumb-ass way to try to disguise your voice."

And then it suddenly hit Harrison like a sucker punch to the gut. He swallowed hard and said:

"Jacobi, how do you think your voice would sound if you had a jaw crammed full of teeth much larger and sharper than the kind found in the typical human mouth?"

Harrison took genuine pleasure in the way Jacobi's face blanched slowly to yellow-white.

He didn't get home again until after seven the following night. The whole department had been in an uproar all day. This was the first break they had had in the case. It wasn't much, but contact had been made. That was the important part. And although Harrison had done nothing he could think of to deserve any credit, he had accepted the commissioner's compliments and encouragement on the phone shortly before he had left the office tonight.

But what was most important to Harrison was the evidence from the call—*Damn!* he wished it had been taped—that the killer wanted to stop. They didn't have one more goddamn clue tonight than they'd had yesterday, but the call offered hope that soon there might be an end to this horror.

Martha had dinner waiting. The kids were scrubbed and pajamaed and waiting for their goodnight kiss. He gave them each a hug and poured himself a stiff scotch while Martha put them in the sack.

"Do you feel as tired as you look?" she said as she returned from the bedroom wing.

She was a big woman with bright blue eyes and natural dark blond hair. Harrison toasted her with his glass.

"The expression 'dead on his feet' has taken on a whole new meaning for me."

She kissed him, then they sat down to eat.

He had spoken to Martha a couple of times since he had left the house twenty hours ago. She knew about the phone call from the Facelift Killer, about the new hope in the department about the case, but he was glad she didn't bring it up now. He was sick of talking about it. Instead, he sat in front of his cooling meatloaf and wrestled with the images that had been nibbling at the edges of his consciousness all day.

"What are you daydreaming about?" Martha said.

Without thinking, Harrison said, "Annie."

"Annie who?"

"My sister."

Martha put her fork down. "Your sister? Kevin, you don't have a sister."

"Not any more. But I did."

Her expression was alarmed now. "Kevin, are you all right? I've known your family for ten years. Your mother has never once mentioned—"

"We don't talk about Annie, Mar. We try not to even think about her. She died when she was five."

"Oh. I'm sorry."

"Don't be. Annie was . . . deformed. Terribly deformed. She never really had a chance."

Open trunk from inside. Get out. The Detective Harrison's house here. Cold night. Cold feel good. Trunk air make sick, dizzy.

Light here. Hurry round side of house.

Darker here. No one see. Look in window. Dark but see good. Two little ones there. Sleeping. Move away. Not want them cry.

Go more round. The Detective Harrison with lady. Sit table near window. Must be wife. Pretty but not oh-so-beauty. Not have momface. Not like ones who die.

Watch behind tree. Hungry. They not eat food. Talk-talk-talk. Can not hear.

The Detective Harrison do most talk. Kind face. Kind eyes. Some terrible sad there. Hides. Him understands. Heard in phone voice. Understands. Him one can stop kills.

Spent day watch the Detective Harrison car. All day watch at police house. Saw him come-go many times. Soon dark, open trunk with claw. Ride with him. Ride long. Wonder what town this?

The Detective Harrison look this way. Stare like last night. Must not see me! Must *not!*

Harrison stopped in mid-sentence and stared out the window as his skin prickled.

That *watched* feeling again.

It was the same as last night. Something was out in the backyard watching them. He strained to see through the wooded darkness outside the window but saw only shadows within shadows.

But something was *there!* He could feel it!

He got up and turned on the outside spotlights, hoping, *praying* that the backyard would be empty.

It was.

He smiled to hide his relief and glanced at Martha.

"Thought that raccoon was back."

He left the spots on and settled back into his place at the table. But the thoughts racing through his mind made eating unthinkable.

What if that maniac had followed him out here? What if the call had been a ploy to get him off-guard so the Facelift Killer could do to Martha what he had done to the other women?

My God . . .

First thing tomorrow morning he was going to call the local alarm boys and put in a security system. Cost be damned, he had to have it. Immediately!

As for tonight . . .

Tonight he'd keep the .38 under the pillow.

Run way. Run low and fast. Get bushes before light come. Must stay way now. Not come back.

The Detective Harrison *feel* me. Know when watched. Him the one, sure.

Walk in dark, in woods. See back many houses. Come park. Feel strange. See this park before. Can not be—

Then know.

Monroe! This Monroe! Born here! Live here! Hate Monroe! Monroe bad place, bad people! House, home, old home near here! There! Cross park! Old home! New color but same house.

Hate house!

Sit on froze park grass. Cry. Why Monroe? Do not want be in Monroe. The Mom gone. The Sissy gone. The Jimmy very gone. House here.

Dry tears. Watch old home long time till light go out. Wait more. Go to windows. See new folks inside. The Mom took the Sissy and go. Where? Don't know.

Go to back. Push cellar window. Crawl in. See good in dark. New folks make nice cellar. Wood on walls. Rug on floor. No chain.

Sit floor. Remember . . .

Remember hanging on wall. Look little window near ceiling. Watch kids play in park cross street. Want go with kids. Want play there with kids. Want have friends.

But the Mom won't let. Never leave basement. Too strong.

Break everything. Have tv. Broke it. Have toys. Broke them. Stay in basement. Chain round waist hold to center pole. Can not leave.

Remember terrible bad things happen.

Run. Run way Monroe. Never come back.

Til now.

Now back. Still hate house! Want hurt house. See cigarettes. With matches. Light all. Burn now!

Watch rug burn. Chair burn. So hot. Run back to cold park. Watch house burn. See new folks run out. Trucks come throw water. House burn and burn.

Glad but tears come anyway.

Hate house. Now house gone. Hate Monroe.

Wonder where the Mom and the Sissy live now.

Leave Monroe for new home and the Old Jessi.

The second call came the next day. And this time they were ready for it. The tape recorders were set, the computers were waiting to begin the tracing protocol. As soon as Harrison recognized the voice, he gave the signal. On the other side of the desk, Jacobi put on a headset and people started running in all directions. Off to the races.

"I'm glad you called," Harrison said. "I've been thinking about you."

"You undershtand?" said the soft voice.

"I'm not sure."

"Musht help shtop."

"I will! I will! Tell me how!"

"Not know."

There was a pause. Harrison wasn't sure what to say next. He didn't want to push, but he had to keep him on the line.

"Did you . . . hurt anyone last night."

"No. Shaw houshes. Your houshe. Your wife."

Harrison's blood froze. Last night—in the back yard. That had been the Facelift Killer in the dark. He looked up and saw genuine concern in Jacobi's eyes. He forced himself to speak.

"You were at my house? Why didn't you talk to me?"

"No-no! Can not let shee! Run way your house. Go mine!"

"*Yours*? You live in Monroe?"

"No! Hate Monroe! Once lived. Gone long! Burn old houshe. Never go back!"

This could be important. Harrison phrased the next question carefully.

"You burned your old house? When was that?"

If he could just get a date, a year . . .

"Last night."

"*Last night?*" Harrison remembered hearing the sirens and fire horns in the early morning darkness.

"Yesh! Hate houshe!"

And then the line went dead.

He looked at Jacobi who had picked up another line.

"Did we get the trace?"

"Waiting to hear. Christ, he sounds retarded, doesn't he?"

Retarded. The word sent ripples across the surface of his brain. Non-human teeth . . . Monroe . . . retarded . . . a picture was forming in the settling sediment, a picture he felt he should avoid.

"Maybe he is."

"You'd think that would make him easy to—"

Jacobi stopped, listened to the receiver, then shook his head disgustedly.

"What?"

"Got as far as the Lower East Side. He was probably calling from somewhere in one of the projects. If we'd had another thirty seconds—"

"We've got something better than a trace to some lousy pay phone," Harrison said. "We've got his old address!" He picked up his suit coat and headed for the door.

"Where we goin'?"

"Not 'we.' Me. I'm going out to Monroe."

Once he reached the town, it took Harrison less than an hour to find the Facelift Killer's last name.

He first checked with the Monroe Fire Department to find the address of last night's house fire. Then he went down to the brick fronted Town Hall and found the lot and block number. After that it was easy to look up its history of ownership. Mr. and Mrs. Elwood Scott were the current owners of the land and the charred shell of a three-bedroom ranch that sat upon it.

There had only been one other set of owners: Mr. and Mrs. Thomas Baker. He had lived most of his life in Monroe but knew nothing about the Baker family. But he knew where to find out: Captain Jeremy Hall, Chief of Police in the Incorporated Village of Monroe.

Captain Hall hadn't changed much over the years. Still had a big belly, long sideburns, and hair cut bristly short on the sides. That was the "in" look these days, but Hall had been wearing his hair like that for at least thirty years. If not for his Bronx accent, he could have played a redneck sheriff in any one of those southern chain gang movies.

After pleasantries and local-boy-leaves-home-to-become-big-city-cop-and-now-comes-to-question-small-town-cop banter, they got down to business.

"The Bakers from North Park Drive?" Hall said after he had noisily sucked the top layer off his steaming coffee. "Who could forget them? There was the mother, divorced, I believe, and the three kids—two girls and the boy."

Harrison pulled out his note pad. "The boy's name—what was it?"

"Tommy, I believe. Yeah—Tommy. I'm sure of it."

"He's the one I want."

Hall's eyes narrowed. "He is, is he? You're working on that Facelift case aren't you?"

"Right."

"And you think Tommy Baker might be your man?"

"It's a possibility. What do you know about him?"

"I know he's dead."

Harrison froze. "Dead? That can't be!"

"It sure as hell *can* be!" Without rising from his seat, he shouted through his office door. "Murph! Pull out that old file on the Baker case! Nineteen eighty-four, I believe!"

"Eighty-four?" Harrison said. He and Martha had been

living in Queens then. They hadn't moved back to Monroe yet.

"Right. A real messy affair. Tommy Baker was thirteen years old when he bought it. And he bought it. *Believe* me, he bought it!"

Harrison sat in glum silence, watching his whole theory go up in smoke.

The Old Jessi sleeps. Stand by mirror near tub. Only mirror have. No like them. The Jessi not need one.

Stare face. Bad face. Teeth, teeth, teeth. And hair. Arms too thin, too long. Claws. None have claws like my. None have face like like my.

Face not better. Ate pretty faces but face still same. Still cause sick-scared look. Just like at home.

Remember home. Do not want but thoughts will not go. Faces.

The Sissy get the Mom-face. Beauty face. The Tommy get the Dad-face. Not see the Dad. Never come home anymore. Who my face? Never see where come. Where my face come? My hands come?

Remember home cellar. Hate home! Hate cellar more! Pull on chain round waist. Pull and pull. Want out. Want play. *Please*. No one let.

One day when the Mom and the Sissy go, the Tommy bring friends. Come down cellar. Bunch on stairs. Stare. First time see sick-scared look. Not understand.

Friends! Play! Throw ball them. They run. Come back with rocks and sticks. Still sick-scared look. Throw me, hit me.

Make cry. Make the Tommy laugh.

Whenever the Mom and the Sissy go, the Tommy come with boys and sticks. Poke and hit. Hurt. Little hurt on skin. Big hurt inside. Sick-scared look hurt most of all. Hate look. Hate hurt. Hate them.

Most hate the Tommy.

One night chain breaks. Wait on wall for the Tommy. Hurt him. Hurt the Tommy outside. Hurt the Tommy inside. Know because pull inside outside. The Tommy quiet. Quiet, wet, red. The Mom and the Sissy get sick-scared look and scream.

Hate that look. Run way. Hide. Never come back. Till last night.

Cry more now. Cry quiet. In tub. So the Jessi not hear.

Harrison flipped through the slim file on the Tommy Baker murder.

"This is it?"

"We didn't need to collect much paper," Captain Hall said. "I mean, the mother and sister were witnesses. There's some photos in that manila envelope at the back."

Harrison pulled it free and slipped out some large black and whites. His stomach lurched immediately.

"*My God!*"

"Yeah, he was a mess. Gutted by his older sister."

"His *sister?*"

"Yeah. Apparently she was some sort of freak of nature."

Harrison felt the floor tilt under him, felt as if he were going to slide off the chair.

"Freak?" he said, hoping Hall wouldn't notice the tremor in his voice. "What did she look like?"

"Never saw her. She took off after she killed the brother. No one's seen hide nor hair of her since. But there's a picture of the rest of the family in there."

Harrison shuffled through the file until he came to a large color family portrait. He held it up. Four people: two adults seated in chairs; a boy and a girl, about ten and eight, kneeling on the floor in front of them. A perfectly normal American family. Four smiling faces.

But where's your oldest child. Where's your big sister? Where did you hid that fifth face while posing for this?

"What was her name? The one who's not here?"

"Not sure. Carla, maybe? Look at the front sheet under *Suspect.*"

Harrison did: Carla Baker—called 'Carly,' '" he said.

Hall grinned. "Right. Carly. Not bad for a guy getting ready for retirement."

Harrison didn't answer. An ineluctable sadness filled him as he stared at the incomplete family portrait.

Carly Baker . . . poor Carly . . . where did they hide you away? In the cellar? Locked in the attic? How did your brother treat you? Bad enough to deserve killing?

Probably.

"No pictures of Carly, I suppose."

"Not a one."

That figures.

"How about a description?"

"The mother gave us one but it sounded so weird, we threw it out. I mean, the girl sounded like she was half spider or something!" He drained his cup. "Then later on I got into a discussion with Doc Alberts about it. He told me he was doing deliveries back about the time this kid was born. Said they had a whole rash of monsters, all delivered within a few weeks of each other."

The room started to tilt under Harrison again.

"Early December, 1968, by chance?"

"Yeah! How'd you know?"

He felt queasy. "Lucky guess."

"Huh. Anyway, Doc Alberts said they kept it quiet while they looked into a cause, but that little group of freaks—'cluster,' he called them—was all there was. They figured that a bunch of mothers had been exposed to something nine months before, but whatever it had been was long gone. No monsters since. I understand most of them died shortly after birth, anyway."

"Not all of them."

"Not that it matters," Hall said, getting up and pouring himself a refill from the coffee pot. "Someday someone will find her skeleton, probably somewhere out in Haskins' marshes."

"Maybe." *But I wouldn't count on it.* He held up the file. "Can I get a xerox of this?"

"You mean the Facelift Killer is a twenty-year-old girl?" Martha's face clearly registered her disbelief.

"Not just any girl. A freak. Someone so deformed she really doesn't look human. Completely uneducated and probably mentally retarded to boot."

Harrison hadn't returned to Manhattan. Instead, he'd headed straight for home, less than a mile from Town Hall. He knew the kids were at school and that Martha would be there alone. That was what he had wanted. He needed to talk this out with someone a lot more sensitive than Jacobi.

Besides, what he had learned from Captain Hall and the Baker file had dredged up the most painful memories of his life.

"A monster," Martha said.

"Yeah. Born one on the outside, *made* one on the inside. But there's another child monster I want to talk about. Not Carly Baker. Annie . . . Ann Harrison."

Martha gasped. "That sister you told me about last night?"

Harrison nodded. He knew this was going to hurt, but he had to do it, had to get it out. He was going to explode into a thousand twitching bloody pieces if he didn't.

"I was nine when she was born. December 2, 1968—a week after Carly Baker. Seven pounds, four ounces of horror. She looked more fish than human."

His sister's image was imprinted on the rear wall of his brain. And it should have been after all those hours he had spent studying her loathsome face. Only her eyes looked human. The rest of her was awful. A lipless mouth, flattened nose, sloping forehead, fingers and toes fused so that they looked more like flippers than hands and feet, a bloated body covered with shiny skin that was a dusky gray-blue. The doctors said she was that color because her heart was bad, had a defect that caused mixing of blue blood and red blood.

A repulsed nine-year-old Kevin Harrison had dubbed her The Tuna—but never within earshot of his parents.

"She wasn't supposed to live long. A few months, they said, and she'd be dead. But she didn't die. Annie lived on and on. One year. Two. My father and the doctors tried to get my mother to put her into some sort of institution, but Mom wouldn't hear of it. She kept Annie in the third bedroom and talked to her and cooed over her and cleaned up her shit and just hung over her all the time. *All* the time, Martha!''

Martha gripped his hand and nodded for him to go on.

''After a while, it got so there was nothing else in Mom's life. She wouldn't leave Annie. Family trips became a thing of the past. Christ, if she and Dad went out to a movie, I had to stay with Annie. No babysitter was trustworthy enough. Our whole lives seemed to center around that freak in the back bedroom. And me? I was forgotten.

''After a while I began to hate my sister.''

''Kevin, you don't have to—''

''Yes, I do! I've got to tell you how it was! By the time I was fourteen—just about Tommy Baker's age when he bought it—I thought I was going to go crazy. I was getting all B's in school but did that matter? Hell, no! 'Annie rolled halfway over today. Isn't that wonderful?' Big deal! She was five years old, for Christ sake! I was starting point guard on the highschool junior varsity basketball team as a goddamn freshman, but did anyone come to my games? Hell no!

''I tell you, Martha, after five years of caring for Annie, our house was a powderkeg. Looking back now I can see it was my mother's fault for becoming so obsessed. But back then, at age fourteen, I blamed it all on Annie. I really hated her for being born a freak.''

He paused before going on. This was the really hard part.

''One night, when my dad had managed to drag my mother out to some company banquet that he had to attend, I was left alone to babysit Annie. On those rare occasions, my mother would always tell me to keep Annie company—you know, read her stories and such. But I never did. I'd let her lie back there alone with our old black and white tv while I sat in the living room watching the family set. This time, however, I went into her room.''

He remembered the sight of her, lying there with the covers half way up her fat little tuna body that couldn't have been much more than a yard in length. It was winter, like now, and his mother had dressed her in a flannel nightshirt. The coarse hair that grew off the back of her head had been wound into two braids and fastened with pink bows.

"Annie's eyes brightened as I came into the room. She had never spoken. Couldn't, it seemed. Her face could do virtually nothing in the way of expression, and her flipper-like arms weren't good for much, either. You had to read her eyes, and that wasn't easy. None of us knew how much of a brain Annie had, or how much she understood of what was going on around her. My mother said she was bright, but I think Mom was a little whacko on the subject of Annie.

"Anyway, I stood over her crib and started shouting at her. She quivered at the sound. I called her every dirty name in the book. And as I said each one, I poked her with my fingers— not enough to leave a bruise, but enough to let out some of the violence in me. I called her a lousy goddamn tunafish with feet. I told her how much I hated her and how I wished she had never been born. I told her everybody hated her and the only thing she was good for was a freak show. Then I said, 'I wish you were dead! Why don't you die? You were supposed to die years ago! Why don't you do everyone a favor and do it now!'

"When I ran out of breath, she looked at me with those big eyes of hers and I could see the tears in them and I knew she had understood me. She rolled over and faced the wall. I ran from the room.

"I cried myself to sleep that night. I'd thought I'd feel good telling her off, but all I kept seeing in my mind's eye was this fourteen-year-old bully shouting at a helpless five-year-old. I felt awful. I promised myself that the first opportunity I had to be alone with her the next day I'd apologize, tell her I really didn't mean the hateful things I'd said, promise to read to her and be her best friend, anything to make it up to her.

"I awoke next morning to the sound of my mother screaming Annie was dead."

"Oh, my God!" Martha said, her fingers digging into his arm.

"Naturally, I blamed myself."

"But you said she had a heart defect!"

"Yeah. I know. And the autopsy showed that's what killed her—her heart finally gave out. But I've never been able to get it out of my head that my words were what made her heart give up. Sounds sappy and melodramatic, I know, but I've always felt that she was just hanging on to life by the slimmest margin and that I pushed her over the edge."

"Kevin, you shouldn't have to carry that around with you! Nobody should!"

The old grief and guilt were like a slowly expanding balloon in his chest. It was getting hard to breathe.

"In my coolest, calmest, most dispassionate moments I convince myself that it was all a terrible coincidence, that she would have died that night anyway and that I had nothing to do with it."

"That's probably true, so—"

"But that doesn't change the fact that the last memory of her life was of her big brother—the guy she probably thought was the neatest kid on earth, who could run and play basketball, one of the three human beings who made up her whole world, who should have been her champion, her defender against a world that could only greet her with revulsion and rejection—standing over her crib telling her how much he hated her and how he wished she was dead!"

He felt the sobs begin to quake in his chest. He hadn't cried in over a dozen years and he had no intention of allowing himself to start now, but there didn't seem to be any stopping it. It was like running down hill at top speed—if he tried to stop before he reached bottom, he'd go head over heels and break his neck.

"Kevin, you were only fourteen," Martha said soothingly.

"Yeah, I know. But if I could go back in time for just a few seconds, I'd go back to that night and rap that rotten hateful fourteen-year-old in the mouth before he got a chance to say a single word. But I can't. I can't even say I'm sorry to Annie! I never got a chance to take it back, Martha! I never got a chance to make it up to her!"

And then he was blubbering like a goddamn wimp, letting loose half a lifetime's worth of grief and guilt, and Martha's

arms were around him and she was telling him everything would
be all right, all right, all right . . .

The Detective Harrison understand. Can tell. Want to go kill
another face now. Must not. The Detective Harrison not like.
Must stop. The Detective Harrison help stop.

Stop for good.

Best way. Only one way stop for good. Not jail. No chain,
no little window. Not ever again. Never!

Only one way stop for good. The Detective Harrison will
know. Will understand. Will do.

Must call. Call now. Before dark. Before pretty faces come
out in night.

Harrison had pulled himself together by the time the kids
came home from school. He felt strangely buoyant inside, like
he'd been purged in some way. Maybe all those shrinks were
right after all: sharing old hurts did help.

He played with the kids for a while, then went into the kitchen
to see if Martha needed any help with slicing and dicing. He
felt as close to her now as he ever had.

"You okay?" she said with a smile.

"Fine."

She had just started slicing a red pepper for the salad. He
took over for her.

"Have you decided what to do?" she asked.

He had been thinking about it a lot, and had come to a
decision.

"Well, I've got to inform the department about Carly Baker,
but I'm going to keep her out of the papers for a while."

"Why? I'd think if she's that freakish looking, the publicity
might turn up someone who's seen her."

"Possibly it will come to that. But this case is sensational
enough without tabloids like the *Post* and *The Light* turning it
into a circus. Besides, I'm afraid of panic leading to some poor
deformed innocent getting lynched. I think I can bring her in.
She *wants* to come in."

"You're sure of that?"

"She so much as told me so. Besides, I can sense it in her."
He saw Martha giving him a dubious look. "I'm serious. We're
somehow connected, like there's an invisible wire between us.
Maybe it's because the same thing that deformed her and those
other kids deformed Annie, too. And Annie was my sister.
Maybe that link is why I volunteered for this case in the first
place."

He finished slicing the pepper, then moved on to the mush-
rooms.

"And after I bring her in, I'm going to track down her mother
and start prying into what went on in Monroe in February and
March of sixty-eight to cause that so-called 'cluster' of freaks
nine months later."

He would do that for Annie. It would be his way of saying
good-bye and I'm sorry to his sister.

"But why does she take their faces?" Martha said.

"I don't know. Maybe because theirs were beautiful and
hers is no doubt hideous."

"But what does she *do* with them?"

"Who knows? I'm not all that sure I *want* to know. But
right now—"

The phone rang. Even before he picked it up, he had an
inkling of who it was. The first sibilant syllable left no doubt.

"Ish thish the Detective Harrishon?"

"Yes."

Harrison stretched the coiled cord around the corner from
the kitchen into the dining room, out of Martha's hearing.

"Will you shtop me tonight?"

"You want to give yourself up?"

"Yesh. Pleashe, yesh."

"Can you meet me at the precinct house?"

"*No!*"

"Okay! Okay!" God, he didn't want to spook her now.
"Where? Anywhere you say."

"Jusht you."

"All right."

"Midnight. Plashe where lasht fashe took. Bring gun but
not more cop."

"All right."

He was automatically agreeing to everything. He'd work out the details later.

"You undershtand, Detective Harrishon?"

"Oh, Carly, Carly, I understand more than you know!"

There was a sharp intake of breath and then silence at the other end of the line. Finally:

"You know Carly?"

"Yes, Carly. I know you." The sadness welled up in him again and it was all he could do to keep his voice from breaking. "I had a sister like you once. And you . . . you had a brother like me."

"Yesh," said that soft, breathy voice. "You undershtand. Come tonight, Detective Harrishon."

The line went dead.

Wait in shadows. The Detective Harrison will come. Will bring lots cop. Always see on tv show. Always bring lots. Protect him. Many guns.

No need. Only one gun. The Detective Harrison's gun. Him's will shoot. Stop kills. Stop forever.

The Detective Harrison must do. No one else. The Carly can not. Must be the Detective Harrison. Smart. Know the Carly. Understand.

After stop, no more ugly Carly. No more sick-scared look. Bad face will go way. Forever and ever.

Harrison had decided to go it alone.

Not completely alone. He had a van waiting a block and a half away on Seventh Avenue and a walkie-talkie clipped to his belt, but he hadn't told anyone who he was meeting or why. He knew if he did, they'd swarm all over the area and scare Carly off completely. So he had told Jacobi he was meeting an informant and that the van was just a safety measure.

He was on his own here and wanted it that way. Carly Baker wanted to surrender to him and him alone. He understood that. It was part of that strange tenuous bond between them. No one else would do. After he had cuffed her, he would call in the wagon.

After that he would be a hero for a while. He didn't want to be a hero. All he wanted was to end this thing, end the nightmare for the city and for poor Carly Baker. She'd get help, the kind she needed, and he'd use the publicity to spring-board an investigation into what had made Annie and Carly and the others in their 'cluster' what they were.

It's all going to work out fine, he told himself as he entered the alley.

He walked half its length and stood in the darkness. The brick walls of the buildings on either side soared up into the night. The ceaseless roar of the city echoed dimly behind him. The alley itself was quiet—no sound, no movement. He took out his flashlight and flicked it on.

"Carly?"

No answer.

"Carly Baker—are you here?"

More silence, then, ahead to his left, the sound of a garbage can scraping along the stoney floor of the alley. He swung the light that way, and gasped.

A looming figure stood a dozen feet in front of him. It could only be Carly Baker. She stood easily as tall as he—a good six foot two—and looked like a homeless street person, one of those animated ragpiles that live on subway grates in the winter. Her head was wrapped in a dirty scarf, leaving only her glittery dark eyes showing. The rest of her was muffled in a huge, shapeless overcoat, baggy old polyester slacks with dragging cuffs, and torn sneakers.

"Where the Detective Harrishon's gun?" said the voice.

Harrison's mouth was dry but he managed to get his tongue working.

"In its holster."

"Take out. Pleashe."

Harrison didn't argue with her. The grip of his heavy Chief Special felt damn good in his hand.

The figure spread its arms; within the folds of her coat those arms seemed to bend the wrong way. And were those black hooked claws protruding from the cuffs of the sleeves?

She said, "Shoot."

Harrison gaped in shock.

The Detective Harrison not shoot. Eyes wide. Hands with gun and light shake.

Say again: "Shoot!"

"Carly, no! I'm not here to kill you. I'm here to take you in, just as we agreed."

"*No!*"

Wrong! The Detective Harrison not understand! Must shoot the Carly! Kill the Carly!

"Not jail! Shoot! Shtop the kills! Shtop the Carly!"

"No! I can get you help, Carly. Really, I can! You'll go to a place where no one will hurt you. You'll get medicine to make you feel better!"

Thought him understand! Not understand! Move closer. Put claw out. Him back way. Back to wall.

"Shoot! Kill! Now!"

"No, Annie, please!"

"Not Annie! Carly! Carly!"

"Right. Carly! Don't make me do this!"

Only inches way now. Still not shoot. Other cops hiding not shoot. Why not protect?

"*Shoot!*" Pull scarf off face. Point claw at face. "End! End! *Pleashe!*"

The Detective Harrison face go white. Mouth hang open. Say, "Oh, my *God!*"

Get sick-scared look. Hate that look! Thought him understand! Say he know the Carly! Not! Stop look! *Stop!*

Not think. Claw go out. Rip throat of the Detective Harrison. Blood fly just like others.

No-No-No! Not want hurt!

The Detective Harrison gurgle. Drop gun and light. Fall. Stare.

Wait other cops shoot. Please kill the Carly. Wait.

No shoot. Then know. No cops. Only the poor Detective Harrison. Cry for the Detective Harrison. Then run. Run and climb. Up and down. Back to new home with the Old Jessi.

The Jessi glad hear Carly come. The Jessi try talk. Carly go sit tub. Close door. Cry for the Detective Harrison. Cry long time. Break mirror million piece. Not see face again. Not ever. Never.

The Jessi say, "Carly, I want my bath. Will you scrub my back?"

Stop cry. Do the Old Jessi's black back. Comb the Jessi's hair.

Feel very sad. None ever comb the Carly's hair. Ever.

Tenants

The mail truck was coming.

Gilroy Connors, shoes full of water and shirt still wet from the morning's heavy dew, crouched in the tall grass and punk-topped reeds. He ached all over; his thighs particularly were cramped from holding his present position. But he didn't dare move for fear of giving his presence away.

So he stayed hunkered down across the road from the battered old shack that looked deserted but wasn't—there had been lights on in the place last night. With its single pitched roof and rotting cedar shake siding, it looked more like an overgrown outhouse than a home. A peeling propane tank squatted on the north side; a crumbling brick chimney supported a canted tv antenna. Beyond the shack, glittering in the morning sunlight, lay the northeast end of Monroe Harbor and the Long Island Sound.

The place gave new meaning to the word *isolated*. As if a few lifetimes ago someone had brought a couple of tandems of fill out to the end of the hard-packed dirt road, dumped

them, and built a shack. Except for a rickety old dock with a
sodden rowboat tethered to it, there was not another structure
in sight in either direction. Only a slender umbilical cord of
insulated wire connected it to the rest of the world via a long
column of utility poles marching out from town. All around
was empty marsh.

Yeah. Isolated as all hell.

It was perfect.

As Gil watched, the shack's front door opened and a grizzled
old man stumbled out, a cigarette in his mouth and a fistful of
envelopes in his hand. Tall and lanky with an unruly shock of
gray hair standing off his head, he scratched his slightly protruding belly as he squinted in the morning sunlight. He wore
a torn undershirt that had probably been white once and a pair
of faded green work pants held up by suspenders. He looked
as rundown as his home, and as much in need of a shave and
a bath as Gil felt. With timing so perfect that it could only be
the result of daily practice, the old guy reached the mailbox at
exactly the same time as the white jeep-like mail truck.

Must have been watching from the window.

Not an encouraging thought. Had the old guy seen Gil out
here? It he had, he gave no sign. Which meant Gil was still
safe.

He fingered the handle of the knife inside his shirt.

Lucky for him.

While the old guy and the mailman jawed, Gil studied the
shack again. The place was a sign that his recent run of good
luck hadn't deserted him yet. He had come out to the marshes
to hide until things cooled down in and around Monroe and
had been expecting to spend a few real uncomfortable nights
out here. The shack would make things a lot easier.

Not much of a place. At most it looked big enough for two
rooms and no more. Barely enough space for an ancient couple
who didn't move around much—who ate, slept, crapped,
watched tv and nothing more. Hopefully, it wasn't a couple.
Just the old guy. That would make it simple. A wife, even a
real sickly one, could complicate matters.

Gil wanted to know how many were living there before he

invited himself in. Not that it would matter much. Either way, he was going in and staying for a while. He just liked to know what he was getting into before he made his move.

One thing was sure: He wasn't going to find any money in there. The old guy had to be next to destitute. But even ten bucks would have made him richer than Gil. He looked at the rusting blue late-sixties Ford Torino with the peeling vinyl roof and hoped it would run. But of course it ran. The old guy had to get into town to cash his Social Security check and buy groceries, didn't he?

Damn well better run.

It had been a long and sloppy trek into these marshes. He intended to drive out.

Finally the mail truck clinked into gear, did a u-turn, and headed back the way it had come. The old guy shoved a couple of envelopes into his back pocket, picked up a rake that had been leaning against the Ford, and began scratching at the dirt on the south side of the house.

Gil decided it was now or never. He straightened up and walked toward the shack. As his feet crunched on the gravel of the yard, the old man wheeled and stared at him with wide, startled eyes.

"Didn't mean to scare you," Gil said in his friendliest voice.

"Well, you sure as hell did, poppin' outta nowhere like that!" the old man said in a deep, gravelly voice. The cigarette between his lips bobbed up and down like a conductor's baton. "We don't exactly get much drop-in company out here. What happen? Boat run outta gas?"

Gil noticed the *we* with annoyance but played along. A stalled boat was as good an excuse as any for being out here in the middle of nowhere.

"Yeah. Had to paddle it into shore way back over there," he said, jerking a thumb over his shoulder.

"Well, I ain't got no phone for you to call anybody—"

No phone! It was all Gil could do to keep from cheering.

"—but I can drive you down to the marina and back so you can get some gas."

"No hurry." He moved closer and leaned against the old

Torino's fender. "You live out here all by yourself?"

The old man squinted at him, as if trying to recognize him. "I don't believe we've been introduced, son."

"Oh, right." Gil stuck out his hand. "Rick . . . Rick Summers."

"And I'm George Haskins," he said, giving Gil's hand a firm shake.

"What're you growing there?"

"Carrots. I hear fresh carrots are good for your eyes. Mine are so bad I try to eat as many as I can."

Half blind and no phone. This was sounding better every minute. Now, if he could just find out who the rest of the *we* was, he'd be golden.

He glanced around. Even though he was out in the middle of nowhere at the end of a dirt road that no one but the mailman and this old fart knew existed, he felt exposed. Naked, even. He wanted to get inside.

"Say, I sure could use a cup of coffee, Mr. Haskins. You think you might spare me some?"

George hesitated. Making coffee for the stranger would mean bringing him inside. He didn't like that idea at all. He hadn't had anybody into the house since the late sixties when he took in his tenants. And he'd had damn few visitors before that. People didn't like coming this far out, and George was just as glad. Most people pried. They wanted to know what you did way out here all by yourself. Couldn't believe anybody sane would prefer his own company to *theirs.*

And of course, there was the matter of the tenants.

He studied this young man who had popped out of nowhere. George's eyes weren't getting any better—"*Cataracts only get worse,*" the doctor had told him—but he could plainly see that the stranger wasn't dressed for boating, what with that blue work shirt and gray denims he was wearing. And those leather shoes! Nobody who knew boats ever wore leather shoes on board. But they were selling boats to anybody with cash these days. This landlubber probably didn't know the first thing about boating. That no doubt was why he was standing here on land instead of chugging about the harbor.

He seemed pleasant enough, though. Good-looking, too, with his muscular build and wavy dark hair. Bet he had an easy time with the girls. *Especially* easy, since from what George understood of the world today, *all* the girls were easy.

Maybe he could risk spotting him a cup of coffee before driving him down to the marina. What harm could there be in that? The tenants were late risers and had the good sense to keep quiet if they heard a strange voice overhead.

He smiled. "Coffee? Sure. Come on inside. And call me George. Everybody else does." He dropped his cigarette into the sandy soil and stomped on it, then turned toward the house.

Just a quick cup of coffee and George would send him off. The longer he stayed, the greater the chances of him finding out about the tenants. And George couldn't risk that. He was more than their landlord.

He had sworn to protect them.

Gil followed close on the old guy's back up the two steps to the door. Inside was dark and stale, reeking of years of cigarette smoke. He wondered when was the last time George had left a window open.

But being indoors was good. Out of sight and inside—even if it stank, it was better than good. It was super. He felt as if a great weight had been lifted from him.

Now to find out who made up the rest of the *we*.

"Got this place all to yourself, ay?" he said, glancing quickly about. They were standing in a rectangular space that passed for a living room/dining room/kitchen. The furniture consisted of an old card table, a rocker, a tilted easy chair, and a dilapidated couch. Shapeless piles of junk cluttered every corner. An ancient Motorola television set with a huge chassis and a tiny screen stood on the far side of the room diagonally across from the door. The screen was lit and a black chick was reading some news into the camera:

"*. . . eriously injuring an orderly in a daring escape from*

*the Monroe Neuropsychiatric Institute. He was last reported
in Glen Cove—''*

Gil whooped. "Glen Cove! Awright!" That was the wrong
direction! He was safe for the moment. "Fan*tas*tic!" he yelled,
stomping his foot on the floor.

"Hey! Hold it down!" George said as he filled a greasy,
dented aluminum kettle with water and put it on the gas stove.

Gil felt the customary flash of anger at being told what he
could or couldn't do, but cooled it. He stepped between George
and the tv set as he saw his most recent mug shot appear on
the screen. The black chick was saying:

*"If you see this man, do not approach him. He might be
armed and is considered dangerous."*

Gil said, "Sorry. It's just that sometimes I get excited by
the news."

"Yeah?" George said, lighting another cigarette. "Don't
follow it much myself. But you got to keep quiet. You might
disturb the tenants and they—''

"Tenants?" Gil said a lot more loudly than he intended.
"You've got *tenants*?"

The old guy was biting his upper lip with what few teeth he
had left and saying nothing.

Gil stepped down the short hall, gripping the handle of the
knife inside his shirt as he moved. Two doors: The one on the
left was open, revealing a tiny bathroom with a toilet, sink,
and mildewy shower stall; the one on the right was closed. He
gave it a gentle push. Empty: dirty, wrinkled sheets on a narrow
bed, dresser, mirror, clothes thrown all around, but nobody
there.

"Where are they?" he said, returning to the larger room.

George laughed—a little too loudly, Gil thought—and said,
"No tenants. Just a joke. Creepy-crawlies in the crawl space
is all. You know, snapping turtles and frogs and snakes and
crickets."

"You keep things like that under your house?" This was
turning out to be one weird guy.

"In a manner of speaking, yes. You see, a zillion years ago
when I built this place, a big family of crickets took up resi-

dence''—he pointed down—''in the crawl space. Drove me crazy at night. So one day I get the bright idea of catching some frogs and throwing them in there to eat the crickets. Worked great. Within two days, there wasn't a chirp to be heard down there.''

''Smart.''

''Yeah. So I thought: Until the frogs started croaking all night. They were worse than the crickets!''

Gil laughed. ''I get it. So you put the snakes down there to catch the frogs!''

''Right. Snakes are quiet. They eat crickets, too. Should've thought of them in the first place. Except I wasn't crazy about living over a nest of snakes.''

This was getting to sound like the old lady who swallowed the fly.

Gil said, ''And so the next step was to put the turtles down there to eat the snakes.''

''Yeah.'' As George spooned instant coffee into a couple of stained mugs, Gil tried not to think about when they last might have had a good washing. ''But I don't think they ate them all, just like I don't think the snakes ate all the frogs, or the frogs ate all the crickets. I still hear an occasional chirp and croak once in a while. Anyway, they've all been down there for years. I ain't for adding anything else to the stew, or even looking down there.''

''Don't blame you.''

George poured boiling water into the mugs and handed him one.

''So if you hear something moving underfoot, it's just one of my tenants.''

''Yeah. Okay. Sure.''

This old guy was fruitcake city. As crazy as—

. . . *Crazy. That was what that college chick had called him that night when he had tried to pick her up along the road. She was cute. There were a lot of cute girls at Monroe Community College, and he'd always made it a point to drive by every chance he could. She'd said he was crazy to think she'd take a ride from a stranger at that hour of the night. That had*

*made him mad. All these college broads thought they were
better and smarter than everybody else. And she'd started to
scream when he grabbed her, so he'd hit her to make her stop
but she wouldn't stop. She kept on screaming so he kept on
hitting her and hitting her and hitting and hitting . . .*

"You're spilling your coffee," George said.

Gil looked down. So he was. It was dripping over the edge
of his tilted mug and splashing onto the floor. As he slurped
some off the top and sat on the creaking couch, he realized
how tired he was. No sleep in the past twenty-four hours.
Maybe the coffee would boost him.

"So how come you live out here all by yourself?" Gil asked,
hoping to get the conversation on a saner topic than snakes and
snapping turtles in the crawlspace.

"I *like* being by myself."

"You must. But whatever rent you pay on this place, it's
too much."

"Don't pay no rent at all. I own it."

"Yeah, but the land—"

"My land."

Gil almost dropped his coffee mug. "*Your* land! That's impossible!"

"Nope. All twenty acres been in my family for a zillion and
two years."

Gil's brain whirled as he tried to calculate the value of twenty
acres of real estate fronting on Monroe Harbor and Long Island
Sound.

"You're a fucking millionaire!"

George laughed. "I wish! I'm what you call 'land poor,'
son. I've got to pay taxes on all this land if I want to keep it,
and the damn bastards down at City Hall keep raising my
rates and my assessed value so that I've got to come up with
more and more money every year just to stay here. Trying to
force me out, that's what they're up to."

"So sell, for Christ sake! There must be developers chomp-
ing at the bit to get ahold of this land. You could make 'em
pay through the nose for a piece of waterfront and all your
money worries would be over!"

George shook his head. "Naw. Once you sell one little piece, it's like a leak in a dam. It softens you, weakens you. Soon you're selling another piece, and then another. Pretty soon, I'll be living on this little postage stamp surrounded by big ugly condos, listening to cars and mopeds racing up and down the road with engines roaring and rock and roll blasting. No thanks. I've lived here in peace, and I want to die here in peace."

"Yeah, but—"

"Besides, lots of animals make their homes on my land. They've been pushed out of everywhere else in Monroe. All the trees have been cut down back there, all the hollows and gullies filled in and paved over. There's no place else for them to go. This is their world, too, you know. I'm their last resort. It's my duty to keep this place wild as long as I can. As long as I live . . . which probably won't be too much longer."

Oh, yes . . . crazy as a loon. Gil wondered if there might be some way he could get the old guy to will him the property and then cork him off. He stuffed the idea away in the *To be Developed* file.

"Makes me glad I don't have a phone," George was saying.

Right . . . no phone and no visitors.

Gil knew this was the perfect hiding place for him. Just a few days was all he needed. But he had to stay here *with* the old guy's cooperation. He couldn't risk anything forceful—not if George met the mailman at the box every day.

And from a few things the old man had said, he thought he knew just what buttons to push to convince George to let him stay.

George noted that his guest's coffee was empty. Good. Time to get him moving on. He never had company, didn't like it, and wasn't used to it. Made him itchy. Besides, he wanted this guy on his way before another remark about the tenants slipped out. That had been a close call before.

He stood up.

"Well, guess it's about time to be running you down to the marina for that tank of gas."

The stranger didn't move.

"George," he said in a low voice, "I've got a confession to make."

"Don't want to hear it!" George said. "I ain't no priest! Tell it somewhere else. I just want to help get you where you're going!"

"I'm on the run, George."

Oh, hell, George thought. At least that explained why he was acting so skittish. "You mean there's no boat waiting for gas somewhere?"

"I . . ." His voice faltered. "I lied about the boat."

"Well ain't that just swell. And who, may I ask,"—George wasn't so sure he wanted the answer to this, but he had to ask—"are you on the run from?"

"The Feds."

Double hell. "What for?"

"Income tax evasion."

"No kidding?" George was suddenly interested. "How much you take them for?"

"It's not so much 'how much' as 'how long.' "

"All right: How long?"

"Nine years. I haven't filed a return since I turned eighteen."

"No shit! Is that because you're stupid or because you've got balls?"

"Mr. Haskins," the stranger said, looking at him levelly and speaking with what struck George as bone-deep conviction, "I don't believe any government's got the right to tax what a working man earns with the sweat of his brow."

"Couldn't of said it better myself!" George cried. He thought his heart was going to burst. This boy was talking like he'd have wanted his son to talk, if he'd ever had one. "The sonsabitches'll bleed you dry if you let 'em! Look what they've been doin' to me!"

The young stranger stared at the floor. "I was hoping you'd understand."

"Understand? Of course I understand! I've been fighting the IRS for years but never had the guts to actually *resist!* My hat's off to you!"

"Can I stay the night?"

That brought George up short. He wanted to help this courageous young man, but what was he going to do about the tenants?

"What's going to happen to you if they catch you? What kind of sentence you facing?"

"Twenty."

George's stomach turned. A young guy like this in the hole for twenty years just for not paying taxes. He felt his blood begin to boil.

"Bastards!"

He'd have to chance it. Tenants or not, he felt obligated to give this guy a place to stay for the night. It would be okay. The tenants could take the day off and just rest up. They'd been working hard lately. He'd just have to watch his mouth so he didn't make another slip about them.

"Well, George? What do you say?"

"I can let you stay one night and one night only," George said. "After that—"

The young fellow leaped forward and shook his hand. "Thanks a million, George!"

"Hear me out now. Only tonight. Come tomorrow morning, I'll drive you down to the train station, get you a ticket, and put you on board for New York with all the commuters. Once in the city, you can get lost real easy."

George thought he saw tears in the young man's eyes. "I don't know how to thank you."

"Never mind that. You just hit the sack in my room. You look bushed. Get some rest. No one'll know you're here."

He nodded, then went to the window and gazed out at the land. "Beautiful here," he said.

George realized it would probably look even more beautiful if the window were cleaner, but his eyes weren't good enough to notice much difference.

"If this were mine," the young fellow said passionately, "I'd sure as hell find a way to keep it out of the hands of the developers *and* the tax men. Maybe make it into a wildlife preserve or bird sanctuary or something. *Anything* to keep it wild and free.''

Shaking his head, he turned and headed for the back room. George watched him in wonder. A *wildlife preserve!* Why hadn't he thought of that? It would be untaxable and unsubdividable! What a perfect solution!

But it was too late to start the wheels turning on something like that now. It would take years to submit all the proposals and wade through all the red tape to get it approved. And he didn't have years. He didn't need a doctor to tell him that his body was breaking down. He couldn't see right, he couldn't breathe right, and Christ Almighty, he couldn't even pee right. The parts were wearing out and there were no replacements available.

And what would happen when he finally cashed in his chips? What would happen to his land? And the tenants? Where would *they* go?

Maybe this young fellow was the answer. Maybe George could find a way to leave the land to him. He'd respect it, preserve it, just as George would if he could go on living. Maybe that was the solution.

But that meant he'd have to tell him the real truth about the tenants. He didn't know if the guy was ready for that.

He sat down in the sun on the front steps and lit another cigarette. He had a lot of thinking to do.

The five o'clock news was on.

George had kept himself busy all day, what with tending to the carrot patch outside and cleaning up a bit inside. Having company made him realize how long it had been since he'd given the place a good sweeping.

But before he'd done any of that, he'd waited until the young fellow had fallen asleep, then he'd lifted the trapdoor under the rug in the corner of the main room and told the tenants to lay low for the day. They'd understood and said they'd be quiet.

Now he was sitting in front of the tv watching *Eyewitness News* and going through today's mail: Three small checks from the greeting card companies—not much, but it would help pay this quarter's taxes. He looked up at the screen when he heard "the Long Island town of Monroe" mentioned. Some pretty Oriental girl was sitting across from a scholarly looking fellow in a blue suit. She was saying,

". . . explain to our viewers just what it is that makes Gilroy Connors so dangerous, Dr. Kline."

"He's a sociopath."

"And just what is that?"

"Simply put, it is a personality disorder in which the individual has no sense of 'mine' and 'not-mine' no sense of right or wrong in the traditional sense."

"No conscience, so to speak."

"Exactly."

"Are they all murderers like Connors?"

"No. History's most notorious criminals and serial killers are sociopaths, but violence isn't a necessary facet of their make-up. The confidence men who rip off the pensions of widows or steal from a handicapped person are just as sociopathic as the Charles Mansons of the world. The key element in the sociopathic character is his or her complete lack of guilt. They will do whatever is necessary to get what they want and will feel no remorse over anyone they have to harm along the way."

"Gilroy Connors was convicted in the Dorothy Akers murder. Do you think he'll kill again?"

"He has to be considered dangerous. He's a sociopathic personality with a particularly low frustration threshold. But he is also a very glib liar. Since the truth means nothing to him, he can take any side of a question, any moral stance, and speak on it with utter conviction."

A voice—George recognized it as belonging to one of the anchormen—called from off-camera: "Sounds like he'd make a great politician!"

Everyone had a good laugh, and then the Oriental woman said, "But all kidding aside, what should our viewers do if one of them should spot him?"

Dr. Kline's expression was suddenly grim. "Lock the doors and call the police immediately."

The camera closed in on the Oriental girl. "There you have it. We've been speaking to Dr. Edward Kline, a Long Island psychiatrist who examined Gilroy Connors and testified for the state at the Dorothy Akers murder trial.

"In case you've been asleep or out of the country during the last twenty-four hours, all of Long Island is being combed for Gilroy Connors, convicted killer of nineteen-year-old college coed Dorothy Akers. Connors escaped custody last night when, due to an error in paperwork, he was accidently transferred to the Monroe Neuropsychiatric Institute instead of a maximum security facility as ordered by the court. The victim's father, publisher Jeffrey Akers, is offering a fifty thousand dollar reward for information leading to his recapture."

Fifty thousand! George thought. *What I could do with that!*

"You've heard Dr. Kline," she continued. "If you see this man, call the police immediately."

A blow-up of a mug shot appeared on the screen. George gasped. He knew that man! Even with his rotten vision, he could see that the face on the tv belonged to the man now sleeping in his bed! He turned around to look toward the bedroom and saw his house guest standing behind him, a knife in his hand.

"Don't even think about that reward, old man," Connors said in a chillingly soft voice. "Don't even *dream* about it."

"You're hurtin' my hands!" the old fart whined as Gil knotted the cord around his wrists.

"I'm putting you down for the night, old man, and you're *staying* down!"

He pulled the rope tighter and the old man yelped.

Gil said, "There—that ought to hold you."

George rolled over onto his back and stared up at him. "What are you going to do with me?"

"Haven't figured that out yet."

"You're gonna kill me, aren't you?" There was more concern than fear in his eyes.

"Maybe. Maybe not. Depends on how you behave."

Truthfully, he didn't know what to do. It would be less of a hassle to kill him now and get it over with, but there was the problem of the mailman. If George wasn't waiting curbside at the box tomorrow morning, the USPS might come knocking on the door. So Gil had to figure out a way to pressure George into acting as if everything was nice and normal tomorrow. Maybe he'd have George stand at the door and wave to the mailman. That might work. He'd have to spend some time figuring this out.

"All that stuff you said about dodging the tax man was just lies, wasn't it?"

Gil smiled at the memory. "Yeah. Pretty good, wasn't it? I mean, I made that up right off the top of my head. Sucked you in like smoke, didn't I?"

"Nothing to be proud of."

"Why not?"

"You heard what they called you on the tv: a 'socialpath.' Means you're crazy."

"You watch your mouth, old man!" Gil could feel the rage surging up in him like a giant wave. He hated that word. "I'm *not* crazy! And I don't ever want to hear that word out of your mouth again!"

"Doesn't matter anyway," George said. "Soon as you're out of here, my tenants will untie me."

Gil laughed. "*Now* who's crazy!"

"It's true. They'll free me."

"That's enough of that," Gil said. It wasn't funny any more. He didn't like being called crazy any more than he liked being near crazy people. And this old man was talking crazy now. "No more of that kind of talk out of you!"

"You'll see. I'm their protector. Soon as you're—"

"Stop that!" Gil yanked George off the bed by his shirt front. He was losing it—he could feel it going. "God *damn* that makes me mad!"

He shoved the old man back against the wall with force enough to rattle the whole house. George's eyes rolled up as he slumped back onto the bed. A small red trickle crawled

along his scalp and mixed with the gray of his hair at the back
of his head.

"Sleep tight, Pops," Gil said.

He left George on the bed and returned to the other room.
He turned the antique tv back on. After what seemed like an
inordinately long warm-up time, the picture came in, flipped
a few times, then held steady. He hoped there wasn't another
psychiatrist on talking about him.

He hated psychiatrists. *Hated* them! Since he'd been picked
up for killing that college chick, he'd seen enough of their kind
to last a couple of lifetimes. Why'd she have to go and die?
It wasn't fair. He hadn't meant to kill her. If only she'd been
a little more cooperative. But no—she'd had to go and laugh
in his face. He'd just got mad, that was all. He wasn't crazy.
He just had a bad temper.

Psychiatrists! What'd they know about him? Labeling him,
pigeonholing him, saying he had no conscience and never felt
sorry for anything he did. What'd they know? Did they know
how he'd cried after Mom had burnt up in that fire in Dad's
car? He'd cried for *days*. Mom wasn't supposed to be anywhere
near that car when it caught fire. Only Dad.

He had *loads* of feelings, and nobody had better tell him any
different!

He watched the tube for awhile, caught a couple of news
broadcasts, but there was only passing mention of his escape
and the reward the girl's old man had posted for him. Then
came a report that he had been sighted on Staten Island and
the search was being concentrated there.

He smiled. They were getting farther and farther away from
where he really was.

He shut off the set at eleven-thirty. Time for some more
sleep. Before he made himself comfortable on the couch, he
checked out the old man's room. He was there, snoring comfortably under the covers. Gil turned away and then spun back
again.

How'd he get under the covers?

Two strides took him to the bedside. His foot kicked against
something that skittered across the floor. He found what it was:

the old guy's shoes. They'd been on his feet when he'd tied him up! He yanked back the covers and stared in open mouthed shock at the old man.

George's hands and feet were free. The cords were nowhere in sight.

Just then he thought he caught a blur of movement by the doorway. He swung around but there was nothing there. He turned back to George.

"Hey, you old fart!" He shook George's shoulder roughly until his eyes opened. "Wake up!"

George's eyes slowly came into focus. "Wha—?"

"How'd you do it?"

"Go way!"

George rolled onto his other side and Gil saw a patch of white gauze where he had been bleeding earlier. He flipped him onto his back again.

"How'd you untie yourself, goddammit?"

"Didn't. My tenants—"

"You stop talking that shit to me, old man!" Gil said, cocking his right arm.

George flinched away but kept his mouth shut. Maybe he was finally learning.

"You stay right there!"

Gil tore through the drawers and piles of junk in the other room until he found some more cord. During the course of the search he came across a check book and some uncashed checks. He returned to the bedroom and began tying up George again.

"Don't know how you did it the first time, but you ain't doing it again!"

He spread-eagled George on the sheet and tied each skinny limb to a separate corner of the bed, looping the cord down and around on the legs of the frame. Each knot was triple-tied.

"There! See if you can get out of that!"

As George opened his mouth to speak, Gil glared at him and the old man shut it with an almost audible snap.

"That's the spirit," Gil said softly.

He pulled the knife out of his shirt and held its six-inch blade up before George. The old man's eyes widened.

"Nice, isn't it? I snatched it from the kitchen of that wimpy Monroe Neuropsychiatric Institute. Would've preferred getting myself a gun, but none of the guards there were armed. Still, I can do a whole lot of damage with something like this and still not kill you. Understand what I'm saying to you, old man?"

George nodded vigorously.

"Good. Now what we're going to have here tonight is a nice quiet little house. No noise, no talk. Just a good night's sleep for both of us. Then we'll see what tomorrow brings."

He gave George one last hard look straight in the eye, then turned and headed back to the couch.

Before sacking out for the night, Gil went through George's checkbook. Not a whole lot of money in it. Most of the checks went out to cash or to the township for quarterly taxes. He noticed one good-sized regular monthly deposit that was probably his Social Security check, and lots of smaller sporadic additions.

he looked through the three undeposited checks. They were all made out to George Haskins, each from a different greeting card company. The attached invoices indicated they were in payment for varying numbers of verses.

Verses?

You mean old George back there tied up to the bed was a poet? He wrote greeting card verse?

Gil looked around the room. Where? There was no desk in the shack. Hell, he hadn't seen a piece of paper since he got here! Where did George write this stuff?

He went back to the bedroom. He did his best not to show the relief he felt when he saw that old George was still tied up nice and tight.

"Hey, old man," he said, waving the checks in the air. "How come you never told me you were a poet?"

George glared at him. "Those checks are mine! I need them to pay my taxes!"

"Yeah? Well, right now I need them a lot more than you do. I think tomorrow morning we'll take a little trip down to the bank so you can cash these." He checked the balance in the account. "And I think you just might make a cash withdrawal, too."

"I'll lose my land if I don't pay those taxes on time!"

"Well then, I guess you'll just have to come up with some more romantic 'verses' for these card companies. Like, 'George is a poet/And nobody know it.' See? It's easy!"

Gil laughed as he thought of all the broads who get those flowery, syrupy birthday and anniversary cards and sit mooning over the romantic poems inside, never knowing they were written by this dirty old man in a falling down shack on Long Island!

"I love it!" he said, heading back to the couch. "I just love it!"

He turned out all the lights, shoved the knife between two of the cushions, and bedded down on the dusty old couch for the night. As he drifted off to sleep, he thought he heard rustling movements from under the floorboards. George's 'tenants,' no doubt. He shuddered at the thought. The sooner he was out of here, the better.

What time is it?

Gil was rubbing the sleep from his eyes and peering around in the mineshaft blackness that surrounded him. Something had awakened him. But what? He sat perfectly still and listened.

A few crickets, maybe a frog—the noises seemed to come from outside instead of from the crawlspace—but nothing more than that.

Still, his senses were tingling with the feeling that something was wrong. He stood up and stepped over toward the light switch. As he moved, his foot caught on something and he fell forward. On the way down his ribs slammed against something else, something hard, like a chair. He hit the floor with his left shoulder. Groaning, he got to his knees and crawled until his fingers found the wall. He fumbled around for the light switch and flipped it.

When his eyes had adjusted to the glare, he glanced at the clock over the kitchen sink—going on 4:00 a.m. He thought he saw something move by the sink when he squinted for a better look, it was just some junk George had left there. Then he turned back toward the couch to see what had tripped him up.

It was the little hassock that had been over by the rocking chair when he had turned the lights out. At least he was pretty sure it had been there. He *knew* it hadn't been next to the couch where it was now. And the chair he had hit on his way down—that had been over against the wall.

In fact, as he looked around he noticed that not a single piece of furniture in the whole room was where it had been when he had turned out the lights and gone to sleep three or four hours ago. It had all been moved closer to the couch.

Someone was playing games. And Gil only knew of one possible someone.

Retrieving his knife from the couch, he hurried to the bedroom and stopped dead at the door. George was tied hand and foot to the corners of the bed, snoring loudly.

A chill rippled over Gil's skin.

"How the hell . . . ?"

He went back to the main room and checked the door and windows—all were locked from the inside. He looked again at the furniture, clustered around the couch as if the pieces had crept up and watched him as he slept.

Gil didn't believe in ghosts but he was beginning to believe this little shack was haunted.

And he wanted out.

He had seen the keys to the old Torino in one of the drawers. He found them again and hurried outside to the car. He hoped the damn thing started. He wasn't happy about hitting the road so soon, but he preferred taking his chances with the cops out in the open to being cooped up with whatever was haunting that shack.

As he slipped behind the wheel, he noticed a sliver of light shining out from inside the shack's foundation. That was weird. *Really* weird. Nobody kept a light on in a crawlspace. He was about to turn the ignition key but held up. He knew it was going to drive him nuts if he left without seeing what was down there.

Cursing himself for a jerk, he turned on the Ford's headlamps and got out for a closer look.

The light was leaking around a piece of plywood fitted into an opening in the foundation cinder blocks. It was hinged at the bottom and held closed by a short length of one-by-two shoved through the handle at the top. He pulled out the one-by-two and hesitated.

Connors, you are an asshole, he told himself, but he had to see what was in there. If it was snakes and snapping turtles, fine. That would be bad enough. But if it was something worse, he had to know.

Gripping the knife tightly in one hand, he yanked the board toward him with the other and quickly peered in, readying himself to slam it shut in an instant. But what he saw within so shocked him he almost dropped the knife.

There was a furnished apartment inside.

The floor of the crawlspace was carpeted. It was worn, industrial grade carpet, but it was *carpet*. There were chairs, tables, bunk beds, the works. A fully furnished apartment . . . with a ceiling two feet high.

Everything was doll size except the typewriter. That was a portable electric model that looked huge in contrast to everything else.

Maybe George wasn't really crazy after all. One thing was certain: The old fart had been lying to him. There were no snakes and snapping turtles living down here in his crawlspace.

But just what the hell *was* living down here?

Gil headed back inside to ask the only man who really knew.

As he strode through the big room, his foot caught on something and he went down again, landing square on his belly. It took him a moment to catch his breath, then he rolled over and looked to see what had tripped him.

It wasn't the hassock this time. A length of slim cord was stretched between the leg of the couch and an eye-hook that had been screwed into the wall.

He got up and continued on his way—carefully now, scanning the path for more trip ropes. There were none. He made it to the bedroom without falling again—

—and found George sitting on the edge of the bed, massaging his wrists.

Dammit! Every time he turned around it was something else! He could feel the anger and frustration begin to bubble up toward the overflow levels.

"Who the hell untied you?"

"I ain't talking to you."

Gil pointed the knife at him. "You'll talk, old man, or I'll skin you alive!"

"Leave him alone and leave our home!"

It was a little voice, high-pitched without being squeaky, and it came from directly behind him. Gil whirled and saw a fully dressed little man—or something squat, hairy, and bull-necked that came pretty close to looking like a little man—no more than a foot and a half high, standing outside the bedroom door. By the time Gil realized what he was looking at, the creature had started to run.

Gil's first thought was, *I'm going crazy!* But suddenly he had an explanation for that two-foot high furnished apartment in the crawlspace, and for the moving furniture and trip cords.

He bolted after it. Here was what had been tormenting him tonight! He'd get the little sucker and—

He tripped again. A cord that hadn't been there a moment ago was stretched across the narrow hall. Gil went down on one knee and bounded up again. He'd been half ready for that one. They weren't going to—

Something caught him across the chin and his feet went out from under him. He landed flat on his back and felt a sharp, searing pain in his right thigh. He looked down and saw he had jabbed himself in the leg with his own knife during the fall.

Gil leapt to his feet, the pain a distant cry amid the blood rage that hammered through his brain. He roared and slashed at the rope that had damn near taken his head off and charged into the big room. There he saw not one but two of the little bastards. A chant filled the air:

"*Leave him alone and leave our home! Leave him alone and leave our home!*"

Over and over, from a good deal more than two voices. He couldn't see any others. How many of the little runts were there? No matter. He'd deal with these two first, then hunt down the others and get to the bottom of this.

The pair split, one darting to the left, the other to the right. Gil wasn't going to let them both escape. He took a single step and launched himself through the air at the one fleeing leftward. He landed with a bone-jarring crash on the floor but his outstretched free hand caught the leg of the fleeing creature. It was hairier than he had realized—furry, really—and it struggled in his grasp, screeching and thrashing like a wild animal as he pulled it toward him. He squeezed it harder and it bit his thumb. Hard. He howled with the pain, hauled the thing back, and flung it against the nearest wall.

Its screeching stopped as it landed against the wall with an audible crunch and fell to the floor, but the chant went on:

". . . *our home! Leave him alone, and leave our home! Leave him . . .*"

"God *damn* it!" Gil said, sucking on his bleeding thumb. It hurt like hell.

Then he saw the thing start to move. Mewling in pain, it had begun a slow crawl toward one of the piles of junk in the corner.

"No, you don't!" Gil shouted.

The pain, the rage, that goddamn chant, they all came together in a black cloud of fury that engulfed him. No way he was going to let that little shit get away and set more booby traps for him. Through that cloud, he charged across the room, lifted the thing up with his left hand, and raised the knife in his right. Dimly he heard a voice shouting somewhere behind him but he ignored it.

He rammed the knife through the damned thing, pinning it to the wall.

The chant stopped abruptly, cut off in mid verse. All he could hear was George's wail.

• • •

"Oh, no! Oh, Lord, *no!*"

George stood in the hall and stared at the tiny figure impaled on the wall, watched it squirm as dark fluid flowed down the peeling wallpaper. Then it went slack. He didn't know the little guy's name—they all looked pretty much the same through his cataracts—but he felt like he'd lost an old friend. His anguish was a knife lodged in his own chest.

"You've killed him! Oh, God!"

Gil glared at him, his eyes wild, his breathing ragged. Saliva dripped from a corner of his mouth. He was far over the edge.

"Right, old man. And I'm gonna get the other one and do the same to him!"

George couldn't let that happen. The little guys were his responsibility. He was their protector. He couldn't just stand dere like a useless scarecrow.

He launched himself at Gil, his long, nicotine-stained fingernails extended like claws, raking for the younger man's eyes. But Gil pushed him aside easily, knocking him to the floor with a casual swipe of his arm. Pain blazed through George's left hip as he landed, shooting down his leg like a bolt of white hot lightning.

"You're next, you worthless old shit!" Gil screamed. "Soon as I finish with the other little squirt!"

George sobbed as he lay on the floor. If only he were younger, stronger. Even ten years ago he probably could have kicked this punk out on his ass. Now all he could do was lie here on the floor like the worthless old half-blind cripple he was. He pounded the floor helplessly. Might as well be dead!

Suddenly he saw another of the little guys dash across the floor toward the couch, saw the punk spot him and leap after him.

"Run!" George screamed. "*Run!*"

Gil rammed his shoulder against the back of the couch as he shoved his arm far beneath it, slashing back and forth with the knife, trying to get a piece of the second runt. But the blade cut only air and dust bunnies.

As he began to withdraw his arm, he felt something snake

over his hand and tighten on his wrist. He tried to yank away
but the cord—he was sure it was a cord like the one he had
used to truss George—tightened viciously.

A *slip knot!*

The other end must have been tied to one of the couch legs.
He tried to slash at the cord with the knife but he couldn't get
the right angle. He reached under with his free left hand to get
the knife and realized too late that they must have been waiting
for him to do that very thing. He felt another noose tighten
over that wrist—

—and still another over his right ankle.

The first cold trickles of fear ran down Gil's spine.

In desperation he tried to tip the couch over to give him
some room to maneuver but it wouldn't budge. Just then something bit deeply into his right hand. He tried to shake it off
and in doing so he loosened his grip on the knife. It was
immediately snatched from his grasp.

At that moment the fourth noose tightened around his left
ankle, and he knew he was in deep shit.

They let him lay there for what must have been an hour. He
strained at the ropes, trying to break them, trying to untie the
knots. All he accomplished was to sink their coils more deeply
into his flesh. He wanted to scream out his rage—and his fear—
but he wouldn't give them the satisfaction. He heard George
moving around somewhere behind him, groaning with pain,
heard little voices—How many of the little fuckers were there,
anyway?—talking in high-pitched whispers. There seemed to
be an argument going on. Finally, it was resolved.

Then came a tugging on the cords as new ones were tied
around his wrists and ankles and old ones released. Suddenly
he was flipped over onto his back.

He saw George sitting in the rocker holding an ice pack to
his left hip. And on the floor there were ten—*Jesus, ten of
them!*—foot-and-a-half tall furry little men standing in a semi-
circle, staring at him.

One of them stepped forward. He was dressed in doll clothes:
a dark blue pullover—it even had an Izod alligator on the left
breast—and tan slacks. He had the face of a sixty-year-old

man with a barrel chest and furry arms and legs. He pointed at Gil's face and spoke in a high-pitched voice:

"C'ham is dead and it's on your head."

Gil started to laugh. It was like landing in Munchkinland, but then he saw the look in the little man's eyes and knew this was not one of the Lollipop Kids. The laugh died in his throat.

He glanced up at the wall where he'd pinned the first little runt like a bug on a board and saw only a dark stain.

The talking runt gestured two others forward and they approached Gil, dragging his knife. He tried to squirm away from them but the ropes didn't allow for much movement.

"Hey, now, wait a minute! What're you—?"

"The decision's made: You'll make the trade."

Gil was beginning to know terror. "Forget the goddamn rhymes! What's going on here?"

"Hold your nose," the talking runt said to the pair with the knife, "and cut off his clothes. Best be cautious lest he make you nauseous."

Gil winced as the blade began to slice along the seams of his shirt, waiting for the sharp edge to cut him. But it never touched him.

George watched as the little guys stripped Connors. He had no idea what they were up to and he didn't care. He felt like more of a failure than ever. He'd never done much with his life, but at least since the end of the Sixties he had been able to tell himself that he had provided a safe harbor for the last of the world's Little People.

When had it been—Sixty-nine, maybe—when all eleven of them had first shown up at his door looking for shelter. They'd said they were waiting for "when time is unfurled and we're called by the world." He hadn't the vaguest notion what that meant but he'd experienced an immediate rapport with them. They were Outsiders, just like he was. And when they offered to pay rent, the deal was sealed.

He smiled. That rhymed. If you listened to them enough, you began to sound like them. Since they spoke in rhyme all the time—there was another one—it was nothing for them to crank out verse for the greeting card companies. Some of the stuff was pretty sappy, but it paid the taxes.

But what next? One of the little guys had been murdered by this psycho who now knew their secret. Soon all the world would know about these Little People. George had doubly failed at his job: He hadn't protected them and hadn't kept their secret. He was just what the punk had called him: a worthless old shit.

He heard Connors groan and looked up. He was nude as a jaybird and the little guys had tied him with new ropes looped through rings fastened high on the walls at each end of the room. They were hauling him off the floor, stringing him across the room like laundry hung out to dry.

George suddenly realized that although he wasn't too pleased with being George Haskins, at this particular moment he preferred it by far to being Gilroy Connors.

Gil felt as if his arms and legs were going to come out of their sockets as the runts hauled him off the floor and stretched him out in the air. For a moment he feared that might be their plan, but when he got half way between the floor and the ceiling, they stopped pulling on the ropes.

He couldn't ever remember feeling so damn helpless in all his life.

The lights went out and he heard a lot of shuffling below him but he couldn't see what they were doing. Then came the sound, a new chant, high-pitched and stacatto in a language he had never heard before, a language that didn't seem at home on the human tongue.

A soft glow began to rise from below him. He wished he could see what they were doing. All he could do was watch their weird shadows on the ceiling. So far they hadn't caused him too much pain, but he was beginning to feel weak and dizzy. His back got warm while his front grew cold and numb, like there was a cool wind coming from the ceiling and passing right through him, carrying his energy with it. All of his juice seemed to be flowing downward and collecting in his back.

So tired . . . and his back felt so heavy. What were they doing below him?

They were glowing.

George had watched them carry C'ham, their dead member, to a spot directly below Connor's suspended body. They had placed one of George's coffee mugs at C'ham's feet, then they stripped off their clothes and gathered in a circle around him. They had started to chant. After a while, a faint yellow light began to shimmer around their furry little bodies.

George found the ceremony fascinating in a weird sort of way—until the glow brightened and flowed up to illuminate the suspended punk. Then even George's lousy eyes could see the horror of what was happening to Gilroy Connors.

His legs, arms, and belly were a cold dead white, but his back was a deep red-purple color, like a gigantic bruise, and it bulged like the belly of a mother-to-be carrying triplets. George could not imagine how the skin was holding together, it was stretched so tight. Looked like it would rupture any minute. George shielded his face, waiting for the splatter. But when it didn't come, he chanced another peek.

It was raining on the Little People.

The skin hadn't ruptured as George had feared. No, a fine red mist was falling from Connors' body. Red microdroplets were slipping from the pores in the purpled swelling on his back and falling through the yellow glow, turning it orange. The scene was as beautiful as it was horrifying.

The bloody dew fell for something like half an hour, then the glow faded and one of the little guys boosted another up to the wall switch and the lights came on. George did not have to strain his eyes to know that Gilroy Connors was dead.

As the circle dissolved, he noticed that the dead little guy was gone. Only the mug remained under Connors.

George found his mouth dry when he tried to speak.

"What happened to . . . to the one he stabbed?"

"C'ham?" said the leader. George knew this one; his name was Kob. "He's over there." He wasn't rhyming now.

Sure enough. There were ten little guys standing over by the couch, one of them looking weak and being supported by the others.

"But I thought—"

"Yes. C'ham was dead, but now he's back because of the Crimson Dew."

"And the other one?"

Kob glanced over his shoulder at Connors. "I understand there's a reward for his capture. You should have it. And there's something else you should have."

The little man stepped under Connors' suspended body and returned with the coffee mug.

"This is for you," he said, holding it up.

George took the mug and saw that it was half-filled with a thin reddish liquid.

"What am I supposed to do with this?"

"Drink it."

George's stomach turned. "But it's . . . from him."

"Of course. From him to you." Kob gave George's calf a gentle slap. "We need you George. You're our shield from the world—"

"Some shield!" George said.

"It's true. You've protected us from prying eyes and we need you to go on doing that for some time to come."

"I don't think I've got much time left."

"That's why you should drain that cup."

"What do you mean?"

"Think of it as extending your lease," Kob said.

George looked over at C'ham who'd surely been dead half an hour ago and now was up and walking about. He looked down into the cup again.

. . . extending your lease.

Well, after what he'd just seen, he guessed anything might be possible.

Tightening his throat against an incipient gag, George raised the cup to his lips and sipped. The fluid was lukewarm and salty—like a bouillon that had been allowed to cool too long. Not good, but not awful, either. He squeezed his eyes shut and chugged the rest. It went down and stayed down, thank the Lord.

"Good!" Kob shouted, and the ten other Little People applauded.

"Now you can help us cut him down and carry him outside."

"So what're you going to do with all that money, George?" Bill said as he handed George the day's mail.

"I ain't got it yet."

George leaned against the roof of the mail truck and dragged on his cigarette. He felt good. His morning backache was pretty much a thing of the past, and he could pee with the best of them—hit a wall from six feet away, he bet. His breathing was better than it had been in thirty years. And best of all, he could stand here and see all the way south along the length of the harbor to downtown Monroe. He didn't like to think about what had been in that mug Kob had handed him, but in the ten days since he had swallowed it down he had come to feel decades younger.

He wished he had some more of it.

"Still can't get over how lucky you were to find him laying in the grass over there," Bill said, glancing across the road. "Especially lucky he wasn't alive from what I heard about him."

"Guess so," George said.

"I understand they still can't explain how he died or why he was all dried up like a mummy."

"Yeah, it's a mystery, all right."

"So when you *do* get the fifty thou—what are you going to spend it on?"

"Make a few improvements on the old place, I guess. Get me some legal help to see if somehow I can get this area declared off-limits to developers. But mostly set up some sort of fund to keep paying the taxes until that comes to pass."

Bill laughed and let up on the mail truck's brake. "Not ready for the old folks' home yet?" he said as he lurched away.

"Not by a long shot!"

I've got responsibilities, he thought. *And tenants to keep happy.*

He shuddered.

Yes, he certainly wanted to keep those little fellows happy.

Sheri S.
Tepper

The Gardener

From the terrace on the fortieth floor, the men struggling with the trees down by the curb were foreshortened into inconsequentiality. Dots. Dots pulling other dots around. Dots grabbing at their caps and cursing loudly— Tower Wills could hear the sense of it if not the words—as they hauled and tugged against the whip of the wind to get the last two potted trees onto the four-wheeled dolly. The trees were wrapped in layers of plastic, as unwieldy as bellying sails. At last the dolly moved slowly toward the building and Tower tore himself away from the low wall which surrounded the terrace on two sides. On his way to the elevator, he stopped once more at the cast stone planter beside the penthouse door to examine the small brass plaque set into its lip. "Landscape design by Tower Wills." It was the first job he had done that he felt fully merited that label. When he and Ted had been kids they'd talked about going into the landscaping business together. "The Wills Brothers," Ted had insisted, ignoring Tower's comment that it sounded like a male vocalist group.

Now Ted was out of it, but Jeanette still talked about "Tower Wills and Associates," with herself as the associate. Tower had long since decided he had no intention of sharing the business with anyone. Not that Jeanette had given up.

"Looking good," she said from the terrace door.

"Almost perfect," he responded in a voice harshened by the wind and the dust. "If this damn wind will just let up."

"You allowed for it."

"Not sure I allowed enough."

"Sure you did. The tree planters are protected from the two windiest sides. Do you want to meet the elevator, or shall I?"

"You go ahead," he told his assistant, turning to examine the terrace from inside the sliding glass doors, checking off items on the list he had carried in his head for months. Stone tiles covering the terrace, with low, broad steps to lend interesting differences of level. Narrow cast-stone planters filled with trimmed privet and yew. Larger planters holding the trees they had planted yesterday. A reflecting pool tiled in various greens and hints of blue which cradled white lilies and a tall, perfect spray of papyrus. White marguerites and geraniums cascading from carved stone bowls. Furniture, too. Though he hadn't been directly responsible for that, he had approved it. Antique wrought iron, upholstered in dark green and ivory, rather formal in tone. A white canvas awning over the dining area.

And finally, the two cast-stone planters at either side of the glass doors next to huge plastic sacks of special potting soil. Behind him he heard the door to the penthouse open and Jeanette's cheerful voice instructing, "Everybody take their shoes off! Right. These carpets are genuine somethings or other. The furniture is all priceless. Figure you knock anything with that dolly, you are in hock for the next ten years. Go through there and do not even touch the walls. Pretend they're made out of spun glass . . ."

Then the three sweating men in their white coveralls were on the terrace with him and he forgot the list in his head for the time it took to lift the two matched kousa dogwoods from the huge fibre pots into their planters and pack the soil around them. All the trees had been selected a year ago. These two were in bud, ready to bloom within days. And the Bryants, whose penthouse terrace this was, would be moving in this weekend and would have their anniversary party next week. There would be fifty people on this terrace. Some of those people would see the little brass label. Someone or ones with lots of money. Other commissions could come from it. Other commissions as expensive and challenging as this one had been.

Lost in this particular dream, he looked up to find the tree branches waving gently over him, a benediction. The men were gone and Jeanette was busy planting ivy both to cover the bare soil and discourage people from using the tree planters as ash trays. Tower found himself momentarily at a loss, with everything done.

"It's marvelous," Jeanette murmured, waving her trowel to indicate the whole thing, trees, flowers, all of it, and glowing with a pride of at least partial ownership. "It's come together beautifully, Tower."

"Money," he replied, knowing he sounded surly, but grudging every word of credit she seemed to take a share of. "What money can do." And me, he thought. Money and me.

"There is that," she admitted as she went back to the ivy, then shamed him by saying, "But money alone wouldn't have done it. You are good, Tow. You know that." She gave him an admiring look and patted his knee in motherly fashion.

He flushed with pleasure. "I can be," he admitted. "If I get a few jobs like this instead of more like Mrs. Silver's patio."

They both laughed, half sympathy for one another, half jeering at themselves. When Mrs. Silver commissioned a perennial garden to surround her patio, she had supplied them with a sample of salmony orange sandstone to be provided by another contractor. Plants had been chosen and planted with that color in mind, but the completed patio had turned out to be quite a vivid rosy pink. "It was a lot cheaper," said Mrs. Silver in explanation when Tower pointed out the inconsistency. "What difference does it make?"

"She couldn't see the difference," Jeanette reminded him.

"Some of her friends might not have been color blind," he

said. "And she would have told them I designed it."

"We only had to change about fifty plants," Jeanette said. "All the dianthus, and the oriental poppies and the helianthemum. Oh, yes. And the iris."

"And half the lilies."

"Right. The lilies. Still, it could have been worse."

He nodded, trying not to remember that the new plants and bulbs and the labor involved had eaten up the small profit on the job, which he had bid too low because he needed the work. It all came down to money. If he was going to do the kind of work he wanted to do, the kind of work the great landscape artists had done, the work the great plantsmen had done, then he had to have money behind him. He'd given up ten years to get that money, his own money, almost half a million dollars of it, but Aunt Henry went on acting as though he were still sixteen. Tower had stayed with her, gambling on being able to win her over long ago, but so far all the winnings were on her side.

"The final payment on this job will make up for the Silver job," Jeanette went on happily. "It'll bring the business loan up to date and maybe we can even start the greenhouse." She pushed the soil carefully around the last ivy plant, stacked the black plastic pots in the tray, brushed a few grains of soil from the edge of the planter, took off her gloves then laid them on the tray as well. "It's beautiful. God. I hope the Bryants are nice people. Only nice people deserve something like this." She flicked a faded leaf from a white geranium which sprawled lavishly in its huge white pot, then stroked a feather of new yew growth, brilliant green against the darkness of the old foliage. "It looks like a garden for . . . for vestal virgins or something. Maybe like something on Mount Olympus. You can't even see the city. Nothing but sky."

"The Bryants seem to be very pleasant people," he said firmly. Also rich as Croesus, he added to himself, adding to the Greek similies. "If you want to take those pots and the plastic bags away, I'll double check everything and let myself out."

"Want to gloat, don't you?" she grinned understandingly.

Tower nodded, as usual, a little annoyed at her assumption of intimacy. Jeanette Miller was a middle aged woman of motherly dimensions who sometimes treated Tower as though he were her son. She was also a wonderful gardener and a competent plantsman, but Tower bridled whenever she overstepped his definition of a business relationship and said something personal. He didn't have a mother, and so far as he was concerned, he didn't need one.

"Sure," he agreed, lying only a little. "I need to gloat."

"Going to show it to Nina?"

The question jarred. He had forgotten that Jeanette had met Nina. "She saw it last week. I showed it to her then," he said stiffly.

"What's her real name again?"

"Ilanina," he replied, opening the door for Jeanette and watching her wander down the hall to the elevator, whispering it again to himself. "Ilanina Gyulas."

"You know, you have a strange name," he had told Nina, shortly after he met her, hot on the chase and busy making conversation. "A strange name for a strangely lovely girl. Ilanina."

"My mother gave it to me. She told my father she liked the sound of it."

It was the first time she had consented to go out with him, and they had been at a small Italian restaurant which was a favorite of Tower's. He could tell she was attracted to him, but she had been oddly reluctant to go anywhere with him. Her reluctance simply made her more exciting so far as Tower was concerned. "Does your name mean something, anything? Does your last name mean anything?"

"My last name means a color, my father has said to me. It is he who has raised me. My first name might mean something. I don't know. Mother died soon after I was born. Lots of the mothers do in our family."

"Lots of the mothers what?"

"Die when they have their first child. In our family, our—what to say, tribe?—many of our women die having the first baby."

"Ah," he had said, with casual sympathy, not really believing her. Many of the things Nina said made so little sense that Tower simply disregarded them as resulting from Nina's occasionally spotty understanding of American idiom. His interest in her wasn't centered on what she said. Besides, Tower had lost his own mother when he was ten, and he could not remember missing her very much. Of course, he had Aunt Henry, such as she was. "Did you have any brothers or sisters?" he had asked Nina.

"No. I was the only one. Just hard luck." She shook her head to and fro. "A lot of our families have just one. Some have two. Some have three. Never more than three."

"That's what I call effective family planning," he had laughed. "And your father never married again?"

"No. In . . . among our people, men usually don't."

"Don't marry again?" He was frankly dumbfounded. "I knew there were traditional cultures where women didn't marry again—India, places like that. I didn't know there was any culture where men didn't marry again."

"Maybe ours is the only one in which this is true." She had smiled at him, that grave, exotic smile which so aroused him, and he had reached out to trace the strange loveliness of her face. Skin like rich, nutshell velvet. Hair drawn back into a smooth bun and so dark that it had blue lights in it. Her upper lip was rather-long, and thin except at its dipped center, but the lower lip was full which made her mouth seem always curved in the beginning of a smile. Her nose was perfectly straight. She had an ancient face, he sometimes thought. An Etruscan face. Old as history. "In our culture, the women do not marry again if their husbands are alive," she said. "The men do not marry again at all."

"Then you'd better live forever," he had laughed easily, letting her infer whatever she liked from this. "I'd hate being uncultural, but I'd hate being lonely, too."

"I don't think my father is lonely," she had said, looking a little puzzled. "Not more than any of the men. I must ask him."

"Why would he be lonely," Tower had been consciously

courtly, which went over well with Nina. "He has you."

That had been months ago. While Tower was still courting her, before their relationship had turned into something both more intimate and more disturbing. Tower flushed, half angrily, as he went back to the terrace wall and leaned on it, peering over it into the street. It was like a canyon down there. The canyon down which Nina had disappeared a week ago, walking away into the noisy, bustling river of the city. When he drew back, the sound diminished. When he went farther back, against the wall of the penthouse, under the newly planted trees, it became quieter still. The trees made a soft lace against the sky. Properly cared for, they would double in size over the next ten years. A lengthy maintenance contract was part of the deal, icing on the Tower Wills cake.

If he could keep the cake. Keep the Tower Wills cake to himself. No partners. No associates. Eat it and have it.

One couldn't always do that, evidently. Not some things. Nina among them. Couldn't eat her and have her.

Beginning with his first sexual affair at fifteen, Tower had developed a strategy for lovers who were about to be ex-lovers. He had a standard, let's-go-on-being-friends monologue he always used when it was time for someone new. The thought of former girlfriends saying derogatory things about him—maybe talking to mutual friends or even future clients—had always bothered him. It was important to be respected, well-regarded, to have a good reputation. He prided himself on taking time to end relationships pleasantly, working up gradually from apologetic neglect to absent minded inattention to matter-of-fact severance in incremental degrees that were nicely calculated to chill an affair without provoking overt hostility. The monologue was always the penultimate clincher, though he usually called a few times after that, just to let women get bored with him.

Nina though! Nina wasn't just another girl. Aunt Henry made that very clear. And then, Nina herself had moved from being exotic to being so unacceptably strange that Tower had wanted out, out now, with no nice increments about it. He had tried to tell her once, pleading the pressure of work, but Nina hadn't caught on. She didn't respond to the usual clues. Hinting wouldn't do it. So, a week ago, he had invited her to see the Bryant Terrace as an object lesson, an illustration for the usual monologue. If she could see it.

He had waited for her here on the terrace. The buzzer had rung, rattling like a lost bee in the far reaches of the untenanted apartment, and he had run for it, stumbling over his own feet, over the carpet. "Yes."

"It is I, Tower. It is Ilanina." The speaker had distorted her voice into something distant and tinny saying ridiculously formal words. Like Donald Duck doing Shakespeare.

He had fought back an urge to laugh. Increasingly he had found himself wanting to laugh uncomfortably at her stylized language or at her fantastic stories, tales she tossed off casually, as though she were describing a visit to the supermarket. He never had laughed, though. Neither with her nor at her. Her gravity inhibited any show of amusement. The mood that surrounded Ilanina was soberly wistful. He had never actually heard her laugh. Even their lovemaking had always been . . . He turned away from that thought.

"Come on up," he had said, pushing the button and keeping it down until he was sure she was in.

He met her at the elevator, keeping his distance, showing politeness but not affection, escorting her through the vacant apartment onto the terrace. "This is it."

She stood bemused, looking around her like some tourist lost in a foreign port, seeking something familiar. "Daisies," she said at last. "Those?"

"Yes. Marguerites, they're called."

"Ah. It is . . . it is all very cool looking. Like a fountain without water."

"There's water," he indicated the reflecting pool.

"You apprehend what I mean to say. It is liquid looking. Green and gray and white. Like a stream."

"Good," he nodded, liking her description. If she found the garden beautiful, it would help explain his work. "It's supposed to be restful."

She nodded. "I will look at more of it." She wandered out

along the terrace wall, examining the steps, the pool, the plantings, all with a cool, serious eye. "Good," she said, returning to him. "It is a good garden, Tow-er."

No one else made an elegant two syllables of his name. Most people made a mushy "Tahr," out of it. Of course, no one was quite like Ilanina. "Do you understand what I meant the other day?" he asked her, trying to be gentle but firm. "Do you understand now?"

"About gardens being important? But, yes, Tow-er. Of course, I do. I understood you when you spoke to me then, too. It is important work. In the Jewish and Christian scripture it tells of the first parents being given the job of gardeners, is that not so?"

"Not a job they kept long, I'm afraid."

"No. Perhaps it was more than they could do, being human. Perhaps it would have been better if their god had told an angel to do the gardening." She turned up the corners of her mouth at him, cuing him that she had made a joke. "It is important work. I know that. You do it very well."

"I know I do. And I will do it better, yet."

"And it is for you to do it better than we must stop being together?" It was asked in the same tone, gravely, without anger, but with that same, puzzled, slightly anxious expression. "This is what you have told me before, and it is this I do not understand."

"I wanted you to see this so you *would* understand," he said lamely, wishing she would get just a little bit angry at him. It would make it easier for both of them. "My career is important to me. More important than anything else. I've got to concentrate on business for a while. The business is all mine. I have no real help. If I'm going to be successful, it will take all the time I've got. I didn't want you to think I was neglecting you for any other reason . . ."

"You want me to go away from you, but you do not want me to think it is because of any other woman, is that not so? You do not want me to be . . . to be jealous of you in that way."

"Something like that. There isn't any other woman." He thought fleetingly of Patty somebody he had picked up at The

Threatened Species two nights before, but decided that didn't count because he really couldn't remember her name. "I wouldn't object if you want to go out with some other man. Perhaps you should."

"But Tow-er, I cannot. I told you. We do not marry again while the husband lives."

He had gritted his teeth, trying to keep his own anger from showing. She did this to him all the time. It was the main reason he had to stop this whole thing. "That's *your* customs, Nina. Not mine, remember? We talked about that!"

"But it is my customs I live by. What other customs would I live by except my own?" She had turned very pale, stricken looking.

"Nina, I did not take advantage of you. Whatever our relationship might have meant in your culture is not relevant. We're not living in your culture. In this culture, we had a love affair . . . are having a love affair," he amended quickly, not wanting her to think this was precipitous. "I'm not saying I don't want to see you ever. I'm just trying to get a little space around me to work in."

She went on staring at him, that wide-eyed, sober, almost childlike look she so often had. "In the country where we lived before we came here, the people had to clear away the jungle to get a space to work in. They chop down all the trees and set fire to them. It is called 'slash and burn.' I learned those words when I went to school there." She looked down, smoothing the sleeves of her dress, running one hand across the back of the other, wrist to fingertips, feeling her own hands as though they were new to her, in a gesture uniquely her own. "Slash and burn, to get room."

She was so serious. He had to pretend to laugh a little, grasping her shoulders. "I'm not slashing and burning you 'Nina. I'm just asking you to be patient. To give me a little room for a while."

After a long, thoughtful silence, she had said, "Tell me, Tow-er. If we do not see each other again, will you probably make love with other girls?"

Why wouldn't she just say, "have sex." She never would.

It was always "make love." He had answered her, a little angrily. "I haven't taken a vow of celibacy, Nina. If we never saw one another again, I probably would, sooner or later."

She had said almost nothing else. Her face had been expressionless, empty. He had asked her if she understood, and she had looked into his face with vacant eyes as she said, "Yes, Tow-er. I do understand. More than you know. The work of your hand is more important than I am. More important than others, too, I think. You cast me away, and them as well. It would be better if you did not do this. I curse your hand, Tower Wills." It hadn't sounded like a real imprecation, more like a habitual utterance: "Up yours," or "fuck you." Still, he had blinked in surprise.

Then she had gone, swiftly, without another word. He had leaned over the terrace wall to see her come out of the door below, see her walk down the sidewalk among a hundred other people, losing herself.

"Losing herself," he had said then, looking down on her with a sense of relief. "Losing herself. Getting lost," he said now, remembering. He would call her in a few days, still keeping to his "let's-still-be-good-friends" pattern. it would be easier on them both if she could accept what he had told her, that he wasn't just throwing her over. Because he wasn't. Not really. Not for anyone else. Not for anyone else in particular. He'd wait a week or two more and then he'd call her. By that time, she'd have had a chance to settle down.

He turned, taking one final look at the garden. Watering would be automatic, controlled by humidity sensors in every planter. Everything had been fertilized with time release fertilizer that would last for six months. Jeanette would make weekly visits every Monday morning to check that everything was doing well, to trim and replace, if necessary.

So. He polished the brass plate with the flat of his hand. So. Maybe someone would see it. Someone definitely would see it. It was time he got lucky.

The luck seemed to materialize out of pure expectation: two new clients by the end of the week. Both of the callers said they had seen the Bryant Terrace. After the second call, from a man named Gray, Tower whooped like a child at the beach, shouting his delight. Jeanette did a war dance, pounding an imaginary tom-tom.

"What do they want?" she gasped at last, falling into a chair. "Not that it matters."

"One townhouse for certain. One country place, maybe. The townhouse's name is Winston. The country place's name is Grayholm. Gray, that is."

"We really need our own greenhouse." Jeanette was suddenly sober. "We need it."

"I know." He frowned at her "we," her continued assumption of at least partial ownership. "That's only one of the things I need." Accumulating the plants for the Bryant job had been an exercise in frustration. He had no central place in which to keep plants or trees in good condition, and suppliers had not been uniformly helpful in saying they would hold material for later delivery. Tower was determined that delivery of plant material, on time and in top condition, was to be the mark of his design work. Any contractor could take a year to dribble in with this and that. Very few could deliver the complete stock at one time. "I'm going to talk with Aunt Henry again."

"She hasn't been real helpful, has she."

For the moment, Tower forgot his resentment at Jeanette's personal comments. "Damn it, Jeanette, mother left dad's money to Ted and me."

"She left her sister in charge of it."

"I was ten years old. Ted was eight. The Wills money was supposed to come to us when we grew up. It was supposed to set us up in business."

"It's a pity your mom didn't attach an age to that growing up bit. I'd say that at twenty-eight you're fairly well grown up. Why is your aunt so reluctant?"

"Oh, I think she's afraid I'll leave her the way Ted did if she lets me have the capital. She wants to feel she controls me." He flushed, having betrayed more than he had meant to do.

"Is that why you still live with her?"

He shook his head. It was the reason, but that was no concern of Jeanette's. He lived there to save money, too. Money for the business. "No. Not really. Living there is convenient."

"Not for your little brother, though?"

"No, not Ted," Tower admitted through gritted teeth. He didn't like to remember the details of Ted's leaving. "Ted didn't like her interference. He told her he'd live where he pleased and do what he wanted . . ."

Ted had never appeared to rebel, not during junior high or high school. He had smiled, never arguing. He had talked rebellion with Tower at night in the secrecy of their room, but during the days he had said "Yes Ma'am" and "No, Ma'am." Ted and Tower had agreed to leave when Ted was eighteen, the date when Ted would begin getting his interest payments from the estate. Tower had been getting his for two years. Aunt Henry had no control over that. With those payments, the two of them could finish their education and go into business together. And on Ted's eighteenth birthday he had gone, as agreed. The day dawned, but Ted had already departed. In the night sometime, "Like a thief," said Aunt Henry. Tower had known he was going. Tower was supposed to go along, but at the last minute he'd changed his mind.

"You could have told me," Ted had said. "You could have told me you weren't coming, Tow. We could have talked about it."

Tower really hadn't wanted to talk about it. There were certain aspects of his decision he didn't want to examine too closely.

"Of course, Ted doesn't want much, that's the difference," Tower said to Jeanette.

"Oh, I don't know," Jeanette said in a judicial tone. "He seems like a nice guy."

"He is a nice guy," he said defensively. "We're both nice guys. It's just that being successful doesn't matter that much to Ted."

"I think he's quite successful! He has a nice family and a good job . . ." To augment the income from the estate, Ted had worked for the parks department of a small suburb. When the parks manager had died, Ted had applied for the job and, to everyone's surprise, had been hired. Since there was a small zoo in the park, Ted had stopped working toward a degree in landscape architecture and had begun studying animals.

"He likes the birds and the beasts," Tower said, half angrily. "I suppose he figures he's got enough landscape education. He can tell the park gardeners how to tell a prunus from a primula."

Or a Sally from a salvia, he thought. It had been Ted's marriage to Sally which had provoked the final split between Ted and Aunt Henry four years before. "You can hold on to mother's money," Ted had said, "until you're blue in the face, Aunty Hen, but you can't control how I live or who I pick as friends. I told you that when I was in high school. Who I pick for a wife comes under the same heading. Sally and I are being married next week. You're invited to the wedding."

Aunt Henry hadn't approved of Sally—Tower could not remember that she had ever approved of any of his or Ted's friends—so she hadn't attended the wedding. Tower had gone to the wedding, though he hadn't talked about it at home. Neither Sally nor Ted had seemed to care that Aunt Henry wasn't there.

"What are you going to live on?" Tower had asked at the time. "I save every dime I can by living with Aunt, but I still don't have enough to go around . . ."

"Hell," exploded Ted, flushed and expansive with inexpensive champagne. "If you hadn't let me down when I was eighteen, Tower, we'd both have more than we do now. We'd be in business together. I'd have been good at it, Tower. As good as you. Maybe even better."

Tower was still trying to think of a response to this when Ted went on. "Anyhow, that's old history. It didn't happen. Now I'm doing something else. The pay isn't much, but they give me tuition money. Right now I'm taking a course on animal populations."

"Sounds fascinating," Tower had said, not meaning it but thankful they were not going to talk old history.

"It is fascinating. All about analyzing ratios of predators to

prey. I may learn a lot about animals and turn out to be the
next Jane Goodall or Konrad Lorenz, who knows? And Sally
has a part time job doing bookkeeping for the parks department.
Our offices are in the same building. We get to spend a lot of
time together, and she gets to take courses, too. We're having
a great time. We'll get by.''

He'd get by. But he wouldn't follow in the footsteps of his
famous father, Michael Wills. Which left those footsteps for
Tower to follow alone. How many species or cultivars were
there with the Wills name attached to them? Twenty or thirty
at least. Salix Willsii. Taxus Willsii. Evodium fraxinifolia
'Willsii.' Michael Wills had been one of the great plantsmen,
a self taught botanist, a world traveler, someone, to hear Aunt
Henry tell it, considerably larger than real life.

Tower couldn't stop himself. ''Managing parks is kind of a
come down for Michael Wills's son.''

Ted, already flushed with wine, turned an angry red. ''Oh,
get off it, Tower. Gunga Din could have been my father for
all I care. You were two when he died. I wasn't even born
yet. We never knew our father.'' Ted had pounded the table,
rumpled his hair, eager to make his point. ''We've had Michael
Wills fed to us like oatmeal, morning, noon, and night ever
since we were babies. Aunt Henry was in love with him, for
God's sake. She met him in Italy or someplace. She brought
him home with her. They were going to be married, then he
married her sister instead. Do you think she got over that?
She's been taking it out on us ever since mother died. She
couldn't have old Dad, but she's got his sons. Sometimes I
wonder what mother's last days must have been like. She only
had Aunt Henry to take care of her, her own sister, but can
you imagine dying with someone as vindictive as Aunt Henry
hovering over you like a vampire? Why do you think I got out
of there as soon as I could? You're crazy to stay!''

Tower hadn't answered. There was no answer. They'd said
it all before. Calming down, Ted had gone on, ''Anyhow,
whether Michael Wills was a great plantsman or a garbage
truck driver, what does it have to do with me? I'm tired of
being told I have to model myself on somebody I never knew.

So, I'll become a great zookeeper instead. Wake up, Tower. There are other people out there besides you and Aunt Henry and the ghost of our father! If you'd get rid of her and the ghost, you'd find you had a life of your own to live."

Which might have been true, but which ignored the fact that Tower had always liked the idea of being the son of a famous father—the famous son of a famous father. "Two generations of famous plantsmen, Michael and Tower Wills." Or better yet, "Michael Wills, father of the famous plantsman, Tower Wills." Aunt Henry might have pushed him in that direction, but Tower hadn't been unwilling to go.

"I'll talk to Aunt Henry," he said to Jeanette again, warm from the flattery of that last phone call. Mr. Gray had called to set up an appointment. Mr. Gray had been very complimentary about the Bryant job.

Aunt Henry did not respond to the question of the Wills estate at all. Instead she asked, "Have you broken off your unfortunate relationship with that strange girl, Tower?"

It was only slightly less offensive than what she had said a few weeks before. She'd been vulgarly specific then, not that he was surprised. He and Ted had always understood Aunt Henry's views on racial and social matters. Whatever had been current bigotry in about 1950 was what Jessica Henry thought now. "Never married, never pregnant, never changed her mind," Ted had quipped more than once.

"What relationship is that?" Tower asked innocently.

"That colored girl, Tower. The one I saw you having lunch with at the Gregory." It seemed to Tower that whenever he went out with a woman in public, Aunt Henry showed up. Sometimes he believed she had him followed.

"If you mean Ilanina Gyulas, she isn't colored. Not in the way you mean." Why was he arguing? He'd broken up with Nina at least partly because of what Aunt Henry thought. No sense making additional problems for himself.

"I believe the current word is Black."

"No, Aunt Henry, she isn't Black. Black means African, and she isn't African or even part African." Annoyance maybe. At himself for caving in so easily, though that was part of his strategy where his aunt was concerned. Give in. Be flexible. Go on living with Aunt Henry as long as possible, saving the money he'd spend on meals or rent.

"Dark skinned, Tower. Whether from Africa or somewhere else really doesn't matter. She is not white."

"White is European. Nina is European. She's a lovely girl. Very sweet, very kind." He said it half heartedly, knowing it would make no difference. He had already given in. Why make a fuss?

"She may be sweet as sugar, but she is not suitable for a Wills. If you are going to continue seeing her, please don't go on asking me again to turn over your father's capital to you."

"As a matter of fact, I'm not seeing her anymore." Capitulation. But calculated capitulation, he told himself. Despite what Ted said, the money was important.

"Very wise of you, I'm sure. People of that type can do you no good in your career, Tower. Your father never associated with people of that type."

Unwisely, he exploded. "Aunt Henry, my father traveled over half the world. Plantsmen don't discover exotic plants by having tea parties with local aristocrats. They go out in the mud, among the peasants! You may have met him in an aristocratic setting, but you weren't with him all the time. He probably associated with all kinds of people. You can't travel like that and hold yourself aloof!" He knew it was a mistake as soon as he said it.

"That will do, Tower."

"We were talking about Dad's money," he went on stubbornly, already knowing he had lost the battle yet again.

"Another time, perhaps. When you are less inclined to be rude."

"A formidable woman!" Ilanina had said, her accent almost but not quite French, when he told her of his Aunt Henry.

"The skinny witch," Sally called her, half laughing.

"Old battleaxe," Jeanette sometimes remarked.

Tower had learned to keep his feelings to himself. Aunt Henry was formidable. She was a battleaxe. Though pictures of her taken thirty years ago showed a handsome woman, now she certainly looked like a witch: narrow visaged, broad shouldered, breastless, hair drawn high into a tight coronet—sometimes decked with artificial blossoms like an aged bride. She had eyes like those of a chicken, sharp and black and expressionless. Her hands were big, and powerful. When Ted and Tower had been boys, she had never used anything to discipline them but those fingers, as effective as any torturers' tongs at pinching and twisting. When they were older, she had quit pinching with her fingers and had started pinching with words. "Another time." It was always another time with Aunt Henry.

She hadn't finished. "If you are insufficiently capitalized, I will be happy to speak to Mr. Sunderson at the bank for you," Aunt Henry said infuriatingly, smiling her cold smile, her huge hands folded across her lap.

"Aunt Henry, Ralph Sunderson has already given me as big a loan as I can afford. He knows it and I know it. I need my own money! It belongs to me!"

"I made you an offer a year ago, Tower."

She had offered to capitalize him herself in return for a controlling share of the business. He turned and left the room, knowing that behind him she was still smiling.

Tower and Jeanette talked to the Winstons on Wednesday of that week. By Friday, they had the contract and Jeanette was singing in the outer office as she sharpened pencils and laid out ground plans. While she burbled, Tower consulted a map of the greater metropolitan area, finding the streets into and out of Cedar Hills, the exclusive suburban enclave where the Gray estate, Grayholm, was located. Mr. Gray had suggested that Tower take a look at it over the weekend. "Alone, Mr. Wills. I don't want people wandering about."

"Gray himself won't be there?" Jeanette asked.

"No. He said he wasn't sure yet about wanting the garden done. He wouldn't be sure for a few weeks, but he'd like me to look at the place. He said the caretaker would show me around."

Though there was no caretaker in evidence when Tower arrived. Or assumed he had arrived. There was a stone gatehouse with an ornate mailbox, as described, but no number corresponding to the address he had been given. Since nothing within a half mile to either side looked more promising, Tower drove between the half opened gates and up the long, curving drive under the limbs of huge, red horsechestnut trees in full, scarlet bloom. "Aesculus carnea," he chanted to himself. "Being a cross between Aesculus hippocastanum and A. pavia." Certain colors made him feel almost as though he were making love, sending spasms of erotic feeling from his head to his groin. The blooms on the trees to his right were the brightest he had ever seen, a brilliant red which seemed to vibrate against the shade, and the trees were fully fifty feet tall, an enormous size for the particular variety which seldom exceeded forty feet even after many decades of growth. "Lavish," Tower chanted to himself. "Very lavish."

The house came gradually into view, first a corner, then a tower, then a line of diamond paned windows glittering in the noon sun. A stone chateau, larger than it first appeared, for as he drove toward it, other wings disclosed themselves; ranks of chimneys appeared, twisting upward among tall oaks and beeches. Enclosed within the curve of the drive was a complex topiary garden, one both appropriate to the scale of the house and hard to improve upon. One didn't replace topiary on a moment's notice.

He parked on the gravel, took his canvas tool bag from the seat beside him and got out, leaning against the car, soaking in the quiet. The voice surprised him.

"Are you just lookin', or are you plannin' to buy the place?"

"Sorry?" Tower turned. Battered-hat and jacket. Faded jeans and disreputable boots. "Mr. Gray asked me to have a look at a place he wanted to put a garden?"

"Oh. You're that Wills fella." Mr. Battered-hat stared at him, up and down, as though memorizing him. "All right. You go around that corner over there and down the stairs. Down at the bottom of the path is a circle of big old trees, and it's inside there he wants the garden. Told me to let you measure it and look at it, he'll decide when he gets back whether he wants you to do the job."

Tower nodded, was nodded to in return, then watched the retreating back of Battered-hat as he disappeared around a corner. As Tower turned to follow the directions he had been given, he caught a glimpse of motion from the house itself. A window? A curtain moving? He stared upward, seeing nothing except a curtain quivering slightly in a second floor window. A maid? Probably. A place this size wouldn't be left completely empty.

Around the corner of the house he found a flight of granite stairs about thirty feet wide. The flight was interrupted by two landings decked with rose trees and carved fountains. The roses were various shades of rich pink and peach, every bush as well tended as though for exhibition.

At the foot of the stairs a gravel path led between clipped hedges to a curving line of oaks, the interstices between the old trees filled with a solid hedge of trimmed juniper. An arch had been carved into this thick, resinous growth, and he stepped through it into the circle of trees . . .

And found nothing. A circular plot, half grassy, half weedy, the center disfigured by a drainage pond about thirty feet across. The circle of huge, well cared for trees surrounded nothing at all. He frowned. Something must have been planned for this plot amid the trees. The trees were at least a hundred years old, perhaps older. Something must have been here once. He kicked the dirt, uncovering a fragment of rock. Paving, perhaps. He stared at the pond, seeing just beneath the water surface the dim outline of a circular foundation. What? Fountain? Sun-dial? It was large enough for a gazebo, though the site left a lot to be desired. One wanted to gaze from a gazebo, and there was certainly nothing to gaze at here.

There was a trowel in the tool bag, along with a roll of plastic bags and a stack of numbered chips. Walking around the circumference of the circle, he took soil samples at fifty foot intervals, numbering each one in sequence, counting off the paces as he went. At the drip line of the trees, the circle was six hundred-fifty feet around, give or take twenty feet. He quartered the area, taking more samples. The earth looked fairly uniform, a sandy loam, somewhat lacking humus, which would

be normal away from the trees. At the water line, he stood for
a long time staring into the pond, trying to make out what had
been there. Mists rose lazily from the water's surface, obscuring
what lay below. Were there steps, leading down? Which would
mean what? A cellar?

Abruptly, he gave up and turned back to the sloping saucer
among the trees. Not a saucer. A flat soup bowl with a wide
rim and a small depression at the center. So. What else? The
area nearest the trees would be tricky. Half a day's sun on the
east and west, full sun on the north, no sun on the south, except
at this time of year. May through July, maybe. The rest of the
site would present no problem.

A cloud crossed the sun and the shadow fled over him. His
skin felt suddenly wet, as though his shirt was soaked. He
backed away from the pond with an exclamation of disgust.
He had stood there so long that his clothes were wet with the
mists. And it smelled, a dank, stagnant smell.

"If he wants me to do the job, first item of business will be
to get rid of that water," he told himself, striding up the slope
and casting about for a moment as he sought the patch that led
out. The dark arch in the shade of the trees was almost invisible
from this side, the path lost in shadow. As he left the circle of
oaks and came into the sun once more, he shivered.

"Find what you wanted?" Battered-hat was with him once
more.

"More or less. Say, do you know what was in the middle
of that place? There's some kind of foundation there."

"Oh, that!" exclaimed Battered-hat. "That was a tomb, that
was. Family vault! Then the spring burst up through there and
floated all the dead ones right out of it." He whinnied laughter,
a kind of muted gargle, ending when he cleared his throat and
spat, juicily. "Floated those deaders right out," grinning sly-
faced, watching Tower out of the corner of his eyes. "You
find your way back all right?"

"Sure. Thanks." And he watched the retreating back once
more. Had it really been a vault, with a spring under it? Even
though he doubted it, he shivered, aware of the clamminess of
his clothes. The center of the oak circle would have to be

drained, or filled, or both. And what kind of garden did Mr. Gray have in mind? The place would be perfect for a maze. Tower had always wanted to design a maze.

When he got back to the office, Jeanette handed him his calls, making a face as she did so. "Where've you been?"

"Why," he asked. "What's the face for."

"You smell," she said. "You smell like a swamp."

He explained about Mr. Gray's estate while she exclaimed and shook her head in wonderment. "Tower, six hundred forty feet around? That's—why, that's over thirty thousand square feet of planting space!"

"He can't want it all in garden," he said. "Terraces, maybe? Maybe some flower beds. I'd love to do a maze."

"You know what we could do?" she asked, eyes wide in the enthusiasm with which she always greeted a new job. "We could do a water garden. Pump up the water to the top of the circle and then let it run down in a spiral, all the way around. We could put in lily ponds, and bog plants . . ."

He laughed, too shortly, wishing she would not be so eager with her suggestions. "Why don't we wait until Mr. Gray tells us what he has in mind?"

"Yeah, but Tower. Lord." Her irrepressible vitality almost made the room quiver. "You know what we could do . . ."

Early Wednesday morning Tower woke thinking of Nina. It was time to call her, ask how she was getting along, act friendly, maybe make a date to take her to lunch. Even though it was a lot more comfortable without her, he didn't want her angry at him.

The voice at the other end of the phone sounded sleepy. "Nina Gyulas? No. She moved away. Two or three weeks ago."

"She what?" He stopped, squinting his eyes, wondering if he had heard correctly. "Moved? Do you have a forwarding address for her?"

"No. She didn't leave any." The voice was remote, uncaring. Wasn't it Nina's roommate? Tower had met her once.

"This is Tower Wills."

"Yes?" No recognition.

"Are you . . . ah," he groped for the name. "Sandra? Her roommate?"

"No. Her roommate moved away too."

"What do you do if mail comes for Nina?"

"I have never seen mail for her. I am the new tenant. I do not know her." The voice was remote, uncaring, a little foreign sounding.

"Thank you," Tower said, breaking the connection with a tentative finger. If she'd moved, why hadn't she had the phone disconnected. Had Nina really intended that he be unable to find her? Surely not. He hadn't expected her to . . .

What had he expected?

He dropped the phone into its cradle and took himself into the shower. He would simply wait until she called him. Which she would do, sooner or later. He wanted her to remember him fondly. He didn't want anyone to really dislike him. Ted might be willing to have people mad at him, but Tower would prefer not.

His irritation continued through the morning, though it began to wear off about noon. He decided to celebrate recent successes by taking Ted and Sally to lunch, a plan that Ted agreed to with enthusiasm.

"Pick us up at the zoo," he asked. "Our car's in the garage having its fuel pump fixed. Besides, you haven't seen where Sally and I work."

The park administration office was also the zoo administration office, a bright and nursery-cheerful room painted daffodil yellow with leaf green counters and floor. "My God, you could go blind in here," Tower mocked. "Not exactly subtle, are you?"

"Who needs subtlety," Sally cried from behind him, enveloping him in a hug that made his ribs creak and enveloping him in a cloud of her particular odor: vanilla, doughnuts, fresh bread, something warm and nourishing and unmistakeably herself. "Old subtle Tower," she teased him. "Everything monochrome."

"With accents," he objected. "I always have accents."

"Sure. An acre of clipped yew with one calla lily, slightly off center."

He laughed. Sally had that effect on him. She was bouncy and brown, freckled and auburn haired, not pretty but always joyous, and she smelled good. She fit Ted like a glove. "How're the kids?"

"The twins are fine, thank you. Enjoying the birthday gift their uncle sent them."

Tower kept his face quiet though he could not keep from flushing slightly. Jeanette had bought the gift and dispatched it for him. He'd forgotten to ask her what she had picked out.

"At this stage, a playpen was exactly what they needed! And what I needed. Thank you, Tower."

"Ah, well," he said, pretending to be knowledgable. "I wasn't sure they were old enough."

"At one year? My dear brother-in-law, you should see those infants move! Like otters. Where are we going to have lunch?"

"I thought the Beggar's Grill?" It was a casual place nearby, with better food than the decor would indicate.

"Oh, yumm. I don't have to change clothes."

"That's why I picked it," he said, slightly snide. Sally was not what his Aunt Henry would call "well turned out." Usually, Sally was barely turned out at all.

"I brought clothes to change into, Tower. I know what you think of my dress sense! Is Nina coming with us? Meeting us there?"

He flushed again, deeply this time, trying to keep it out of his face with no success.

"You haven't broken up," she cried. "Oh, Tower, no. You're *always* breaking up with women. Nina's so . . . so sweet! So different! I like her so much!"

"No," he protested. "We haven't broken up. We've just cooled the relationship down for a while. I've got a lot of work pending, and not enough time for everything." He was conscious of how defensive it sounded, even more conscious of the skeptical expression on Ted's face. It was the expression Ted usually got when the subject of Tower's relationships was under discussion, but Tower didn't intend to let the subject surface today. "Let's go," he urged them. "Our reservations are for ten minutes from now."

They ate curried lamb with all the trimmings. Tower relished Indian and Szechuan and Mexican cooking, strong sweet-hot flavors that filled mouth and nose. During lunch, Nina's name came up twice. The first time, Tower changed the subject by asking for more chutney. The second time, Sally would not be derailed. "Does Nina still live at the same place?"

"No," he answered, curtly. "She moved."

"Give me her new address, will you Tower. I'd like to stay in touch with her."

"I don't have it with me, Sal. I'll call you." Then he changed the subject once again. "Are you doing any landscape design work at all, Ted?"

"Bits and pieces. I've done a playground display for the Home and Garden Show. Plus a couple of city office buildings."

Tower knew the kind of thing. One newport plum and three junipers, two yellow vicaris, one flat of ground cover, five square yards of black plastic and six sacks of bark chunks to cover it. He smiled politely and said he'd look in on the Garden show. He would have done that anyhow, just to keep up with who was doing what.

When he got back to the office, there was a message from Mr. Gray setting a date for a meeting with Mr. Wills. Mr. Gray was still not one hundred percent sure he wanted to do the garden. He would make up his mind in a few days, before he returned to the country.

"Probably still in Europe. Must be nice," sighed Jeanette. "I've never even been out of the U.S."

"You went to Hawaii."

"That's the U.S. It's just Southern California with east coasts."

"More rain than Southern California."

"Okay, so it's Florida with luaus."

When she went out into her own area, Tower shut the door after her before unlocking the narrow door behind his desk. It led into his secret room, the only place of his own where he

could be completely private. Though she'd never been invited
into it, Jeanette knew it was there. He'd never mentioned it to
Ted and Sally, and he'd carefully kept it secret from Aunt
Henry. Tower himself hadn't been in it since Nina left. Almost
three weeks ago now. The closet-sized kitchenette still held
their two coffee cups, half full of dried coffee and drowned
flies. The bed still bore the impression of her body, her scent,
musky and somehow wild. He pulled the linens off the bed
and thrust them into a laundry bag, remembering the last time
they had been here.

The phone had rung, and Nina had reached for it to stop its
intrusions on their loveplay. "Sorry," she had said in her
formal, accented voice. "You have reached a wrong number."
It had been a Saturday afternoon, with Jeanette safely at home
and the place locked up tight. Nina had been naked except for
the veil of her hair which had slipped away from her breast as
she had replaced the receiver, frowning.

He had laughed at the frown and at her formal tone. "You
sound like a phone company recording, Nina love. Sooo polite."

"The person wanted someone named Sara," she replied
seriously. "There is no Sara here, is there?"

Sara had not been there for three months, though at one time
she had spent a good many evenings and weekend afternoons
in Tower's private room. When Tower was eighteen, he'd been
able to afford an occasional motel room. When he was twenty,
he'd borrowed the apartment of an acquaintance who was often
out of town. Since he'd started the business five years ago,
he'd had this comfortably furnished back room as his hide-a-
way. Sara, like others before her, had been a frequent visitor,
but Sara, like others before her, had been gently moved on.
"No Sara here," he had said to Nina. "Just one Nina and one
Tow-er and nobody else at all."

"Oh, yes," she had said, pulling a veil of blue-black hair
over her naked breasts. "The spirits of my people are here."

Even though Nina often said very strange things, always
with an air of complete belief, this was stranger than usual.
He had stared at her, open mouthed. "What?"

"It is so, Tow-er. When one of us marries, all the people come to witness."

"Marry?" he said, his voice sounding ugly. "Who said anything about marriage?"

She shook her head. "I don't mean your customs, Tow-er. I have seen how your people marry on television, on the soaps. I mean my customs. I told you all about it. My people marry as we have done."

"And how is that again?" he had asked, not remembering that she had told him anything of the kind. Of course, she might have done. While Nina chattered, he often didn't listen.

"Among our people, when a man tells a woman that he loves her, she thinks about it carefully, because it is her life she is laying down, then if she has had enough of being young and a girl, she tells him that she accepts his love. And they tell their people and everyone knows, and they are married, that's all. And the spirits assemble. They come when babies are born, too, it is said. It is the way it is done. In accordance with my customs, you and I have become married."

More of her craziness. There was enough craziness in her that he drew back from time to time, startled, sometimes a little put off. "But not by my customs," he said. "Right?" relieved when she nodded. "And no one in your culture ever goes to bed together if they aren't married? I find that hard to believe."

"Of course they do. My people have sex and do sinful things just like people in this country. For heaven's sake, Tow-er, we are pretty human too, you know."

"But that isn't marriage?"

"Not unless love is vowed. Without love, there are no children. We do not vow love without meaning it. That is..." she searched for a word. "That is risky. That would be very wrong."

Then she had come into his arms while he told her he loved her and agreed that it would be very wrong not to mean it. Unthinkable, in fact. She had seemed reassured by this. Still, even though they had been together only three or four times, scarcely time enough for Tower to have had enough of her, the exchange had troubled him enough that he had not brought her to the room again. There were other women who might be less lovely but who were a lot less complicated to have sex with.

On Saturday, even though it would be another week before he met with Gray, Tower drove out to Grayholm again. Battered-hat was nowhere in evidence, though the covering of the same upstairs window quivered for a while after he had parked the car and while he was walking around the house. He watched the shaking curtain, hoping he was making his observer uncomfortable.

In the oak circle, the water was lower, exposing some of the old foundations. He didn't really believe it had been a tomb. Battered-hat was having his little joke. And yet, what could it be except some kind of vault? He tried to see through the water and couldn't. The surface seemed clear, but there was a murkiness gathered just below it. The stone sides of the stairway could barely be glimpsed, and they wavered as though they were flexible, as though they moved.

Which was ridiculous. He shook himself. Since the water level was lower this week, evidently the pond resulted from surface drainage as much as from a spring. There had been no rain at all during the week. Perhaps draining it wouldn't be as much of a problem as he had feared. He made the circuit of the grove once more, imagining what could be put into it. Anything, really. A formal garden. A maze. An informal garden. A specimen garden. A series of gardens for differing habitats. The soil was good, very slightly acid. He sat by the pond and stared at it, hypnotized by the sparkle of sun on the ripples, flakes of light that seemed to originate in the stone littered depths and rise like fireflies. Half an hour later he came to himself and realized he had fallen asleep.

There was still no one at the house as he passed. The curtain did not move.

On Sunday he decided to go to the Home and Garden Show early, before the crowds poured in. He made a quick circuit of the garden displays, assaulted by the bright colors, the crowd noise, the odors of caramel corn and hot dogs. He sought Ted's design and found it—a playground for children. Swings and a sandbox. Varying lengths of soil pipe standing on end, each spilling a topknot of plumy grass. A tree with a clever treehouse in it. Bright flowers marching along the edge of a retaining wall, out of reach of little hands. Another set lower down, where they could be picked by those same little hands.

"Isn't it wonderful," breathed a voice at his ear. He turned to see a very pregnant woman leaning on her husband's arm. "We could do that in the backyard, Bill."

"Get the guy's name," he said. "We'll find out."

"No, I mean we could do it ourselves."

"So, let's see the guy and find out what kind of grass. And what kind of tree. This one isn't real. It'd have to be a real tree."

Typical, Tower told himself. Typical for Ted to do a design that any yahoo could duplicate, and that Ted himself wouldn't get a dime out of. Which was only one more reason why it was better that Tower was on his own. If Ted were in business with him, Ted would be giving the business away.

"Tower!" someone called. Sally. Bearing down on him with one twin on each arm. "Ted's back there somewhere with the stroller. We got impatient, didn't we, chicks."

One baby girl grabbed for her glasses while the other made a whooping noise. Ted emerged from the growing crowd, and the babies were restored to the wide stroller. "What do you think of it?" Ted asked, indicating the display.

"Very practical. Should be a hit. I heard a very pregnant lady saying nice things about it."

Ted beamed. "The city says I can have all the material after the show so we can duplicate the set-up at home. You remember that rotten old maple tree behind our house? I trimmed it up and filled the cavities, and it looks like it'll live another fifty years. Great for a tree house. I always wanted a tree house."

So had Tower. Aunt Henry hadn't wanted one, however. Not a tree house and not skiing lessons and not a horse. "Too dangerous, Tower. Too risky, Ted. Not our kind of thing."

"Tower, I saw Nina," said Sally, reaching out for his hand, jerking it to get his attention. "I saw her over at the college.

She said you weren't seeing each other at all!''

He attempted a laugh. "Well, since she moved without telling me where . . .''

"You didn't tell me that!''

"I was a little embarrassed to admit it. Anyhow, she moved. She left no number and no forwarding address. That seems to indicate she'd rather I didn't . . .''

"Oh, I don't think it means that at all. She's there every Monday and Wednesday morning, Tower. At the modern languages building. She's taking an Italian course . . .''

"I'll try to get over there next week." He felt his lips curve without feeling a smile at all. It was a lie. He wouldn't go to the college. He had tried to reach her, and that attempt was enough. He could always say he had tried. She had taken the final step. He wasn't the one who had moved without leaving a forwarding address. The suggestion that he should go running after her annoyed him slightly, so he excused himself, mentioning business. Sally was an inveterate do-gooder, a constant meddler in other people's business, always set on matchmaking or mending relationships or getting people together. Tower decided to avoid her for a few weeks until the Nina business became ancient history and Sally forgot about it.

His resolution did no good. Next morning he found Ted waiting for him at Tower's office.

"Wanted to talk to you," Ted muttered. "Sally thought I should. Where's Jeanette?''

"Monday's her day for maintenance on some of our installations.''

"Good. I mean, I wanted some private time with you." Ted was embarrassed. It showed in his face.

"I don't have a lot of time, Ted . . .''

"Time enough for this. Listen, Tower, Sally's really upset about you and Nina.''

"Isn't me and Nina my business?''

"Sure it is. I told Sally that. She knows that. But she's afraid Nina could be badly hurt, Tower. Nina isn't exactly your average American girl, you know.''

"She's a grown woman. She's twenty-two years old.''

Tower grabbed the figure out of the air. He had no idea how old Nina was. He had never asked her.

"Twenty-two or forty-two, she's naive and a lot younger than her age emotionally. Whatever her culture had been, it hasn't really prepared her for the U.S. She's gullible. She believes all kinds of strange things. If you told Nina the sky was red, she'd believe you. And Sally says she looks awful. Yellowish. As though she's sick."

Sick? Making herself sick, maybe? Fussing? Grieving? Instead of getting on with her own life. "Still," Tower replied, trying not to get angry, "that's my business or Nina's. Not Sally's. Not yours."

"Well, it's sort of our business, Tow, in that you introduced her to us and we like her. She told Sally she didn't really believe you loved her until you introduced your people to her, then she knew you were telling the truth. Sally—both of us, actually, we feel responsible. We just don't want her to be hurt. You're not always really sensitive to people's feelings."

"Oh? Since when?"

"Since always. God, Tower, I shouldn't have to tell you. Like when you and I planned to leave Aunt Henry's, and then you decided to stay without even telling me. That hurt. It's like you decided you wanted to be rid of me, so you talked me into leaving. And it hurts to have you living there, listening to Aunt Hen make remarks about me or Sally without protesting or telling her she's off the wall. And there's the way you treat Jeanette, sort of off-handedly, as though she were some kind of robot. You were like that even back when mother died, Tow. I remember the same day she died, you were talking about going to the beach."

"I'm some kind of monster because I didn't cry for weeks or something? Because I didn't have hysterics like you had?"

"Hell, I didn't say that. No. You're no kind of monster. I didn't even imply that. I'm just saying you use people kind of like groceries, Tower. Eat them up and then forget them easier than I can. And maybe a lot easier than Nina can, which is the point I'm trying to make."

"Not all that easily. I still miss Nina."

"For God's sake, man, aren't you listening? That's what I mean. You say you miss her, but you're not doing anything about it. You used to say you missed me, too, but you didn't do anything about that. Damn it, Tower, you've had twelve or fifteen women in the last three or four years. You keep telling me you've stayed friends with them, but let me tell you, the reason you broke up so easily with them is that they haven't cared enough about you to get angry at you. Nina's different. Nina's in love with you, or was. You acted like it, too, for a while. You gave her reason to believe you meant what you said, Tower!"

Tower bridled, angrily. "Of course I did . . ."

"I know what happened. I can hear it. I'll bet Aunt Henry made a few cracks about dark skin and inferior races—don't tell me she didn't. I know Aunt Hen, and she wouldn't miss an opportunity like that to save her life—next thing Sally and I know, you've broken up with Nina just to keep Aunt Hen happy. When are you going to admit Aunt Hen won't ever let go!"

"It wasn't because of Aunt Henry," he half lied. "It was because I needed more time, that's all. Nina was getting too . . . too demanding."

"She loved you. Loves you. She wants to be part of your life. That's what people do when they love each other. It isn't 'demanding.' It's sharing. It takes work!"

"I don't have time right now! I'm not ready for that yet."

"When the hell will you be?"

"When the business is a success. When I'm . . . when I've made a name for myself."

"In landscape design?" Ted looked angry, resentful.

"Of course, landscape design. Just because you gave up on it."

"I didn't give up on it. I just wasn't willing to sacrifice my life to it. God, Tower, don't think I don't know what you're doing. Ever since I left, you've been trying to get the whole inheritance released to you. One of the other trustees called me. Evidently Aunt Hen told them, 'Tower Wills, following in his daddy's footsteps, needs all his daddy's money.'"

"I'd pay you higher interest on it than you're getting now, Ted. When I'm successful, you'd profit from it."

"If you're planning on being successful, don't ever lose Jeanette, brother. Without her, you're sunk."

"What do you mean! I do the design work. Jeanette is merely an assistant."

"You ought to have given Jeanette a raise and put her name alongside yours two years ago, Tower. She's the one who breathes life into your designs. Without her, you're lost. Lifeless as a corpse. She's the one who knows what people need. How they feel. You just talk people into things without ever finding out what they want."

Tower didn't stay to hear any more. He stormed out of his own office, angrier than he could ever remember having been before, brushing past Jeanette without even seeing her, without realizing she had come back in time to hear the conversation through the open door. He didn't come back to it until afternoon, and by that time the office was empty.

Though Tower did not believe what Ted had said, he couldn't forget it. He found himself watching Jeanette, listening to her, analyzing everything that she said. She had always bubbled a lot, saying nothing much. There were many times she said nothing at all, only sang to herself in a barely audible voice.

"Jeanette?"

"Umm?"

"What's that you're singing?"

"Singing? Me? I can't sing. Couldn't carry a tune in a bucket."

Still, it sounded like singing. Tower found himself listening for it, interrupting it when it happened. "Jeanette where's the file on that Smith job we did last year?" "Jeanette, could you bring in some coffee." He kept doing it, without knowing why he was doing it. As the days went by, he heard the happy sound less and less often. He still heard it out in the yard, sometimes on the job, but hardly ever in the office.

"You know what we could do?" she said, excited, tapping the Winston plan with the eraser end of a pencil. "You know what we could do? We could put some species tulips under that ground cover. A wonderful April surprise. They won't even know they're there until the bulbs sprout!''

She'd said the same kind of thing about the Bryant job. ''You know what we could do? We could put sweet alyssum and that short blue salvia along the base of that yew. The salvia blooms a long, long time, and it'll come back every year. It doesn't take any time at all to stick a few cheap alyssum plants in every spring . . .''

And the huge pots of white geraniums. Those had been her idea. When the Winstons had called, they had mentioned the geraniums.

''No,'' he said calmly, coldly. ''Let's keep it clean. As little as possible that has to be seasonally maintained.''

''Won't that look sort of sterile?''

''Clean,'' he repeated, still calm. ''Good masses. Good foliage color. Good lines. That's what's important.''

She made a few more suggestions about the Winston job, and he vetoed them all. There wasn't going to be any question about this project. It was going to be Tower Wills from start to finish. Ted had had no business saying what he did, and Tower intended to show him that it wasn't true.

Gradually, over the next few days, the sound of Jeanette's singing in the yard diminished, as well.

''When is the Gray job supposed to start,'' she asked.

''He's supposed to be back from his trip this week. I'm going up there this weekend.''

''Do you want me to go along?'' A few weeks ago she would have simply assumed she'd be included.

''He said just me,'' Tower replied. ''Don't need to interrupt your weekend to find out what he has in mind.''

The drive to Cedar Hills seemed longer than before. It was a cloudy day, overcast and still. He was let into the house by a butler. The place was enormous, cavelike, somewhat dim, expensively furnished. Mr. Gray sat in a wheelchair on an enclosed porch, blinds drawn over every window, a tray of snacks on a table before him and a portable bar nearby. The one thing Tower could tell about him was that he was tall. A blanket hid his legs. Dark glasses hid half the man's face and a dark beard hid the other.

"Forgive my appearance, Mr. Tower. I have both arthritis and an allergy to sunlight. I cannot do without the dark lenses, and I cannot shave without much difficulty. In the winter, things are better for me. When there is not so much daytime, you understand?"

"I understand, Mr. Gray. It must be difficult to plan a garden when sunlight bothers you."

"No. Not this garden. Sit down, Mr. Wills. Take a little something on a plate. Pour yourself whatever you will drink. I enjoyed seeing the penthouse garden you did. I was there at night, of course. Now. I will tell you of my little conceit."

"Conceit?" Tower poured himself a weak scotch and soda, took some tiny salmon sandwiches.

"My name. Gray. The name of my house. Grayholm. Also a conceit. Now, I would like you to design a garden for me. Another conceit. A garden to be viewed after sundown and in moonlight. A gray garden."

Tower could not keep the expression of astonishment from his face.

"Aha! I have surprised you, have I not? Yes. A gray garden. I have been reading a little about horticulture. There are many plants and trees with gray foliage or foliage that is mostly gray. A little green, a little blue, but mostly gray. Some are desert plants. Some are shrubs. Some are very large, others are tiny, so I have read. It is in my mind for you to create for me a gray garden."

"In the oak circle?"

"Yes. The gardener tells me you've looked at it a time or two. I wanted you to do that. The space is otherwise unused and very ugly. Did you not find it ugly? There was a little stone house there, all fallen to ruin. A springhouse, I am told. I had the top of it taken down. Now the place collects water and breeds insects."

So much for Battered hat's little joke about the tomb. Tower mused, "Had you given any thought to the style of garden?

Do you want any bloom at all? White flowers are striking at dusk, and in the moonlight.''

"White," the bearded man mused, his lips twisting under his beard. "A virginal color. Not appropriate, I'm afraid. No. No color. Not even white. You understand?"

"I do understand. I'm just not sure what kind of thing we're aiming for. A rock garden? A maze garden? A desert garden?"

"Rock garden?" The tone in which it was said told Tower more than the words themselves.

"Excuse me, but English is not your native tongue?"

"Oh, no, my dear Mr. Wills. No. Your language is not my native language. Often I find words I do not know."

"Well, a really good rock garden looks like a natural rock outcropping. It may be dry, or it can have water running over it or through it, just as stones in the high mountains or near rivers often do. A good rock garden has many intriguing changes of level and scale, and, of course, it is planted with interesting plants in order to look like a natural landscape."

"I see. Would you put a rock garden in the oak circle?"

Tower thought deeply. "I think . . . I think if it were mine to do—and if the budget would allow—I would put a rock garden at the entrance to the circle, so that one would enter the circle through the stones, down shallow, very natural looking steps. I would pump water from the spring up and through it, so it would have small falls and pools to reflect moonlight and to make a soft sound. In that way we can use both plants that prefer a dry environment and plants that prefer a wet one. If we are using only gray plants, having both wet and dry environments would expand our choices. Then, I would build a small pond somewhere, preferably not in the middle where it is now, which would allow us to use marsh and water plants. There are some lovely marsh plants, reeds, some are sweet scented, and in the dusk they will appear to be dark gray or black. Then, I would take up some of the remaining area with big plantings of trees and shrubs, as background. The feeling would be of a gradual descent out of a canyon. It's a large area. It's going to be expensive to fill. If you want it to stay gray, things that bloom are going to have to be trimmed back constantly. It's going to need to be maintained."

"Oh, of course. Anything worth doing is worth doing to the limit of ones resources, don't you think?" The man's voice quivered with emotion, so much emotion that Tower paled with the force of it, unable to reply.

He decided not to acknowledge the emotion. "How soon would you want it done?"

"It must be completed by the spring. By June."

"Twelve months. That's scarcely time. Just locating plants can sometimes take months."

"I know I have delayed you in starting, but I did not know until this week whether . . . whether the garden would be truly needed. But it must be done by then. Or not done at all."

Tower bit his cheeks, wondering what to say. "Mr. Gray, believe me, I'll certainly do what I can if you understand that I can't guarantee perfection in that time period. It does sometimes take months to locate things and get them shipped in."

The man stared at his feet through the dark lenses for a time, one foot swinging back and forth, like a metronome. "Oh," he said at last. "Perhaps I can help you. I am in the import business, all manner of things, from many places around the world. If you will let me know what is needed, I can expedite their shipment. Perhaps some of my contacts can even make suggestions . . ."

It was not the kind of involvement Tower wanted from a client. Too many opportunities for intervention. Too many ways things could go wrong, out of his control . . .

The man in the chair interrupted his thought. "Have you any idea as to costs, Mr. Wills? My own, uneducated estimate is in the vicinity of a million and a half. Am I anywhere near the figure you would estimate?"

A million and a half. Yes. Tower realized he had been hiding that figure from himself, thinking it, not admitting it. He nodded, ready to cut it in half if the man objected.

"It sounds reasonable to me. If you will guarantee the completion date."

Stunned, Tower nodded. "I think . . . if your overseas contacts will help us . . ." He had just relinquished total control, something he had sworn he would never do again. But if Gray was good for that kind of money, the garden could make the covers of every horticultural magazine in the country. "Shall I draw up a contract?"

"Leave your usual contract with me. I will have my own man of business amend it as necessary."

"I won't have final estimates of costs for some time."

"It doesn't matter. We will write the contract on a 'not to exceed' basis, and you will tell me later what that figure is."

As Tower was being ushered out, the man in the chair stopped him once more. "Mr. Wills. At the center of the circle, where the pond is, I want to do something of my own. You understand?"

Tower frowned, then erased the frown. "Whatever you like, of course."

"In your plans, provide for building a fence around the center. A circle—oh, say forty feet in diameter. That should be large enough. Plan to plant a thick hedge around the fence. Make it part of your design."

"You don't want to be able to see the center? The hedge and fence are to be permanent?"

"The hedge, yes. Permanent. Something tall. Yes. What lies inside is to be a surprise. For those who walk through the garden. They will not know it is there, until they come upon it."

Puzzled, Tower nodded. Like the center of the maze, without the maze. It would create design problems, but he wasn't going to argue with the man.

Tower got home without knowing how he got there, half floating.

That evening, Sally called him.

"Tower, have you gotten over to the college to see Nina?"

"No, I haven't," he said off-handedly, not thinking about Nina at all, reminded of what Ted had said and angry all over again.

"I saw her again," she said. Her voice sounded muffled, as though she had been crying. "She said some very odd things. You really ought to see her, Tower."

This time he didn't even feel angry. "If and when I do, I'll manage it without your instructions, Sal." He hung up without waiting for her to respond.

Five minutes later he had forgotten the call.

He did the preliminary Gray plan at home, not admitting to himself that he didn't want to hear what Jeanette had to say about it. He temporized with her.

"He's not sure what he wants," Tower muttered. "We'll meet several more times, talk about things."

She was uncharacteristically incurious. "I'm sure it will be fine."

"How's the Winston job coming?"

"They don't say much."

"What do they say?"

"They say . . . they say it seems a little . . . a little frozen, I think Mrs. Winston said. A little stiff. I told her things would loosen up as they grow."

He frowned. There wasn't much in the Winston plan to loosen up. "The dwarf maples?"

"Those. Yes." Defiantly. "I told her she should plant some bulbs along the front of the planting. And some other perennials."

He stared at her, hard. "I thought we talked about that."

"We did. But she wasn't happy. The idea of bulbs and flowers made her happy. I gave her a list. Species tulips. Dwarf columbine. Blackberry lilies. Anemone japonica."

"And we're supposed to maintain what she plants?"

"I told her we wouldn't maintain the flowers, only the shrubs. In order to allow her to be involved individually."

"She bought that."

"Yes. She did." Jeanette went out of the office, closing the door behind her. She had not usually closed the door, not before. He found himself staring after her uneasily, wondering what it was that made him at all uneasy.

He spent the morning making lists of plant material, browsing through *Hortus Three*, examining back issues of *Horticulture* magazine, checking his supplier's list for people who specialized in exotic material. Not that everything had to be exotic. There were some old standbys. Cerastium tomentosum. Artemesia stellerana. Russian olive. Colorado spruce—supposed to be blue, but just as often a silvery gray. There were many gray junipers. Gray sedums. Cactuses, of course. He needed some things that were almost black, for contrast. That would be difficult. Things with black bark weren't difficult to find, but black leaves? Would Gray allow dark wine? It would look black in the dusk. Cotinus, maybe? Or very dark green. Taxus. Yew, or holly. Male holly, without the berries.

He had once bought some large, silvery boulders from a farmer north of town. At the time Tower had noticed a larger outcropping on the property. As Tower recalled, the stones were thickly lichened in dark gray and silver. Some red. He could kill the red with a sponge dipped in chlorine solution. If he moved the entire ledge, he thought it would occupy just about the right amount of space.

"Photographs," he noted for himself. He would have to photograph the natural outcropping, number the pieces as they came off, then reassemble them with a crane. Like moving that Egyptian temple! Except that when he was finished, everything should look as though it had always been there.

He went home early, taking the stack of materials with him.

"Working on something special," cooed Aunt Henry.

"Possibility of a big job," he admitted. "Only a possibility. I don't even have an estimate yet."

"Who for?" Aunt Henry wanted to know.

"A man who lives out in Cedar Hills . . ."

"Oh, really." No one but the very rich lived in Cedar Hills. "Anyone I've heard of?"

"His name is Gray. First initial A. He's foreign. I mean, not born in this country." Too late, he remembered Aunt Henry's opinion of foreigners.

"Not . . . not colored?"

"Not colored. No. Russian, maybe? One of those countries around the Black Sea. I can't place the accent. He doesn't have much of one. More as though he'd learned his English from a book. Perfect pronunciation, but the word choice is a little odd."

Her face changed oddly. She looked almost wistful. "I knew a lovely man once who spoke exactly like that," she confided. "I think he was Yugoslavian or Rumanian . . ."

"Umm," Tower acknowledged.

"The man I knew was of royal blood," she said archly. "Quite a handsome man. He was quite attentive to me. Of course that was over thirty years ago."

"What happened?" he blurted. "Couldn't he marry a commoner?"

"His wife had only recently died," she said. "He was in mourning. Otherwise—well, who knows. We had many things in common." She sighed, for a moment sounding almost human, "When we parted, he told me one day he would give me my heart's desire." Then, sharply, "I'm glad you're improving the quality of your associates, Tower."

Perhaps it was Jeanette's apparent total lack of curiosity that spurred Tower to tell her about the Gray job. He explained the situation over coffee, casually, as though it didn't matter terribly. He made little jokes about the man who was allergic to sunlight.

"How awful," said Jeanette, her eyes filling with inexplicable tears. "How dreadful. But still, that's no excuse . . ."

"No excuse for what?" he asked, too sharply, wondering what she could possibly be thinking.

"For spending all that money on a dead garden," she said. "I don't think I can do it."

"It's not dead, and you aren't being asked to do it." He turned a stack of papers on their sides and tapped them sharply together, a noise like a slap. "I am."

She reacted as though he had struck her. It was some time before she answered, carefully, as if talking to someone unbalanced. "I know nobody asked me to take part. But, I don't think you ought to do it either, Tower. There's something . . . Sick, I guess. There's something sick about it. Morbid."

"Nonsense. All the plant material I'll be using will be perfectly natural. A lot of it will be stuff we use all the time."

"Stuff we use all the time with other things," she said. "With other things that have color. With other things that bloom. Half the plants you've mentioned do bloom, and you'll have to keep them sheared to keep them gray."

"So. I'll keep them sheared."

"I can understand the man's desire for a garden he can be comfortable in, but he could have white. White isn't a color. And it's beautiful in the moonlight."

"He doesn't want white. He wants gray. Dark gray, medium gray, charcoal gray, dove gray, pale gray. It's a play on his name. Gray."

"White roses. You could grow them behind a rock so you couldn't see them, but you could smell them. Or lilies . . ."

"Jeanette," he said warningly, angrily. "The job is worth a million and a half. Our profit will be enough to pay for the greenhouse. And the man wants gray."

She sighed. Sighed again. "It's a lot of money," she admitted. "Still, I don't think I'd do it, Tower. It's like . . . it's like a betrayal. It's a kind of denial. A denial of color. A denial of the senses. Just because he has a vision problem . . . Well, I just wouldn't." She left him, going out sadly. It had been days since he had heard her singing.

None of which bothered him later that week when he sat with Mr. Gray on the enclosed porch once again, talking about the stones for the garden. ". . . silvery gray stone, naturally weathered into a rugged outcropping. Lots of little crevasses in it where things can be planted. Also, it breaks naturally into two groupings, so we have a place to bring the stairs down through it."

"Stairs?"

"We'll need to build some. A few steps, then a long stretch, then a few steps more. The steps should be made out of the same stone, and the path between them should be graveled in the same color, perhaps with some flat stones set into it. I've been making lists of plant material and calling my suppliers." Tower had been amazed to find a number of gray and black plants available which he had never heard of before. When he started calling around, people called back from here and there, offering things. "We could do it rather quickly if we used only ordinary things, but that's not what you had in mind."

"No." Gray shook his head slowly. "It mustn't be ordinary."

"Still, more readily obtainable stuff will do for the background plantings. I can begin getting in some spruces, some cypresses, as soon as we agree on the layout."

"You have plans?"

"Preliminary sketches." Tower excelled at renditions, and he had worked through the night on the ones he had brought with him. One showing the rock garden from below. One showing the massed plantings. One of the pond. All dim, misty, a Scottish highland light.

"So." Gray peered at the renditions through his dark glasses. "You will leave these with me?"

"Of course. You'll want to study them."

"Will the amount we spoke of be satisfactory?"

Tower swallowed. "It will take all of it. It's going to cost a quarter million just to move the rocks. The spruces must be selected for color. They'll cost up to a hundred a foot, planted, and we need a lot of them. I'm allowing for extraordinary expense in procuring the more exotic material. I may have to fly quite a few miles to pick it up." And profit, he reminded himself silently. At least a quarter of a million dollars profit.

"Can you handle this without an advance, Mr. Wills?"

"No, frankly, I can't. I'll need to pay suppliers and laborers . . ."

"I'll have an account set up for you to reimburse expenses. I presume you're willing to wait until completion for your own fee?"

Wordlessly, Tower nodded.

"Then we can complete your contract. I have signed it. Will you sign it now?"

"What have you added to it?"

"Only the completion date," Gray said. "It must be completed in June. There would be no reason for it if it were not finished by then."

"We should be able to manage, with the help you've offered."

"It must be then."

"A date that has meaning for you?" Tower pried gently, thinking it might help him with the design. "Perhaps an anniversary?"

"Perhaps," the man smiled, full lips showing briefly between the beard and moustache. They were purplish, as though in someone with heart trouble. "All dates are anniversaries of something, are they not, Mr. Wills?"

Tower waited for more, but Mr. Gray did not bother to explain. Tower flipped through the contract, finding nothing to take exception to. The clause specifying the completion date merely said that Tower would guarantee personally to complete the garden in June of the following year. He reached for his pen.

"No," said Mr. Gray. "Please sign it over there."

"Where?" Tower looked up, surprised.

The man rolled his chair toward the window, reaching forward to open the shade which had shut out much of the light. When it was raised they could look down the wide stairs, down the graveled path, and through the notch in the trees to the center of the circle. Light glimmered from the wind riffled pool, sending bright shards of light into his eyes. Someone was walking there, but the dazzle of light hid anything but the outline. Tower grunted. "I do know what it looks like."

"There are three parties to this contract, are there not? There is the buyer, that is I. And the designer, you. And the—what shall we call it? The subject? Which is to be immortalized by your talents? All three should be present at the time of agreement." He handed Tower his pen. Tower took it, then dropped it with an exclamation, shaking his hand.

"What happened, Mr. Wills? Ah, you've cut yourself. Look, there's blood on the paper. Ah. I see. The pen clip is broken. Nasty. May I get you a bandage?"

Tower pressed his handkerchief into his hand. It was only a shallow cut about an inch long in the center of his palm. Nothing serious. Only a pinhead of blood had flecked the paper.

"I'm fine," he said. "Fine." He took his own pen and signed his name, obscuring the tiny bloodstain.

The bearded man closed the blind and rolled back to his former place. "Tell me, Mr. Wills, do you love your work?"

"I enjoy it a great deal."

"Do you love it?"

"I've never been quite sure what that word means," Tower laughed unconvincingly. "I have an assistant who loves ice cream and loves puppy dogs and loves to plant anything. I'm not like that. But I'd rather do what I'm doing than anything else I know of, if that's love."

The purple lips showed briefly through the beard, then Mr. Gray took one copy of the contract and handed another ceremoniously to Tower. "I pray you will take great pleasure in this project, Mr. Wills."

Summoned by some silent signal, the butler came to usher him out. Tower found himself on the front steps, the door closing behind him. It had happened so quickly that he was unable to feel the elation he had expected. There was no warm glow from the contract in his inside jacket pocket. Still, it was signed. The renditions were provisionally accepted. The budget—Lord, what he would do with that million and a half. And what he would do with the profit!

As he drove down the avenue of horsechestnuts, he noted half consciously that the scarlet candles of bloom had faded to a corroded, metallic pink. It was an odd color, not one he had seen before, one he found difficult to associate with anything living.

"I shall be sixty next week," said Aunt Henry with an air of satisfaction. "I am giving myself a birthday party. I want Ted and what's-her-name to come."

"I thought you didn't approve of Sally." Tower replied, annoyed. He didn't want to talk about his relationship with Nina again, but Sally would be sure to bring it up. Tower had dropped off some papers at Ted's office only the day before—thankful to see the place had been repainted in more subdued colors. He had timed his visit to coincide with Ted and Sally being out to lunch. Instead they had been having sandwiches at Ted's desk, and Sally had immediately started harassing him about Nina. Tower had fled then, and he wanted to flee now. "Why are you inviting Ted and Sally?" he demanded.

"We must let bygones be bygones," Aunt Henry said placidly.

It wasn't what she had said last month; it wasn't what she would say next week. It was what she was saying today because she knew it would irritate Tower. How did she know? How had she always known? If it was something that would make Tower or Ted uncomfortable, she had known, that's all, ever since they were children, ever since she had come to take care of their mother. If Tower had begged her to invite Ted and Sally to join them for dinner, Aunt Hen would have objected. Because Tower didn't want them, she did.

All he could do was pretend indifference. "Fine," he said. "Do you want me to call them, or will you?"

"You," she said in a firm tone, only slightly surprised by his attempt at nonchalance. "You do it. Friday night. Eight o'clock. Dinner. No gifts. Ted probably couldn't afford a gift anyhow."

This was more in her usual tone but "No gifts," meant she would be mortally offended if she didn't receive something rather nice. Though the three of them could put their names on one gift. She could hardly object to that.

"For your aunt?" Jeanette asked. "Gee, I don't have any ideas at all, Tower."

He had asked her, casually, as he had asked a hundred other favors, if she would mind picking out a gift.

"You do it so well," he said. "Sally loved the playpen you got for the twins."

"Oh, well, babies are different. I know about babies. But I don't know about your Aunt. I'm afraid I'll have to pass on that one, Tower."

She had never before refused to do anything he had asked her to, or even anything he had suggested. The refusal left him momentarily at a loss. "What are you working on?" he asked.

"That apartment house courtyard you didn't want to be both-ered with. And those two little show houses."

"Any problems?"

She shrugged. "I'm sure you'd do them better than I will, Tower, but they'll do well enough." When she left, she shut the door behind her.

Tower gritted his teeth and called Ted, receiving the response he would have expected.

"I can't believe she asked you to invite Sally and me."

"Well, she did. Now all you have to do is tell me whether you'll come or not."

"I'll talk to Sally. She thinks Aunt Henry is a dirty joke, and she's pretty pissed at you."

"This has almost nothing to do with me. I'll be there, but it isn't my idea, it isn't my birthday, it isn't my party. I'll find some kind of gift for the three of us to give her—that is, if you don't object—and we'll spend a couple of hours eating Mrs. Shandle's cooking, after which you can forget it ever happened." Mrs. Shandle was Aunt Henry's long time and ageless cook. "Just do me a favor and ask Sally, please, to stay off the subject of my personal relationships."

"Fine by me, bro. I'll tell her but I can't answer for her. Never could. That's one of the things I like about Sally."

"Do what you can," Tower said. "By the way, I like the new paint job on your office."

"What new paint job?" Ted asked, sounding puzzled.

Tower's other phone rang and he merely laughed and said goodbye.

"Why don't you ask that nice assistant of yours to dinner with us," suggested Aunt Henry.

"I don't like to mix business and social life, Aunt. Sorry. No."

He had so seldom said no to her that she actually looked shocked. She did not raise the subject again, which was unusual for her. Aunt Henry's persistence was legendary, though both Ted and Tower had called it other things from time to time. When the birthday evening came, Aunt's continued silence was explained by Jeanette's arrival. "Your aunt called and invited

me,'' she said. "I didn't have anything else to do tonight."
She had also brought a gift, a set of Irish linen handkerchiefs
which Aunt Henry, ignoring her other gifts, exclaimed over
again and again.

"So *thoughtful*," she beamed. "Real Irish linen. I don't
think I've had a linen hanky since I was oh, fifteen or sixteen.
What a nice gift."

After glasses of sherry shared in an atmosphere of false
sociability, they went in to dinner. Though Tower usually enjoyed Mrs. Shandle's excellent cooking, he found the meat dry
and flavorless, like cardboard. The ornate birthday cake, with
tactfully few candles, also tasted of nothing much.

They had coffee in the drawing room. Coffee and brandy.
Sally sat almost silently beside the unnecessary fire, refilling
her glass from time to time. Ted was at the low bookcases
under the window, calling out the titles of books he remembered
from his childhood. Jeanette was on the windowseat, remembering a few favorite titles of her own. Tower sat at a corner
table, drumming his fingers on the polished mahogany. Aunt
Henry excused herself. "Such an exciting time," she said in
her cold, placid voice. "Such a nice evening. Now you young
people stay on as long as you like." And she drifted out, leaving
a deadly silence behind.

Jeanette broke it. "I'd better be getting along home. By the
way, Tower. I'll be a little late tomorrow. There's some personal business I have to attend to."

"The Myersons are coming in first thing tomorrow," he
objected.

"I know, but you don't need me for that. I'm sure they'll
want to deal directly with you, not with some assistant." She
shook hands with Ted, exchanged cheek kisses with Sally and
was quickly gone, the sound of the front door echoing down
the hallway and into the room.

"Me, too," yawned Sally. "Come on, old Ted-bear. Take
the lady home."

"Who's a lady? I don't see any lady."

"Sure you do, this drunk lady, right here."

"You have kind of been tossing them down."

"Well," she said judiciously, trying to get her left foot back into the shoe she had shed under the coffee table, "it was the lesser of two evils. You told me not to talk to Tower, so I drank, instead."

"Oh, come on," Tower tried to laugh. "You're just trying to wash down that tasteless meal. I can't imagine where Shandy got that meat! Or this coffee, either."

"The meat tasted fine to me," said Sally. "Juicy and tender. I wish we could afford beef like that. I'd have it every day."

"It tasted of sawdust," he said definitely. "And so did the cake."

"You're probably coming down with something," Ted remarked. "A cold, maybe. I can never taste anything when I have a cold."

"I don't have a cold," Tower said stubbornly. "It did taste like sawdust."

"Come on, sweetie," said Sally, tugging at Ted's arm. "Early day tomorrow.

"Why are you in such a hurry," demanded Tower. "You don't need to run off just because of me."

"You and I are not going to get into it," she leered at him, slightly drunkenly. "On orders from the Lord and Master, here. I am not to discuss Nina with you. I am particularly not to tell you all the stuff Nina said to me the last time I saw her. Because, the Lord and Master says, if you wanted to know what she had to say, you would hear it from her yourself."

Tower agreed but found himself saying, irrationally, "What did she say? Why did it upset you so?"

"Sally," said Ted, warningly.

"No," she replied. "He asked. You heard him ask. That means he's interested, so I can tell him."

"That wasn't the deal."

"New deal, then," she said, plopping herself back down on the sofa. "Nina said to me that you betrayed her, Tower Wills. She said you told her you loved her and she thought that meant you really did. So she said she gave her life to you. Those were her words, not mine."

"This is none of your business," Tower exploded.

"Right. Ab-so-lutely. But you asked. More important, Nina thinks she is pregnant. She was crying. She said that one third of the women in her family die having first babies, so she's scared. That's what Nina says. She also says her family knew all about you just as we knew all about her, and her family are very upset because—get this, Tower, it'll blow the girdle off Aunt Hen—they don't approve of mixed relationships."

"Crap," he said, unfeelingly. "If there was any group of people where one third of the women died with first babies, they'd be written up in *Discover* and you'd see the story on NOVA with sixty scientists dramatically searching for a cure. Nina always made up stories, unbelievable stuff, and that's just what they are, stories. 'The women sometimes don't reach puberty until they're in their forties or fifties.' 'If the women die, the men never remarry,' she told me. 'If the men die, the women can remarry,' 'Some of the men live to be hundreds of years old.' How about that? Crazy enough for you? She's a hysterical girl who lives in a dream world. She's schizzy. I was perfectly right tô break it off. Can you imagine what that would be like to live with?"

"I can imagine what it would be like for you to live with, yes," said Sally, getting to her feet once more. "But I don't think she's crazy. I think she's just . . . exotic. At one time people used to believe in devils and witches, even educated people. It didn't mean they were crazy, it just means they were raised to believe in those things. There are people in the far east who believe in demons as part of their religion. So, maybe Nina is superstitious, or gullible, or believes in myths. You knew that when you sweet-talked her, Tower my friend, and don't tell me you didn't, because your reputation as a wom-anizer is virtually legendary. At least with your awe-struck brother, it's legendary. According to me, you aren't a legend, you're just a waster. You seduce and throw away—what did Nina call it? Slash and burn. You did it to Ted, even though he's too sweet to hold it against you. You're doing it to Jeanette. You did it to Nina and you've done it to a whole string of other women, even though most of them didn't care much. Mark my words, Tower Wills. You're building a real vaccuum around yourself. Nature abhors a vaccuum, and if you chase all the good people away, something bad will come along to fill it. I've seen it happen to people before. And that's all I have to say on that matter.''

"For which I am very grateful," he snarled.

"That's all right, poopsie," she said, patting his face with infuriating calm. "If I had to live with Aunty Hen, I'd be nasty tempered and sexually unethical, too." She leaned forward and hugged him, then tugged Ted away by one hand and fled the room, staggering slightly and laughing about it.

Something. Something missing. He couldn't imagine what. Something in that last few words . . . Something she didn't . . . He took a deep breath. She hadn't smelled like Sally. Nothing. No scent at all. He sniffed, experimentally. He couldn't smell anything. Ted was right. He was coming down with something.

Tower photographed the rock outcropping and arranged to have it moved. He began to order material, drawing against an account that Gray's business manager had set up for him. He did ten renditions of various views from the garden looking toward the center before he found one that pleased him. Before anything else had been done, the fifty-foot circle in the center of the space had been surrounded with a solid, dark-painted board fence about twelve feet high, around which he had planted thick cypresses. The resultant mass presented definite design problems. The best solution seemed to be to plant clumps of trees around the central core, clumps of different sizes and heights, the varying shapes and types of foliage effectively camouflaging the dark block of hedge and the fence behind it. The barricaded central space was accessible now only by a tall, solid gate, tightly padlocked, which Tower never saw opened.

"What's he got in there," Tower asked Battered-hat.

"A sump pump," snarled the man. "Wouldn't you?"

It was obvious the man would provide no responsive answer. Tower set his curiosity aside. He was too busy to play games.

Since he had chosen not to involve Jeanette in the project, he had no help with it, and the details seemed to take endless hours. He began to receive letters describing plant materials, offering trees, offering shrubs, most of them with pictures, from Africa, from Australia, from the Far East. Still, amid the continual phone calls and paper work he made time to see a doctor about his vanished senses of taste and smell. Sometimes he could almost taste something, almost smell something, like a sensation recalled, but then it would slide away, elusive as a dream. The doctor found nothing obvious and went on to speak of brain scans and possible tumors. Tower submitted his skull to the latest electronic diagnostic marvel. It made enigmatic pictures of his head, but the doctor merely frowned and consulted colleagues and confessed himself at a loss.

"We can't find anything," he said. "You haven't used chemical inhalers to excess? You're not taking drugs you haven't told us about? Normally this kind of thing is a neurological problem but . . ."

"You're losing weight," said Aunt Henry.

"When nothing tastes good, you don't eat much," he snapped. It was true. Everything tasted like sawdust and left a dead feeling in his mouth.

He decided to see Nina. Not because Sally had urged it, but because he kept dreaming about Nina, long, tortuous dreams in which she was trying to tell him something. In the dream, he couldn't hear her. He thought if he saw her, it would put an end to the annoyance. He could hear for himself what she had been telling Sally.

He went to the Modern Languages Building on Wednesday morning, knowing she had an Italian class at ten. She wasn't among those leaving at the end of class. He stopped a studious looking girl and asked her if Ilanina Gyulas was in the class.

"Nina Gyulas? She was. Sure. But she got to looking really terrible. Some of us thought maybe she had cancer or something because she dropped out, last week I think. No. It was the week before. Are you a friend of hers?"

He nodded, wondering what to do next.

"She sure looked as though she could use a friend. You might ask at the administration office. They may have an address for her."

The administration office had a numbered post office box as an address. "You can write to her," said the grandmotherly type, unhelpfully. "It says here she's dropped out temporarily for reasons of health."

Write to her. What would he say? "Dear Nina, I've heard you're ill and I'm sorry." "Dear Nina, Sally says you think you're pregnant?" "Dear Nina, what makes you think it is mine?" "Dear Nina, here's the address of a good abortion clinic, and if you need money for the procedure, I'll provide it."

"Dear Nina, I do love you. Come back to me."

None of them seemed any truer or more appropriate than any other. He didn't write any of them.

He had to meet Ted at the bank for a meeting with the trustees. Ted invited him to lunch afterward, with the air of one making amends. Tower couldn't think of a way to refuse without seeming churlish.

"I know you don't want to talk about your ex-girlfriend, but you know that funny thing Nina said about mothers dying?" Ted asked. "Something came up in the class I'm taking, and it reminded me of that. The class is on population dynamics of predator-prey populations. Kind of fascinating, actually. In the context of that class, the scenario Nina outlined could make a certain amount of sense. If you had a population that needed to be strictly controlled, it could be accomplished if one third of the females died with their first pregnancy, one third with the second, and one third with the third . . ."

"What the hell are you talking about," snarled Tower. The report on the trust funds had not put him in a good humor. Aunt Hen had not been as careful as she should have been about approving investments.

Ted went on calmly, "What Nina said, about one third of the women in her family dying with their first babies. I was just thinking that from an environmental point of view, it could make sense in providing a strictly controlled population. Maybe the one third maternal death rate is true of some animal or bird population where Nina came from. She could have picked up the information and applied it to her own family. Or someone might have told her it was true, and she believed it. Where did she come from, anyhow?''

"Someplace in Europe. I'd never heard of the town. Some name like a dirty word . . .''

"What dirty word?'' Ted laughed.

"I can't remember. Just that I thought at the time it was a four-letter word. But they've lived all over. She lived in Brazil for a while.''

"Well, that story of hers is interesting if you consider it in the light of population dynamics. The females dying that way would keep reproduction at an average of two young ones per couple which would be mere replacement. No more, no less.''

"That's fine if you're talking about lemmings or rhinoceroses. Nina happened to be talking about people.''

"I know,'' Ted mused. "It doesn't make real sense applied to people. Unless there were some other reason. I haven't figured that out yet. Even the rest of it sort of makes sense.''

"What rest of it?''

"The part about if a husband died, the woman would remarry. She'd need to, because she would need to complete her reproductive quota to keep the population stable.''

"But she said if a woman died, the man wouldn't remarry. What kind of sense does that make?''

"I don't know,'' Ted sighed, running his finger down the menu. "Maybe it's like geese. Maybe the men mate for life, and if the wife dies, he just goes on alone.''

"You're not eating,'' said Aunt Henry.

Tower played with the dressing on his plate. Turkey and dressing and Mrs. Shandle's brown gravy, and it tasted like nothing at all.

"Even if you can't taste it, Tower, try to eat something. You have to have nourishment.'' Aunt Hen sounded tentative, strangely tentative, as though she could not make up her mind whether to admonish him or let him alone.

Jeanette came into his office. "Tower, I've had an offer from Schmidt's nurseries. They're opening a new design department and would like me to head it up." She played with the pencils on the edge of his desk, not meeting his eyes.

"Ted used to work for Schmidt. Did he put you onto it? Did they offer you more money?" he asked at last, the words coming harshly from a raw throat. "Did they?"

"I haven't even talked to Ted," she said. "I thought of talking to him, just to find out what Schmidt's are like to work for, but quite frankly, considering that he's your brother, I didn't feel that would be at all appropriate. No, Mr. Schmidt called me and asked if I'd be interested. And no again, it isn't any more money."

"Then why would you . . ."

She clasped her hands in front of her and set her jaw. "The reasons I would consider it are that you don't include me in projects the way you used to. You've quit accepting any of my ideas or suggestions. I feel like I've been demoted, and I want to be more than just an assistant. Then, you're spending all your time on a job I'm not in sympathy with, and to tell you the truth, it hasn't been much fun working here lately." The words came out carefully, without emphasis, neatly strung together and obviously thought out beforehand.

"Well," he said at last. "You're in charge of the checkbook. Write yourself a severance check."

"Is that all?" Her eyes were scrinched half shut as though to close in tears. "We've worked together for almost five years, but you don't say anything but 'write yourself a check.'"

"What is there to say? You say you're leaving."

"I hadn't really said that," she sighed, wiping her eyes with a grubby tissue. "Not until right now. Now I'll say it. Tower, please accept my resignation as of the end of next week. I think I can get everything I'm involved in caught up by then."

He didn't see her go out. He didn't hear the door close.

"Dear Nina,

"I heard from Sally that you are not well. I came to the university looking for you and was told you've dropped out for health reasons. Nina, I never intended that we not see one another again. I'm sorry you didn't understand that. Please

write giving me your address so I can see you, even if it's only
to say goodbye.

"As ever,

"Tower."

"Dear Tower,

"I did understand you. I explained to you how it was with
our people. You just didn't want to believe I meant *me* when
I talked about our people. Among us, when a man says he
loves, it means forever. I explained that, over and over, before
we made love. You said, yes, yes, you understood, you agreed.
You always laughed and said you understood, you agreed. You
even took me to meet your people! When one of our men
speaks of love, he knows he is asking for a life. He knows the
woman may die, maybe soon, maybe a little later. He asks for
the sake of children, for continuity. It's the way we are. I was
honest with you, Tower, but you didn't pay attention. You lied
to me.

I do not need to say goodbye. Our people do not say 'Goodbye.' We do not say 'Farewell.' We do not say, as the Spanish
do, adios, go with God. Our separations are forever. They are
not good-byes, we do not fare well, we do not go with God.

"I do not give you an address. I am with my people and
they say there is no reason to see you again now.

"Ilanina."

Throughout the fall Tower immersed himself in the Gray
garden. What could be planted in the autumn, he planted, using
a pick-up crew of men whom he had to watch every minute to
be sure they did things correctly. Tower installed a drip system
to water the plants as well as a tiny waterfall to begin at the
top of one ledge and trickle down from ledge to pool to streamlet
to ledge to pool once more, finally running back under the
fence to be pumped to the top once more. Battered-hat had
handled the installation of the pump. Tower still hadn't seen
what Mr. Gray was doing behind the fence. Whatever it was,
it evidently hadn't yet included draining the pond.

The rockgarden occupied the entire north quadrant of the

circle. The south quadrant was virtually filled with large trees and shrubs set on beams of varying heights to lend the feeling of a receding landscape. The west quadrant was being planted as a desert garden, and the pond and marsh occupied the eastern part of the circle. The whole was integrated by a network of paths steps with seats here and there. Though only half done by the end of October, one could still see the shapes emerging, contrasting hard and soft, line against curve, mass against mass.

From time to time, almost idly, Tower found himself wondering what he would do when the Gray commission was finished. He had had no time to take on any other work. Without Jeanette, there was no one to do anything he could not handle himself. He kept telling himself he would hire someone else, but the weeks fled by and he had no time to do so.

He fell into bed at night exhausted. Weekends went by without even one visit to the places he had used to frequent. He was too tired to look for female company. He drove to and from work in a daze, spending more than half his time on the site. It was as he was driving home late in October that he was brought to himself cars honking angrily behind him. He looked at the light, thinking it might have changed, and saw that it was out of order. Cars were pulling out to go around him. He pulled across the intersection and stopped, shaken.

"Whassamatta, stupid, you can't see green!" demanded a driver who had been blocked behind him. "Open yer eyes for chrissake."

Tower walked back to the intersection and peered at the light. A winish glow. Then an amber glow, faint as a distant fire. Then nothing for a while. Then a winish glow again.

"Excuse me," a kindly voice. "Do you need some help?"

He turned, half snarling.

"Oh," she said, backing away. "I'm sorry. The way you were peering, I thought perhaps your vision . . . that is that you . . . I thought you couldn't see." She fled.

He waited through another cycle. Winish glow. Amber. Nothing. All the cars and trucks moved on nothing, stopped on wine.

A strolling couple stopped near him. "Excuse me," he said,

his voice trembling on the verge of a scream. "I'm ah having trouble with my eyes. Is there a green cycle on this traffic light?"

"Just come along with us," the man smiled. "We'll tell you when it's green." They moved on in a moment, beckoning.

Tower looked at the traffic light. There was nothing there. No color. He turned and ran to the car, drove slowly down the block where he turned onto a side road and followed its winding and unregulated length three extra miles toward home.

He pawed through a bureau drawer looking for a favorite green sports shirt. It wasn't green anymore. It was a nothing color, no color at all. His bright red tie was now wine colored, so deep a wine as to look almost black. His blue shirts were still blue, but the color seemed lost in mist, as though seen from a great distance.

The purple hall carpet outside his room was black. The row of marigolds along the back walk were a dark bronze. There was virtually no color he could see, no color he could find. The world had become a sepia photograph, a faded image, frozen in time. He found himself walking up and down the stairs, back and forth through the halls, dry mouthed, filled with a hysterical desire to laugh or cry or scream. Instead he walked, walked, his feet stumbling after one another as though he had been drunk. A landscape gardener who couldn't tell green from gray? A plantsman who couldn't identify the hue of a bloom?

"Tower? Tower!"

He looked up into Aunt Henry's face, her eyes intent upon him, her expression speculative.

"What's the matter with you. What are you doing?"

"Color," he said, a grating whisper. "I can't see color any more."

"You didn't need to take the time to visit me." Tower pushed himself higher in the hospital bed. "It feels silly lying down all the time when all they're doing is tests." His voice was surly. He didn't want visitors and he'd said so. He felt he was living in some old black and white movie, and he needed time to get used to it.

"You probably needed the rest," said Sally, not reacting to his tone, determined to be pleasant. "Ted and I've both thought you've looked very tired lately."

"What are they finding out about you?" Ted asked. "Any results at all?"

Tower shook his head. He didn't feel like answering questions, either. "Nothing. No tumor. No neurological damage they can find. They're telling me to go back to work, hire someone to identify colors for me if I need someone . . ." He fell silent, thinking of Jeanette.

"Jeanette quit her new job," said Ted, reading Tower's mind. "She called me a couple of weeks ago to tell me she was moving to the coast. She has a daughter and granddaughter there, and she said she wanted to live closer. She never should have left you in the first place. She was really happy there when she started out."

Tower shook his head, not answering. Jeanette had left because Tower wanted to control his own business, which he had a perfect right to do. He didn't want associates. He didn't want partners. He did not feel repentant. There was an accusatory silence. More to break it than out of any desire to tell Sally what he had done, he said, "I wrote to Nina, you know."

"You did! Tower, that's wonderful."

"She wrote back. She doesn't want to see me again."

"Oh." Her face sagged. "Well. I guess that's that, then." She twiddled her fingers, stared out the window. "You guys have a chat for a few minutes. I have an errand down in the gift shop." She left the room, rather hurriedly, eyes brimming.

"I know Sal's intruded in your private affairs," Ted admitted. "Even I don't understand what Sally and Nina had going, but Sally really liked her. I don't know what it was, some kind of immediate empathy between the two of them, maybe. Maybe it's just that Nina thought the twins were wonderful. She was a real nut on babies. She sent little gifts to them, asked about them when she called . . ."

"I didn't know that."

"Even though they never got to know each other well, Sally thought of her as a friend."

"Weird," muttered Tower. "Both of them."

Ted bridled, then decided not to make an issue of it. "Nina was weird, maybe. You remember, I was saying the other day how that business of the mothers dying would make sense in an absolutely stable population. And you said that was great for lemmings but not for people."

"Ted, I've told you she didn't make sense."

"I got to thinking about it. She did make sense, Tower. Of a kind."

Tower sighed inwardly. He seemed doomed to hear about Nina for the rest of his life.

"It makes sense," Ted crowed, "if you're a predator."

"It what?"

"It makes sense if you're a predator. Listen, I learned all about it in that class I'm taking. It takes a large population of herbivores to support each predator, and if you're going to be a successful predator, you need herbivores who are generally rather placid."

"So you can jump them while they're having lunch," Tower said, trying to make a joke of it.

"No, now listen. If you have too many predators, the herbivores will get jumped every five minutes and they'll be so wary it will be very hard to make a kill. So, predator populations cannot be too large or they make the herbivores nervous."

"Which has what to do with Ilanina Gyulas?"

"I know it's a little unusual, but maybe her family has a history of predation on other people. There are certain tribes or groups that are predatory, right? Gypsies, for example."

"Wouldn't she have said if her family were gypsies?"

"Not necessarily gypsies. There are others. Snake Oil salesmen. Con men, and pickpockets, you know what I mean? I've read about whole generations of certain families making their living in ways like that."

"I don't get your point, Ted."

"You're not listening, Tower. Look, all of us get burglarized or get our pockets picked once in a while, say every three or four years. And as long as it's every three or four years, we forget about it in between. Oh, we get mad when it happens, but the rest of the time we forget about it. Now, suppose it happened every other week.'' He stared at Tower expectantly.

''Suppose my pocket got picked every other week?''

''Right.''

''I'd be madder than hell.''

''Yes. And you'd retaliate against pickpockets somehow. You'd put shockers in your pocket or learn to grab the guy's hand or quit carrying any money.''

''What are you saying, Ted?''

''I'm saying that just like animal predators, human predators have to figure on not making the population really mad. They have to pick one off here and one off there, but not too often, because otherwise the human herbivore population would rebel and retaliate against the predators, right? So, to keep the herbivore population placid, the population of predators has to stay fairly low. Am I right?''

''I don't see what that has to do with Nina.''

''It just kind of fit in with what Sally learned about Nina's people. They frown on mixed marriages. They keep themselves to themselves. They wander around so that the number of them in any given place is rather small. And they have small families, average two to the family. That's just what a predatory culture would do.''

''You're not saying one third of their women *really* die in childbirth.''

''No. I don't know. What I'm saying is, if keeping the population of predators very small and constant were important, that's one way it could happen. It could actually be a survival mechanism to prevent there ever being enough predators to make the population really upset. If the gypsies don't want to get wiped out, they need to be sure there aren't too many of them.''

''I don't think Nina was a gypsy.''

''I don't either, Tower,'' Ted agreed. ''I was just using that as an example.''

''Well, then what was she?''

"I don't know. You knew her, for God's sake. Didn't you ever ask her?"

Tower tried to remember. "She was European. That's all she ever said. That she was from this dirty-word town in Europe."

"What country in Europe?"

"I don't know. I don't think she ever said."

"If the name of the town was a dirty word, you ought to be able to find it. In the back of an atlas or something. Look up all the four-letter words."

"I suppose," Tower mumbled, suddenly weary of the whole thing. "It doesn't matter, does it? So, her family were predatory, like gypsies."

"How did you meet her, anyway?"

Tower yawned. "She was at a concert. Sitting next to me. I was with Soph Kimball, and Soph went off with some old friend at the intermission. So I talked to this girl." His eyes closed. He could remember Nina's face. So serious. So intent. As though she had never been in a concert hall before. As though everything in the world was a new experience.

"Tower," said Ted. "Tower?"

Tower did not answer. He was too tired. He only wanted to sleep.

Two weeks later, equipped with bottles of this and vials of that, energizers, vitamins, anti-depressants which the doctor wanted to try on the theory that Tower had a neuro-transmitter disorder which one of the anti-depressants might affect, Tower returned home.

"I missed having you here for Christmas and New Years," said Aunt Henry accusingly, as though it had been his fault.

"I didn't even know it was Christmas," he replied, trying to keep his eyes open. The anti-depressants acted like sleeping pills. He was constantly fighting lethargy.

"Can I have the cook bring you something? Some fruit juice? Some soup?"

"Aunt Henry, I can't taste it. If I can't taste it, I don't want it. I'll eat something when I get hungry, but it doesn't matter what.''

"Well, why don't you rest, then.''

"Rest,'' he growled. "Is what I've been doing. I have to finish a landscaping job. There's a completion date in the contract, and I can't afford not to collect.''

"Surely you've made something on it thus far?''

"Not a dime. Every dollar spent has gone for material or to pay for labor. My profit comes at the end of the job. It says so in the contract.''

She sat there, bolt upright, staring at him with a strange intensity. Not like herself. When he saw himself in the mirror next, he thought he understood why. It was like looking into the face of a mannequin, something constructed. He looked only marginally alive.

"You've been ill?'' asked Mr. Gray.

Tower nodded. It was too much effort to explain. The cold air bit at his lungs, and he wondered what had brought the invalid out of his house on such a chill day in February.

"You're going to finish on time?''

"Oh, yes,'' Tower murmured. "I'll finish on time. Beginning in mid-April, we'll plant all the remaining material. One of your contacts offered me some interesting trees that I changed the design for. Most of the basic labor is done . . .''

"So glad,'' the man in the the wheelchair said, staring at Tower through his dark glasses. "You don't look at all well, Mr. Wills. What has been the trouble?''

"A neurological problem,'' Tower answered. He had no intention of telling his only customer that he could neither taste nor smell nor see color. He changed the subject. "What are you doing with the central space, Mr. Gray?''

The invalid shrugged, expressively. "A surprise. You'll see it later.''

"Is it finished? Whatever it is?''

"Oh not quite. It needs a few finishing touches.'' He raised a gloved hand in farewell and murmured to his attendant who pushed him up the path, back through the juniper arch and down the path to the house. A ramp had been constructed at one side of the stairs for the chair. Tower looked after him as he disappeared into the house.

Upstairs the curtains quivered. Tower stared at them incuriously, no longer caring who it was who watched him almost every time he came and went. Someone with few amusements, obviously. Someone who preferred watching people to watching television.

Winter came, hard winter, cold and snow, days of wind and bleared skies. Tower went to the office each day, just to get away from Aunt Hen, but he had no energy to go after new jobs. He spent his time reading through catalogues and making tentative designs on odd pieces of scrap paper. He could have the Gray garden photographed in May or early June. He could have the copy ready before that. He sent a few letters to the architectural magazines, asking if they would be interested in an article, enclosing pictures he had taken last fall.

His weight had stabilized. He ate when he was hungry. Pencils and paper at the office were labeled as to color. Sally had insisted on coming in to do that for him. She had quit talking about Nina, though Ted still worried away at the subject, certain there was some body of fact which underlay Nina's crazy stories. Tower surprised himself by beginning to scan the birth notices. If Nina had become pregnant in June, late in their relationship, the baby could be born in March. There was no notice in March. Nor in April. Though that didn't mean anything. She might have gone away. She might have changed her name. He had broken with her in June. The baby couldn't be born later than March or April. He wondered what she would name it. Boy or girl? It would be raised in her culture, of course . . .

A son. Third generation Wills. Who could have been a great plantsman, like Michael Wills.

"Why don't you go out, have some amusement?" Aunt Henry asked him. "You haven't been out in months! I've never known you to go without a girlfriend before, Tower." She said it without expression, not with her usual sneer. Still, there was something strange in her expression.

He started to reply as he had about eating. "I'll eat when I'm hungry," he'd said. "I'll get a girl when I want one," he started to say, only to stop, mouth open, confronting a fact he hadn't realized until now.

He hadn't had sex for months. No kind. Hadn't had it, hadn't wanted it. There had never been a time since he was a teenager that he hadn't had sex of some kind every few days, but months had gone by . . .

Since Nina.

"Our men don't marry again," she had said. "Don't marry again."

Perhaps couldn't marry again.

"You'll think I'm crazy," he said to his brother.

"All right, so I'll think you're crazy. Tell me. I'll try to help."

"Do you believe in curses? Hexes? Do you believe someone can put a hex on someone else?"

"Don't ask me what I believe. Just tell me what the problem is."

He fumbled telling it. Fumbled and flushed and backed up to start over.

"You think Nina hexed you?"

"The doctors can't find anything!" he cried. "I can't taste anything, smell anything. I can't see color. I don't feel any sex urge at all. Why? It all happened after I broke up with Nina."

"It happened after Jeanette left," said Ted. "Maybe it could have been her."

"Jeanette wouldn't . . ." he flushed. "She wouldn't care about my sex life. She . . ."

"You're probably right."

"Nina cursed me. She said, 'I curse your hand, Tower Wills.' Funny thing. I cut it soon after that, and I thought about her at the time." He held out his hand to Ted, prodding at the palm where the scratch had been. There was only a faint scar cutting across the center of his hand.

"Well, if she caused that, all she did was chop your life line a little," Ted laughed.

"My life line?"

"Palmistry. Never mind, Tow. You asked do I believe in curses. No. I don't. I don't believe Nina hexed you, either. I met her, and she's not the kind of girl who would do that. Sure, she might say, 'I curse your hand,' but that has the flavor of some traditional saying. There's a Yiddish curse like that, something about 'May you grow with your head in the soil like an onion.' Sally's mother always says, 'May your children never give you a moment's peace.'"

"It started with Nina," said Tower stubbornly, almost hysterically. "It did."

"Oh, I agree. But I don't think she did it. I think you did it. Have you considered the fact that you might have hexed yourself, Tower? You know, there are such things as psychological blindness and psychological paralysis. Couldn't there be psychological tastelessness? Psychosomatic color blindness?"

Tower felt wetness on his face. "I'm scared," he said, the words wrenched from him, without volition. "Oh, God, Ted, I'm scared."

He was in his brother's arms, crying, as he could not recall crying before. He was mourning, mourning his lost sight, his lost senses.

"There, there," Ted was saying over and over again. "We'll find out, Tower. We'll find out."

"Why don't you take a vacation?" asked Aunt Henry, examining Tower through the lower part of her glasses, as though he were a specimen under a microscope. "It's May. The weather's perfect. I think Ted's right. You need to get away somewhere quiet."

"When this job is finished," he replied. "When the Gray garden is done."

"When will it be done?"

"Next month," he said. "The middle of next month. June."

"You should go away now," she said.

"Give me my money and I can. Give it to me, Aunt Henry."

Her face closed up, remote and closed. Little beads of moisture appeared on her upper lip. She tried to say something and couldn't.

"You'd rather I died, wouldn't you?" he asked, knowing she would never admit the truth and yet it was the truth. "You'd rather I died. I remind you of my father, don't I? You're getting even. You've always been getting even. You don't want me to die because it will all be over, but you'd rather have me die than be free of you . . ."

She turned and left him there, and he felt the room sway and quake around him. Everything he had said was true, but only Ted had had sense enough to escape in time. Who was it really who had cursed him?

"Next month," he told himself. "June. I'll leave this town and never come back."

Tower came to himself out of a fitful sleep, lying on the bed in the private room behind his office, alerted by the buzzing of a bee. Bee. No bee. The radio, set on the classical music station, now making a noise like a chorus of monotone insects. He turned it off in irritation and lay staring at the pool of light on his table as he had been doing off and on for the last several hours. Light he could see. Light and dark. It seemed important to have light where he could look at it, to reassure himself he wasn't actually blind. He hadn't gone home since that last confrontation with Aunt Henry. He could have gone to Ted's. They would have taken him in, but even now he rejected that, rejected giving up his independence, even if it was only his independence to skulk in this back room, eating tasteless frozen dinners, drinking tasteless coffee.

Another sound broke the quiet, and it took him some time to identify it as the phone. The periodicity and length of the sound cued him, not the sound itself. The realization that within the last hour, while he had slept, he had gone tone deaf came with a dull sense of inevitability. The phone stilled as he bit his tongue, trying not to scream, making harsh *ungh ungh* sounds which felt as ugly as they sounded. He stopped the

sound, appalled. After a long silence the phone rang again and
he was able to answer it, speaking to the caller who went on
at some length, saying yes doctor, no doctor, that's fine, yes.
Test results, all negative. No answers. No theories. A visiting
specialist who wanted to look at him. Yes doctor. No doctor.
When the call was over, he got up and went out into the office.

The paper work for the last three projects of the Gray garden
lay on the desk. Last fall someone had called to tell him there
were a dozen huge recumbent spruces—either Picea abies Re-
pens or Dumosa—on an estate that would be leveled this summer to make way for a housing development. Earlier this week
his workmen had gathered up the pendulous, silvery branches
and tied them to tall stakes to keep them out of the way. Two
days ago the largest tree spade available had begun to dig them
and make the dozen round trips between the estate and the Gray
garden. The last one had been planted the day before. At noon
yesterday Tower had met a plane bringing some rare succulents
from the mountains of Africa—someone had written him about
them, a name he didn't recognize. Word of the project seemed
to have spread. Almost a third of the material he had used had
been volunteered by people Tower didn't even know.

And at this moment six Vietnamese gardeners were busy
setting out the last of five hundred flats—over twelve thousand
plants—of ground cover on sloping ground that had been
sprayed for weeds and tilled repeatedly over the last six weeks.
The final thing. The last thing. Finis.

He whispered the word to himself. "Done." "Finished."

"I'd like to be paid when the job is completed," he had said
to Mr. Gray. "If you don't mind. My doctor thinks I ought to
get away for a while . . ."

Mr. Gray had inclined his head, as though to invite further
confidences. Tower hadn't provided them. Mr. Gray nodded
then, a decisive nod. "I'll have your check ready—why not
at the first viewing of the completed garden? There will be a
full moon on June 15th. On that evening, I will take off my
dark glasses and get out of this chair—which I can do from
time to time if I am careful—and explore the beauty you have
created for me. Will that be satisfactory?"

Tower bowed, murmuring. Yes. Oh, yes, it would be satisfactory. Anything would be satisfactory if he could only escape. Escape Aunt Henry. Escape Ted's and Sally's solicitude. Escape whatever this thing was that was eating him.

Today was the fifteenth. He would go out there now. No, he would go later this afternoon. After the men had finished. He would check everything one last time. He ran his fingers over the buttons on the phone, feeling nothing. He hadn't been able to feel anything much for two days now. Pressure. Heat and cold. But nothing delicate.

It was like a wheel turning, a sanding wheel, stripping away layer after layer. Color first, then taste and smell, then sex, then feeling, then sound. Or maybe there had been something else first. Something he hadn't even missed until it had been gone a while. Companionships. Friendship. Jeanette had been his friend. He had had others. People he used to see all the time. He hadn't seen any of them for weeks.

Even hostility, he whined to himself, ashamed at the abject, sniveling self he was becoming, ashamed but unable to do anything about it at all. Even hostility was wearing away. He couldn't even hate Aunt Henry.

The phone rang again. This time he recognized it for what it was.

"Tower? Listen, remember we talked about that city you said Nina came from."

He didn't recognize the voice, the tinny, toneless voice. "Who is this?"

"Ted. It's Ted."

Ted. Why was Ted still talking about Nina?

"Tower. It's important. Remember?"

"I remember," he said.

"You said it was a dirty word? Was it Turdas?"

He thought. Turdas. Funny name. Yes. Yes, that's the place Nina had mentioned. Turdas. How peculiar. "Yes, Ted. I think that was it."

"It's in Romania, Tower. It is in gypsy country. Remember, I was talking about gypsies?"

"In Romania," he repeated dully.

"Just south of the Carpathian mountains."

"That's interesting, Ted."

Silence, a voice in the background. Sally, saying "Ask him to come to dinner."

"Sally wants you to come to dinner."

"Can't," he mumbled. "The Gray job's finished. I have to go out there and collect my check."

"Oh. Well. I thought you'd want to know about that city," Ted said lamely. "I looked in the encyclopedia to see if there was a group where the women died having babies, but I couldn't find anything. I thought I'd tell you. That's all." His voice trailed away.

Tower hung up without saying goodbye. So, Nina came from Romania. He had no very clear idea of where Romania was. Near Hungary, wasn't it? And Nina came from there.

Tower still read the birth notices, out of habit. Though it was foolish to assume that Nina would have had a baby in the normal way, in a hospital, with doctors and nurses and others intruding upon her strangeness. No. She would have a child as a tiger has a cub. Alone. In a lair, somewhere. With her people gathered around, howling at the moon . . .

He stopped, appalled. Where had that idea come from? Still, it seemed fitting. There would be no one to put a notice in the paper. Born to Mr. and Mrs. Tower Wills, a son, a daughter, a daughter, a son. Maybe she would have a litter of them. Maybe she already had. Maybe she had died.

If she had died, would this curse die with her?

"There's no such thing as a curse," Sally had told him, holding his shoulders, shaking him gently as though she were afraid he would fall apart. "No such thing, Tower. You're an educated man. You know better."

"I knew a lot of things," he replied. "I knew I was better at what I did than Ted was. I knew I was smarter than him, not to get myself tied down, to take my time, build a career. I knew I was going to be famous. I knew I was going to follow in my father's footsteps. I knew, I knew . . ."

"Shhh," she had begged, holding him.

"I knew I could manage Aunt Henry somehow, get her to

give me the inheritance, my part and Ted's, too. I didn't know she hated me, but she does. She'll never let loose of that money. It's her way of getting even with us, with Ted and me, with mother for having married dad. Maybe it wasn't Nina who cursed me at all. Maybe it was Aunt Henry . . .''

"Shhh," she said again, tears in her eyes.

"I knew I could have any women I wanted," he babbled on, the words running off his tongue like molten metal, drip, splat, drip, splat, flowing unstoppable. "I figured, what the hell, there was always another one along . . .''

Another one along, he told himself. Not since Nina there hadn't been. Not another one along. He ran his fingers over his face, trying to feel it, feeling nothing. So. Tonight. Tonight would finish it. Then he would go away. Somewhere by the water, where he could rest. Let the doctors consult and mumble all they liked. If he could just lie down near running water and let the sound . . . well, the sight of it wash all this away.

"Tower?" A voice from the door.

"Jeanette?"

"I heard you were ill. No one would tell me what was wrong, so I came back to see for myself. You weren't at home. Your Aunt said you might be here." She moved forward and stared at him. "Lord, Tower! Look at you! What is it?"

"Nothing that needs concern you," he heard himself saying, the "nothing" hanging on the air like a bad smell, not falling into silence but reverberating. Nothing.

"Of course it concerns me," she cried, he thought she cried, her mouth was wide open as though she had cried it though he couldn't hear any change in the dull monotone of her voice, not really.

"Sick," he explained. "But I'll get better. Just as soon as the Gray job is completed. Tonight. Collect my money and run." He felt himself giggling. "Run."

She came around the corner of his desk, put her hands on him. He couldn't feel them, but he saw them on him. "Tower, don't finish it. Please. I have this terrible feeling about it. Don't finish it."

"But it's done," he said, staring at her. "Everything's done. Complete. The last of it was done today."

"I wish you hadn't. I wish you'd just planted hundreds of gardens for Mrs. Silver. I wish you'd done anything else . . ."

"All done." He nodded owlishly. "About a million dollars worth done. And a quarter million coming to me. You run on. Don't worry about me. I'll be fine."

"Tower. I'm staying at a hotel here in town. Will you come with me? Will you come there with me now? Will you let me take you back with me when I go? I always felt you were like a son to me, Tower. Please?"

He shook his head. What was the crazy woman babbling about? "Go on, Jeanette. You left. Rat deserting the ship. Go on. Get out of here. Go live with your family. I'm not your son. I'm not anybody's son."

She was holding him, hugging him. As his mother might have hugged him once. "Oh, Tower . . ."

"Right," he nodded. "Ted was right. You were right. Everybody right except me. Sorry."

She said something else, but he didn't hear her. After a while, she went away. Outside, the sky darkened. He picked up his briefcase and went down to the car.

He began the drive, slowly, carefully, watching for signals from other drivers to know whether lights were red or green, watching his hands and feet to know what he was doing. It would take time to get out there. The window was open, and he could feel the coolness of the night air. Heat and cold. He could still feel heat and cold. And pain. He could still feel pain. He pinched himself experimentally to be sure. Oh, yes. It was like living in an old television broadcast with earmuffs on. Earmuffs and a bad cold. He was still functioning, though. Still moving. If he could get past tonight, somehow it would all come right. There would be enough money to leave Aunt Henry, enough money to make Tower Wills famous. Famous.

Outside the TV show unreeled itself against the evening sky, shadowed masses of tree and shrubbery, the black diagonals of house roofs, the mantis arms of antennae, all outlined against a thousand different grays which were probably roses and ambers and violets. The evening rush was over. The streets were almost vacant. When he turned into the road which led to Cedar Hills it was as though he had reserved it for himself. No cars. No people. A dog barking behind a fence, making abrupt sounds which conveyed neither anger nor warning. Rarp, rarp, rarp, over and over, like the tap of a shallow drum. Nothing else. Silence and more silence. He could barely hear the sound of the car moving or the sound of the engine. He moved in dream, inexorably forward, just getting past the next moment, the next five minutes, the next hour . . .

The gates of Grayholm were open. Battered-hat stood beside them, waving the car down.

"Mr. Wills? Nice night, isn't it. Mr. Gray said you was to go right on in. He's waiting for you up at the house."

Battered-hat moved away toward the circle of great oaks. On the car seat beside Tower was his camera. He had meant to come out earlier so he could take pictures. Well. Well. When he came back from his vacation, he would take photographs. His contract allowed him to take photographs at any time in the next five years. He would have pictures, text. It would make a good article. It would attract clients.

The car slid on up the driveway and around the circle before the house. Mr. Gray was there, in his chair, waiting. When Tower got out, the man rose from his chair and came toward him, leaning heavily on a cane. "Right on time, Mr. Wills. Moonrise will come shortly. We want to be in the garden at moonrise, but we have some business to transact first."

He held out a slip of paper. Tower took it, noted the amount, the signature. Paid in full. Oh, yes. He would never go back to Aunt Henry's. Never again.

"Just leave your car here. The maintenance man will take care of it. Shall we walk down?"

Tower folded the check and put it carefully away in his wallet. When he looked up, Battered-hat was getting into his car and Mr. Gray was already some distance ahead of him, going around the corner of the house. Feeling as though he were moving in water, Tower followed. The blackness and whiteness of his affliction had no meaning here. All was gilt and shining. All was black and gray and silver.

At the top of the stairs he stopped, impressed by the view. Hard shadow and soft light. Rose trees like small, tethered clouds of bloom, the colorless, scentless petals gleaming. He passed between them, following his host. The gravel crunched beneath his feet, scarcely audible, and he passed on down the length of the path to the dark arch beneath the junipers, the pathway through the mighty oaks which made a solid, unyielding mass against the sky.

Then they were through, standing where Tower's work had begun, the gray mounds of spruce piling upward at either side, the ledges of stone pressing inward, decked with spreading masses of silver star and tumbling falls of gray lamb's ear and lighter gray sage.

"Cryptanthus Lacerdae," Tower murmured to Mr. Gray. "Stachys Byzantina. Artemisia . . ." His mind still worked. He could still remember. "Artemisia . . ." he tried again.

"Stellerana," replied Mr. Gray. "Isn't that what you told me?"

They went down the path, seeing the ripples of moonlight as water fell into small pools, as water flowed away downward, glittering around carefully selected stones and the stems of blackrush. "Typh . . ." Tower said, to himself. "Typh . . ."

"Typha melanofolium," Mr. Gray said. "Very effective. It really is almost black, isn't it. Where did you get it."

"Rare cultivar," Tower said, trying to remember where he had obtained it. Someone had called to tell him about it. "Very rare."

The path turned downward once more, past clustered knobs of stone decked with Ek . . . Ek . . . Tower couldn't remember.

"Echevaria," said Mr. Gray. "It seems to be doing very well."

Tower stopped for a moment, panting. The total drop from the edge of the oaks to the central fence was only about six feet, but he felt as though he had been climbing down, straining to hold himself erect against the pull of the earth. Over the oaks the moon was rising. Behind him the garden glowed and pulsed. There were people walking in it. He could see their dark shapes moving in the silvered light. Men. Women. One tall woman who looked almost familiar in silhouette.

"Some of our family and friends," murmured Mr. Gray. "Enjoying the beautiful moonlight."

"Beautiful," Tower told himself.

"Dead," whispered a remembered voice. "A denial . . ."

He turned resolutely downward once more. Someone was waiting for them at the foot of the stairs, close to the gate in the fence, someone with a bundle. Mr. Gray went forward and took the bundle as the anonymous figure turned back through the gate. It was open. Tower had never seen it open before. He stood and stared at the gaping opening, unable to go on.

Mr. Gray came back to him. He held out the burden he carried.

"I thought you might like to see your son," said Mr. Gray.

Tower was too stupefied to answer. At last he managed to gargle, "My son?"

"Yours. So Ilanina assures me and our women do not lie about things like that. Ilanina is my daughter, Mr. Wills. Hadn't I mentioned that?"

"Her name is Gyulas."

"So is mine. I use 'Gray' for convenience."

"She . . . how is she?"

"She is well. She survived. Our people gave her their support. Not as a beloved husband could have done it, but to the limit of their abilities."

"All that stuff . . . about dying . . ." he fumbled.

"Quite true. All of it. Our womenfolk stay young for many decades. They have a long and lovely youth. When it is over, when they fall in love, they risk death to give birth. A time for rejoicing. A time for grief. There is a certain amount of sexual dimorphism with us. Our women look very like your women, and they die relatively young. We menfolk are not quite like your men, and we have a lonely age, but a very long one. Having been the cause of one death, we choose never to cause another."

"My brother looked up the city you come from. Turdas. In

Romania. He couldn't find anything about any group in Romania like that.''

"Well, we don't think of it as Romania. It used to be called something else. And we are careful not to be much talked of. Aren't you going to look at the baby, Mr. Wills?''

Tower held out his arms unwillingly, feeling the weight of the child on his hands like the weight of the world. A baby. Just a baby. Asleep.

Tower looked away from the sleeping baby toward the enigmatic face before him, its eyes hidden. ''Ted talked about predators. He said that's why the women died. To keep your population small.''

''Your brother is very astute.''

''Gypsies, he said. Something like that.''

''Not quite like that. No.''

''I told him we would have heard of any group like that.''

''Oh, you have, Mr. Wills. Fiction, mostly. And lies. They say we are bloodsuckers. Any banker can be a bloodsucker, isn't that true?'' He laughed, a thin, papery laugh, like the shaking together of dried leaves. ''Any usurer can be a bloodsucker.''

Tower stared at the sleeping child. ''Vampires, you mean? I never believed in vampires. Sucking blood. Turning other people into vampires by sucking blood. Silly.''

''I quite agree. Silly. Why would one want all one's victims hanging about, living forever. And why suck blood? Blood isn't that rare.''

''Not rare,'' Tower agreed. He was so tired. The baby was too heavy to hold. ''Where is Nina?''

''Waiting for us. Down in the center of your lovely garden. I said it was to be a surprise.''

''Not sucking blood,'' Tower repeated, dazedly, holding out the baby.

''No,'' Mr. Gray agreed, taking the child onto his shoulder. ''Not blood. Something rarer than that. Life, Mr. Wills. Sensation. The life of color and smell, of taste and sound. The life of feeling, of intelligence. We suck it all away. It's what keeps us young. It's what lets us menfolk live such a long, long time.''

"How?" Tower asked, stumbling along behind the man, unable not to stumble along. "How do you?"

"A spell, a hex, a curse, a drop of blood on a contract. A lifeline cut on a palm. One way or another. We're moderate in our demands. We pick and choose. We take those with something to offer. Or those who give us no reason to hold back. In your case, I owed a favor to someone. And then, you betrayed and insulted one of us. Ilanina should never have met you, but she so wanted to experience your society. Having met you, she should have been wiser. Ah, well, what is done is done. We don't take many victims. Not so many as would cause a stir. Not enough to bring out the villagers with their traditional Transylvanian torches, storming our castles." He laughed again, a fuller laugh, one of genuine amusement. "Not that we live in castles any more."

They had reached the gate. It stood open. "Look at your garden, Mr. Wills," Gray urged. "Take a last good look at it. Afterall, it will bear your name."

Tower turned and stared back the way they had come. The full moon flooded it with pale light—gray stone, gray of leaf, gleam of water, shapes moving, sound of wind and water dropping, sound of silence walking, sound of . . . nothing. Jeanette had called it a dead garden. It was. There was no life in it. No bloom. No seed for tomorrow.

Gray's hand was on his arm. They walked through the fence, down the scruffy turf to the place where the pond had been. No pond now. Just a layer of cracked mud and the slimy stone foundation standing clear in the light, the stone steps leading down as he had seen them before. "Down," said Gray. "Down, my boy."

Down stone steps into the damp, rank vault lighted by dim candles. Gray candles in tall holders of twisted iron. Nina was there, taking the baby from her father, smiling, that serious, sweet smile he had loved to see. "Have you seen your son, Tower? Good. I wanted you to see your son."

The baby wakened and turned to stare at Tower out of glowing eyes, red eyes, unearthly eyes. Mr. Gray took off his glasses and examined Tower with similar eyes.

"You're tired aren't you," he asked. "We've taken a very long time with you. Among our people pregnancies last almost a year. I'm afraid we've worn you out. Why don't you lie down."

There was a place there for him to lie. He had to lie there, of course. She would want to marry again, and she wouldn't be able to, otherwise. Not if her first husband was alive. What was left of him. The words were carved on the stone, telling him where. "Beloved husband of Ilanina Gyulas." No name. Not there. His name should be somewhere. On the garden. They'd forgotten, but he had a right to have it on the garden.

He started to say so, but then he saw they hadn't forgotten it and the sight of it took all the breath he had. It was the last thing he saw before they lowered the lid upon him and screwed it shut, before he heard the monotonous gurgle as they let the water back into the vault.

The little brass plate on the inside of the lid. Fastened with four, bright screws that glittered one last time in the candlelight.

> "Landscape design by Tower Wills—
> and Associates."

Ray
Garton

WARMLY DEDICATED TO

Susan Davis
Glenda Harcourte
Nancy Alvord

Who, during this writing,
poured my coffee, made me laugh,
and made me wish I could
have the delightful pleasure
of meeting them all
for the first time
again and again

Monsters

Until that cold early morning in the munch room, Roger never realized that blood had such an overpowering smell. But then, he'd never been near so much of it.

Blood was splashed in deadly Rorscharch designs all over the wall above the dying man—

Jesus Christ, Roger thought, hugging himself in the corner, *he's still alive, dear God his chest is open how can he STILL BE ALIVE?*

—and dribbled to the floor in long thin black-red streaks. Dark strands of it shot from the man's chest and tattered throat in rhythmic spurts. His blood-gloved hands slapped the cement floor leaving smeared hand prints and the heels of his boots thunked together spastically.

The alcohol in Roger's stomach burned as it tried to come back up and his own babbling voice sounded unfamiliar to his ears. He was babbling not only because of the bloodshed before him, but because of the cause of it all.

The creature that hunkered over the convulsing body was only vaguely human in shape. Its patches of mangey hair were clotted with blood; bits of flesh clung to its jagged teeth like chives; tremors of pleasure passed over its leathery skin as it plunged a clawed hand into the man's chest and tore something out with a moist ripping sound.

When it began to eat, Roger lost consciousness...

1

The drive from L.A. was like sliding naked along the edge of a razor blade. He hadn't stopped once in nine hours. A rusty nail was imbedded deep in the small of his back, he was sitting on crushed glass, and somewhere along the way he'd swallowed a rock. The rock had gotten stuck between his throat and stomach, and remained a lump of dull pain in his chest. He didn't always feel the pain—mostly just when he heard the wrong song on the radio or began to worry about returning to the Napa Valley.

Which was most of the time.

2

The valley was getting ready to change color when Roger arrived that late Thursday afternoon. Fall was a footstep away and with it would come the crush, when the entire Valley would smell like a freshly opened bottle of chilled wine. But now the green of the trees had darkened on the verge of brown and the grapevines, full with leaves ready to be pruned, clung to their trellises as if shocked by the changing of their color.

St. Helena remained cradled among the vineyards, a small town that still seemed uncomfortable with blacktop rather than cobblestone streets.

Why shouldn't it, asshole? Roger asked himself. *You were only gone six years, and they didn't exactly log your departure in the fucking town records.*

The town had changed slightly in places.

Jim's Country Kitchen, a coffee shop on the south end of town, was now Molly's and looked like a giant enclosed gazebo instead of the noisy, smelly, greasy spoon it had been.

Taylor's Hardware was now a video store.

And so, he was sad to see, was Hollywood North. It used to be a store that sold only Hollywood memorabilia—posters, stills, lobby cards, decorations, greeting cards, and toys—and had been run by Josh Draper. Roger had spent many an afternoon sitting behind the counter in Hollywood North with Josh, drinking coffee, and talking about movie trivia. Josh's specialty was horror films; one whole wall of the store had been covered with posters and stills of old Frankenstein and wolfman movies and nearly all of the Hammer vampire films, some of which were valuable originals that were not for sale. Roger was sorry to see the store closed and wondered what had become of Josh.

The sidewalks were busy with fashionably dressed shoppers who crossed the narrow Main Street indiscriminately, slowing traffic to an uncertain stutter.

Roger was glad to see that the most welcomed sight in town had not changed at all: the barber's pole in front of DiMarco's Deli.

He parked his gray Accord behind the deli and went in the back way past the stacked cases of beer and soft drinks and—

—suddenly he felt as if he'd just driven over from his house on Sulphur Springs Avenue after spending a few hours at the typewriter.

Suddenly, he hadn't decided—after finding his mutilated dog hanging over his back porch—to pack up late one night six years ago and drive to Los Angeles without telling anyone. He hadn't attended a single meeting with a preoccupied director or producer and hadn't once been told, "It's just not what we're looking for." He'd never had a gun in his mouth and he'd never *heard* of the Sylmar Neuropsychiatric Hospital, let alone seen its sterile white interior.

It was as if he'd never left St. Helena.

The place still looked more like a garage sale than a delicatessen. In the front was the candy counter and register, then the meat counter, shelves of groceries, coolers of drinks, and the sandwich counter. Above it all were shelves and shelves of souvenirs, knick-knacks, mementos, photographs, drawings, and other objects unidentifiable from any distance. The walls were covered with posters, postcards, letters, photographs and notes. Nothing was arranged in any particular order but it did not look sloppy. It looked somehow . . . right. As if the place couldn't possibly be any other way.

Roger was halfway to the meat counter when he heard a hoarse shriek.

"Roger Bernard Carlton!"

Betty DiMarco was already rushing toward him when he turned, her arms open wide. She laughed as she embraced him, the cigarette between the first two fingers of her right hand trailing a thread of smoke.

"Holy God!" she cried, her voice muffled against his shoulder. "How long has it been?"

"A long time, Betty. How are you?"

"Well, I'm—oh, you know how I—Jesus, but it's good to—let me *look* at you!" She stepped back, a hand on his shoulder.

Betty, a small, spare woman, wore a red plaid shirt and a pair of bluejeans that still looked good on her in spite of the graying of her curly blond hair and the deepening of the lines around her eyes and mouth.

"Come on in the back," she said, tugging his arm. "Come *on*."

She led him through a door over which a sign read THE MUNCH ROOM and seated him at a rustic picnic table. It was the very same table where he used to sit each morning drinking coffee, reading the paper, and writing.

"A sandwich?" Betty asked.

"Yeah, I was just gonna—"

"Let me. What kind?"

"Roast beef and dill cheese on dark—"

"Dark rye, no onions, no sprouts. Right?" She grinned before hurrying out of the room.

The same pictures hung in the munch room: Nixon and Agnew dressed as Batman and Robin, posters for a local rock group, an art show, a wine tasting, all several years old, a few old beer logos and a painting of Betty and Leo. Mickey Mouse ticked away the time on a wall-sized wristwatch.

The far end of the room was partitioned off and held a large metal sink, a cutting board, and shelves of cutlery and containers.

A few hours ago, at lunch time, there wouldn't have been an empty seat in the room. Patrons would have been shouting to be heard above the din of voices and the single restroom would have been free for only seconds at a time.

Roger remembered sitting at the same table one day during just such a busy lunch hour. A young couple walked in, college age, both neatly but plainly dressed. He didn't recognize them, but knew immediately that they were Seventh-day Adventists— probably students from the college up the hill—and looked away from them, went back to his writing.

A moment later, he realized they were standing by his table facing him. He looked up to see them staring, lips parted, eyes wide below frowning brows, sandwiches held before them on paper plates. He started to ask them what was wrong when the girl spit on him.

The voices in the munch room silenced and all eyes turned to Roger and the couple.

"You're the writer," the girl said quietly with a mixture of fear and awe, as if she were standing before a movie star who also happened to be a serial killer. "I caught my brother reading your book once. I burned it." Her voice lowered to a whisper. "You're sick." She turned and walked out, followed by her boyfriend. They threw their sandwiches into the garbage can by the door as they left, as if unwilling to eat the food of an establishment that would serve Roger.

The eyes of the other patrons remained on Roger for several silent seconds, then he said, somewhat nervously, "Probably kept the book and underlined the dirty parts."

A brief chorus of laughter broke the uncomfortable silence and the chatter continued. A man asked if Roger was really a writer; when Roger introduced himself, the man said he'd read his novel and eagerly awaited his next. They talked for a while, had a laugh over religious nuts, and the man even bought Roger lunch.

But, pleasant as the conversation had been, the lunch had not gone down well. In fact, on his way home, Roger was struck by a pain in the lower right side of his abdomen, a pain so severe that he had to pull over to the side of the road and sit a while. It was a dreadful scraping pain, as if a claw were scooping out his insides. At home that day, he'd vomited his lunch and kept retching until blood splashed red in the toilet.

It was the first sign of an ailment that would elude countless doctors. He spent the next three years undergoing test after test, none of which showed the slightest sign of an ulcer or intestinal problem, and all of which inspired the doctors to suggest he see a therapist. Although he would do so later, he wasn't quite ready to go that route when it was initially recommended.

Instead, he would sometimes spend entire days in bed curled into a ball, either waiting for the pain to go away or fearing it would return, all the while imagining it to be an ugly gnarled claw that scraped through his insides, trying to gut him like a fish . . .

Betty hurried back into the room and seated herself across from him, taking his hand.

"The sandwich is coming, now how *are* you? Where have you *been*, what's the—*oh*!" She held up his left hand and examined his fingers. "You're not married?"

"Uh, no." He gently pulled back his hand and drummed his fingers on the tabletop. "That . . . um, didn't work out."

"Oh. Well. I must admit, I'm glad to hear that."

Roger chuckled. "Should've said something *then*."

"Oh, I did. But when you're in love, honey, you'll hear a gnat fart before you'll hear your friends' warnings. You were deaf to 'em. And understandably so. She was a very appealing, very pretty girl."

"She was selfish," Roger said, shaking his head gently. "She was . . . deceitful . . . unfaithful . . ."

"She was a Seventh-day Adventist."

After a pause, Roger said, "That, too."

"That in *particular*."

"Oh well. That was . . . Jesus, that was over five years ago." He shook his head again; he hadn't thought of Denise in a long time.

Betty asked how long he'd be in town and if he needed a place to stay, and Roger explained that he'd already rented a house on Beakman.

"Have you even seen it yet?" she asked.

"Not lately, but my friend Bill Neiborg—remember Bill? The musician who believed in better living through litigation?"

"Sued Springsteen?"

"Tried to. Over a song. But it got thrown out of court. Anyway, he's lived in this house for the last two years or so and now he's moving to L.A. I needed to come *here*, so I grabbed it up."

"Why are you here?"

"I got a teaching job through Napa Community College. Creative writing and a short story class. Night classes here at St. Helena High."

"Well, that's good." She took an uncertain drag on her cigarette, cocking a brow. "Isn't it?"

"Yeah, sure. Sure it's good." He tried to give her a genuine smile as he thought, *Better than bouncing around in a rubber room or using a gun to repaint my bedroom a deep shade of brainmatter*. "I've always wanted to try my hand at teaching."

"But you're still writing, aren't you?"

Roger half-shrugged.

"Well, you *are*, aren't you?" Betty was beginning to sound stern and motherly.

Someone came into the munch room and placed a sandwich and a Michelob in front of Roger, saving him from having to reply. He looked up to say thank you but could only stare silently for a moment at the most beautiful, loving, and frightened eyes he'd ever seen.

"Thank . . . um . . . thank you," he stuttered after a moment.
The girl quickly turned to leave, but Betty waved her back.
"Sondra, Sondra, c'mere."

The girl stopped suddenly, as if disappointed she hadn't
escaped, slowly turned and came back to the table.

"Sondra, I want you to meet Roger Carlton, the writer
you've heard so much about?" She turned to Roger. "I talk
about you all the time and I came in here screaming my head
off the morning after you were on Letterman." To Sondra:
"Remember that?"

Roger was touched that she still seemed interested in him
after he'd made no attempt to stay in touch for so long. But
he gave that little thought; he couldn't take his eyes from the
girl.

Her hair was the color of creamed coffee and her eyes—he
couldn't stop watching them—were a deep dark brown, a solid
brown that seemed to darken naturally into the black of her
pupils.

She leaned over Betty's shoulder, holding out her hand cautiously, as if he might bite her.

"I knew who you were soon as you came in," the girl said,
her eyes turned downward to the table. "I didn't see—" Her
mouth was dry, so she stopped to swallow. "I didn't see you
on TV but, but I saw your picture in the paper."

Betty said, "The Chronicle ran your picture when they re-
viewed *Ledges*. It was a terrible picture, Roger. You should
have another taken."

Roger figured Sondra was about seventeen; she wore no
make-up and her skin was unblemished and fair. There was a
darkness about her eyes that made eyeshadow unnecessary and
somehow made her look worried.

As Roger shook her hand, her eyes met his for just a moment
and he saw something in them: flecks of gold, like miniscule
slashes, tiny slits in the brown that opened up to something
else.

She pulled her hand away and—Roger wasn't sure, but he
thought he saw her wipe it on her apron.

"Nice to meet you," she said quickly, then spun around and hurried out.

Roger noticed as she left that she was quite tall, maybe taller than he.

"I just love watching the brains drip out of men's ears when she walks through the room," Betty laughed, putting out her cigarette. "Isn't she a stunner?"

"Yeah," Roger breathed. "Is she new?"

"No. She's been here about six months. That's a long time for the girls who work here. But then, everybody here's new to you. You've been gone too long." She reached over, took his face between her hands, and gave him a big kiss. "Glad you're back, kiddo." Standing, she pointed a finger at him and said, "Tonight. Our place. Seven. We've got a lot to talk about. I'll tell Leo you're here."

After Betty went back out front, Roger took a back-issue of *American Film* from the basket of magazines on the floor and absently thumbed through it as he ate, just scanning the pictures and reading captions. He couldn't start an article because each time Sondra whisked in to wash some lettuce in the sink or slice some tomatoes, he had to look up and watch her go by.

She smelled only faintly of a sweet perfume—the kind of perfume a teenager would wear—and quickly rushed by him as if he weren't there, afraid that he might speak to her.

The sandwich was delicious, but Roger couldn't finish it.

The rock in his chest was hurting him again.

3

Ten years before, when Roger was going to the Seventh-day Adventist college on the hill and living in the dormitory, DiMarco's Deli was a refuge, a place that served real meat, played rock and roll over the P.A. system, and where no one damned you for drinking a beer. Of course, if you weren't careful, you might be spotted by one of the school's many narcs who occasionally came into DiMarco's for a vegetarian sandwich and a can of fruit juice, and who would immediately report your transgression to the dean.

When Roger quit college to write full time and moved down the hill to St. Helena, he frequented DiMarco's even more. It became a second home, the DiMarcos a second family; his own small house was too enclosed and too empty.

He'd moved to St. Helena for two reasons; he loved the town and he wanted to be close to his friends at the college. He'd grown up with most of the people he knew there because he'd gone to Seventh-day Adventist schools since first grade. The Adventists are a very close-knit, self-contained group; they have their own schools, their own hospitals, even their own towns. One of those towns was just eight miles north of St. Helena.

Manning is populated solely by Seventh-day Adventists and closes up from sundown Friday till sundown Saturday—the Sabbath. Most of the students who moved off the hill settled in Manning.

By the time Roger left school, though, he considered himself an Adventist by association only, and decided it would be a lie to continue associating with them. He went to movies and bars, smoked and drank, ate meat—and worse, pork and seafood—and he didn't want to live in a community that would expect him to hold to *their* lifestyle, which included none of those things.

When he moved to St. Helena, he had a job in a Napa bookstore and drove there four days a week. The rest of the time he spent writing his book, trying to finish it as quickly as possible, hoping to sell it and raise enough money to quit his job.

He'd told only his two closest friends at the college of the *real* reason he quit school—his writing—telling everyone else that he was just taking a break.

There was a reason for this secrecy and it had nothing to do with shame. Rather than flaunt his choice to write fiction—let alone his chosen genre—Roger wanted to keep peace. As far as Seventh-day Adventists are concerned, fiction of any kind is *not* a peacemaker. In fact, according to the writings of Ellen

G. White, a self-proclaimed prophet and the voice and conscious of the Seventh-day Adventist Church since the mid–1800's, the writers of fiction of any kind (and she includes fairy tales, comic strips, and even history books in the lot) are directly inspired by Satan to teach their unsuspecting readers to properly serve the Prince of Darkness. She even goes so far as to say in her writings that some people have been stricken with physical paralysis simply from reading too much fiction; the victims were kept in such a state of excitement by their reading material, claims Mrs. White, that their brains simply shut down and their bodies ceased to function.

Needless to say, reading fiction is not approved in Adventist circles; *writing* it is openly condemned.

So Roger decided to keep his intentions to himself.

But somehow, word got out; then everyone wanted to know *what* he was writing.

The book was called *Restraints* and Roger knew it would not be well received by Adventist friends and acquaintances. There were a few close friends who would probably appreciate it, but not many.

His novel was an erotic murder mystery that centered around a secret dominant-submissive relationship between a man and woman. When the woman is murdered, her sister—a straight-laced church organist—is determined to see justice done and find the killer herself. In the process, she discovers a dark, sexual side of herself that she never knew existed.

Roger had hoped to at least keep the book's plot under wraps, but knew that would be impossible, having had first-hand experience with the Adventist grapevine. So he prepared himself for the criticism.

It started as a quiet murmur on the hill.

What a disappointment Roger had turned out to be . . .

To think he'd been president of his senior high school class and used to sing in the church choir . . .

What a shame he was using his God-given talent to titillate and disturb rather than uplift and encourage . . .

He got stares when he went on campus to visit friends—stares from people he didn't even *know*. Roger thought he was imagining it at first until one day, while waiting for a girl in the dorm lobby, he was approached by a young man in a suit who asked hesitantly, ''You're the writer, aren't you?''

Startled, Roger nodded; the boy stared at him for a moment, then walked away.

He tried to ignore it at first, but when he noticed that his friends were becoming increasingly unavailable—always too tired or too busy to see him—he could ignore it no longer.

Lying in bed one night, he realized he should have known this would happen, that his work, if he chose to continue it, would require him to cut himself off from the church and its people entirely—just as he should have known how difficult that would be.

As a child, Roger was taught—as was every other child he knew—that the Adventist church was the only true church, the ''remnant church,'' and that he was fortunate to have been born into an Adventist home. He was taught to cling to his faith as if for his life—because some day it *would* be. Some day, he was told by his parents and his friends' parents, his ministers and Sabbath school teachers and school teachers—even his *gym* teachers—the government would band together with America's churches and decide that *everyone* should worship on Sunday. Because Adventists worship on Saturday, they would be considered criminals. They would have to flee their homes and hide out in forests and caves, living off the land while their enemies—all the other churches of the world— hunted them down like animals to be shot and killed on sight. This ''time of trouble,'' as it was called, had been foreseen by Ellen White and written about at length in her many books. It was to take place just before the Second Coming of Christ; He would descend from the clouds to save His people—the Adventists—and punish everyone else by throwing them into the Lake of Fire (Adventist's don't swear, so they can't call it Hell).

Ellen White's writing, with its purple prose and lofty words, conjured powerful and frightening images in young minds, images not soon forgotten and difficult to stop believing in. Every other child Roger knew was affected by these teachings;

on the school playground, it wasn't uncommon to hear one child say to another, "I'll be the Adventist, you be the Catholic, and you try to kill me, okay?"

Throughout his childhood, Roger was hounded by nightmares of cowering in reeking garbage bins and dark, filthy abandoned buildings while the footsteps and gunshots of his hunters sounded all around. The nightmare always ended the moment he was discovered and about to be killed.

He had another recurring nightmare as a boy. It involved a picture his parents hung on his bedroom wall.

It was a picture of the U.N. Building; beside it stood a giant ghostlike Christ as tall as the building and wearing a white robe and sandals, His knuckle crooked, preparing to gently knock on the building, the hole in His palm clearly visible.

It wasn't a very good picture—it looked like a paint-by-number—but was very popular with Adventists and showed up in nearly every Adventist home. Posters were issued to Sabbath school rooms and school offices; there was even a wallet-sized picture available in Adventist bookstores.

Roger knew the artist had intended the giant Jesus to look gentle and benevolent, but in bad light, it did not.

In shadows, the beatific bearded face seemed to take on a sneer, a sinister grin held in check. The crooked finger seemed about to crash through a window and drag out whoever was unfortunate enough to be too close.

Christ seemed to be about to say, "I'm back, folks . . . and guess what I'm going to do to you for killing me the *last* time?"

Roger used to dream of waking to a tremendous rumbling and the agonized screams of people outside; a loud, angry voice that seemed to come from everywhere shouted, "Where's Carlton? Where is that little shit? I'm here for Roger Carlton because he reads *comic books* that he buys with his Sabbath school offering, and he watches TV on the *Sabbath* when his parents aren't around, and sometimes at night he *plays with himself*—DON'T YOU, ROGER? Where *is* the little *shit*?"

In the dream, Roger always went to his bedroom window and, with fear-weakened hands, pulled aside the curtain—

—to see two gigantic, ghostly, sandaled feet crushing cars

and houses and people. There would always be a bloody hole through each foot.

The feet were always headed straight for Roger's house as the voice roared on . . .

"Where's Carlton? Where *is* the little *shit*?"

It was not easy to get out from under such dark clouds . . . the threat that the Time of Trouble might come and Roger might not be ready . . . the image of a gigantic enraged messiah tearing up a whole town just to find Roger . . .

Even now, at the age of 28, he sometimes tensed when a television program was interrupted by a special news report, certain that Dan Rather was about to announce that a national Sunday law had been decreed and that those who break it— "Like you Seventh-day *Ad*-ventists," he might add with a hateful sneer—would be executed. Even though Roger considered himself the farthest thing from an Adventist—he even held a burning *hatred* for them—the thought of such a broadcast chilled something in him, as if, although he'd shed the beliefs the church had instilled in him, he could not rid himself of the fears it had created.

When it came time for him to sever his ties to the church, he couldn't do it at first. It was like trying to stop smoking, something he'd failed to do; just as he needed a cigarette after a meal, he needed the approval of his Adventist friends. They were his whole life, the only friends he'd ever had. In order to disconnect himself from the church, he would have to disconnect himself from the first twenty years of his life.

Completely.

Roger needed to know that his friends didn't think there was something wrong with him—because there wasn't. He was just doing something he enjoyed, something he did well: telling stories.

As he continued writing the book, he tried to reassure his friends.

One of his closest and oldest friends was Marjie Shore. She'd been his first kiss in grammar school, his first girlfriend in high school, and his first lover in college. (In spite of stern doctrines prohibiting sex outside of marriage, Adventists—particularly of that age—are no less active, just less obvious.) They'd never gotten too serious, always dated other people, but they remained the closest of friends.

She knew he'd always planned to be a writer, she knew he wrote mysteries and thrillers; it had never seemed to bother her before and he asked her why she was suddenly uncomfortable with it *now*.

"I always thought you'd outgrow it," she said. "I never liked the stuff you wrote. I've always loved your *writing*— you're very good, God has blessed you with a wonderful talent. But I never liked the stories. All the violence and . . . and sex."

"But it's real. I mean, look around you, there's violence everywhere, we live in a violent world. Read a paper lately? And sex—well, Marjie, what was it we did, the two of us, remember? When—"

"I know, but it's . . . different. The things you write are wrong. You dwell on them, wallow in them, and they're . . . they're *sick*. They're wrong."

"But all those things you read, that was . . . *me*," he said. "My writing was a part of *me*. Yeah, they were thrillers and stuff, but they were *important* to me. I thought you knew that."

"I never understood it. I thought it would go away."

"You *read* them. You seemed to *enjoy* them."

"But I always prayed it would go away."

Roger felt like putting his face in his hands and bawling then. It was as if his entire relationship with Marjie had been a charade; she'd been waiting for him to turn into another person, and when she realized he wasn't going to—when he got serious about his writing and tried to do something with it—she just quit waiting.

She wasn't the only one.

That was the night he began to see the bridges burning all around him.

All of his friends—friends he'd known since he was a toddler—were no longer waiting for Roger to change; in their eyes, he was hopelessly lost.

Fortunately, his family gave him their support, although they remained active in the church. They told him to forget about those people, that they were never friends in the first place.

But that was what hurt the most. In spite of the histories they'd had, in spite of all they'd shared, they'd never really been his friends; they'd been waiting for Roger to shed his scaly, soiled skin, when all along, that skin had been Roger.

That was the night they began to hurt him.

Then he sold *Restraints*.

That was when they began to terrify him . . .

4

Roger spent the evening with Betty and Leo, sitting at the bar in their kitchen and talking over wine.

He'd spent a few hours settling into his new house; most of his things were in storage, so it didn't take long.

Leo, an enormous, solid man with a shiny bald head and a fringe of silvering black hair over his ears, pounded a hammer-like fist on the bar after finishing his fourth glass of wine, and rumbled, "Read your last book. You know, the one with the, uh—" He snapped his fingers twice in Betty's direction. "—what was it?"

"*Ledges*," Betty replied.

"Yeah, yeah. God*damn*, son, that was a horny book. Had me jumpin' on this broad every night that week," he laughed, leaning over to kiss Betty's hand. "But the movie—"

"Oh, please," Roger groaned, "let's not talk about that. It never should have been made." He sipped his wine and said, "Speaking of movies, I noticed Hollywood North is gone."

Betty and Leo exchanged a dark glance and Betty said, "You haven't heard."

"Heard what? Is Josh all right?"

Shaking her head slowly, Betty said, "He's got AIDS."

Something in Roger's chest seemed to deflate, collapse. "How bad is he?"

"Pretty bad. I saw him Sunday. He likes visitors but doesn't get many. Everybody's too scared they're gonna *catch* it,'' she added with quiet bitterness.

"S'a scary thing," Leo mumbled.

"Is he still living in St. Helena, Betty?"

"When he's not in the hospital. It won't be long before he'll need constant care. It won't be long, *period*, according to his doctor."

Roger finished his wine with a gulp. He hadn't been in contact with Josh in six years, but their long visits together were fond memories and he'd always meant to give Josh a call someday.

"*Meant* to," he murmured angrily to himself as he poured another glass.

"What?" Leo said.

"I'm just pissed at myself. I kept meaning to write him or call, but . . ."

"Go see him," Betty said enthusiastically. "He'd love that. He sits in that little house and watches old movies day and night. Pretty soon he won't even be able to do *that*. He'd love to see you."

"Yeah, I'll do that."

They talked for another hour about other people in town—who'd moved, who'd married, who'd died—then Leo lifted his bulk from the barstool and slurred, "I'm through for the night, kids. See ya tomorrow."

After they heard the bedroom door close, Betty said, "So what's eating you? Why aren't you writing?"

"I didn't say I'm not writing."

"You didn't say you *are*."

"I am, I'm working on a new book, but it's . . . slow. The teaching job will do me good. I need a break."

"You've *had* a break. It's been—how long since your last book?"

"Almost two years."

"And the next one?"

"Whenever it's finished."

"Which will be—when?"

"I . . . don't know. Look, Betty, I need the break, okay? For however long it lasts, I *need* it." He blinked in surprise at his own words; he hadn't meant to sound so harsh. He picked up his crumpled pack of cigarettes, found it empty, and took one of Betty's and lit up. "The last couple years have been pretty . . . rough."

"Wanna talk about it?"

He thought about that for a few moments. Betty was just about the most understanding person he knew; she'd given him her support in everything he'd done, and always made him feel like she was on his side. But she knew nothing of Sylmar Neuropsychiatric or of his reasons for going there.

Sometimes even the most understanding people cocked a brow when they learned a friend—however close—had spent some time in a mental hospital . . .

"No," he said. "Someday, but not yet."

"Whatever you say."

"So. Who's that girl in the deli? What's her name—Sondra?"

"For God's sake, Roger," she laughed. "She's only seventeen."

"No, that's not why I'm asking. She's just . . . interesting, that's all. She seems so afraid, as if she's used to being hit every time she walks into a room. You know much about her?"

"Not much. She's awfully quiet. She's from Berrian Springs, Michigan."

"An Adventist?" Roger asked. Berrian Springs was another predominantly Adventist community.

"I think so, but I'm not sure. She always wears dresses, never pants, no jeans, no jewelry. She probably is."

"I'm surprised she's allowed to work there."

"I don't think they have much choice."

"Her parents?"

Betty shook her head. "Her parents were killed over a year ago. Maybe two. Some kind of accident, I think. She moved here to live with her cousin."

"Who's her cousin?"

"Her name's Annie. She comes in to get Sondra at the end of the day. Another quiet one, never says anything. I get the impression money's tight. I suspect Sondra never sees much of her paycheck, if any.''

, "Is her cousin married?"

"Yeah, but the way Sondra talks about him, he's been hurt, or he's crippled, or something. Whatever's wrong, he can't work.''

Roger thought about Sondra's eyes, how they never met his for more than a second at a time, of the golden flecks in them that looked like tiny puncture wounds.

Punctures from the inside, he thought.

Sipping his wine, he muttered, "Poor kid."

5

When Roger walked through the back door of DiMarco's the next day, someone was screaming. The deli was dead silent except for the radio and wailing sobs of a girl who was leaning on Leo at the register, her fingers clutching his big shoulders and her face pressing to his chest.

Two girls behind the sandwich counter stared at her; customers stood in the middle of the store gawking at the crying girl.

Someone had died, Roger was certain.

Betty hurried by him from behind, patting his shoulder and saying, "In a minute, hon." She went to the girl's side and gently pulled her away from Leo, whispering something in her ear.

Roger stepped out of the way as Betty led the girl back to the munch room whispering, "Just come in the back and sit down till we can reach your parents, okay honey? Okay?"

The girl had long red hair and a face sprinkled with freckles and wet with tears.

Roger went to the meat counter where Leo stood beside the slicer shaking his head as he watched Betty lead the girl into the munch room.

"What happened?" Roger whispered.

"Shelly's fiance was killed. The boy's parents are out of town, Shelly's parents are at work, so they called here. I went down and . . . and identified the body." He pulled his palm across his lips, closing his eyes a moment. "Hope I never again have to . . ." He didn't finish.

"What happened?"

"They're not sure yet and they don't want me to talk about it." A line had formed at the counter; voices mixed with the radio's music; the deli was back in order.

"Roast beef and dill?" Leo asked.

"Uh, no. Just coffee for now."

A few tables were occupied; a cup of coffee sat beside the morning paper at Roger's usual place. As he seated himself, Betty came out of the restroom and joined him.

"Christ, what a horrible thing," she sighed.

"Is she okay?"

"Oh, it'll be a while before she's okay, I think." She lit a cigarette and blew smoke hard from her lungs. "They were gonna be married here. In the deli. Right up front between the potato chip racks and the cash register, can you imagine that? They met here, so they wanted to get married here." She laughed humorlessly.

"How long were they together?"

"Not long, about three months. She's—" Betty lowered her voice. "She's pregnant. But they say they would've gotten married anyway. That they loved each other and . . ." She waved her cigarette before her face as if to say, *You know the rest.* "I never liked the boy. Benny Kent was his name. He was nice enough, but didn't seem the marrying kind, didn't seem . . . faithful. He'd come in here wearing his jogging clothes—he always wore jogging clothes, but I don't think he ever really jogged—and start flirting with the girls. When Shelly was around, he'd flirt with her, but when she *wasn't*— well, he got along very well with the others when Shelly was gone. He especially liked Sondra. Can you imagine someone trying to pick up Sondra? He asked for her phone number once and I thought she was gonna have a stroke; scared her silly. I tried to talk to Shelly about him, but . . ."

"She wouldn't listen."

"Sound familiar? Well, I better go back and be with her till someone comes. Later."

Betty returned to the restroom and Roger opened the paper before him, but he couldn't concentrate on the words. Instead of giving any thought to the girl whose fiance had been killed, Roger found himself thinking about Sondra.

He wondered what she was so frightened of . . .

Roger was still in the deli two hours later. He'd chatted with a man in the wine business; he watched Shelly's mother arrive wearing a red grocery store apron and nametag, complaining about being pulled away from work and telling Betty, a bit too loudly, "I never could stand that boy, anyway." He finally read the paper and decided to have a sandwich.

When he went out front to order, he spotted Sondra coming in the front entrance.

"You're early," Leo bellowed.

She seemed to whither a bit at the attention Leo's voice drew to her.

"They . . . they closed school early," she said softly. "When they heard about B-Buh . . . the boy."

Roger thought it odd that she referred to him as "the boy" instead of by name.

As she hurried by him, hugging her school books to her breasts, he noticed there was something different about her. Something . . .

"Hello, Sondra," he greeted her, smiling.

She turned her head away from him and breathed, "Hi," then went into the munch room.

Roger got his sandwich, a beer, and went back to his table.

An old man sat at the back table noisily chewing his sandwich.

Sondra was the only other person in the room; her books were spread out on a table across from Roger. She sat hunched over her books, her long hair hiding her face, her index finger tracing sentences as she read.

What had he seen about her that was different from yesterday? Was it something about the way she walked? Something about her hair?

Her hair seemed stringier than yesterday, perhaps greasy, unwashed.

"Are you a senior this year?" he asked.

Without looking up, she nodded.

"Are you going to college next year?"

"No."

"Do you plan to go at all?"

Sondra slowly lifted her head a bit and looked at him through strands of her hair. There were blotches of darkness beneath her eyes; her face looked drawn and weary. Her voice was fragile as a spider's web: "I don't think we'll ever be able to afford it. I . . . I might take a few classes . . ."

"What would you like to study?" he asked, spreading a napkin over his lap.

She straightened a bit and pulled some of the hair from her eyes. Sondra seemed to puzzle over that question, as if she'd never given it a thought.

"I . . . I don't really know," she whispered, looking at the floor.

"What are your best subjects?" he asked.

Well . . . She frowned a moment. "All of them, I guess."

"You get straight A's?" he asked, somewhat surprised; she seemed too afraid of everything to be as aggressive as most straight A students.

She nodded, looking at her book again.

"Then you'll have a lot of choices," he said. "In choosing a major, I mean."

She said nothing and didn't look up.

"Have you ever considered teaching?"

Sondra shook her head with a jerk, as if startled.

"Neither have I," Roger chuckled. "I *tell* people I have. I mean, that I'm looking forward to it. But you know what?"

Roger waited a long moment until she finally said, "What?" in a voice thin as silk.

"I'm scared to death," he said, leaning toward her a bit.

Nothing for a long time. Then she slowly lifted her head and turned her eyes to him, met his own.

"Really?" she whispered. "You're really scared?"

"Sure."

"Why?"

"Well, who am I to tell these people whether or not they can write? Just between you and me, most of them probably *can't*—but I had teachers tell me I was bad, that I'd never sell a word, so . . ." He shrugged and realized she was still looking at him, looking him right in the eye; but it was the way a deer looks into the eye of its hunter when the hunter snaps a twig or disturbs the earth. "Do you know what I mean?"

"Your teachers told you that?"

"Mm-hm."

She shook her head slightly and whispered, "But you went to school up—" then stopped suddenly and looked away.

Roger chuckled. "Up on the hill?"

A faint nod.

"Yeah, and most of my teachers didn't like *what* I wrote anymore than *how* I wrote it. Did Betty tell you that?"

No reply.

"Hm?"

He thought he saw her shake her head once.

"How did you know?"

Her book closed with a *crack* and she stood suddenly, scraping her chair over the concrete floor.

"I've gotta get to work," she said as she hurried out.

He noticed her clothes—a simple brown skirt, maroon sweater and white top—were mussed and in need of a wash, as if they'd been slept in.

She was an Adventist, all right. If Betty hadn't told her he'd gone to school up there, then one of *them* probably had. They'd probably been expecting him—probably already knew he'd arrived. Why had he, for one moment, thought otherwise?

They always knew where he was, where he was going.

They watched him.

In fact, they'd followed him all the way into a breakdown.

Now they were apparently waiting for him, smiling, on the other side.

6

News of the sale of *Restraints* spread quickly on the hill, then through Manning.

The first sign of it was a phonecall. It was a little after one a.m.; Roger was up working.

"Hello?"

" 'Whatever is true, whatever is honorable, whatever is right, whatever is pure . . . let your mind dwell on these things.' Does *that* sound familiar?"

It was a woman, but he didn't recognize the voice.

"Who is this?"

"It's the Word of *God*! 'Whatever is true . . . whatever is pure.' What you're doing is a perversion, it's dangerous, mind damaging—"

Roger wanted to hang up but was too shocked and fascinated.

"—and God will *damn* you for it. And you were *given* the truth, *raised* in it, and—and—" She sounded almost too frustrated to go on. "God *damn* you for it!"

The loud slam that came over the line made Roger jerk the receiver from his ear; when he heard the dial tone, he replaced it in the cradle.

He called Marjie then, mostly out of habit. He hadn't seen her in three months but couldn't get out of the comfortable habit of calling her now and then. He knew her schedule enough to know she'd still be up studying; she had no morning classes the next day.

A second after Roger said hello to her, Marjie hung up the phone.

Roger stared at the receiver a while, reached down to call her back twice, but decided against it. Instead, he called Bill Dunning.

He'd known Bill since first grade when they got in trouble

for fighting over a crayon; they'd been best friends ever since.
They'd roomed together in boarding academy, where they'd
raised no end of mischievous hell without getting caught once;
they'd always been a couple of teacher's pets and no one ever
suspected them of the pranks that befell the school during their
two years as students.

Bill was now an engineering major. They were still close
but conflicts in their schedules and interests had put a wedge
between them. Bill was a motorcycle enthusiast, Roger couldn't
stand them; Bill was a sports fan, Roger wasn't; and rather
than growing away from the church as Roger had, Bill had
become more devoted to it.

That night, Bill was working the desk in one of the men's
dorms; Roger called him there.

Bill immediately hung up on him.

He didn't sleep that night; he sat in front of the television
staring blankly at the screen.

Two days later, he found the two front tires of his Accord
slashed and flattened.

The following week, someone smeared dog shit all over the
front seat of his car. He cleaned it off with trembling hands—
it took days to get rid of the smell—and drove to DiMarco's.

Betty told him to call the police.

An officer came to the deli and talked with him; he took
notes as Roger spoke.

"I don't know what to tell you," he said afterward, tapping
his pencil on the table. "You really have no proof of—"

"I have two slashed tires and three rags covered with dog
shit."

"They won't do us any good. And even if they would, our
hands are tired because nothing was actually *done* to you *personally*."

"But they slashed my tires and—"

"That's vandalism, not necessarily a personal threat. We
don't know why these people—"

"But I *told* you—"

"You can't prove that."

"So . . . what has to happen before you *can* do something?"

"They have to be caught hurting you, or trying to. And if they're from that church, like you say, you have to be able to prove it."

He never could prove it, even though it continued to get worse.

A rumor spread on the hill that Roger had broken into the biology lab late one night and stolen a dead cat to use in some kind of sexual satanic ritual.

Several nights after he heard about the rumor, he got a phone call around nine in the evening.

"So what're you gonna steal next, devil worshiper?" a breathy male voice asked. "Babies out of the hospital? Or would you rather—"

Roger hung up, got in his car, and drove up the hill to Bill's dorm. He looked at no one as he hurried upstairs to Bill's room, not wanting to see the staring eyes, the sneering glances of those around him.

Bill's door was open wide and Bill lay on his bed studying. On the wall above him was a poster of the picture Roger had always hated so much: the giant spectral Jesus about to knock on the U.N. Building.

"Will you tell me what the hell is going on, Bill?" he asked, standing in the doorway on trembling legs. For a moment, he couldn't move; he was paralyzed by the alien look in Bill's eyes.

When he lifted his gaze from his book to Roger, his eyes flashed, in rapid succession, three reactions: surprise, sudden fear, then the dawn of the solid assurance—the cold steel *conviction*—that he had nothing to fear after all.

"I'd appreciate it if you didn't come in here, Roger," he said, reaching out to swing the door shut.

Roger caught it with his foot, stepped inside, and closed it behind him.

"Bill, why are you *doing* this?" Roger asked in a firm but quiet voice.

Sitting up on the bed, Bill said, "I'd really rather you go, Roger."

"We used to be so close, you and me. And Marjie? The

three of us were—'' Roger felt his voice weaken and start to crack; he took a breath. ''—we were inseparable. Ever since we were *six*, for Christ's sake.''

''Don't talk like that in *my* room,'' Bill snapped, standing.

''*What*?'' Roger was genuinely surprised. ''My swearing's never bothered you before.''

Bill seemed to carefully choose his words as he shuffled his weight from foot to foot.

''I've lost patience with you,'' he said finally.

''Lost patience?''

''You were always interested in such . . . bad things. Fiction, movies . . . all things that you knew were wrong—and you *knew* that as well as *we* did, Roger, you *still* know it,'' he added quickly, as if he thought Roger might interrupt. ''You were raised and taught the same way we were. But you kept rejecting the truth. No matter how much we prayed. You . . .'' He shook his head sadly. ''You're our failure.''

''Fai . . . failure?'' A moment before, Roger had feared he might cry; now he felt an anger stronger than anything he'd felt before.

''Maybe not as a writer. But you know, Roger . . . you *know* what you write is wrong.''

Roger turned around and pressed his clenched fists to Bill's desk.

''It's not of God, Roger. And there's only one other source.''

On the desk, Roger saw a paperweight he'd given Bill in highschool. It was a scorpion encased in a clear half-sphere of plastic about the size of a large man's fist.

Roger touched it with his fingertips; it was hard and cool.

''Your work is evil, Roger,'' Bill said. ''Evil.''

Without a thought, Roger swept up the paperweight, spun around, and threw it blindly.

He regretted it even as his arm was slicing the air.

Bill threw himself on the bed.

The paperweight hit the poster and stuck in the gypsum wall behind it with a loud *thwack*, tearing a gash in the side of Christ's ghostly head.

Roger stared at Bill silently; he'd shocked himself.

Bill slowly rose from the bed, gawking open-mouthed at the paperweight sticking out of Jesus's head. Then he turned to Roger, looking at him as if Roger had just committed cold-blooded murder, and breathed, ''I'm calling campus security.''

''I-I'm sorry, Bill, really, I'm . . . I'm j-just so *frustrated*!''

Bill went to the phone on his dresser and began dialing as if Roger weren't there.

Roger moved toward him, saying, ''Wait, Bill, just listen for—''

Looking over his shoulder, Bill said, ''Don't come *near* me.'' His voice was unsteady and his hands trembled as he dialed; Bill was terrified.

''Just tell me who's calling me at night, Bill, just tell me—''

''Jesus Lord, protect me now from this evil,'' he whispered, hunching over the phone. ''Shield me from whatever demon has—hello, security?''

Roger heard no more; he hurried out of the room and down the hall.

''Stay away from him!'' Bill shouted from his doorway.

Doors opened and heads began to peer out.

A young man wearing a bathrobe stopped on the way to his room and stared as Roger passed.

''He's evil! Stay away from him! He tried to kill me!''

Roger resisted the urge to turn around and shout back; *what* he would shout he did not know. In the stairwell, he could still hear Bill, no matter how hard he tried not to.

''He's evil! Stay away from him! He's evil!''

He sometimes heard him still . . .

7

Josh looked as if he'd died some time ago but refused to admit it. He stood in the doorway pale as fishmeat, his skin hanging from his bones like clothes he hadn't changed in a year. His brown hair was wiry and unkempt now and there seemed to be less of it.

His smile came slowly as his drawn, skull-like face craned forward on his wrist-thin neck.

"Roger?"

"Hey, Josh." Roger tried to smile and almost held out his hand to shake, but a sickening image flashed in his mind that held his hand back: Josh's arm breaking off in his hand, snapping at the elbow with a crisp, hollow crack.

Josh held out his hand anyway, and Roger could not ignore it; the hand was featherlight and too cold.

Pulling his bathrobe together in front, Josh led Roger into the house where Humphrey Bogart was shouting at Edward G. Robinson on television.

Josh walked slowly and carefully, as if his body might, at any moment, crumble into a heap of splintered, broken parts.

The temperature in the small house was cloyingly warm and Roger could smell pungent, stinging medicines.

Josh fell into a chair and turned off the television and VCR with the remote control.

Roger seated himself on the sofa and looked at Josh, wondering if he should have come. This was not the same man he'd known six years ago; he was a whithered stalk of flesh and bone. Roger didn't have the foggiest idea what to say; *so how've you been?* was out of the question.

A tune from the seventies ran through Roger's head, but with slightly altered lyrics:

What do you say to a dying man?

But Josh managed to make him comfortable. Eventually.

"Did you call?" he asked.

"No, I'm sorry. I should have—"

"Oh, no, I was just wondering. I haven't checked the answering machine lately. I sleep a lot these days. Practicing, I guess."

Roger winced.

"You should hear my tape," he said with a paper-thin laugh. " 'I'm sorry, I can't come to the phone right now. I'm in the bedroom rehearsing my Greta Garbo death cough.' " He laughed again, but it turned into a fit of coughs.

The joke made Roger fidget; it was funny, but he couldn't bring himself to laugh.

"You would've laughed at that a few years ago, Roger."

"But you weren't sick then."

"I am *now*, and if *I* can laugh at it, so can *you*." Then, after a moment: "Please."

Their conversation was peppered with Josh's razor-sharp jokes about his illness; it wasn't long before Roger was laughing with him.

They talked about movies, about Roger's work, then the topic of Josh's impending death moved in like a storm cloud.

"This isn't going to take me," Josh said quietly. "The doctor doesn't give me long, but I know I've got longer than he thinks. I can feel it." He placed a skeletal hand on his chest. "Inside. It'll be a while before I run out of life. But when I do . . . it won't be because of this."

"What do you mean?"

"I have a gun. I've never used it before, but I know how. When I feel I don't have much longer—when I *know* I'm going to die soon but while I'm still able to get around—I'm going to disappear."

"Where?"

"I'm the only one who needs to know that."

"But . . . why?"

"I don't want to be found here, in my home. I don't want to leave a . . . a mess someone else will have to clean up." He cocked his head, looking at Roger thoughtfully. "You're the first person I've told. About my plan. Keep it to yourself, okay?"

"Sure, Josh, but . . . well, the thought of you—"

"Don't think about it. I probably shouldn't have told you. But believe me, Roger the thought of this thing, this sickness, taking me when *it* wants to . . ." He shook his head. "It has to be *my* decision."

"I understand," Roger said quietly, remembering the sensation of cold gunmetal against the roof of his mouth. "Believe me, Josh, I understand."

8

Although the police would confirm nothing, word spread that Benny Kent had been shredded like a life-size paper doll, and that parts of him had been eaten.

The police did make a brief statement, however, saying only that Benny had been attacked by a wild animal while jogging and had bled to death before he was found.

Roger knew the press would stay with the story for weeks to come, ferreting out every rumor and speculation, getting as much from it as they could. As he read about it in Saturday's paper, Roger kept remembering what Betty had said about Benny Kent:

He always wore jogging clothes, but I don't think he ever really jogged . . .

. . . *don't think he ever really jogged* . . .

. . . *ever really jogged* . . .

The funeral was going to be Tuesday; the high school would be closed for half a day so students could attend.

. . . *I don't think he ever really jogged* . . .

Roger tried to shake it from his mind; he had a habit of turning unanswered questions into mysteries with which he became obsessed, pursuing them at the expense of his work, and sometimes his sleep.

He didn't need that now.

More than anything, he needed his sleep.

9

Roger's last two years in St. Helena were like riding a roll-ercoaster that only went down—*straight* down.

The story of his visit to Bill's room was blown out of proportion and spread like a plague. It went like this:

Roger burst into Bill's room and began spouting some sort

of evil spell in an ancient tongue; a paperweight flew across the room, untouched and of its own volition, destroying a picture of Christ. The evil force that had, for years, been so subtly inspiring Roger's unholy stories of lust and murder, was clearly making itself known. The monster inside him was finally awakening. Roger Carlton was *obviously* possessed by Satan.

The late night phonecalls doubled.

"Are you keeping the *Sabbath*, Roger?"

"Do you know you're going to *burn*, Roger?"

"Take your demons somewhere *else*, Roger, your evil isn't welcome here."

"The Bible says—"

"Sister White says—"

"*God* says—"

The voices were male and female, sometimes familiar, sometimes not. He had his number changed twice, always unlisted, but the calls continued.

After the girl spit on him in DiMarco's, Roger began to spend more time at home with his dog Larry, a mutt he'd found outside the deli one evening.

Stories of Roger's "possession" began to spread among non-Adventists; while they were not familiar with the church's beliefs and taboos and did not accept the stories as gospel, they still looked askance at Roger, apparently deciding that there must be *something* strange about him to generate so much talk.

By the beginning of the last year, he saw Betty and Leo only at their home or his; DiMarco's Deli was no longer the refuge it had once been.

He began to drink more than he should and write less.

The phonecalls did not stop—he kept his phone off the hook most of the time—and the police said there was nothing they could do unless the calls were specifically life-threatening.

His tires were slashed again and one morning he awoke to find a red cross painted on his front door; beneath it, written crudely, was a Bible verse: Exodus 22:18. He went to the library to look it up because he no longer owned a Bible.

It read, "Thou shalt not suffer a witch to live."

He filed yet another report with the police, but they did not see it as a threat.

That was when he finally began to think it was time to leave in spite of his love for the Napa Valley.

Two nights later, feeling restless, he drove to a coffee shop in Calistoga. On his way back, as he drove through Manning, headlights appeared bright in his rearview mirror; a car parked behind a large tree sped onto the road and followed him. The headlights drew nearer, filling the mirror, and, a few hundred yards farther down the road, two gunshots rang out behind him.

The next few minutes became a blur as Roger slammed his foot on the accelerator and doubled the speed limit the rest of the way through Manning, hoping he would attract a patrolman. Rivulets of sweat cut chilly trails down his neck and back as he hunched over the steering wheel as if hugging it for protection, breathing, "Oh God, oh God, oh God," over and over. He tensed in anticipation of another gunshot, of the sensation of a chunk of lead tearing through his flesh, nicking his bone—

—but the headlights were growing smaller in the mirror and the sound of the car's roaring engine was fading away.

Roger did not slow down; he went from Manning to St. Helena, where he parked in front of the police station and ran inside, nearly sick with fear. After a glass of water and a cigarette, he calmed down enough to tell the on-duty officer—a man named Miller with a barrel chest, thick glasses and thin brown hair—what happened.

Afterward, Miller began asking questions, shaking his head slightly after each reply.

No, Roger could not identify the car or its driver or passengers.

No, he did not see the license plate.

No, he didn't actually *see* a gun, but it sure didn't sound like an engine backfiring.

"Look," Roger said, "this has been going on for more than two years now. Not as bad as this, but—well, I've reported everything."

After checking a file and shuffling some papers, Miller returned to his desk and said, "You sure have." He kept glancing from the papers to Roger and back again, noisily chewing some gum. "You've reported a lot of stuff, haven't you?"

"Everything that's happened."

"But you had no proof *then* that these things were being done by Seventh-day Adventists."

"But the things they say on the phone, the cross and—"

"Those don't mean a thing. Listen, I've lived here most of my life, and you can't do that without getting to know a little about the Adventists. They're kinda strange—no movies, no coffee, no jewelry or dancing—but maybe it works, because they're good people. They do a lot for the community. They—"

"Yeah, I know, they collect clothes for the poor and food for the hungry, they help people stop smoking—they've got *great* PR." Roger stood. "But they're like *spiders*, Officer Miller. They eat their own."

Miller leaned back in his chair and shrugged. "Well, even if the people who shot at you *were* Adventists, you've got no ID on the car or driver, no witnesses. You've got nothing."

Frustrated, Roger started to leave.

"Wait, Mr. Carlton, I'd like to make a suggestion."

Roger stopped and turned wearily.

"Don't take this wrong, now. I'm on your side. I believe that *somebody's* got it in for you and your work. And God knows I've dealt with enough religious nuts in my time—of *all* religions—but you need solid proof. And it might be a good idea if you didn't report any more of these things till you *have* that proof. Think about it. Some kid on the hill gets a wild hare up his ass and burns down one of the school buildings. We've got no leads, don't know who did it, but we *do* have a stack of reports filed by some guy who thinks the Adventists are out to get him but can't *prove* it. Turns out *you* were home alone the night of the fire. No witnesses. No alibi. And we *know* you don't like them. Wouldn't be too good for you. That's why I'm telling you—for your own good. Think about it."

The short drive home was terrifying; each time he saw head-

lights in his rearview mirror, Roger's body buzzed with adrenaline.

When he got home, his front door was open a crack. With
his heart pumping its way up his throat, he cautiously entered,
turned on the lights, and looked around.

The lock had been broken; no one was inside and nothing
seemed to be missing.

But he couldn't find Larry.

Not at first, anyway.

Larry was hanging by a rope over the back porch. All four
of his legs had been twisted and broken; his abdomen had been
cut open down the middle and his insides lay splashed on the
concrete.

Roger moved to Los Angeles that night.

10

Sunday was covered by a shroud of gray clouds.

Around one, Roger bought a paper and went to DiMarco's.
Sunday was always slow; there were a few people in front but
the munch room was empty except for Sondra, who was seated
at a corner table studying and drinking apple juice. She sat
straighter than she had the day before; she looked a little healthier, more rested. Roger got a bowl of minestrone and took a
seat at the table closest to hers.

"On a break?" he asked.

She nodded without looking up.

"What are you studying?"

"American history," she whispered.

She didn't seem interested in talking, but Roger didn't want
to give up while she was on a break. He wanted her to talk,
have a whole conversation with him; he wanted to put her at
ease.

"Where do you go to school?" he asked.

"St. Helena High."

"Really? Why not the prep school on the hill?"

She slowly lifted her eyes to him.

"You are a Seventh-day Adventist, aren't you?"

The light from the small lamp on her table glistened among the golden gashes in her brown eyes.

"How did you know?"

"Just a guess. I'm familiar with them and . . . well, a pretty girl like you should be wearing a little make-up, maybe a nice necklace—"

You're making an idiot of yourself, he thought.

"—but you aren't. So, I thought maybe . . ."

"You used to be one," she whispered, turning away from him.

"That's right. How did you know?"

"I . . . heard."

"Like you heard that I went to school on the hill?"

She suddenly seemed out of breath as she gathered up her things from the table.

"Where did you hear that?"

"Around."

"Is your break over?"

"Uh, no, I just have to . . . I have to, uh . . ." She pushed away from the table, stuttering, then stopped; she couldn't lie. "No, it's not over."

Roger turned his chair toward her. "Are you afraid of me, Sondra?"

She bowed her head again and blushed. "Well . . . not . . . not really. But . . . they say I should be."

"Who?"

"People at church."

He nodded. "Do you believe them?"

"I . . . don't know." She whispered this secretively as she took her seat again, as if afraid of being overheard. "You don't *seem* . . . um . . ."

"Evil?"

She nodded.

He waited because she seemed about to ask him something. Finally she looked at him and, like a fearful schoolgirl asking the principal if he *really* kept a spiked paddle in his bottom drawer, Sondra asked, "Are your books inspired by Satan?"

"No," he smiled. "If anything, they're inspired by news-papers. I write about the things people do to each other—mostly *bad* things—and about what happens to them afterward."

Here I go again, he thought, *defending myself against their lies.*

"But . . . if they're bad things . . . why write about them?"

Roger chose his words carefully. "Because if we don't write about them and read and *think* about them, they'll only get worse. We'll never figure out a way to make them stop because we won't look at them long enough to figure out why they happen. Unfortunately, everyone in the world doesn't do the things Adventists *think* they should do."

Including some Adventists, he thought.

"Don't you ever write about . . . good things?"

"Sure. About good people and bad people. Good things happen in my books, but bad things happen, too—and some-times to good people. Because that's just the way it is. Think about it, Sondra, have you ever had a single day when only *good* things happened to you?"

As she thought about that a while, her face slowly changed, softened, and Roger thought he saw a glimpse of something that made him want to smile; she understood. It seemed to make sense to her; something he'd said had cut through prob-ably seventeen years of Adventist teaching and thinking—Ad-ventist *living*—and had *reached* her.

This is how a teacher feels, he thought, still wanting to smile—to *grin*—but not sure how she would interpret it.

She stood with one hand on the table and said, "Well, I guess I'd . . . better go." She started to walk away but quickly turned and whispered to him, "Do . . . do you really think I'm . . . pretty?"

"Very," he said, meaning it. Before she could go, he put his hand on hers, stopping her, and said, "Would you like to read one of my books? I've got some copies at home."

Her eyes moved downward to his hand and lingered there for a long time. So long, in fact, that Roger thought she was getting angry, thinking that he was making a pass, and he pulled his hand away.

Her hand followed his, gently brushing it with her fingertips, then jerked away as if burned. Sondra's entire body jolted once and she stepped back, bumping her chair and pressing her hand to her stomach.

"*Sondra?*" Roger said, concerned. "Are you—"

"I'm fine," she whispered, backing away, still holding her stomach. "Fine, just . . . I just . . . have to . . ." She bolted for the bathroom and slammed the door behind her.

Something fell to the bathroom floor with a *smack—*

Her books, he thought.

—and muffled retching sounds came from behind the door.

Roger lost his appetite, thinking perhaps he'd said something that had upset her, made her sick, and he pushed his soup aside.

A moment later, Betty called him from out front. As he left the munch room, Leo passed him coming in, grumbling.

"Where the hell are those *boxes*, goddammit?" he snapped as he passed, heading for the restroom. "*Sondra?* Where the hell is Sondra?"

As Roger walked through the door, Betty took his arm and led him past the grocery shelves.

"Somebody I want you to meet," she said.

"Betty, Sondra's pretty sick, I think. She just—"

"Oh, it's just—" She leaned toward his ear and whispered. "—just her period. It always hits her hard, poor kid."

Betty introduced Roger to a customer who was a fan of his books. They chatted at the register for a moment, Roger answering all the usual writer questions, then froze when they heard Sondra's scream.

They stood in place for a moment, as if paralyzed, until she screamed again:

"*Leooo!*"

Roger dashed back through the munch room and spotted Leo's legs sticking out of the bathroom door, jerking.

He was curled on the floor, clutching his chest, pain shattering his red sweating face with countless lines and wrinkles.

He was groaning, writhing miserably, wheezing for air, and as Roger knelt beside him, Leo vomited onto the concrete floor.

Sondra pressed herself into the corner, hugging her books, her face ashen.

"Call an ambulance!" Roger said in a thick voice.

She didn't move.

"Go *now*!"

Betty passed her on the way in, crying, "Leo! God, oh, Leo, oh—"

"Betty, see if there's a doctor out front—somebody who knows what to do! I think it's his heart."

Her hoarse crying voice faded as she hurried out.

Leo's face was darkening as he struggled for air; he vomited again with a long, agonized groan.

Roger had never felt so helpless, so useless; tears burned his eyes as he watched Leo's body perform its violent mutiny. "Leo, oh Leo, just . . . if you could just . . ." He didn't know what to say.

Suddenly, Leo gripped Roger's shirt with a meaty hand and pulled him closer, sucking air to speak. His words were wet and garbled:

"What . . . *is* . . . she?"

"I don't . . . who?"

"Son . . . *dra*"

Roger saw more than pain in Leo's face, in the way his mouth stayed open and his tongue darted around, in the way his eyebrows rose high above his bulging eyes; he saw fear.

"What . . . what about Son—" Leo wouldn't let him finish.

"I *saw* . . . her. I-I came in and . . . and she . . . she was—"

Leo's big body stiffened and he cried out in pain, tearing Roger's shirt with his fingers.

"What . . . *is* she?" he gasped.

Leo released a long sigh that seemed to come from every inch of his body; his hand relaxed against Roger's chest.

The room filled with the smell of bodily wastes as Leo's hand slapped to the floor.

11

Roger got no sleep for the next twenty-four hours.

Betty crumbled when she returned to the restroom and found Leo dead; she was taken to the hospital at the request of her family doctor, who came to the deli as soon as he heard.

Roger stayed behind to take care of things at the deli; fortunately, the girls knew what they were doing and didn't need much help because he was not up to supervising. He knew Leo kept a bottle of scotch in a box under the back room sink; after things had calmed down a bit, he had a couple of drinks to warm the cold trembling in his limbs.

When he went out front, he found Sondra sitting at the table by the front window, staring out at Main Street. Roger quietly seated himself at the table.

"Would you like to go home, Sondra?"

"My cousin is coming to get me during her next break." She was silently crying.

"Are you okay? Can I get you something?"

"No, I'm okay."

He chewed his lip a moment, debating his next question.

"Tell me, Sondra . . . what happened in there?"

She took a deep breath and said, "He . . . he came in and . . . he grabbed his chest and . . . fell over and . . . and . . ."

"Did something startle him? Were you talking when it happened?"

She stared out the window a long time, then shook her head, wiping away a tear.

What . . . is she?

Leo was in a lot of pain, he thought. *He was probably hallucinating.*

Another tear tumbled down her cheek as she whispered, "I didn't do anything."

"There was nothing *any* of us could do, Sondra. It was a bad one. It took him—"

Roger stopped when he noticed she was wringing her hands

on the table, squeezing until the knuckles paled. Pearls of sweat clung to her forehead and her lips were a tense, straight line.

She didn't mean she was sorry that she didn't do anything to save Leo from his heart attack; she was denying that she'd done anything to cause it, and making the denial for no good reason Roger could see.

What . . . is she?

"Well," he said, looking at her differently now, curious about the guilt she was failing to hide, "remember what I said about bad things happening to good people? This is one of them. But Leo wouldn't want us to spend too much time crying over him." Roger stood. "He'd want us to keep the boxes stacked and the slicer clean."

The bell over the door clattered and a small, weary-looking woman came in wearing a white rectangular nametag on her pink-and-white striped smock. She smelled slightly of medicine and disinfectant, like a doctor's office. Her brown hair was pulled back snugly into a ponytail. Large brown eyes were set deep beneath a worried brow. Her cheekbones were like blades beneath her pale skin. She clutched her purse before her in both hands.

"Ready to go, Sondra?" she asked in a small voice, ignoring Roger.

He saw in Annie the same fear he saw in Sondra and found it fascinating.

Sondra left the table and went to the door. Roger wasn't sure he'd heard her whisper "Goodbye" or if it was just a soft exhalation.

"Sorry about your loss," Annie muttered, leaving with Sondra.

Roger watched them through the window for a moment. Sondra's shoulders were stiff and a bit hunched, as if she wanted to close in on herself.

Roger thought, *What could she have done in that bathroom?*

In the following days, Roger helped Betty arrange for Leo's cremation. She refused to hold any kind of ceremony, claiming that Leo would hate to be the reason for any man to have to put on a suit and tie. Instead, she held a gathering at her house the following Tuesday.

DiMarco's Deli had been opened in St. Helena by Leo's grandfather seventy-five years ago; the DiMarcos were a prominent family in the area and Betty received visitors from all over the valley.

Roger spent that day at the deli. Debi, the cashier, showed him how to clean the slicer and change the coffee filter.

Sondra came in late that day and said little. Whenever Roger spoke to her, she acted as if she didn't hear and hurried away.

Betty had given him the key to lock up at the end of the day, but after everyone had gone, Roger sat in the munch room, listening to the radio, sipping scotch, and smoking while he stared at his blank-paged notebook.

An hour later, Betty came in the back door and walked unsteadily to his table smiling.

"Jesus, I've never had so many people in that house," she said, slurring her words.

"Did it go well?"

She lit a cigarette and nodded. "Everybody seemed . . . comfortable, you know? Leo would have liked it. Everybody was . . . well, *drunk* is what everybody was. Me, too, I guess." Her smile turned downward and tears began to fall. "Roger, I don't know what I'm gonna do. I think I . . . want to stay this way for a while. Drunk. You know? I was wondering if you'd mind . . . taking care of things here for a few days? Or weeks. I don't know how long. I'd *pay* you, of course. Just for a while, Roger, I promise."

"Sure, Betty. I don't know if I'll do you any *good* . . ."

"Oh, you'll be fine. I don't know about *me*." She laughed as she cried, putting out her cigarette and standing.

"Can I drive you home?"

"No, I'd like to walk."

Roger imagined Benny Kent's torn and bloody body lying in a cold muddy ditch—

I don't think he ever really jogged.

—and became uncomfortable with the idea of Betty walking alone after dark.

He drove her home.

12

Roger met Denise in Los Angeles.

He moved in with Tony Gavin, an ex-Adventist he'd known for years. Tony constructed sets for movies and television shows and, like Roger, had bitter feelings toward the church.

The week Roger moved in, Denise Long moved in two doors down. She was a speech therapist from Colorado.

And a Seventh-day Adventist.

Roger didn't discover that until their third date. By then, it was too late. They got serious fast and on that night, when Denise made a joke about her Adventist upbringing while they were tangled on the sofa in a half-prone position, it didn't seem very important. She knew about his writing; he decided if it disturbed her, she would have mentioned it already. She was probably a lax, back-slidden Adventist.

He was right; she went to church sporadically, was very liberal in her observation of the Sabbath, and she danced and went to movies.

And she had nothing against living together before marriage, a topic that came up sooner then Roger expected.

Three months after they moved in together, Roger announced their engagement to his parents and sister, as well as to Betty and Leo. Shortly after that, Denise read his book in progress in bed one night. She didn't talk about it until two weeks later.

During those two weeks, something changed between them. Denise seemed preoccupied and frowned a lot. Sometimes Roger would find her staring at him as if he were a total stranger.

He thought little of it. He was happy for the first time in a long while; he was in love and his writing was going beauti-

fully. The pain that had made him so miserable for a while
had not reared its ugly head in months. He decided Denise was
just buried in her work, maybe not getting enough sleep. The
possibility of it all going sour seemed remote.

Until he came into the bedroom one night to find Denise
reading a volume of *Testimonies* by Ellen White.

"Roger, why do you write what you write?" Denise asked
suddenly.

He took his time replying, trying to give her a clear explanation for his interests in crime and the macabre.

"Why?" he asked after trying to answer her question.

She hesitantly told him that his novel had disturbed her, that
she'd confided in a friend about her feelings.

"A . . . pastor," she said. "From Glendale. He's heard of
you. *Lots* of people have, it seems. And none of what they've
heard is good."

As Roger tried to decide where to begin his explanation of
his reputation, she asked, "Are you *always* going to write this
kind of stuff?"

"Probably. I don't know."

"Because if you are . . . I can't stay with you."

They did not go to bed that night; they stayed up talking.
Their conversation, which seemed to go in circles, moved from
the bedroom to the kitchen to the living room and back to the
bedroom, Denise saying that, even in her disinterested, back-
slidden spiritual state, she could not justify his work, could not
understand how a person with his upbringing could use a God-
given gift toward such unpleasant ends.

It was the same thing he'd heard from Marjie and Bill, and
when he realized that, he couldn't fight anymore. He stopped
arguing and started packing; his things were back in Tony's
apartment the next day.

But it wasn't that easy. She only lived two doors down. He
knew when she walked by the door because he recognized her
footsteps in the tile corridor, he saw her car in the parking lot;
sometimes he thought he could smell a faint whiff of her perfume.

Roger began to look for another apartment. He couldn't

really afford it, but he had a royalty check due any day. It was already four months late.

He found a studio apartment in North Hollywood. On the evening he was moving his last few boxes of things out of Tony's apartment, he got a phonecall.

"We wanted to wish you luck in your new apartment," a man said.

"Who is this?"

"Because you're gonna need it, devil worshipper."

Although he had an unlisted phone number, he began receiving the calls at his apartment after he moved in.

His tires were slashed again, all four this time; the following week, someone painted a red cross on the hood of his car.

He decided not to buy a pet.

Roger drove nightly to Studio City where he spent a few hours writing over coffee in Tiny Naylor's. He was unable to spend much time in his apartment; the clamber from Tiny's kitchen and the chatter of the waitresses was comforting and preferrable to the confinement of his apartment.

He got to know several other writers who frequented the coffee shop for the same reasons. One was a screenwriter who interested Roger in writing for the movies and even arranged a couple of meetings so Roger could pitch some ideas. Neither meeting was successful, but Roger told himself it was good experience if nothing else.

The pain returned with a vengeance and brought with it horrifying nightmares. Roger remembered little of what happened in those nightmares except for two things: looking at his hands and seeing, instead, hideous blood-soaked claws and the burning sensation of his skin changing its texture.

He began to renew his relationship with alcohol, which had gone ignored during his months with Denise.

When the calls increased in spite of the fact that he'd changed his number, he spent more and more time at Tiny's, never looking forward to going home.

One morning, Roger awoke to find his apartment door open a crack. The lock had been broken during the night and the contents of his open closet were scattered on the floor. With his head pounding from a hangover, Roger went to the closet and fell against the wall suddenly, afraid he would be sick.

His clothes were splattered with blood; clots of it clung to shirt-sleeves and had dribbled into small puddles on the floor.

But it wasn't blood. It was red paint.

All but the clothes in his hamper were ruined.

As he stared in disbelief at the closet, the phone rang.

"Most people have *skeletons* in their closet," a man said. "You've got *blood* in yours. And we want *you* to know . . . that *we* know."

Roger hung up.

Later that day, he bought new locks and an answering machine.

From then on, he went out only to buy groceries or go to the post office. Even then, he tried to make his errands as brief as possible; sometimes he got the unshakable feeling that people were staring at him, maybe even whispering about him behind his back. The pain in his gut became a companion that clawed his insides at the most unexpected moments, doubling him over, sometimes sending him retching to the nearest bathroom. Sometimes he lay in bed waiting for the pain, afraid of it.

Tony came over one afternoon and pounded relentlessly on the door until Roger let him in. Tony looked around the messy apartment and stared at Roger like a stranger, muttering, "Shit, man, what's wrong?"

Roger tried to smile. "Caught me on a bad day, I guess."

"Bad day my ass. You need help."

Tony insisted Roger see a therapist and, reluctantly, he agreed.

Her name was Dr. Yee—"But please, call me Laurie." —a soft-spoken Asian women in her thirties whose interest turned to confused shock as Roger told her of the harassment and threats he'd been receiving.

Shortly before the end of the session, she frowned and said, "Tell me more about this pain in your stomach."

"Well, it has no pattern that I can see, it's not brought on by food or—"

"Stress? Anxiety?"

"Maybe, but I'm not sure."

"Tell me again what it feels like."

"Like . . . like a claw scraping out my insides."

"Picture the claw in your mind and describe it to me."

"It . . . it has long bony fingers . . . knobby joints . . . coarse, leathery skin and . . . and . . ." He stopped, afraid that talking about it would stir it up, bring it to life. "Razor sharp talons are growing out of the ends of the fingers."

"Is it always there?"

"No. Sometimes it . . . well, it's like it curls up in a ball and just . . . waits."

"For what?"

"I don't know."

"What is it trying to do, Roger?"

"Well, it . . . Jesus, this sounds crazy."

"Go on."

"Sometimes I feel like it's . . . trying to get out. Like it will tear right through my stomach."

He saw Laurie again that week and she continued asking him about the pain. After searching his face for a long thoughtful moment, she said, "What is it about yourself that you're afraid of, Roger?"

"I'm sorry?"

"Look at the way you're sitting. Arms folded in your lap, hunched forward, like you're covering something up. Or . . . holding something in."

"I don't understand."

"What do your Adventist friends think of you now, Roger?"

"They think I'm evil. That I'm some kind of monster."

"Do you agree?"

"Of *course* not."

"But Roger, you were raised to believe that the things you're doing now are wrong, *very* wrong. This was pounded into your head from birth. Aren't you just a little afraid that maybe the Adventists are right?"

He didn't respond.

"I'm not saying they *are*. But you can't just throw away more than two decades of being taught what's right and wrong.

Especially when you've still got people *telling* you how evil you are. You know what I want to do here, Roger? I want to help convince you that what's inside of you—the real Roger Carlton—is *not* an evil, clawed monster. Because I don't think you're too sure yet.''

She assured him he would not see immediate results, that it would take some time, and that he should be patient. But patience did not come easily. He wanted whatever was wrong with him to go away now.

When that didn't happen—when the pain grew worse and the calls continued and someone left a large dead rat at his door with a crucifix on a chain around its matted neck—Roger bought a gun.

He told himself he was just buying it for protection, but when the man in the store told him he couldn't have it for two weeks, he suddenly knew the truth.

"Why two weeks?" Roger asked.

The broad black man behind the counter flashed two rows of bright teeth and said, "California law. We call it a cooling off period. Say you get really pissed at the wife, decide to blow her head off, and buy a gun. Two weeks later, maybe you'll be cooled off. But then again," he chuckled, "maybe not."

"Two weeks," Roger muttered, thinking, *That'll give me plenty of time to decide how to do it.*

Two weeks later, Roger knelt over his bathtub and eased the trembling barrel of the .25 caliber automatic pistol into his mouth as rain thrashed against the windows.

He stayed that way for a long time, feeling disoriented, wincing at the jagged-edged fragments of thoughts that cut through his mind.

The phone rang three times—three long meandering rings—and the answering machine picked up; it was Barry Leese, one of his writer acquaintances from Tiny's.

"Hey, Rog," he said, "if you wanna try your hand at screenwriting, I think I can get you something. It's just a cheap-shit horror flick, but maybe it'll get you out of your cave. Give me a call tonight."

All Roger heard was, "Maybe it'll get you out of your cave." He heard it over and over as his sweaty palm slid against the butt of the gun.

Something about the call jarred him and he sat up and pulled the gun away. His stomach was hurting and he realized he'd shit his pants.

He called Laurie.

By mid-afternoon the next day, Roger was admitting himself to Sylmar Neuropsychiatric Hospital.

"I really think it's the best thing for you now, Roger," Laurie told him. "You can't be alone, and you know that. It's entirely voluntary, so you can spend a night there and if you don't think you'll benefit from a stay there, you can leave. Any time you want. I promise."

Laurie was unable to keep her promise. She was called out of town shortly after Roger was admitted. "A personal emergency," her service said. "She's turned her caseload over to Dr. Stanwyck until she returns next month."

Next month.

Roger repeated those words to himself as he waited to see the chief of staff, Dr. Lyle Abbott, who said, "A voluntary admission means nothing if you're still suicidal, Mr. Carlton. And I'm not so sure you've passed that stage yet."

He repeated them as he waited to see Dr. Stanwyck, a short stern gray-haired woman who told him, "You've only been here two days, Mr. Carlton, and I sense no sign of improvement over the symptoms described in these records."

He repeated them silently to himself as he was questioned by Dr. Abbott:

"What do you think of when you see the color black?"

"What does 'a rolling stone gathers no moss' mean to you?

"Do people talk about you behind your back?"

Next month, next month, he thought, wishing Laurie could hear the words.

She returned almost seven weeks later. Roger was polite and reserved when she came to see him; he smiled a lot and answered all of her questions positively, hating her all the while. Pleased with his disposition, Laurie authorized his release. He made an appointment to see her later that week at her request but had no intention of keeping it. He returned none of her calls; he couldn't even bear to listen to her messages on the answering machine. Her voice was no longer pleasant and sincere; now it seemed the very sound of deceit and conspiracy. It was the voice of a used car salesman or a carnival barker and, because he once trusted it, he could no longer listen to it.

As before, he spent most of his time alone in his apartment trying to write, drinking, and thinking a lot about that gun in the closet . . .

13

Leo had been dead for more than a week. Betty did not come into the deli; she slept until one or two in the afternoon and drank until she went back to bed.

"Should I be worried about you?" Roger asked her one evening.

"Probably. But don't be. Give me just a little more time."

Each night, Roger went to the deli after watching the *Tonight Show*. There he would write, listen to the radio, and sometimes sip a little scotch. He found it easier to work at his table in the lunch room where he used to, even easier at night when it was quiet and dark except for his small lamp. The novel was beginning to unfold and draw Roger into its pages. It was called *Personal Sacrifices* and was about a frustrated young man who, as an act of rebellion against his strict religious upbringing, joins a satanic cult, never for a moment taking it seriously. The cult members, however, are *very* serious and he is drawn into an underworld of human sacrifice and ritualistic child abuse.

One afternoon, Roger took a break from the deli and drove to the bookstore in Napa where he used to work; there he picked up eight books on devil worship and satanism, hoping to give his novel as much authenticity as possible.

He immersed himself in his work each night and usually lost track of time, sometimes looking up to find it was four A.M. when just a moment ago it hadn't even been one. He usually left the deli about the time Sidney, the bread man, delivered the day's supply from the bakery in Rutherford. Sidney let himself into the storeroom in back, usually whistling a tune, and greeted Roger as he left the deli with, ''Hey-hey, still at it, huh?'' Roger would get a couple hours' sleep, then shower and go back.

Although he was not accustomed to a nine-to-five routine, he didn't mind getting up in time to open the deli. He tried to tell himself that he even looked forward to it; secretly, he knew he looked forward to seeing Sondra.

Roger found her very attractive, but knew better than to try starting something. Still . . . there were times when he had to clench a fist to keep his hand from touching her face, her hair, her slender neck.

For God's sake, Roger, he remembered Betty saying. *She's only seventeen.*

While she still seemed very guarded, Sondra had relaxed somewhat over the past week. Her smile came easier and she held her head a bit higher; more than once, she quickly turned away when Roger caught her staring at him from across the deli.

They talked during her breaks; she asked questions about him and his writing and he ended up doing most of the talking. He was unsuccessful in his attempts to get her to talk about herself; although she no longer looked as afraid or guilty when he asked about her as she had before, she still remained closed to him.

But something was coming. Roger wasn't sure if he was imagining it or not, but he sensed that she was slowly developing trust in him, that soon she would take him into her confidence. He didn't know if that was a good idea, but, against his better judgement—which, in this case, was speaking in a very hushed voice—he welcomed it; he wanted to get to know her. Spending time with Sondra was like spending time with himself as he was ten years ago, like having a conversation with his own past.

Except Sondra was much prettier.

Frequently she asked, cautiously but with great interest, about his background in the church. She seemed especially curious about his reasons for abandoning his faith, about his initial feelings of doubt toward the church. He wondered if Sondra were beginning to ask herself the same questions he'd once asked himself:

If there are so many different Christian denominations, how could only one be the true church?

What kind of God would slaughter everybody except the members of one little group?

What kind of God would slaughter any *of His children?*

He *hoped* she was asking herself those questions, because they were the only things that could save her from a life of confusing guilt and oppressed dreams.

It wasn't until the second week after Leo's death that his suspicions were confirmed.

Roger and Sondra were sitting in the munch room during her break on a slow Wednesday afternoon; she'd asked him about his two years at the Adventist boarding academy in Healdsburg and he was telling her about the time he and a friend played an AC/DC tape over the chapel P.A. system during services, when she interrupted him.

"Did you ever think there was something . . . wrong with you back then?" she asked. Her fingers were tangling nervously on the table and she sounded near tears.

"Sure," he said, puzzled by the sudden change in her behavior. "All the time. I didn't fit there. I used to think it was my fault, that there was something wrong with me. But I eventually realized the only thing wrong was that I didn't fit. And the only thing wrong with *that* was that I was pretending I *did*."

For a moment, Sondra's big eyes darted all over the room as if searching for words, and her mouth worked to find a voice, but she said nothing. She finally nodded, as if in agreement.

Roger leaned toward her and whispered, "Are you pretending you fit, Sondra?"

Her nostrils flared and tears glistened in her eyes as she nodded. Through her tears, the golden flecks in her eyes seemed to grow a fraction larger, as if the gashes were opening to reveal what lay beyond.

"I know how that feels," he assured her. "I went through it and it can really hurt."

She shifted in her chair, turning away from him, and wiped her face with a palm, trying to compose herself.

Roger ached for her then; he ached with sympathy and, he was half ashamed to admit, desire. He wanted to hold her, tell her she was going to to be okay in a few years, maybe a couple decades, *if* she could get out from under whatever cloud the church had put over her.

"Look, Sondra, I realize this isn't the place for it, but if you ever need someone to talk to—" He took her hand. "—I'm always willing to—"

"Stay away from me," she hissed, pulling away.

Roger blanched, shocked.

"I'm sorry, but . . . you really should. Stay away from me. I'm bad. For you. For everyone." She quickly left the munch room and went back to work.

Sondra did not speak to him again all day.

14

Roger taught his first class that night. It was small—only nine people—but after twenty minutes of talking about writing with his students, Roger decided they were all genuinely interested and not just taking creative writing to avoid a standard English class.

Then Marjie walked in.

Roger felt a surge of vertigo and had to check his surroundings to make sure he wasn't back in college standing in the

biology lab where he and Marjie had dissected so many frogs
and cow's eyes together.

She stood in the doorway a moment wearing a rust-colored
skirt and brown sweater, a notebook cradled in her arms, a
denim bag slung over one shoulder. Her hair was longer now,
but otherwise she looked exactly as she had the last time he'd
seen her. When a breeze whispered through the open door from
behind her, he realized she even wore the same perfume.

Her smile seemed big enough to swallow her whole head as
she stepped inside and said, "Sorry I'm late, but I was held
up at work and . . ."

They stared silently at one another long enough to make the
students fidget at their desks.

Marjie finally seated herself and Roger spent a few minutes
stammering through the course outline, then dismissed the class
early for the first of its three hourly ten-minute breaks.

The students headed for the restrooms and smoking areas
except for Marjie, who remained in her seat smiling at Roger.

"I can't believe you're taking this class," he said, sitting
on the edge of his desk. He did not return her smile.

"Oh, it's not for the grade or anything. I've always wanted
to take a shot at writing." She stood. "And I wanted to see
you." Moving toward him, she said, "Don't I get a hug?"

"No."

Her smile went away.

"I can't believe you're doing this, Marjie."

"Doing what?"

"Acting like you're glad to see me, like we're old friends."

"I *am* glad. And we *are* old friends."

"We *were*."

"Please, Roger," she said softly, her eyes becoming sadly
apologetic, "that was a long time ago."

"Six years is not my idea of a long time, but even if it were
twenty-six years, this would be a surprise. Your . . . *convictions*—" He spat the word. "—seemed pretty firm back then."

"Oh, you know how it is, Roger, you've been through it.
They hold a Week of Prayer on campus, get some loud, char-
ismatic guest speaker to give two sermons a day and call every-

body to the altar to surrender themselves to Christ and burn
their novels and rock albums and get re-baptized. You get . . .
well, you know, on fire for the Lord and try to clean up your
life, read the Bible every day. It's like . . . like *brainwashing*,
almost. Except it doesn't last.''

"There was no Week of Prayer then, Marjie."

"I know, but . . . well, it's the same principle. I was going
through one of those stages."

"Did you chase off any other friends during that stage?"

Marjie sighed and moved closer to him. "I tried to find you,
Roger. I called your parents, but they wouldn't tell me anything. I wrote a letter to your publisher, but they never wrote
back. You just disappeared."

"I *had* to disappear, and don't act like you don't know why."

"I know, there were some people who . . . overreacted."

"*Overreacted?* Jesus, I'm glad they didn't get *pissed*, they
probably would've firebombed my car."

"A lot of people were . . . disappointed in you, Roger. I don't
condone what they did, but they didn't know how to handle
it."

"Well, they still don't know how to handle it because they
followed me all the way down to L.A."

"I'm sorry," she whispered. "But I promise you . . . I had
nothing to do with any of that. I . . . I've missed you."

When she was finally close enough to put her arms around
him, Roger could not resist. Six years quickly melted away as
he held her, smelled her, heard her sigh against his ear.

"I've missed you, too, Marjie," he said, startled by how
good it felt to say her name aloud again. He whispered, "But
you really hurt me."

"I always prayed—"

. . . *it would go away* . . .

"—I'd get to apologize to you for that." She moved back
and placed a hand to his cheek. "You're—"

. . . *sick* . . .

"—still very important to me. Hey, you're—"

. . . *sick sick sicksicksick* . . .

"—my childhood sweetheart. You don't just forget your childhood sweetheart, you know."

Roger lost his feeling of comfort when he heard the old echo of her words and remembered how much they'd hurt; he gently pulled away from her. Suddenly, he couldn't even look at her and he felt a twinge of pain in his side.

No, no, he thought, *not now, please not now*.

He put a hand over his stomach, preparing to double over, waiting for the claw inside him to emerge from its sleep and tear at his organs. It never came.

The students began to file back into the room and Roger tried to continue his class without looking at Marjie. Afterward, she approached him again and put her denim bag on his desk, removing a hardcover and paperback copy of each of his books. With a grin she asked, "How about signing them?"

Roger told himself he would not see Marjie outside of class. He did not give her his phone number or address and asked her no personal questions, hoping she would do likewise. The very thought of renewing a friendship with Marjie made the claw stir ever so slightly . . .

But he had to admit, it was sure good to see her again.

15

Sondra called in sick the next day. Roger was considering calling her to see what was wrong when Marjie breezed into the deli and kissed him on the cheek.

"It's my day off," she said. "I thought I'd come for lunch and see if you still hang out here."

"I work here now."

"I heard about Leo. I'm sorry. I know you were friends."

Over lunch, Marjie told him she was now living in Napa working at a property management firm where she was quickly climbing the ladder.

As Roger listened, thinking, *I'm doing exactly what I told myself I* wouldn't *do*, he noticed tiny studs glistening in Marjie's earlobes.

"What's this?" he asked, pointing to them.

"Oh, yeah," she chuckled, covering her ears with her hair. "Guess I'm gonna burn in hell, huh?" She blushed like a child caught smoking. "I even have a sip of wine now and then. I'm a big girl now."

But, Roger noticed, she was not so big that she didn't keep toying with her hair self-consciously to make sure her pierced ears were covered.

She gave Roger her number on a napkin, saying she wanted to get together for dinner soon. Before she left, Marjie glanced around the munch room bashfully, then leaned forward and gave Roger a long kiss on the mouth; he didn't respond, but neither did he resist.

"I *really* want to see you," she whispered soberly, touching his neck.

After she left, Roger realized she was going through the opposite of what he'd experienced. Just as he had tried for so long to fit into Adventist circles, she was now trying to fit in with her co-workers by wearing jewelry and having "a sip of wine now and then." Judging by her self-conscious behavior, she was not succeeding.

Fine, Roger thought with a touch of gleeful bitterness. *See how you like it.*

He tossed her phone number into the trash.

16

Shortly after four the following morning, Roger sat in the munch room squinting at the notebook before him. The radio was playing and the deli was dark except for the pool of light shed by the small lamp on the table. His writing was getting sloppy and the scribbled words were doubling before his bleary eyes. He realized he'd been drinking more than his usual occasional sip and it had gotten the best of him.

Roger decided to quit for the night but, before he could close his notebook, someone banged on the back door.

He found Sondra shivering in the misty alley.

"Sondra, what's wrong?" he asked, closing the door as she came in.

She stumbled past him, crying and out of breath, and fell into a chair in the munch room. Her tall shapely body was swallowed by a huge wool coat and she sat forward with her arms over her stomach as if in pain.

"Are you all right?" Roger asked, sitting across from her.

"I'm scared."

"Of what? What's happened?"

"Something's wrong with me, something *horrible*." Sondra shook with sobs and rested her forehead on the table.

Roger figured it was probably finally hitting her. She was beginning to realize all the things she could never do or be if she remained entombed in her faith. She'd begun to question the logic and fairness of such a senselessly restricting lifestyle and now, because of her doubts, she probably thought there was something wrong with her.

That's how it works, he thought. *That's how they want it to work*.

He poured a couple swallows of scotch into his glass and put it before her.

"Drink this," he said.

"No, I really shouldn't."

"It'll calm you down. Come on, drink it."

She took a sip and coughed a few times.

"How did you get here?" Roger asked.

"My bike."

"Does anyone know?"

"They were asleep when I left." With less reluctance than before, Sondra tipped the glass and finished the scotch. She was still sniffling, but her sobs had calmed.

"Now, will you tell me what you think is wrong with you?"

Her face twisted as she whispered, "I don't know," then she pounded a fist on the table, crying, "I don't *know*, I don't *know*!"

"Hey, whoah." He poured another shot of scotch and she drank it with a scowl that slowly relaxed. "Take off your coat."

"I can't. I'm . . . I didn't change. I'm still in my night gown."

"Okay. If you'll tell me what's wrong, Sondra, maybe I can help."

"*I* don't even know what it is, I don't understand it. But I know it's not gonna go away. It just keeps coming back again and again."

"Have you talked to your cousin?"

"She won't do anything."

"What *could* she do?"

"Take me to . . . to a doctor."

"You're sick?" He remembered the sound of her vomiting in the restroom a few weeks ago and noticed she was still holding her stomach; he wondered if it was something more serious than just a strong period.

She nodded, pouring a bit more scotch.

"Hey, maybe you should go easy on that stuff," he said.

"Just a little more, please." Her hands shook as she drank and a small tremor passed through her afterward.

"Sondra, if you're sick, maybe you should go to a doctor right now. I can take you to—"

"*No.*"

"But don't you want to—"

"No, I can't. I shouldn't even be telling you any of this."

"Yes you should. I *want* you to."

She started crying again. "You'll . . . you'll have me . . . put away."

That scared Roger. He suddenly realized this was more than just a physical illness or a self image problem; this was serious.

"Why would I want to do that?"

"Because I'm dangerous."

"Why do you think that?"

"I *know* it. So does Annie, but she doesn't talk about it. Neither does Bill."

"Her husband?"

She nodded. "They're scared of me. They *hate* me."

As she began to cry again, Roger wondered if he really wanted to hear any of this; he'd planned to keep a very low profile in the Valley this time and not get involved with Adventists in any way. But Sondra looked so lost, so hopeless. Her tear-filled eyes were heavy from the scotch and she rested her head in a palm. Roger could not bring himself to turn his back on her.

"Why are they scared of you?" he asked.

She scrubbed her face with her hands, then reached for the bottle again.

"That'll make you sick if you're not used to—"

"I've drunk before. A little," she said—but not without guilt—taking another swallow.

Roger was surprised.

She sucked in a deep breath, as if for courage, and began:

"When I was a little girl, I wanted to be a dancer. I had this friend, see, a neighbor girl named Rosa who wasn't an Adventist. She was a little older than me and so pretty. I worshipped her. She took ballet classes and every week after her lesson, we'd go into her garage and she'd teach me what she'd learned. Her mom—she was such a nice lady—bought me a pair of ballet slippers and some leotards. I had to leave them at Rosa's house so my parents wouldn't find out. I was so scared they'd discover I was learning to dance . . .

"Well, they *did*. Mom came to the house one day while I was in the garage with Rosa. The look on her face when she saw me dancing . . . I thought she was gonna hit me. 'You're lucky Christ didn't come while you were prancing around in there,' she said when we got home. 'You looked like some kind of a . . . a *pagan* doing that.' The thing is—" She stopped to swallow some tears. "—I thought I was doing so *well*. I was getting *good*. Even Rosa's mother said so.

"Mom and Dad wouldn't let me leave the house for weeks after that, except for school. They stood in my room each night to make sure I studied my Sabbath school lesson and said my prayers. They . . . they took my bedroom door off so they'd be able to see if I danced in my room at night.

"I hated them for that. And I hated the church for saying

dancing was wrong and I hated Mrs. White for writing all those books and . . . and most of all, I hated myself for feeling so much hate. I prayed for God to take away my love for dancing, but the more I bottled it up inside, the more I wanted to do it.

"Then I got sick. My stomach started hurting once in a while. Not my stomach, really; it was more in my side. I'd get such awful pains, sometimes I couldn't even *walk*. A few times, I even threw up and . . . and there was blood in it."

Roger chilled, feeling the fear he could see so clearly in her eyes as she spoke.

It's something else, he thought. *She's talking about something else. It* can't *be the same thing.*

"The doctors couldn't find anything," she went on. "They said it was all in my head. Mom and Dad said it was a punishment from God because I was so preoccupied with worldly things. Like dancing.

"The worse it got, the more they ignored it. Sometimes I'd be sitting at the dinner table saying grace and it'd hit me so hard I'd fall out of my chair and run to the bathroom and throw up. After a while, I figured they must be right—I was being punished. I still wanted to be a dancer. I read books about it, I dreamed about it. No matter how hard I tried to change, I couldn't.

"The pain—" She held her stomach and her eyes tensed as she talked about it. "—was like—still *is*—like something's inside me. Moving. Cutting me."

Roger moved back from the table as he listened, not really wanting to hear anymore but unable to ask her to stop.

"It's like there's something inside me . . . trying to get out," she said.

Something with a claw, he thought, vividly remembering the claw he had imagined, so many times, to be ripping through his insides.

"It kept getting worse and worse until . . . about three years ago . . ." She poured another drink. "It got out."

Roger didn't protest this time; in fact, he was considering having more of the scotch himself.

"I had a pony," she went on. "Three years ago, almost

four, it was killed. I had this nightmare, see, this horrible, bloody nightmare. It didn't make any sense at all, but when I woke up—'' Her face lost its color and her voice cracked; she seemed about to be sick. ''—I was covered with blood. In my hair, in my mouth. My nightgown was torn up on the floor. And I could smell my pony.

''I cleaned up and threw my sheets in the wash before Mom and Dad woke up. That morning, Dad found my pony in pieces, partially eaten. They said a wild animal had done it.'' She stared into her drink with distant eyes; the flecks of gold among the brown seemed on fire and about to spread. ''A wild animal,'' she whispered.

When Roger found his voice, he asked, ''What—''

What . . . is she?

''—are you telling me, Sondra?''

She shrugged. ''I *said* I don't understand it.''

''Well, I'm sure you had nothing to do with the pony,'' he said, certain of nothing.

''Or the neighborhood dogs? Or the little boy down the street who was always offering me his allowance if I'd show him my pussy?''

He could not reply.

''After every one, I woke up the same way, from an awful dream. Covered with blood. When my mother found one of the pillowcases, I think they started to suspect. They became afraid of me. I think they thought I was possessed. When they died, then I knew.'' She squirmed in her chair, clutching her stomach hard with one hand, in pain. ''I'd hear them whispering when they thought I wasn't around, talking about how maybe I should be exorcised or annointed by the pastor, or something. Then they found my dancing books. They went crazy. Mom started screaming at me for bringing the devil into their house, Dad started praying, and all of a sudden the pain hit me like a train and I passed out. Sort of. I . . . I remember hearing screams. Seeing lots of blood. Then . . . then when I came to . . . they were all over the walls . . . on the floor in pieces . . . and there were police at the door.''

Roger was feeling light-headed. He tipped the bottle to his lips and took a swallow.

Some kind of accident, I think, Betty had said of the death of Sondra's parents.

"There have been other times," Sondra said. "Each one's worse than the last. And now they're not just worse, they're ... different."

Roger's fingers toyed with the bottle and scotch sloshed in his burning gut as his mouth worked to ask her *how* it was different; his throat felt tight and the question came out with effort.

"It used to happen just when I was angry," she replied. "But now ... well ... remember the day Leo died?" Her voice caught and she didn't go on for a moment. "I ... I was talking to you in here and ... you told me I was pretty and you took my hand and ... I wanted so much to touch you," she whispered. "I *wanted* you. But then it started and I ran to the bathroom. I was so sick I forgot to lock the door and ... I was on the floor and it was happening to me, the change, and I was fighting it ... then Leo walked in. And saw me. And ... and ... he ..."

Sondra started to cry again and Roger wanted to comfort her but could not. He could only stare at her, wondering if he should help her because she was crazy or fear her because she was telling the truth.

"Sondra, have you talked to anyone about this?"

"Only you. I thought ... well, after all you've said ... about thinking there was something wrong with you ... I thought you'd understand."

Roger pressed a hand to his stomach, thinking of the horrible pain, the claw, the blood he used to spit into his toilet, the awful nightmares ... the bloody, sickening nightmares.

"You need help," he said. "You know that."

"Who's going to help me? I'm ... I don't know *what* I am. What could anyone do?"

"What do *you* think you are?"

"A ... a monster. Like Mom and Dad said. Maybe I am evil. Possessed. Maybe, when I kept wanting to dance so much, maybe God just . . . turned His back on me. Maybe . . .'' She couldn't continue.

Roger took her hand as she cried, quickly checking his watch; Sidney would be delivering bread in about twenty or thirty minutes. It would not look good for him to find Roger alone with Sondra at that hour, and with a three-quarters-empty bottle of scotch on the table, particularly if Sondra's problem, whether real or imagined, later came to light. He felt he should call someone but knew of no one but Betty. As much as he hated to wake her at such an hour, he decided he had no choice.

''You sit right here, Sondra, okay? I'll be back in a minute.''

He went to the phone behind the register and called Betty. It rang a dozen times before she answered.

''Betty? This is Roger. Sorry to wake you, but I've got a—''

She made a deep, gargled noised into the phone.

''Betty?''

''Whum?''

''Betty, this is Roger. *Please* wake up.''

''Rah? Whum.''

''Listen, Betty, I'm at the deli and Sondra's here with me . . . Betty?''

She'd hung up.

Roger dialed again, certain she'd been drinking all day and didn't know what she was doing.

''Betty, *don't hang up*!'' he shouted. ''Listen to me. Sondra is here with me and—''

''Hoozis?''

''It's Roger. Look, can you get up and—''

She hung up again.

''God*damn*!''

As Roger was dialing again, he felt two arms slide around his waist and firm breasts press to his back.

''Don't call anybody,'' Sondra whispered huskily.

Her breath smelled heavily of scotch and her words were slurred; when he turned around, he looked into her big, heavy brown eyes and knew she'd finished the bottle.

''Sondra . . .''

"C'mon, let's go back here."

She took his hand, leading him back to the munch room; he followed without protest partially because he knew he'd never get through to Betty and partially for reasons he did not want to think about.

Her coat lay over the back of a chair and she wore only a powder blue nightshirt that not quite reached her knees and was slit up the sides to her waist.

Before he could take a seat, her arms were around him and she was trying to kiss him.

"Hey-hey, Sondra, *wait*—"

"It's okay," she said, her voice thick as honey. "I've seen the way you look at me. I *know*."

"Uh-uh, no, just—"

Her mouth was on his and his eyes, wide with surprise, slowly closed as her tongue lightly traced his closed lips and—

It feels sooo good . . .

—it was only seconds before his tongue met hers—

It's been sooo long . . .

—and his arms slid around her, his hands moving over her back. Sondra's mouth opened and closed over his, drew his tongue in and sucked on it hungrily. One hand clutched his neck and the other squeezed his buttocks, pressing his hardening crotch to her. Their breathing grew frantic as they bumped the table.

Fighting the warmth that was growing inside him, Roger gently pushed her away but she moved forward again, kissing his throat and face, mumbling, "Don't you like it? Huh? Don't you?"

"Look, Sondra, we can't do this."

"Why not?"

"We . . . we *shouldn't*. We've both had too much to drink and—"

"Not *too* much. Is there any more?"

"Sondra, *stop*."

He firmly held her at arm's length as he tried to regain his composure.

"You *do* like it," she purred drunkenly, closing her hand

over the bulge in his jeans. She stroked it as she kicked a chair aside and sat up on the table, hugging one knee to her chest and gathering the nightshirt around the waist.

"Sondra . . ." Roger's voice lost some of its forcefulness as his eyes traveled up her long smooth thighs to the small thatch of sunset-colored hair that glistened with moisture. "Put your coat back on," he whispered.

She leaned back and tried to pull his head down between her legs.

"*No.*"

"Do you want me to suck this then?" She squeezed his erection. "That's what Benny wanted."

"Buh . . . Benny?" Roger stuttered, his mouth dry.

. . . I don't think he ever really jogged . . .

"You were with Benny?" Roger whispered.

"Just once." She leaned her head back and slid her fingers through her long full hair.

He especially liked Sondra . . .

"Just . . . once . . ." She frowned and gently rubbed her hand in circles over her stomach. Her face seemed to have less color than a few moments before.

Roger knew he had to get her out of there and back home to bed, but didn't know how to do it without getting himself into trouble. He cursed himself for giving her the scotch.

"Come on, Sondra. I'm taking you home."

She turned desperate eyes to him and gripped his collar. "No, please don't do that. Fuck me. Right here. Nobody'll know."

"I can't do that."

"Why? You *want* to." There was a desperate pleading in her voice and her eyes welled with tears. "Is there something wrong with me?"

What . . . is she?

"You said, you said—" Her words were nearly lost in sobs. "—that I was *pretty*, you *said* that."

"You are, Sondra, but I can't—"

"*Please!*" she shouted, clutching his shirt. "I want to so bad—"

With her other hand, she unbuckled his belt—

"—so *bad*, I *need* to—"

—unbuttoned his pants—

"—please let me know what it feels like—"

—and reached underneath to touch him.

"—before it happens, *please*!"

"Before what happens?" Roger's voice cracked when her fingers closed around his cock, pulled it from his pants, and began stroking it tremulously.

She didn't answer, just gasped and sobbed.

Roger gently pushed her arm away and said—

It feels sooo good . . .

—"No, Sondra."

She began touching herself as she reached for him again, whimpering between words as she frantically said, "Please put it in me, puh-*please*, before it's . . . before it's . . ."

Her body stiffened, she bucked a couple times, and Roger thought she was coming, but then she made a sound that changed his mind.

She slapped a hand over her stomach and let out a long wretched groan, turned over on her side and vomited onto the table, knocking over the small lamp and tossing light over the walls like dancing ghosts.

Blood speckled her nightshirt and was smeared over her lips and Roger panicked, reached out to support her so she wouldn't fall off the table, but she faced him as her eyes rolled back in her head and her body curled into a ball as if cramped and she grunted, "Too late."

The lamp rolled back and forth over the table throwing light wildly.

Sondra's head craned back and her throat worked, making dry clicking sounds, as her tongue began to flap rapidly in and out of her mouth. Strands of blond hair writhed like tentacles as her head thrashed from side to side and she began to tear the collar of her nightshirt as if it were a tightening noose.

Roger leaned over her shouting, "Sondra, what's *wrong*? What can I *do*?" and her arm sliced the air, hitting the side of his head like a club and sending him against the wall and to the floor.

Pain throbbed through his skull like a drumbeat and he lay face down for a moment, blinking his eyes and trying to see clearly again.

Sondra made the ragged, throaty sounds of an animal in pain as Roger raised himself to his hands and knees; he heard the nightshirt rip as he got to his feet.

His first thought was to go to the phone and call an ambulance but Sondra fell from the table and landed in a crouch between him and the door and Roger stumbled backward in horror.

Sondra's teeth—now jagged and tapering to deadly points—protruded from her mouth, pushing her lips outward into a kind of snout. Bloody saliva dribbled from her mouth, glistening in the still-shifting light. Her nightshirt hung from her bare body in tatters; her knees jutted upward on each side of her body and her hands scraped the concrete floor between her sneakers, making a harsh sound.

Something was wrong with her fingers.

They were longer and knobby, as if arthritic, and—

—clawed.

A curved, razor-like talon protruded from the tip of each finger.

A claw . . .

As they scraped over the concrete, sparks flashed and died in the shadows.

Like . . . like a claw scraping out my insides . . .

Sondra sounded as if she were strangling, her chin jutting forward, eyes clenched in pain. Her lips writhed over her hideous fangs, her tongue squirmed in her mouth like a pink dying worm—

—and she seemed to be trying to say his name.

"Raaaw . . . Raaaw . . . juuhhh . . ."

Roger could not speak, felt cold and paralyzed with fear, numb . . .

He groped for something to hold onto as Sondra moved backward into the funnel of light that spilled from the toppled lamp.

Her skin was horribly mangled now, as if burned, and tufts of thin hair had appeared in patches over her body. Her breasts were whithered tubes of useless flesh that dangled between her arms as her tortured body quaked.

What . . . is she?

When he was finally able to move, Roger stepped backward, knocking over a chair as he babbled, trying to find his voice. There was no other way out of the munch room and he couldn't bear to get closer to Sondra.

Or what had once been Sondra.

He thought of the knives lined up in cutlery boards by the sink and tripped around a table to get to them, afraid to take his eyes off the creature that was now on all fours before him.

Roger was turning toward the sink when a distant sound froze him in place and made him sob with a combination of relief and dread.

Whistling.

The door to the storeroom in back clattered open and Roger could hear the engine of Sidney's bread truck idling.

"Oh, God," Roger groaned, "oh dear God, *Sidney*!"

The whistling stopped.

"Sidney, get help!"

"Mr. Carlton? That you?"

"Get *help!* Call the *police!*"

"What? Can't hear you. Where are you?" His voice was closer, inside the deli now.

Roger screamed the words again so loudly that his chest hurt.

The beam of Sidney's flashlight cut through the darkness beyond the munch room doorway and his feet scraped heavily over the floor.

Sondra's eyes opened then and she was suddenly alert. The golden flecks had spread like fire through her eyes and glowed with hunger in the darkness.

"Don't come in here!" Roger screamed, his knees weakening. "Get *help*, Sidney, don't come—"

Sidney stepped into the munch room, sweeping his flashlight

in an arc before him, holding it on Sondra, who turned toward
him with a throaty growl.

"What in the fuh—"

She was on him.

Warm blood spattered Roger's face and his legs gave way.
He leaned against the wall swallowing his gorge as bones
snapped and gristle tore.

The wet smacking of Sondra's lips was the last sound he
heard . . .

17

He heard Sondra crying before he opened his eyes.

Roger had no idea how long he'd been unconscious and, for
a moment, wasn't even sure what had happened.

Light from the lamp and flashlight on the floor fell on black
puddles and soggy lumps.

Warm moisture clung to Roger's face and hands.

Trembling, he struggled to his feet and limped to the light
switch, his shoes slopping over the wet floor.

When the fluorescent lights flickered on, Roger wanted to
scream but could only murmur like a frightened child.

Pieces of Sidney lay scattered about the floor. Patches of
tattered skin were indistinguishable from the shreds of his
blood-soaked clothes. One limb—Roger couldn't tell if it was
an arm or a leg—remained attached to the torso, which lay
open like a huge misshapen melon. His head was propped
against the wall two feet away from the body, the face in a
mask of blood, mouth yawning, only one eye remaining, wide
and glazed.

Roger took a long deep breath, fighting to hold onto his
consciousness as he thought to himself, *It's not a person anymore, it's not a person, not a person* . . .

It didn't help.

Sondra was huddled, naked, bloody, and shaking, beneath

a table, hugging herself and rocking, sobbing then laughing in turns.

Blood dribbled down the face of the Mickey Mouse clock on the wall, which read three minutes to five.

The bread truck idled faithfully in the alley outside.

The room reeked of blood and excrement.

Sondra's huge eyes were frightened and strangely innocent in spite of the tears of blood that trickled over her now smooth cheeks. The flecks of gold were invisible from where Roger stood and her eyes were once again a deep brown. Although she was staring at him, Roger knew she was not seeing him.

"Sondra?" he called hoarsely. "Are you hurt? Sondra?"

She whispered something unintelligible, something that was not directed to Roger.

He moved closer and realized she was singing softly to herself. It was a song he remembered singing as a child in Sabbath school.

"Jesus loves me . . . this I know . . ."

Careful not to step on anything, Roger went to the table, bent down, and cautiously reached for her.

". . . for the Bible tells me so . . ."

He took her arm and gently tugged.

". . . little ones to Him belong . . ."

"C'mon, Sondra," he whispered, and she let him pull her out, but kept whispering the song.

". . . they are weak . . . but He is strong . . ."

He seated her in a chair and told her to stay put, although he knew she wasn't hearing him.

". . . yes, Jeee-zus loves me . . . yes, Jeee-zus loves me . . ."

Roger surveyed the bloody mess again, then looked at Sondra, who rocked in the chair like a retarded child, and knew he had to help her. For her sake as well as his own.

". . . yes, Jeee-zus loves me . . ."

He began to look for cleaning supplies and garbage bags as the bread truck continued to idle outside.

". . . the Bible tells me soooo . . ."

18

By the time the girls began to arrive at the deli to prepare for another day of work, Roger was exhausted but buzzing with acid-like adrenaline.

His fear that he'd overlooked something that one of them might notice was so great he was barely able to speak when they greeted him.

"Hey, Roger," Michelle called as she came out of the munch room tying her apron, "what happened to the Batman and Robin poster?"

"What?" He felt his heart moving up his throat.

"It's gone. The Batman and Robin poster. Did you take it down?"

"Oh, that. Yeah. Betty wants to start replacing all that stuff in there." He'd had to throw it away; it was the only wall hanging that had been irreparably bloodied.

"She's gonna remodel the munch room?"

"I guess so." Somehow, he would have to cover for that lie. Among others . . .

After a few minutes of agonizing over where to start, Roger had filled a garbage bag with the remains of Sidney the bread man and stuffed it into a bin at the south end of the back alley. He made sure Sidney had delivered the day's bread in the store room, then, wearing a pair of Playtex gloves, he drove the bread truck to the north end—the direction in which it had been headed—and killed the engine. He wanted to give the impression that Sidney had simply left his truck and decided he might be more successful if he didn't leave the keys. He dropped them into his coat pocket.

Once Sondra was coherent, Roger led her to the big sink in back, took a cloth soaked in warm soapy water, and gently began to clean her up; he slowly moved the cloth around her neck, over her face, across her breasts and belly, speaking soothingly to her, trying to hide the horror and disgust he felt at the sight of her beautiful young body covered with blood and strips of human flesh. When he had her rinse her mouth with water, she gagged and spit up a hank of Sidney's hair.

After using cold water to remove the few streaks of blood on her wool coat, Roger put her bike in the back seat of his car and drove her home, following as many back roads as possible. He stopped the car half a block from her house to drop her off.

"Now, you're sure you're okay?" he asked.

She nodded and when she spoke, her voice was hoarse and strained. "I may not come to work today."

"Sondra, you *have* to come to work. And go to school. Do *nothing* unusual, do you understand?"

"But I'll be so tired." Her casual, weary tone suggested this had happened before and she'd simply walked away from it, just as she'd said. It gave Roger a deep, profound chill, as if he'd stepped through a door and suddenly found himself standing on the edge of the Grand Canyon, naked and cold in the middle of the night. He heard no regret in her voice, not even a hint of understanding of what she'd done.

"I promise you, Sondra, you won't have to do much. Just look busy, that's all."

Roger watched her walk the bike down the sidewalk until she turned into the drive, then returned to the deli where he spent the next few hours vigorously scrubbing the munch room.

When he was finished and everything was put away, he stood in the middle of the room and scanned the walls and floors, searching for the slightest tell-tale sign.

Then he went to the bathroom, kneeled over the toilet, and threw up until he could barely stand.

Now, as he sipped his coffee, having gone home for a shower and a change of clothes, he thought about what he'd done and the fear began to eat into his bones like termites into wood.

The keys to Sidney's truck were in the back corner of his bottom dresser drawer, about a dozen of them splayed from their ring like the stiff, barbed legs of a metal spider waiting to pounce on the next person to pull the drawer out.

Roger knew that, had he called the police, there would have been no way to explain the killing. They would not have believed the truth—*Roger* still did not believe it—and he had the feeling that the blame would somehow fall on him.

But there was another reason he helped her, one he could not pinpoint; it seemed to hover on the edge of his thoughts, unwilling to be discovered.

It had something to do with the claws that Sondra's hands had become, with the talons that had grown from her fingers.

He'd seen them before in his imagination; he'd watched them, with his mind's eye, tearing through his insides as he lay curled in his bed, clutching his abdomen in agony.

It had something to do with the fear he'd felt as Sondra spoke of her mysterious illness, described the painful symptoms and the equally painful circumstances under which they'd arisen.

He'd felt an unsettling bond with Sondra when he saw her huddled beneath that table splattered with blood, a sort of empathy, as if he had been in the same situation himself once.

That, of course, was ridiculous.

But when he thought of those claws and of the pain that used to cut through him until he bled inside, when he thought of the way he used to dream of changing, his skin burning as it writhed and squirmed into something that was not human, he wondered if he'd been close—perhaps *very* close—to experiencing the same thing . . .

19

Late that morning, a man from the Rutherford Bakehouse called to ask if Sidney Nelson had made his delivery that morning. When Roger said that he had, trying to hide the dryness in his throat, the man said Sidney had not yet returned; he was going to call the police and they might come by and ask Roger a few questions. Roger said that was fine, hung up, then went to the back and quickly drank a glass of wine to calm his tattered nerves.

A police officer did indeed come in that afternoon—officer Chuck Niles, a boyish, freckled man—and asked if Roger had spoken to Sidney, if the delivery man's behavior was in any way unusual, if he'd been angry or mentioned quitting his job, if he'd been alone.

Roger answered the questions calmly and with assurance, saying that Sidney had simply come in, said hello, made his delivery, then left.

When the officer left, Roger had more wine, only because there was no more scotch.

Sondra came in a few minutes late looking weary and pale, just as she had the day Benny Kent's body had been discovered. The confidence she'd developed over the past weeks, however small, was gone; she would not look at Roger.

Although he had not slept, Roger was not tired; instead, he was jumpy and irritable and could not think straight. He dropped things and bumped into things and once looked up at the sign over the munch room doorway and began to giggle uncontrollably; remembering the sound of Sondra's wet, sloppy chewing early that morning gave new meaning to the munch room sign and he found it horribly funny.

Shortly before closing time that evening, Roger spotted Sondra going into the bathroom with a broom and followed her.

"Did you get caught this morning?" he asked quietly, half-closing the door.

"No. They were asleep."

"How do you feel?"

"The way I always feel afterward. Tired. Shaky." Her eyes never met his.

"How many times has this happened?"

"I don't know."

"How often? What brings it on?"

"*I don't know*," she hissed.

"You killed Benny Kent, didn't you?"

After a long moment, she nodded and began sweeping as if he weren't there.

"What happened?"

"He wanted to . . . to . . . be with me. We met that night by

the footpath? Between here and Manning? And we started to
. . . you know . . .''

"Did you want to?"

"*Yes*, I wanted to. Just like with you. But when we started
. . . I . . . like always, it happened."

"Sondra, you've got to do something about this. I know
you're scared, but you've got to see someone or—"

"Forget it."

"What? What do you mean, for—"

"Thank you for helping me, but . . . you have to forget it
because . . . I'll be looking for a new job now."

"What? Why?" He was speaking in urgent whispers now,
fists clenched at his sides.

"They don't want me to work here anymore."

"Annie?"

"And Bill. I shouldn't even be talking to you like this. She
could come in any minute and—"

"Because of me? They want you to quit because of me?"

She started for the door but Roger stepped in front of her.

There were heavy footsteps in the munch room, obviously
not those of one of the girls.

"What do they know about me?" Roger asked.

"I have to go, let me *go*," she snapped, moving around him
and leaving the bathroom.

Roger followed her into the munch room where he froze
when a familiar voice said, "Sondra, you ready?"

Bill Dunning stood before them leaning on a cane.

A silence as solid and cold as stone fell over the room.

Sondra stopped, folded her arms protectively over her
breasts, and stared at her shoes.

A second, minute, or hour could have passed as Roger stood
in the doorway, his eyes locked with Bill's; he wasn't sure and
didn't care.

Bill's face was solid now, the boyish roundness it had in
college replaced by a stern, jaw-clenched look of bitterness. It
might have been because he was looking at Roger, but Roger
didn't think so. The look was not a temporary one; it was
chiseled into the bones beneath his skin, carved into his jaw.

He was thicker; stubble sprinkled the lower half of his face.

And his right leg was gone.

The leg of his black pants was filled out but stiff, and when he shifted his weight once, the leg clicked. It was a prosthesis.

"Come on, Sondra," Bill said, his voice low and level, his eyes still on Roger. "Let's go. Annie's waiting."

Sondra was hurrying for the door before Bill was finished.

Bill remained for a moment, eyeing Roger warily.

Swallowing a clot of felt in his throat, Roger tried hard to smile, to sound congenial when he stepped forward and said, "Well, hey, Bill, it's been—"

"Sondra won't be working here anymore," Bill said. "Thought I'd let you know." As he turned and walked out, leaning heavily on his cane, Bill's right leg clicked softly with each step and he muttered, "Getting a job someplace else."

Roger listened until he heard the front door rattle shut behind them, then he sent the others home and closed up for the night.

20

A thin mist crept into the Valley that night and spread itself through the vineyards like a blanket of cobwebs. The stars were hidden by gathering clouds and the air had fangs of ice.

When he turned down his street, he noticed a car pulling up in front of his house.

Roger suddenly felt sick.

It wasn't a police car, but it was unfamiliar.

As Roger pulled into his drive, the driver's door of the car opened and a woman got out.

Marjie.

"*There* you are," she called happily as he got out of his car. "I was afraid I'd come up here for nothing. Hope you haven't eaten yet." She lifted two grocery bags from her car.

Hiding his annoyance, and the fact that eating was the *last* thing on his mind, Roger helped her carry them inside.

"Spaghetti sound good?" Marjie asked as she emptied the bags on the kitchen counter.

"Sure, Marjie, but I really don't—"

She held up a bottle of wine. "Do you want this before, during, or after dinner?"

"Right now, please," Roger sighed, sitting at the table. "How did you find me?"

"I've got a friend in payroll at Napa College. She looked your address up for me. Why, did I come at a bad time? You look terrible, are you sick?"

"No, just tired," he yawned.

She opened the wine and poured two glasses, then busied herself with the groceries, preparing dinner.

It wasn't until he'd finished his first glass of wine that Roger realized how beautiful Marjie looked.

She wore a tight black skirt, a red and black top with a scooped neckline, and a dark gray blazer. Her hair was up in the back and gently curled strands of it fell to the sides of her face.

"You look nice," he said, pouring more wine. "What are you all dressed up for?"

"For you," she said, sounding disappointed that he would think otherwise.

As she darted around the kitchen, chatting about work and her two cats, Roger watched her and realized this was not just a friendly visit; this was a *very* friendly visit. She meant to start something. Roger thought it might be nice to spend the night in her arms—*God, it's been so long*, he thought—and forget about everything else for a while. But he wouldn't; he couldn't. He knew he shouldn't even be having dinner with her, but he couldn't very well tell her to take her spaghetti dinner and go home. Things had happened between them that no amount of explaining or apologizing could erase and, knowing that the average backslidden Seventh-day Adventist could undergo a spiritual about face at any time, he didn't want to open himself up to more of the same.

Over dinner, Marjie brought him up to date on some of their former schoolmates.

Clearing his throat, Roger asked, "What ever happened to Bill Dunning?"

"Oh, what a sad story *that* is. He's married now, you know. Married some girl from Michigan just out of college. Annie Something. A little wallflower. He got *really* religious and was planning to go right back to school—the seminary—and become a minister. Then he had an accident on his motorcycle. Lost his right leg, couldn't work. Annie's a receptionist somewhere in Manning. And if Bill was religious before . . . well, he and God are on a first name basis now. The accident . . . I don't know, I think it maybe made him a little, you know, wiggy. Annie's cousin from Michigan is living with them now. She's got a job somewhere in St. Helena and helps pay some of the bills.''

"Not anymore."

"Oh?"

Roger told her about Bill's visit to the deli that day.

"Then you know the girl," she said.

"Not very well." He suddenly felt uncomfortable with the subject.

"I met her once. I hear she's a real trouble-maker."

Roger swallowed a black, morbid chuckle.

"A horny little devil, I understand."

"I . . . wouldn't know."

There was a pause filled with the clatter of forks against plates, then Roger asked, "Are you sure Bill lost his leg in a motorcycle accident?"

"Yeah. I mean, there aren't too many ways to lose a whole leg, you know. Why?"

He shrugged. "Just wondering."

"No, really, tell me why you asked. You seem . . . I don't know, troubled. Did Bill say something today that—"

"Never mind, Marjie. I really don't want to talk about it."

After dinner, they had ice cream and Marjie turned on the television and cuddled up beside Roger on the sofa, after opening another bottle of wine.

Roger stiffened, forcing himself not to respond.

"What?" Marjie asked, puzzled. "What's wrong?"

"I . . . don't think it's such a good idea, Marjie."

She pulled away from him, smiling, and removed a baggie and a small pipe from her purse on the floor.

"You just need to relax, that's all," she said, waving a lump of marijuana under his nose.

Roger had tried to get her to smoke pot with him the summer of their senior year in high school, but she'd refused politely, saying she had no intention of ever trying it.

"Like I said before, Roger, I'm a big girl now," she whispered conspiratorially, as if reading his thoughts.

They each took a few hits and began laughing at some vapid sitcom on television until Marjie spilled some wine on herself.

She stood, giggling, "Shit, oh shit," as she brushed at the spreading stain. "Do you have a robe, or . . ."

"Sure." Roger went to his room.

"Where's your washer? Do you have one?"

"In the garage, through the kitchen."

Roger returned to the living room with his bathrobe and was about to sit down again when he remembered his blood-splattered clothes stacked on the washer and he bolted through the house after her.

"Roger, what *happened*?" she asked as he stepped down into the garage. She was holding up the shirt splashed with Sidney Nelson's blood.

"Oh, that," he said, trying to calm himself, thinking fast. "I hit a, a-yum deer last night. I had to, you know, move it out of the road." His hands were trembling and he was beginning to perspire as he took the shirt from her and tossed it aside along with the pants. "It was, it was a mess. A mess." When Marjie had her shirt off, Roger handed her the robe and quickly started the wash, then led her back into the house.

"That must've been awful," she said. "Hitting a deer. I did that once and thought I'd never stop crying."

On the sofa once again, Roger suddenly felt giddy at having succeeded with his lie.

They smoked some more, drank some more, and kept laughing at the television show, but now Roger's laughter was deep and heartfelt and not in response to the sitcom they were watch-

ing. They leaned on one another as they guffawed with the
laughtrack, her arm around his shoulders, his arm resting across
her thighs.

Then they were kissing.

Minutes later, they were in bed.

Laughter continued from the television set, blending with
their sighs and whispers, and with the sound of the rain that
had begun to fall gently outside.

When Roger closed his eyes, holding Marjie's body beneath
him, beside him, above him, moving his hips in crescendoing
circles, it was not Marjie who filled his mind.

It was Sondra.

21

When Roger woke the next morning, Marjie was gone. She'd
left a note: *It's still as good as before. Soon—M.*

Over coffee in the deli, Roger searched the paper for any
mention of Sidney Nelson. A small article said only that the
delivery man's truck had been abandoned in the alley; a tiny
smear of blood hinted at foul play and a check was being run
to see if it matched Sidney's type.

Roger grew faint for a moment, but was relieved to read
that the police suspected Sidney had been attacked and robbed
and was perhaps wandering around, injured, lost, and confused;
they expected him to turn up within twenty-four hours.

Roger called Betty, woke her, and told her Sondra had quit
and she would need to hire a new girl. He was not familiar
with the procedure and said he would be more comfortable if
she came in and did it herself.

"Oh, sure, honey," she said groggily. "You've been awfully good to me. I should've come back before this. I'll be in
this afternoon. Why don't you go home and relax."

He did. He watched a Godzilla movie on television that
afternoon, munching on pretzels; he read through some of the

books on Satanism he'd bought and leisurely wrote pages of helpful notes; he finished a chapter that had been stumping him for days.

Marjie called him from work and said she wanted to see him again that night.

By the time she arrived, Roger had set up a tray of take-out Chinese food in the bedroom and they took turns eating one another between courses.

The next week was smooth as glass, and so were the days following it. Roger enjoyed teaching his classes; he had regained an old friendship—and then some; and he was thinking hardly at all of Sondra. He was able to enter the munch room without seeing Sidney the bread man scattered over the floor and walls. He began to feel as if it had never happened.

For the first time in years, Roger's life was good. He would even go so far as to say he was happy.

That worried him.

It had been so long since Roger had felt happy that he began to wonder what would happen to end it; surely it could not last long.

It didn't.

22

Roger tore himself from a nightmare—

Sondra was peeling a bloody sheet of skin from the back of Sidney the bread man, who was convulsing on the munch room floor and who had an enormous set of antlers growing from his skull.

I hit a deer last night . . .

—He sat up in bed gasping in the dark.

"What is it?" Marjie pressed warmly against his back and her breath was hot on his neck.

"Night. Mare." He was still out of breath.

"Get you something?"

"No." He lay back down and Marjie curled up beside him, kissed him, and whispered, "Be right back."

She went into the bathroom and he heard her urinate, flush, wash, then go to the kitchen for a drink.

After a few moments of silence, Roger started to doze.

"Roger, what are these books?"

He opened his eyes and saw her standing in the rectangle of soft light spilling in through the door, holding a book in each hand.

"*The Satanic Bible*?" she said in a tiny voice. "*Satanic Invocations*? Roger, what are you—"

"Research." He rolled over.

"Roger," she whispered, "this is . . . these are . . . I can't believe you—"

"C'mon, Marjie, it's just research for the book I'm writing, that's all."

"But why so many? You've got *more* out there. What are you *writing?*"

"Another thriller," he mumbled into his pillow. When she didn't return to bed for a while, he sat up and saw her still standing in the doorway looking at the books. "Marjie, it's just research. What's the problem?"

Still she did not move for a while, then put the books on his dresser, turned off the hall light, and slowly returned to bed. They were silent for a while, then, her voice cautious and just a little afraid, touched with a nervous chuckle, she asked, "Roger, that . . . that blood on your shirt the other night . . ."

But Roger was asleep.

23

At noon the next day, Roger was hunched over his notebook in the munch room when some of the high school students began to crowd into the deli for lunch. The noise level rose as they took up the tables around him, laughing, swearing, and constantly smoking.

Roger hardly looked up from his work; it was going too well, he was in too deep—

—until he hit bottom. It happened even when he was on a roll: a line of dialogue that didn't ring true or a description that was murky, sometimes even something as small as a single word that didn't fit.

He leaned back in his chair with a sigh, chewing on the end of his pen and, as if drawn to the very spot where she sat, his eyes fell on Sondra.

She saw him, too, apparently at that very moment because she was half-smiling at something someone at her table had said and the smile froze for a moment, then slowly chipped away until it was gone.

She looked weary; her beautiful bright eyes seemed dimmed and had puffy half-moons beneath them. She looked just like she had the day Benny Kent's body had been discovered.

Their eyes remained locked like the bumpers of two cars that had collided and Roger became deaf to the voices in the room. He was suddenly afraid that if he were to look around him, he would see Sidney's blood splashed on the walls and he tried hard to keep the memory of that night from seeping into his mind. But it wasn't easy. He hadn't seen Sondra—had hardly even *thought* of her—for nearly two weeks, two wonderfully comfortable, content weeks that had passed mercifully slowly. Seeing her now brought it back, reminded him how she'd touched him that night . . . how her breasts had felt beneath his hands as he washed the blood from them . . . how much—how very achingly much—he'd wanted her . . .

Movement twitched over her face, as if searching for a hold, then her lips curled upward at the ends. The smile warmed slowly, grew, and for a moment Roger thought she was going to cry.

Then she stood and quickly left.

24

His writing didn't take off again that day. He pieced together a few more paragraphs, then gave up.

When he got home, the red light on his answering machine was winking lecherously and he played his messages.

There were three hang-ups.

He called Marjie at her office and invited her out to dinner that night.

"Um, I don't think so, Roger," she said. "I'm kind of, you know, um, tired."

"We have been pretty active the last few nights, haven't we?" he laughed, but she didn't respond. Silence hissed over the line. "Is anything wrong?"

"Things are kind of hectic here today, really busy, you know? I'll probably have to work late, and . . ."

She didn't finish.

"Well, if you change your mind," he said, "give me a call."

"Yeah, sure, that's a good idea. I'll call you. If not tonight, then . . . well, maybe tomorrow. But . . . things look pretty thick here for the whole week. I don't know . . ."

"Whatever. I'll see you in class tomorrow night, though, right?"

"Yeah. Sure."

He stood by the phone for a while after hanging up, puzzled; Marjie sounded as if something were definitely wrong.

The phone rang and Roger picked it up immediately.

"Hello?"

"Leave the Valley."

It was unfamiliar, a low male voice, so low it was almost a growl.

"You didn't learn your lesson the first time, demon-lover. Don't make us teach you another one."

The voice hung up.

Roger slowly replaced the receiver. He turned on the stereo

and found a San Francisco station that played hard rock and roll—none of that middle-of-the-road cotton candy—turned it up loud, and started doing some housework.

He didn't let himself think about the phone call. He didn't let himself wonder if it had anything to do with Marjie's odd behavior, if the three hang-ups had been the caller, waiting for Roger to answer. Each time he started to think, *It's happening again,* he stopped himself by singing loudly with the radio or dancing hard to the beat as he vaccumed.

He decided he would ignore it.

He would ignore it if it killed him.

25

The phone didn't ring again until shortly before two o'clock the next morning as Roger was typing.

He'd spent the entire evening cleaning and the house was immaculate. After a few hours of television, he'd gone back to work, having pushed the phonecall far into the back of his mind, deciding it was an isolated incident.

Before the third ring, he'd gone through all the possible reasons someone might be calling him at such an hour and decided to let the machine get it, just in case . . .

By the fifth ring, he realized he hadn't turned the answering machine back on . . .

By the ninth ring, he decided perhaps it was important and answered.

"Your lights are on. Don't you ever sleep? Or *can* you sleep?"

Roger slammed the receiver down so hard the phone gave a startled little *ding!* sound, then he went to the front window and pulled the curtain aside, peering out at the early morning darkness.

The street lamp across from his house was out and he could see nothing.

He turned off his porchlight and went out front, walked down the drive, shivering in the cold. The street was silent and life-less.

Roger tried to remember if he'd heard a car drive by earlier, but couldn't.

When he got back inside, he was still shivering.

But not from the cold.

26

Betty was miraculously herself again. She bounced around the deli hugging the regulars and treating new customers as if they had reservations.

Roger heard her before he saw her when he went to Di-Marco's late the next morning. She gave him a big hug, then frowned.

"Jesus Christ, Roger, you look like *death*," she said.

He stroked his sandpapery chin. "Forgot to shave."

"Is that all?"

"I didn't get much sleep last night. I was up working." It was true, he hadn't slept a moment. He had not, however, gotten any work done after the second phone call; he'd sat before the television watching movies.

"Well, comb your hair and look sharp," Betty said. "The law's waiting for you in the munch room."

"Huh?" Roger felt his jaw drop and smacked his mouth shut again.

"Chucky Niles. He's waiting for you."

"Niles," he murmured as a block of ice exploded in his chest.

Officer Niles was seated at Roger's table sipping coffee. He nodded his greeting, meeting Roger's eyes for only an instant.

Roger put his notebook on the table and seated himself, forcing a smile.

"Something I gotta do, Mr. Carlton," Niles said hesitantly, almost shamefully.

Roger willed his heart to keep beating, willed his eyes not to tear up.

"If I don't," Niles went on, reaching under the table and bringing up a heavy brown paper bag, "I'll be sorry, believe me." He removed hardcover editions of three of Roger's novels and plopped them onto the table. "I *said* I didn't want to bother you, but since I told her I met you a couple of weeks ago, my wife talks about nothing else. She's a fan." He offered a pen to Roger and sheepishly asked, "Would you?"

Warm relief spread through Roger's body like urine spreading through his pants and he grinned. "*Would* I. I'd *love* to." He'd never enjoyed signing anything more than he did those three books for Ellen Niles. He felt so good as he scribbled in them that he was able to ask the next question without losing his smile. "Have you found Sidney yet?"

"Um, no. Not exactly."

"Oh? What do you mean, 'not exactly'?"

"I'm, uh, not at liberty to discuss it."

"Then you *do* know something."

"Well, not myself, exactly, but . . . yes, they have made some progress. They say . . ."

Roger finished, put down the pen, and saw Niles's face squirm uncomfortably.

". . . I really can't discuss it. I'm sorry."

Keep the smile, Roger ordered himself with dread.

"Well, I hope he's okay."

Niles shook his head hopelessly.

After the officer left, Roger stared at the table top a long time, wondering how much they knew.

27

Roger held up his class for five minutes waiting for Marjie to arrive. When she didn't, he clumsily began the first hour's discussion on characterization, glancing now and then at the door, hoping to see Marjie sheepishly peering through the window.

He ended up letting the class go early, unable to shake the feeling, the *fear*, that something was terribly wrong. He suspected that something more than an unusually busy day or a flat tire had kept Marjie from the class. After her behavior on the phone yesterday, he wouldn't be too surprised to find she'd dropped the class.

As he pulled into his drive and his headlights passed over the front of his house, he saw what looked like a small sack on his porch with two short sticks protruding from the top.

He got out of the car and headed up the walk, his pace slowing as he neared the object. In the glaring yellow glow of his porchlight, there seemed to be two glistening marbles stuck to its sides and something dark and wet was puddled around the bottom of what Roger no longer thought to be a sack.

The puddle dribbled over the edge of the top step and onto the next.

Roger moved closer, squinting in the poor light, and when he was certain what it was, small clicking noises sounded in his throat as he swallowed dryly again and again. He gingerly touched the toe of his shoe to the severed goat's head and it fell heavily to one side, the freshly hacked neck pulling away from the concrete with a gentle moist sound.

Light glinted off the yellowed teeth revealed by curled back lips and the eyes were comically wide and bulging, a morbid caricature.

Roger stepped over the head, avoiding the blood, sucking cold air deep into his lungs. He turned his back on the front door and kicked the head onto the front lawn. It hit with a heavy thunk and rolled over the grass.

Inside, he poured himself a drink and finished it in a couple gulps, then poured another. He leaned on the kitchen counter, waiting for the liquor to soothe his trembling.

"No," he said quietly, flatly, as the pain in his side returned for a moment, just an instant, then disappeared. He took another drink, then spit it into the sink, crying out like a child when the pain hit again, the worst since his stay in Sylmar, chewing through his insides like a ravenous demon, silently screaming at him in a mocking nails-on-a-blackboard voice:

I'm back, you jelly-assed motherfuckerrrrr, I'm back and it's been TOOOO LOOOONG!

28

When Roger shuffled into the deli the next day, exhausted from lack of sleep, Betty stared at him open-mouthed for a moment, took his hand, and led him into the munch room and sat him down.

Roger fidgeted as she watched him, chewing her lip.

"What's wrong, honey?" she asked somberly.

"I didn't sleep well last night. I was working on—"

"Don't jerk me around. What's wrong?"

Roger tried to look puzzled; he lifted his brows high over his eyes and when he saw she wasn't buying it, he smiled. "C'mon, Betty, I'm just tired."

"Roger, you look like *hell*. You're pale, you're... you're..." She chewed a thumbnail nervously. "A police officer was just in here. It wasn't Chucky, it was someone I don't know. He was asking... questions about you."

Roger's stomach twisted.

"I'm not sure," she went on, "but I think it has something to do with Sidney."

"Well, that makes sense. Apparently I was the last one to see him."

She shook her head. "It sounds like more than that, Roger. Please. Tell me. Just between us. Did something happen here? Is there something I should know? Do they... *suspect* you of something?"

"Jesus, Betty," he laughed, "what *is* this? The guy came, said hi, delivered the bread, and *left*. That's *it*."

She tugged at her lower lip, searching his face.

"Betty, I'm telling you, there's nothing to—"

Glass shattered out front and someone screamed.

"*Jesus!*" Roger blurted as he dashed out of the room, Betty close behind.

There was a jagged hole in the window facing Main Street. Michelle stood frozen behind the register, both hands over her mouth. Broken glass was scattered over the floor and on the front table, which was fortunately unoccupied.

A brick lay among the pieces of glass; attached to it with a rubber band was crumpled piece of paper.

"Is everyone okay?" Betty called.

No one was hurt.

Except Roger, who felt a needle-like squirming in his side as he stared at the brick, afraid to pick it up.

Betty did before he could. She took the paper off and straightened it out. Her eyes scanned it, then looked at Roger.

"What is it?" he asked.

She handed it to him.

In crude block letters, the note read: ROGER CARLTON IS EVIL. HE BROUGHT DEATH HERE.

He couldn't look at Betty, at *anyone*. He wadded the note in his fist, spun around, and went back to the munch room and gathered up his things, feeling sick.

Betty followed him, calling his name. In the munch room, she said, "Roger, we'll call the police."

"No."

"Where are you going? We should report this to——"

"I'm going home. Don't report it to anyone. I'll pay for the window."

"Roger, *wait!*"

He didn't wait. He had to get out. The pain was coming.

29

When he got home, he began to drink, pacing the house like an expectant father, chain smoking and muttering to himself under his breath.

What had happened to bring it all back? Everything had been going so well . . .

He wondered what the police had asked about him, what they knew, what they'd found.

He couldn't have felt more confined, more enclosed, if he were hunkering in his closet.

The drinks started to hit and he started getting sloppy-drunk, crying like a barfly, sitting on the sofa, elbows on his knees, hands hanging between his thighs. He got sick of his own company, decided he had to get out of the house and talk to someone, and cleaned up, then drove to Josh's.

The cold day smelled sweet, which made the odor of death in Josh's house even more overwhelming.

Roger had spoken with him on the phone twice since their last visit, but the dying man's voice, although weaker and more hollow, could not have prepared him for the visible progression of Josh's illness.

His face seemed to be collapsing, his skull deflating like a balloon with a slow leak. He walked with two canes now. When he walked.

The shock Roger felt showed on his face and Josh chuckled—it sounded like someone slowly wadding a sheet of waxed paper—and said in his trembling, pencil-thin voice, "I'm dying, for Christ's sake, what'd you expect, the cover of *GQ*?"

Josh nearly fell in the living room and Roger quickly reached out for him, felt the skeleton beneath the robe, the ribs and fragile joints, the sticks that would serve as limbs for only a short while longer.

Later, Roger would remember the clothes—a long-sleeved shirt, pants, a heavy sweater, and an overcoat—neatly laid out on the sofa. He would even remember seeing Josh's car keys on the coffee table. But his eyes passed over them blindly at the time; his head was too crowded with his own problems for him to realize the significance of what he saw.

"Did Betty get my flowers?" Josh asked.

"Yes. She wanted to thank you, but—"

Josh held up a twig-fingered hand. "I understand. So. What brings you here?"

"Haven't seen you in a couple weeks. I thought I'd drop by."

"And I appreciate that. But what's *wrong*?"

Roger laughed and said, "You sure are . . ." He was going to say *sharp for a dying man,* but a great muddy sob sprang from his center and snatched the voice from his throat and he put his face in his hands and bawled . . .

Roger had never discussed his problems with Josh; their conversations had always been limited to movie trivia and Hollywood gossip, talk that Roger hadn't gotten from his other friends and which—having been a movie fan long before he ever mustered the courage to risk his soul to hellfire by entering a movie theater—he craved. Roger had always talked to Josh to forget his problems, not stir them up or work them out, so Josh knew nothing of his ordeal with the church.

Roger told him; he covered everything up to the time he left Sylmar.

"After that I did some screen work, sold *Ledges* and wrote a draft of the screenplay. I kept busy and made quite a bit of money, but . . . nothing changed. It went on. Phone calls, vandalism. Finally, I just sort of disappeared for a year," he sighed. "Didn't even go home for Christmas. I spent New Year's Eve watching Dick Clark on a black and white television in some roach-eaten motel outside Kansas City. I told no one where I was. I put my parents in charge of my finances—they were very understanding—and had them wire money to me as I needed it. I wanted, *needed*, to be away from everyone, everything. I needed to be unreachable. I got no more obscene phone calls because I had no phone. I found no surprises in my closet because I had no closet, just my suitcases in the trunk of my car. I just drove and stopped and looked and ate and slept and drove. It was nice, a relief. For a while, anyway."

"After all that happened," Josh asked, "why in God's name did you come back here?"

"I love it here. I missed the Valley. It made me angry that I'd allowed myself to be chased out of a place I loved. And I got sick of being alone. I wanted to prove to myself that it was over—I figured it *had* to be after all that time away—and to prove to the people here that there's nothing wrong with me. I guess I came back to clear my name.''

''Is the pain gone now?''

Roger shook his head. ''It's . . . come back.''

''Then it's not over.''

After a long moment of thought, Roger decided to tell Josh everything. He knew it would go no further than the room and Josh would take it with him to the grave—probably sooner than most.

He told him about Sondra, about Sondra's parents and Benny Kent and Leo and Sidney Nelson, and Josh was silent for a long time.

''You're afraid I don't believe you,'' Josh finally said.

''What sane person would?''

''Listen to me, Roger. All my life, and without even realizing it, I have lived, thought, and acted as if I would never die, would live forever. Well, now I'm sitting here at Death's table and we're having a drink. I mean, I'm *dying*, here. It's no longer just a distant possibility, a *myth*. It's real. And suddenly, a lot of other things are beginning to seem real. Suddenly . . . flying saucers don't sound as silly. Big-foot and the Loch Ness Monster seem to be possible, even likely. Things don't seem as . . . as *absolute* as they used to. If I can die, then I guess *anything* can happen.''

''Then . . . you do believe me?''

''Go to the bookcase. Third shelf, far left, the black one.''

Roger removed a trade paperback titled *Lon Chaney, Full Moons, and Lycanthropy*. There was a picture of Lon Chaney as the wolfman on the cover.

''I bought it because I thought it was about movie werewolves,'' Josh said. ''You know, 'Even a man who is pure of heart and says his prayers by night . . . ' That sort of thing. It is, in a way. But it's more than that. It turned out to be much more serious than I expected.''

''Really?'' Roger thumbed through it quickly.

''Did I ever tell you I was a Mormon, Roger?''

Sitting down again, Roger shook his head.

"Well, I was. A good one, too. I loved my church, grew up in it. But when I got to junior high . . . ah, those were hellish years. I knew I was . . . different than the others. I went to a church school so everyone was Mormon and everyone was pretty much alike. Except me.

"When all my friends started noticing girls, I started noticing all my friends," he chuckled, "the *guys*, you know. I got so scared. I didn't understand what was wrong with me, and I didn't dare tell anyone.

"I was taking piano lessons then from Mr. Coswell. A kinder, gentler man never lived. He knew something was wrong and started to pry a little. Didn't take him long to figure it out. He was gay, too, see, but no one knew. God forbid. He would've lost his job, been cast out of the church. It was a while before he gathered the courage to tell *me*. We became very good friends. Not lovers, though. He wasn't like that. Mr. Coswell was in his forties when I knew him, and I don't think he'd had a lover since high school. No, he was only gay in his head, not in his pants." Another chuckle. "He helped me understand myself and accept myself. Yes, he was a good man." Josh's eyes looked past Roger, past the walls of his house, and focused on something far away.

"Anyhow, Mr. Coswell helped me to believe that there was nothing wrong with me. I wasn't a pervert, a monster. And the . . . the summer before I went to college . . . I told my parents.

"Have you ever heard of the Doctrine of Blood Atonement, Roger?"

"No."

"It's Mormon. A lot of people deny it, some have left the church because of it and formed little offshoot churches. Very controversial. Some people take it very seriously.

"It's like this: Some sinners have committed a sin *so* heinous, or have sinned unrepentantly for *so* long, that they cannot be forgiven. Their only hope for salvation is death. Their life must be ended, their blood spilled, in order for them to be accepted into the Kingdom.

"So, I told my parents. We'd always been so close . . . I

guess I thought they would accept me unconditionally. But no. My father went insane. Tried to kill me. Chased me out of the house with a knife. Destroyed all my belongings. He even called the college I was planning to attend—a Mormon college—and told them I was a homosexual. I was not accepted, of course.

"I lost all of my Mormon friends and the church—the church I loved and had actively contributed to all my life—no longer wanted me." He smiled. "I don't have to tell *you* how that felt, do I?"

Josh carefully shifted in his chair and took a deep, labored breath.

"I was the same person I'd always been," he went on, "but suddenly everyone in my life—including my family—felt differently about me, was rejecting me. I was bitter for years. I hated God and Christianity and any organization that vaguely resembled a religion.

"I feel a little better about it now. Mostly because of that book, silly as it may seem. There's a section in there—you'll know it when you find it—that made me think long and hard about all this, and I found some answers to my *why's*. I'm at peace with them now.

"People like you and me, Roger, we're the lucky ones. We went through hell, and yours isn't over yet, but we're *still* lucky. There aren't many like us."

"I don't understand," Roger said, "why are we lucky?"

"*They* are being controlled, those people. So, in turn, they try to control others. It's like a sort of pecking order. Ever since their childhood or since some other vulnerable time in their lives, they were led to believe in the importance of a list of rules. Some of the rules are contradictory, some are impossible to follow, but they have become all-important to these people, whether they're Adventist rules or Mormon rules or Catholic rules. So they are under the control of this list and the people who enforce it.

"Then along comes someone like you or me who very innocently breaks one of those rules. You wanted to be a writer, I learned to accept the fact that I'm gay. It doesn't matter how innocently we broke them—we *broke* them. These other people—Adventists, Mormons, whatever—see that we're not following the rules that control *their* lives, so they try to enforce them. They try to scare us, or *hurt* us, into keeping those rules. They try to control us as they are controlled. They do this by convincing us we're sick, evil monsters.

"Do you know why that so often works, Roger?"

Roger shook his head.

"Because if you tell someone he's a monster long enough, he *becomes* one.

"And if you claim it's evil to be gay, then gays have to find their companionship in a dark, secret place and it *becomes* dirty. Evil.

"If you tell a writer it's evil to write stories because stories that aren't true make people ill, depress them—I believe Mrs. White says something along those lines, doesn't she?—then harrass him and tell him he's going to burn in hell for doing something he loves, well, pretty soon it affects his work. The stories become bleak tales of doom, stories of pain and violence. Evil stories, if you want.

"You see, Roger, their little plan is really quite beautiful. With all those rules, they *create* their own monsters. Otherwise, they would have nothing to fight or control.

"But they didn't get me," he smiled. "That's why I'm one of the lucky ones. And they haven't gotten you yet, even though they're still trying. But this girl, Sondra . . ."

Josh shook his head and his eyes darkened. His sunken face soured into an expression of bitterness. It was so bitter, in fact, that Roger asked, "What's wrong? I thought you said you're at peace with them."

"Oh, no-no. I'm at peace with my *why's*. I'll never truly be at peace with the Mormons. Or *any* of them, actually." He paused a while, resting his face against a palm, then said, "My father called about six months ago, when he found out I have AIDS. I hadn't heard his voice since the day he chased me out of the house, but I knew it immediately. He laughed at me and said, 'God always finds a way to spill the blood of the sinners.' See . . . *that's* what bothers me the most. He thinks I'm being punished for my wicked life. I don't; I just happened to get this horrible sickness that gave me five to seven years and I got the short end of the stick. But after I'm dead, he'll smile, and all his friends will smile, and all the people who used to be *my* friends . . . and they'll think they are victorious.

"I'm at peace with myself in spite of how they tried to make me feel. The truth is, I'm *right*. But there are only a few like me. Most people are controlled, or are controlling others. The only truth to them is that list of rules. So . . . nobody ever believes the truth.

"In the end, they always win." He thought about what he'd said and turned to Roger with a warm smile. "Don't get me wrong, I'm not saying every single Seventh-day Adventist or Mormon is like that. They're not. In fact, there's a young Adventist couple who visits me every week. They bring books and magazines—regular ones like *Time* and *People*, no religious tracts—and just talk. *Most* people are scared to walk on my side of the *street*; not them. They're good people.

"But it doesn't matter. The good people are outnumbered.

"In the end, *they* always win."

Roger sat in confused, overwhelmed silence for a while, drained by what Josh had said. He thumbed through the book glancing at the black and white stills from old werewolf movies, the sketchy illustrations of bodies writhing through hideous transformations.

Josh said, "Take it."

"I'll bring it back."

Josh laughed dryly and said, "Keep it, Roger, I have no use for it."

"Are you sure?"

"Positive." He stood with effort, as if his frail body were several times its actual weight. "I think there are some things in that book that you'll find interesting. I wish I could be of more help."

"You listened."

"Happy to."

"Sorry to dump on you like—"

"Hush." He struggled away from the chair. "I don't mean

to be rude, Roger, but why don't you take off now. I'm very tired . . .''

Roger closed the book and said, "Oh, sure, Josh, you gonna be okay?'' He realized, even as he was speaking, how stupid the words were.

"No," Josh laughed.

"Jesus, I didn't—"

"Don't *worry* about it." He hobbled toward Roger, his shoulders rising and falling slowly above his stiff arms like the pistons of a dying engine. He stopped, lifted his arms, swayed slightly, and lowered them around Roger's shoulders, embracing him as he said, "Thank you for coming by, Roger. You take care.''

Roger felt a sliver of the realization that would later stab him and make him feel so stupid, so selfish. He cautiously returned Josh's embrace, afraid he might break, and said, "Well, I'll come back in a couple days and let you know what I think of the book.''

Josh smirked as he pulled away. "You do that.''

It was the last time Roger would ever see him.

30

Roger went home, made some coffee, and sat down to read the book.

It was poorly written and not even bound very well, but once Roger skimmed through the first three chapters—all of which dealt with the Hollywoodized myth of lycanthropy—he began to find passages that rang chillingly true.

There were several different theories behind the physical transformation that allegedly plagued victims of lycanthropy.

Some attributed it to supernatural curses: a gypsy's hex, a witch's spell.

Others claimed it was a rare disease that caused hair to grow over its victim's body at regular intervals, made him unable to walk upright, and caused him to crave raw meat.

It was a sub-heading in bold print near the end of the chapter that fully captured Roger's attention: LYCANTHROPY AND RELIGION. He read the section slowly, then re-read it again and again.

A psychiatrist in Boston had linked religious repression to a mental and physical aberration that resembled lycanthropy.

"Often, one who is raised in the confines of a fundamentalist faith," Dr. Regis Maine said at a 1978 psychiatric conference in Washington, D.C., "will, at some point, begin to doubt or reject the doctrines of his church. This independent thinking is inevitably met with severe negative reinforcement from family and friends who try, through various means of exclusion and harassment, to convince the subject that the fault is with *him* rather than the church."

"No shit," Roger muttered as he read.

Dr. Maine claimed to have several patients who, after extensive counseling, admitted that they were "werewolves" and were physically transformed with increasing regularity—some at times of anger, others with feelings of sexual arousal or even simple happiness and contentment. He even claimed to have *witnessed* one of these transformations.

"While the physical alterations were nothing like those seen in films or on television, they were, without doubt, complete and inhuman—animal-like—and the patient became extremely violent and exhibited a drastic increase in physical strength."

With continued therapy, Dr. Maine learned that each patient, all of whom were raised in ultra-conservative fundamentalist homes, had been the subject of what he called "intense reconversion or ostracization campaigns" designed to either woo the backslidden, wayward patient back into the fold or shame or frighten him into re-dedicating himself to Christ. During this process, the patients became convinced they were in some way monstrous or even possessed, that they were indeed evil and deserved the treatment given them. It was during this time that they began to experience mysterious physical ailments— usually severe abdominal pains—all of which escaped the diagnosis of doctors, even after extensive tests. These eventually developed into the physical metamorphosis which Dr. Maine suggested had, for centuries, been identified by the superstitious and fanatically religious as a demonic curse that turned its victims into ravenous wolves.

"It was not a curse at all," Maine said, "but quite likely a severe mental *and* physical condition imposed upon its victims by the very people who feared it most."

Dr. Maine proposed a treatment: if the patient were convinced that the desires and aspirations considered to be so evil and monstrous—artistic goals, sexual longings—were perfectly natural and healthy, if they were encouraged and ultimately acted upon, the patient would come to accept and love himself and learn to reject the harmful accusations and teachings of the religious zealots surrounding him.

No one took Dr. Maine seriously. In fact, according to the author, by the time Dr. Maine went public with his theory, he was exhibiting some rather bizarre behavior himself. He'd lost a great deal of weight, his hands shook as he stammered through his address, and his fellow psychiatrists speculated that Dr. Maine was nearing a breakdown.

They were right.

Only weeks after the 1978 conference where Maine shocked his colleagues into an embarrassed silence with his "findings," he was forcibly admitted to a mental institution, hysterical and violent, after being found running naked down a city street babbling wildly about monsters, "horrible flesh-eating monsters."

31

Dr. Maine was a small man with wiry hair the color of a silent film and, because it seemed appropriate to Roger's subconscious, he spoke with a stereotypical German accent. He sat facing Roger in a naugahyde chair hugging himself in a straitjacket and clamping a sweet-smelling pipe between his teeth. A strip of perspiration glistened like jewels above his wide darting eyes.

"Sumzink is vorryink you, no?" the doctor asked through clenched teeth, puffing smoke. "Ze monster, perhaps?"

"Yes."

"Yours or hers?"

"I'm sorry?"

"Your monster or *Zondra's* monster?"

"I don't understand."

"Vell, zat *is* ze problem, no?"

"The problem?"

Dr. Maine began rocking in his chair. "You und ze girl, you are zo much alike, no? Und your zymptoms are zo much alike, no? You *vant* her, und yet you *fear* her. She brings you too close to *zem*. You fear zat, had you not fought zem, *fled* zem, had not continued to exorcise your demons on paper, ze pain would have continued. Vould have come *out*. Like *hers*."

"Come out?"

"Like *zat*," Dr. Maine laughed, nodding toward Roger's stomach.

Roger looked down to find he was naked and his belly was bulging, leaking blood as it tore open and a hideously gnarled claw ripped its way out of him, dangling bracelets of viscera . . .

When he woke from the nightmare, he was sitting up, holding his belly and grunting; the pain was snacking on his guts again.

Roger had re-read the section titled LYCANTHROPY AND RELIGION until he knew it by heart, and then had run it through his mind again and again.

It seemed as if that section of the book had been written specifically for Roger, *meant* to be read by him.

Meant to frighten him.

And frighten him it did.

He tried to go back to sleep and did drop off a couple more times, but his sleep was shallow and diseased with nightmares he'd thought long gone . . .

He heard the thunderous footsteps of a giant raging messiah destroying the neighborhood as He bellowed, "Where's Carlton? Where *is* that little shit?" . . .

He hid in black filthy corners—a child again, weak and

terrified—as the Adventist hunters stormed around him with bright flashlights and powerful guns shouting, "There's one over there!" and "Hah—I got another one!" . . .

He writhed in bed as he dreamed his skin was moving over his body, changing, twisting . . .

And the claw. He saw it when the pain came in his sleep, its curved nails dark with blood . . .

He finally gave up and sat at his bedroom window with a drink, watching the sun rise behind a thick veil of raining clouds that glowed a dull steel gray. As he watched the day begin, he imagined Sondra waking, showering, eating breakfast as Bill limped silently around the house on his clicking leg. She would go to school, go from class to class, eat lunch with friends, acting like just another high school senior, a shy and silent teenager.

Acting as if she'd never hurt a soul, ended a life, or tasted blood.

Until it happened again.

And when will that be? he wondered.

Roger decided he had to talk with Sondra soon.

Today.

32

Roger parked outside the high school and waited for thirty minutes. Shortly before three o'clock, students began to spill down the front steps and scatter in the parking lot to board buses and speed away in cars. When he spotted Sondra, he honked his horn and called to her out the window.

She approached the car warily.

"We have to talk," he said.

"I can't. I've gotta go to work."

"I'll drive you. Get in."

"Roger, I'm not even supposed to—"

"Get. In."

Once she was in the car, he turned to her and asked how she felt.

"I'm . . . fine, I guess."

"You look tired."

She shrugged.

"Has it happened again?"

"Roger I told you to forget it."

"I *can't*. And neither can you. It's only going to get worse unless you try to do something. Look, I think I know what's wrong. What's causing it. It's not your fault, Sondra. It's—"

"I have to go to work." She opened her door and Roger reached across and pulled it shut, then started the car.

"Where?"

"Vintage Video."

Jesus, he thought. *First they let her work in a deli serving food they'd never let her eat, then they let her work in a store that rents movies they'd probably never let her watch. They may say I'm evil, but at least I'm consistent.*

As he drove, he told her what Niles had said about Sidney.

"They know something," he said. "I'm afraid maybe they've found him."

She seemed not to hear.

He parked the car in front of the video store, getting angry.

"Goddammit, Sondra, quit acting like nothing's wrong, like nothing's happened!" he snapped. "I think I can help you. I need to know if Bill knows about—"

Sondra gasped, looking out her window.

Bill stood outside the video store glaring at them.

"Oh, no," she breathed, closing her eyes, "oh no, no, no . . ."

"Jesus," Roger hissed. The dread in Sondra's face made him ache for her. He reached over and squeezed her hand as Bill began to hobble toward them. "Listen, Sondra, *listen* to me, you can get my number from Betty and call me anytime, I want to help you. Is there anything you should tell me?"

She looked at him with terrified eyes and whispered, "You should be very careful. Be careful of—"

Bill opened the door.

"C'mon," he said, his voice low and ominous.

Sondra quickly got out and Bill leaned into the car.

"I *had* to talk to her, Bill," Roger said quickly, "please believe me—"

"You've got nothing to say to her."

"Bill, *we've* got to talk, it's important, *very* important, it's about Sondra and I'm afraid that—"

"You've got nothing to say to me, either. And if I ever . . . *ever* . . . see you with Sondra again . . ." His lips trembled with quiet rage.

"Listen, Bill, we *have* to put our differences aside and talk about—"

"Just don't let it happen again." He stared at Roger with stony eyes a moment, then shook his head and said, "You were stupid to come back here." He slammed the door so hard the car shook.

As he drove home, Roger pounded the wheel with his fist, furiously cursing God, the church, and Bill Dunning.

33

When Roger got home, he was useless; he was angry and afraid and exhausted. He searched his bedroom, hoping to find a little pot to go to sleep by; he finally found a pipeful in his closet—

—along with his gun.

It was in its box, wrapped in a red cloth, where it had been since he'd lived in North Hollywood. He stared up at the closet shelf where it lay under a stack of books and, a few moments later, took it into the living room.

As he filled a pipe, Roger stared at the gun lying on his coffee table. He took a few hits, then picked it up, hefted it.

The phone rang and Roger had the urge to aim the gun and stop the noise with one shot, but the gun was empty.

The answering machine picked up.

A dial tone hummed into the recorder.

It would be nice to end his problems with a single gunshot, but shooting the phone wouldn't do it; they'd find another way to contact him. He could shoot *them* until his trigger finger fell off, but there would always be more to replace them.

There was only one person he could shoot to end it all.

God always finds a way to spill the blood of the sinners . . .

One person . . .

He returned to his closet and got a box of bullets, then started loading the gun.

Before he could finish, Roger heard someone crying outside his door. The bell rang and he recognized Sondra's voice calling his name.

He went to the door, pulling his robe closed and tying it.

She was covered with blood and her left eye was nearly swollen shut. Her clothes hung in tatters on her otherwise naked body and she was hugging herself, shaking violently. She looked very much like she had after killing Sidney Nelson and Roger wondered who had died tonight.

"I'm cuh-cuh-cold," she whimpered, falling into his arms.

The blood was cold and sticky, clinging to Roger's bare chest when his robe fell open. He kicked the door shut and carried her into the bathroom.

The remnants of her clothes peeled from her body easily, like tender meat from the bone, and he tossed it onto the floor.

"What happened?" he asked, holding a washcloth under hot water.

"I . . . I'm really not sure."

"Are you hurt bad?"

"Just my face."

"How?"

"Bill."

"He hit you?"

She nodded.

The dirty copper smell of blood was turning Roger's stomach and he flipped on the fan, then began to gently dab the blood away with the cloth.

"He beat up on you often?"

"Never this bad." She flicked her tongue over a loose tooth

and muttered, "I think I'm gonna lose that one."

"And the blood . . . where did it come from?"

"Some . . . man, I think. Out in the woods."

"The woods? Where?"

"Off Silverado Trail."

"Jesus Christ."

Once her face was clean, Roger hunkered down in front of her, took her bloody hands in his and spoke softly.

"You've gotta let me try to help you, Sondra. You can't keep doing this. And it'll *never* stop if you don't at least let me try."

With a slight shake of her head, she said, "That's why Bill beat me up. Because he found me with you."

"Why was he waiting for you at work?"

"To catch me doing something wrong." She pushed a blood caked strand of hair from her eyes. "He was afraid you'd try to see me because . . . well, he's been worried about you, because . . ."

"About *me*? Why?"

She looked away from him and said, "I want to wash."

Roger let it pass. He handed her the wash cloth, pulled back the curtain, and turned on the faucet. Pouring some bubblebath into the water, he said, "I'll leave you alone. Is there anything I can—"

"Don't leave me alone." she whispered, standing and pressing herself against him, crying softly. "Please don't."

Roger helped her into the tub, sat on the edge, and began passing the cloth over her back.

"Why is Bill so concerned about me?" he asked.

"He has been ever since you came."

"I didn't tell anyone I was coming. How did he know?"

She shrugged, then laid back in the tub, wetting her hair.

The same way somebody always managed to learn my phone number even when it was unlisted, Roger thought, *and the same way they always knew where I lived no matter where I went*.

Roger averted his eyes when her nipples broke the surface

of the water and rose through the foamy suds, erect as pencil erasers atop her pale breasts.

The marijuana had made him uncomfortably loose, just loose enough for the sight of Sondra's wet and soapy body to give him an erection despite the fact that the bathwater was brown with the blood of a dead stranger.

"I'm not going back," she whispered as Roger shampooed her hair. "I won't live with them anymore. With *him*."

"Where will you go? What will you do?"

"I don't know, but I can't live like that anymore." After a long silence, she said, "Can I . . . could I stay with you?"

He wanted to say yes immediately, say it without a second thought, but he couldn't.

"How about if we go see Bill together and I'll talk with him."

"Oh, God, no," she gasped. "No, he'd . . . he'd . . . no. You can't do that." She turned to face him, her head crowned with bloody suds. "They've been talking about you. A lot. Bill and some of the men from the church, elders and deacons. Especially lately."

"Why lately?"

"Marjie's been coming over."

"*Who*?" he asked, certain she wasn't talking about Marjie *Shore*.

"Marjie Shore. She told him . . . she said you had some books."

He remembered Marjie's reaction to his research books; he realized that was when things had changed between them, when she found the books, and he cursed his stupidity.

"She said you had some bloody clothes and . . . well, they all figured you were, you know, doing it again."

"Doing *what* again?"

"The rituals. Worshipping Satan."

"Jesus H. *Christ*, Sondra, I've *never* worshipped—"

"*I* know that. But they're convinced. That's why Bill was so upset with me. See, my whole family . . . all of them . . . have always thought there was something wrong with me, that I was evil, 'cause I've always been such a black sheep. Then

. . . when *this* started . . . you know, the *change* . . . they figured I was possessed, like I told you before.'' She laughed humorlessly. "So now they figure you and I are gonna get together, y'know? Have demon parties and maybe give birth to the anti-Christ, or something.'' Another laugh.

Roger was still shocked about Marjie. If she really thought he was serious about Satanism, why didn't she *say* so? Why didn't she confront him with it so he could defend himself instead of going to Bill—especially after talking about Bill as if he were crazy and she'd written him off—and stirring up ridiculous stories that weren't true.

You asshole, Roger thought to himself, *you knew the risks, you knew what might happen if you got involved with her again, you* knew, *goddammit!*

"Do you love her?'' Sondra asked.

Roger blinked his eyes rapidly, shaking off his thoughts. "Uh, no,'' he said. "Well . . . we used to be close, but . . .'' He didn't finish; he kept thinking, *How could she? How could she when things were going so well?*

He finally stood and said, "I'll get you a towel.''

Roger put her in his bed.

"Do they know where you are?'' he asked, pulling the covers up around her.

"No.''

"Should I call them? Let them know you're all right?''

"No, *please* don't!''

"Okay, okay. We'll wait until morning.'' He went to the door and turned out the light. "If you need anything, just call.''

"Roger?''

"Hm.''

"Please . . . stay with me.''

He sighed at the temptation, turned it over in his mind, but decided he'd already made one mistake too many.

"Get some sleep,'' he whispered, closing the door.

34

Roger made himself a drink, sat down in front of the television, and chewed on what Sondra had told him about Marjie until his feeling of betrayal had become a smoldering anger.

Two drinks later, the doorbell rang and Roger somehow knew that it was Marjie.

"Is she here?" she asked when he opened the door.

"Who?"

"Please, Roger, don't play with me. If she's here, let me take her home. If you know where she is, *tell* me. Please."

"I don't understand why it's any of your business, Marjie."

"I'm doing this for your own good, Roger."

"Oh? Running to Bill and telling him I'm worshipping *Satan*, for Christ's sake—was *that* for my own good, too?"

With a frustrated sigh, Marjie bowed her head and said, "Bill told me what happened today, and I thought—" Her words caught in her throat and she gasped, "Oh, my God!"

There were blood stains on the cream colored carpet.

"What have you done?" she breathed.

"Nothing, it was—it's just—she—"

"Sondra?" she called, scared now.

"She's fine, Marjie, she's sleeping."

"*Get* her." She was trembling, apparently from anger as well as fear.

"I'm going to take her home in the morning, don't worry. I'm going to talk with Bill about—"

"You *can't* take her home in the morning, Roger, *dammit*, will you listen! Right now Bill is getting some men together to come over here looking for Sondra and if they find her with you . . . Please, won't you just let me take her home. It'll save a lot of trouble."

Roger was livid. "They're coming over *here?* Jesus, like some fucking holy posse! And what will they do, *lynch* me? Hang me in a public place, maybe?" His voice was raising slowly to the level of a shout. "Very *Christian* of them, and certainly in keeping with everything else they've been doing, like the goat's head on my porch and the brick through DiMarco's window. Were you in on that, Marjie? Did you play along, huh? Maybe the goat's head was *your* idea. Inspired by my books, were you?''

"I had nothing to do with that. I didn't even know about it.''

"Uh-huh, sure.'' He stepped toward her and she moved back frightened. "I don't suppose you mentioned to Bill that you've been *fucking* the neighborhood Satanist, did you? Because if you did, the son of a bitch'd probably be throwing things through *your* window too, you ever think of that? *Huh?* Did it occur to you that you're dealing with a very sick person, here?

"Roger, h-he's a f-friend,'' she said, trying to hold in her tears. '' . . . *all* of us used to be f-friends.''

"And what brought that to a screeching halt? I never had any friends, Marjie. For the first twenty years of my life I never had any friends. Jesus, and to think I let you . . . all over again, I let you . . .'' Anger constricted his throat and he could say no more. He kicked the ottoman and it slid over the carpet and slammed into the coffee table, knocking off a full ashtray. "Get out of here.''

Moving back toward the door, Marjie shook her head and said, "No, Roger, I'm not—''

"Get the fuck *out* of here!''

Wringing her hands in front of her, she tried to sound calm and reasonable. "I'm not leaving without—''She looked over his shoulder. "Sondra!''

Roger spun around to see Sondra standing in the hall holding his robe before her.

"Sondra,'' Marjie pleaded, "please come with me. Bill is furious.''

She stepped back into the shadows, shaking her head.

"Sondra, *please!*'' She turned to Roger, her face red with anger.

"She's only seventeen, for God's sake, how could you . . . how *could* you?''

"How could I *what*? You think I'm fucking her? Well, I'm not. I'm trying to help her. No one else will. Maybe you've heard of it, it's called decency. You could use some." He turned toward the hall. "Go back to bed, Sondra." Stepping past Marjie to open the door, he said, "And you—go."

"I will not."

He grabbed her elbow and jerked her toward the door but she pulled away, screaming, "Let *go* of me! What's wrong with you, Roger, don't you see I'm trying to help you? I'm thinking of *you*." Her face twisted and tears rolled from her eyes as she massage her elbow. "You act like I hate you, or something, b-but I duh-*don't*." Her words garbled by sobs, she lowered her voice to a raspy whisper. "I've never for a second stopped loving you. And *admiring* you. You weren't afraid to do what you wanted to do even though everyone was telling you it was wrong. I . . . I never had that kind of strength. I'm a . . . conformist, Roger, a weak, spineless conformist. I've always admired your independence. I never *really* believed all that Satanist stuff, not back then, but I was . . . concerned about you. I was different back than, I bought it all, the whole philosophy, being saved, *all* that. And because you were breaking the rules . . . I wanted to *save* you. I'm not that way anymore. Well . . . not quite. But when I saw those books here . . . I looked through them and they're *awful*. I got scared. I thought maybe . . . maybe it *was* true. And those bloody clothes out in the garage . . . it made sense, sort of. I started to worry again and I talked to Bill. You say he's crazy—and he *does* have problems, I don't deny that—but he is a sincere Christian, a good Adventist and . . . I thought he could help, could tell me what to do. I was worried about you, Roger, that's all."

"Worried? That I was committing some great sin? Breaking a few commandments? Not following all of good old Sister White's rules? Is that what you were worried about while you were sipping wine like a *big girl*?" He spit the words mockingly, hurtfully, and Marjie's pain bled from her eyes; Roger enjoyed it. "Were you worried about that while you were smoking *pot*? Or sucking my *cock* out of *wedlock*?"

She pressed a fist to her chest and released an agonized cry.

"*You* were worried about *me*?"

"I was, I was wrong," she cried. "I was tuh-trying to, to *fit*, Roger, I *told* you I'm a conformist. I was trying so hard to fit into an environment that's still new to me. I don't really believe in that kind of life, I don't believe in . . . in . . . I don't know *what* I believe in. I'm always trying so duh-desperately to *fit*."

"You fucking hypocrite," he growled through gritted teeth just an instant before the pain tore through his guts. He doubled over, fell, tried to get up but fell again, groaning as it wrenched his insides.

"Roger?" Marjie sputtered.

He rolled over the floor, retching.

"Roger, what's wrong? Roger?"

"Go," he grunted. "Get out."

"Roger, what . . . what should I do? What's *wrong*?" Her tears were subsiding and the pain in her voice was replaced by urgency.

"Go . . . away." He tried to sit up but curled into a ball instead, releasing a high-pitched wail of misery.

It had never hit him so hard, had never been so intense. The pain exploded in his abdomen, sending shrapnel upward into his throat and downward into his testicles, down his arms to the very tips of his fingers. He screamed a shrill jagged scream, opening his eyes to see Marjie and Sondra standing over him, their mouths working soundlessly, and he realized he could no longer even hear his own voice, just a bone-deep throbbing in his ears, a powerful liquid rush that threatened to send his eyes shooting from their sockets.

He tried to speak, to plead for help, but he had no control over his tongue; it was a thick numb chunk of meat and his teeth were gritty pieces of stone that sliced at his lips like razors and his hands—

Sweet merciful Jesus my haaaands! his mind screamed.

—were cracking open, the fingertips splitting to make way for deadly hook-like claws.

When he looked up, Sondra was smiling as if she'd found a long lost friend, smiling and crying at once, and Marjie was pressing her fists to her mouth, shaking her head as she stumbled backward—

—and as the pain reached a crescendo, Roger felt a hatred for Marjie, a hatred so heavy and thick he felt he could vomit it up like a steaming lump of half-digested food and he swung his arm through the air clutching at Marjie's leg.

She turned to run but her foot struck the ottoman and she fell, arms and legs splayed as she hit the floor.

A thin veil of red covered Roger's vision as he crawled on all fours toward Marjie, the throbbing growing louder in his skull, the pain in his center turning into a deep, engulfing hunger. The red darkened to a rust . . .

. . . then to brown . . .

. . . then black . . .

35

Laughter.

High, musical, crystal-clear laughter.

Roger's vision returned slowly, rising from a dark sludge to a soft glow, from blurred light and colors to a slowly growing clarity.

The drumming pain in his head began to subside as physical sensations returned.

The floor beneath his back . . .

The carpet against his palms, strangely wet and warm . . .

And something else . . .

Something wonderful . . .

Roger moaned and slowly lifted his hips from the floor—

What's happened?

—sliding his cock deeper into the warm sucking mouth that held it.

Why am I here? On the floor? Doing this?

The sensation stopped, the laughter rang out again, then the sucking continued, the voice humming warmly, hands cupping his testicles and stroking his thighs . . .

"You're like me," the voice said, breath hot on his genitals. "We're the same . . ."

He tried to lift his head but was too weak, drained, empty . . .

"We're alike, Roger . . ."

It was Sondra.

Her hands moved over his stomach, his chest, up to his shoulders as she crawled up his body like a cat. Her fingers wrapped around his cock and she impaled herself on him, crying out in gleeful pain.

He tried to speak but only made a hoarse, clogged sound in his throat—

—and tasted the blood.

It slicked the inside of his mouth like oil and he coughed, retched, turned his head and spit as she moved on him.

"Aaahhh, yes, just alike . . . you and meeee . . ."

She leaned forward and placed her open mouth on his throat, licking and sucking, nibbling gently, her heavy breasts brushing his chest and abdomen.

Sitting up again, she reached behind her and held his testicles, squeezed, tugged . . .

There were spots on the ceiling, dark red spots that had not been there before, but he noticed them only peripherally because of the powerful warmth growing between his legs, spreading upward slowly . . .

Must be drunk, he thought, because he remembered nothing and didn't know how this had started. But he didn't care.

He found the strength to lift his head just enough to see her towering over him, grinding herself against him, her body covered with dark wet smears, one hand stroking a breast . . .

Her left hand . . .

On her right arm . . .

What's happened?

He blinked, squinted, certain his eyes were not seeing what he thought they were seeing . . .

Sondra held the left arm in her right hand. It was torn off at the elbow, the skin pale, the fingers splayed and slightly bent just enough to cup her breast, lift it, press it hard against her ribs . . .

"What . . . what's . . ." Roger croaked.

"We're the same," she breathed through a smile, eyes half closed, hair flowing over her shoulders . . .

Roger turned his head to the right, groaning when he saw the splash of blood on the side of the recliner . . .

The other arm beneath the coffee table . . .

The leg not far from that, a lump of bone protruding from the tattered glob of black-red meat above the thigh . . .

And the head . . .

Marjie's head rested on its side, mouth open in a scream, tongue hanging from the corner . . .

Roger screamed as he came, but it was not a scream of pleasure.

36

Sondra slid off him and curled up beside him on the bloody carpet, nuzzling his neck, purring like a kitten.

"No, no, no," Roger hissed, rolling over and getting on his knees, looking around at the scattered gory mess that used to be Marjie Shore, his first kiss, his first date, his first girlfriend. "I . . . I *did* this?" he cried. "Did *I* do this?"

Sondra embraced him from behind. "Mmm-hmmm. You're like me, Roger."

"No," he croaked, stumbling to his feet, "no, I . . . I couldn't have." But he knew he had. Marjie's blood was in his mouth; bits of skin and hair were stuck beneath his finger-nails. If he thought about it, if he were to close his eyes and concentrate on it, he knew he would remember doing it in the same murky way he might remember a bad dream.

He limped into the bathroom and splashed cold water on his face, then began to clean himself off so he could decide what to do next.

37

"We have to clean this up," he said, his voice unsteady, standing in the hall and facing the mess.

Sondra stood at the window staring at the night, twisting a strand of her hair around a finger.

"They'll be coming soon," she muttered softly.

A burst of adrenaline surged through Roger because he knew she was right and he clapped his hands together sharply and said, "C'mon, *c'mon*, get cleaned up, let's *go*."

Roger felt a crank-like rush as he dashed to the window and looked out to see Marjie's car parked on the street. He paced the room as Sondra slowly made her way down the hall.

This would be much more difficult than Sidney the bread man . . .

The phone rang and Roger ignored it.

"Roger?" It was Betty and she sounded very upset. "Roger, if you're there, *please*—"

He picked up. "What is it, Betty?"

"Oh, Roger, *Roger*—" He could tell she'd been drinking. "—it's the police, they're *everywhere*! Running around with their chemicals and little brushes and—"

"Betty, what are you talking about?"

"The police! They're here at the deli going over *everything*! They called me, got me out of bed, said they had a search warrant and that they, they've brought some men in from San Francisco, *lab* men, they said. It sounds like they're looking for *blood*!" she hissed, lowering her voice. "They're in the munch room, talking, whispering to each other, and Roger, they keep talking about *you*, Roger, they keep saying your *name*! I'm scared, Roger, what's going *on*? What have you *done*?"

Roger clutched the receiver so hard, his knuckles ached and he was struck with the urge to laugh, to throw back his head and guffaw; it was so *absurd*, all of it.

"Look, Betty, just . . . just . . ."

"You're keeping something from me," she said. "What *is* it? Does it have something to do with what happened here? With the brick through the window?"

"No, no, that's something . . . that's a . . . Jesus. Oh, Jesus." He did laugh then, a giggle at first that built to a deep belly laugh, and he had to sit down, holding his sides with one arm, his eyes filling with tears as Betty spoke his name again and again.

And then he heard the voices.

There were several of them outside, all male; first one spoke, then another, then all of them at once, as if in disagreement.

Then silence.

Footsteps.

Roger stopped laughing in time to hear one of them say, "I still think we should call the police."

Another said, "Well, as long as you don't *use* that gun, we'll be okay."

Gun?

"Betty," Roger whispered, "hang on a sec." He put down the receiver with Betty's pinched, insect-like voice still coming from the earpiece. Pulling the curtain aside slightly, Roger peered out the front window and saw five men coming across the lawn toward the house. Bill was leading them with a shotgun cradled in one arm. "Christ," Roger hissed, returning to the phone. "I'm sorry, Betty, but I've gotta go."

"You *can't*! I don't know what's—"

"I'm sorry," he said again before hanging up and rushing to the bathroom. Sondra stood naked before the mirror brushing her hair, her eyes heavy-lidded and distant as she whistled tunelessly through her teeth. "C'mon, we've gotta go," Roger said.

"Hm?"

"Get *dressed,* we have to—shit, you don't have any clothes." He led her to his bedroom where he took a pair of sweats from the closet; they were baggy on her, but there was no time to be choosy.

The doorbell rang.

Sondra turned to Roger with panic in her eyes.

Roger put a finger over his lips. "The back door," he whispered.

The bell rang again, three times in rapid, impatient succession.

After putting on his coat, Roger went to the living room and got his gun from the coffee table, loaded it, and stuffed it in his pocket, got his car keys, then led Sondra through the kitchen, out the back door and around to the side of the house. A drizzle was falling and an icy breeze made Sondra's teeth chatter.

As they rounded the front corner of the house and approached the car, Roger could hear Bill's deep, unfriendly voice:

"Roger? Open up. I've come for Sondra."

Sondra took Roger's hand and squeezed fearfully.

He quietly opened the door on the driver's side and waved Sondra in. Behind the wheel, he softly clicked the door shut and slid the key into the ignition.

Someone pounded on the front door and Bill shouted, "Roger? Sondra!"

"Let's go, Roger," Sondra whispered frantically, "please, please, *please* hurry, let's *go*, if he takes me home he's gonna be so mad . . ."

Roger started the engine, punched the car in reverse and sped out of the drive.

Even in the car, Roger could hear the burst of voices from the porch. The men turned and jogged to a pick-up truck and an old Pinto parked across the street. Bill hobbled behind them on his cane, glaring at Roger as he put the car in gear and drove away.

"He has a gun," Sondra said, frightened. "He means business. We have to go to the police, Roger, we have to—"

"No. Not the police."

"Why *not*?"

"I just killed somebody, remember? And now they think I killed Sidney Nelson, too." He quickly told her about Betty's phone call, glancing in the rearview mirror to see the truck and Pinto turning around to follow him. "If they've got a warrant to search the deli and they've brought a bunch of lab guys in from San Francisco, *they* mean business, too.''

"Then . . . then what're we gonna *do*?"

Roger took a sudden left off Beekman, then another left on Watson.

"First, we've got to lose them," he said, taking yet another turn, zig-zagging past warmly lit houses with smoke rising from the chimneys. "Then we've got to get rid of this car."

Then what? he thought. *Leave town? Hide out? Take a minor across the state lines and up your sentence?*

Headlights appeared in the rearview mirror.

"Damn!" Roger barked, hitting the wheel.

"Where are we going?"

He rounded another corner, increasing his speed, making his way toward Silverado Trail. He thought about that, going over his options, which didn't take long, then said, "To see my friend Josh."

38

Josh lived in one of a row of small bungalow-like houses on the south side of town, behind which ran a narrow alley.

Roger parked his car in the alley where it would be invisible from the street, went through the gate that opened onto the small rectangle of grass that served as a back yard, and knocked on the back door. When there was no answer, no sound from inside at all, he knocked again and called for Josh.

"Maybe he's gone," Sondra whispered, shivering as she looked around them nervously.

"No, he's very sick." Roger knocked again.

They'd managed to stay far enough ahead of Bill and his friends to get to Josh's without being tailed, but now Roger began to think perhaps they'd gotten there for nothing.

When he tried the door, it opened easily.

"Josh?" Roger called, taking Sondra's hand and going inside. He checked all the rooms, but the small house was empty. When he looked out the front window, he muttered, "His car's

gone. But where could he . . ." Then he turned to the sofa
where he'd seen the neatly placed clothes the day before—
—and he knew.

I'm going to disappear . . .

Roger slumped onto the sofa and scrubbed his hands over
his face, hating himself for being so blinded by his own problems that he didn't see what Josh was about to do—even after
Josh had *told* him what he was going to do.

"My . . . God . . ." Sondra whispered.

Her voice startled Roger; he'd forgotten he wasn't alone.
She stood across the room looking at a row of pictures on the
wall.

"What?" he asked.

"Him." She pointed at one of the pictures, backing away
slowly crying.

Roger stood and looked over her shoulder at the picture; it
was Josh at Disneyland, a much healthier Josh but still quite
obviously ailing, standing between Mickey and Minnie, arm
in arm, grinning like a thrilled little boy.

"It was him," she whispered. "The man. In the woods.
Tonight. It was *him* . . ."

39

Roger stumbled backward and fell onto the sofa again, his
arms loose at his sides.

"He's . . . the one . . . you killed?" He weakly lifted an arm
and pointed at the picture. "That was his blood?"

Fingertips covering her mouth, tears sparkling in her eyes,
she nodded. "He looked really sick, but yeah, it was him."

"He was sick," Roger breathed. "He had AIDS."

Sondra turned to him slowly, very slowly, her jaw slack,
face blank, eyes disbelieving.

"Whuh . . ." She swallowed dryly, leaning against the wall.
"What did you say?"

Roger repeated himself.

They looked at one another for a long time, their eyes speaking for them, both thinking of the same things—the blood that had covered Sondra when she arrived at Roger's, their love-making on the floor earlier—then Sondra crossed the room, her steps small and clumsy, and knelt before Roger, lips trembling.

"I'm sorry," she rasped.

"You couldn't have known."

She took his hands in hers and made a futile attempt to smile.

"We're gonna die anyway," she said.

"I know."

The gun resting heavily in Roger's coat pocket suddenly felt comforting, not as a means of defense, but of escape.

They held each other for a long moment until they heard engines slowing outside and Sondra pulled away from him and said, "That's Bill's pick-up."

40

When Roger looked out the window, Bill was limping toward the house. He met Roger's eyes with a smile as cold as a tomb and called, "I figured you'd be here with your fag friend," his voice padded by distance. He still held the shotgun in his arm, but appeared to be alone now.

Roger dropped the curtain and turned to Sondra.

"Let's go!" He grabbed her arm and rushed her back out to the car. She got in and slammed her door as Roger hurried around the front of the car—

—and staggered to a halt.

The left front tire had been slashed and was now flat and useless.

So was the right.

And the two in the rear.

"Out, out," he stammered, waving her from the car, "they've slashed the tires."

"What?" she cried, panicked.

"C'mon." He pulled her out and, holding her arm, led her toward the north end of the alley—

—where two men were headed toward them taking long rapid steps. One of them carried a baseball bat, the other a flashlight.

Sondra backpedaled, gasping, "No, no, no, no . . ."

"Just give us the girl," one of the men said.

They walked with such purpose, such force, that Roger wanted to cringe, frozen in place. Instead, he steeled himself and led Sondra in the opposite direction; his heart battered his ribs as he broke into a jog.

For an instant—a terrifying, brain-searing instant—he was a child again, the child of his nightmare, weak-kneed with fear, the debilitating fear of a hunted animal looking for a place to hide.

He reached into his jacket pocket and clutched the cold, heavy gun, holding it like a lover in a last embrace.

Sondra began to cry, coughing sobs that made her stumble against Roger and nearly fall; he held her up and dragged her with him until they reached the cross street.

"This way," he gasped, pulling her to the right—

—and scrambling to a stop when Bill rounded the corner before them.

His stiff leg clicked as he neared them, hefting the shotgun threateningly.

Once again, Roger and Sondra began to walk backwards, clinging closely to one another.

"Sondra!" Bill shouted. "Come here. Now. Annie's worried sick."

Roger said, "Bill . . . Bill, you've gotta listen to me."

"No. No, I don't." He aimed the shotgun at Roger.

"You don't want to do that, Bill. You'll take us both out with that thing."

"Maybe that'd be good. You're both as evil as the night is dark."

Roger thought with chilling certainty, *He's insane.*

"Listen, Bill, Sondra is *sick.* What you're doing is only making her worse. She needs help. She needs—"

"She needs to get away from you, that's what she needs. She's always been a problem, but you've only made it worse. She needs to get down on her knees and plead for God's forgiveness. Isn't that *right*, Sondra?"

Digging her fingers into Roger's arm, groaning miserably, Sondra leaned forward, clutching her stomach, and Roger put an arm around her shoulders to support her.

"No, Sondra," he whispered, "hang on, don't let it happen now."

There were hurried footsteps behind them; the other men were closing in.

Roger remembered the baseball bat and, holding Sondra close to his side, he drew his gun, spun around and leveled it at the man who was holding the bat over his head, preparing to strike.

The bat clattered to the sidewalk.

The yellow sodium glow of the tall streetlights above them cast deep shadows over the shocked faces of the two men; they were both large, like lumberjacks or truck drivers, but they backed away cautiously, keeping their eyes on Roger's gun.

"Stay back!" Roger barked, waving the gun suddenly. Both men were startled and one fell backward into a patch of bushes growing along a fence.

Sondra struggled in Roger's embrace as he turned toward Bill. She hid her face against his shoulder, her voice a muffled growl as she began to chew on his jacket.

"Why have you done this, Bill?" Roger cried, his voice strained. "Why do you—"

Sharp teeth broke through his jacket and pierced his flesh; Sondra writhed in pain against him and Roger felt blood trickling down his arm beneath his clothes, felt her teeth gnaw deeper into his arm, and—

—zhe felt something else: a blade-fingered fist of pain closing around his entrails, squeezing, crushing . . .

No, Roger thought, *no, not now, please not now!*

The pain raged and Roger dug his elbow into his side as hot bile rose in his throat. He swallowed, coughed, and continued:

"Why do you *keep* doing this?"

Bill started toward them as they staggered backward, the shotgun aimed at Roger's midsection; an icy smirk broke the surface of his hard face, but he said nothing.

"It's gone on too long," Roger gasped, trying to conceal his pain. "It's time to stop now, time to . . . to just . . . leave me alone."

Still no response.

Roger screamed, "*What do you want from me, a fucking apology?*"

A door slammed somewhere on the block and a voice shouted. "Take it home or I'm calling the cops, asshole! People are tryna sleep!"

Bill spoke softly: "It's too late for repentance now, Roger. You're too far gone and you've taken too many souls with you." His prosthetic leg clumped as he walked; the rubber end of his cane made sloppy kissing sounds on the wet sidewalk. In a monotonous droning voice, he began to recite: "The books you've written, Roger . . . they're evil. 'Developed by agents of Satan.' Recognize those words, Roger. Know what that makes *you*, Roger? An agent of Satan. Bewitching the minds of your readers 'with theories formed in the synagogue of Satan.' Recognize *those* words, Roger?"

Roger was crying now, overwhelmed by the pain as he stumbled into the street with Sondra leaning on him heavily, her cries garbled against him, her fingers digging into his chest now, tearing his shirt.

"They were written by Ellen White. God's prophet. Heaven's scribe. Leader of the Remnant Church. She used her gifts for *Him*, for *His* glory. But you . . . *you've* used yours for the Prince of Darkness. *You* are an agent of Satan. *You* have put his words into every bookstore and supermarket in the country and you have trampled on the Truth to do it! You've rejected God's word and His plan for you in favor of leading precious souls to the lake of fire!" His voice was raising, trembling with righteous indignation. "Every person who reads one of your books is a step closer to eternal damnation and you are responsible for their loss!" He kept coming steadily: step . . . *clump* . . . step . . . *clump* . . . "You're a disease, Roger, and you're spreading, infecting minds, turning thousands—maybe *millions*—away from the plan of salvation by corrupting them with the Devil's dictations!''

The man who had fallen into the bushes struggled to his feet and warily approached Bill saying, ''Bill . . . c'mon now, Bill, that's enough, don't you—''

''Back off, Matt!'' Bill snapped, then turned to Roger again, lifted his cane and pointed an unsteady finger at him, bellowing, ''*You . . . have to be . . . stopped!*''

Sondra pulled her teeth from Roger's shoulder; he couldn't feel the bite because it was eclipsed by the pain that was spreading inside him, digging its way into his testicles and down his arms as it had earlier that night.

Bill dropped his cane and lifted the shotgun to his shoulder.

''Run!'' Roger cried, pushing Sondra across the street toward the alley that continued on the other side.

''No, Bill, wait!'' one of the men shouted, afraid now, apparently unaware that Bill would go to such an extreme.

Roger ran after Sondra in a half-crouch, the intensity of his pain making him unable to stand upright. He felt spittle dribbling down his chin, felt himself quickly losing control over his own body.

He cried Sondra's name but it came from his mouth a thick and mangled sound: ''Shon-daaahhh!'' As he reached the alley, he heard the shotgun explode . . .

41

Time slowed to a heavy crawl after the gunshot.

Roger tried to run fast when he heard the shotgun go off, hoping to round the corner and duck into the alley for protection before he was hit, but he felt the burning sprinkle of buckshot over his back and legs and he fell, skinning his palms on the ground. His skin felt like fire and his clothes clung to his small bloody wounds.

He didn't stop moving; Roger crawled for a bit, sobbing as

he looked down at his hands scrambling over the ground below him and saw the black claws scraping the pavement.

"No. *No!*" He fought the pain and the changes that were quaking through his body, tried to hold them off by biting his lower lip until he tasted his own blood, trying to use one pain to battle another.

On his left was a tall brick wall and on his right a cyclone fence that separated a row of backyards from the alley. He hooked his clawed fingers into the fence wire and pulled himself up. The fence was crawling with ivy through which webs of soft light from the houses on the other side cut into the murky alley. He pushed away from the fence and staggered on toward Sondra, who was even farther ahead of him now.

Every few yards, a garbage bin hunkered against the wall like a giant metal toad patiently waiting for a passing morsel; a cat dove from the top of one of the bins and shot across the alley in front of Roger.

Up ahead, Sondra careened back and forth down the alley like a pinball, slamming into the fence, then the wall, her arms joined over her abdomen and her miserable cries echoing in the night.

Roger called her name again, more clearly this time, gaining on her in spite of the flames of pain licking his back and legs.

The sound of a scuffle broke out behind him.

"Go then!" Bill shouted. "Don't take part in the Lord's work! *Let* evil spread like a—"

"This is not what we came to do!"

"No," a third voice insisted, "Bill's right, he *is* evil, he's—"

"It's what *I* came to do," Bill growled. "It's what I'm *supposed* to do. It's part of His plan for me . . ."

Roger glanced over his shoulder but could not see them; they hadn't reached the alley yet. He wondered where the other two were.

Sondra collided with a corner of one of the bins, spun like a top, and sprawled onto the ground face down.

Kneeling beside her, Roger rolled her over.

Bits of gravel clung to her forehead and her left eyebrow

was bleeding from a deep gash and she was shaking like a junkie in need of a fix.

Her skin was moving over her face, shifting into a leathery distortion, then smoothing again; her chin jutted as her mouth snapped open and shut, open and shut, like a deadly trap, spitting and snarling.

Roger put the gun back in his pocket and helped her up; she couldn't stand but was able to sit up, leaning against him. Her eyes seemed to notice him for the first time and she clasped his wrists in her hands.

"Roger, Roger!" she gasped, speaking as if through a mouthful of barbed wire. "Make it stop, please, make it go away!"

Her fingers tightened painfully on his wrists and her knuckles became knobby and purple before his eyes; at the same time, Roger realized that *his* hands were his own again—the claws were gone.

"Please make it stop, Roger, kill me, kuh-kill me now before I—" Her head fell back and she gurgled in her throat; her teeth ground together loudly as they lengthened, sharpened, splitting her gums—then they returned to their normal shape and size. She began to thrash and pummel Roger's chest with her fists— which were once again dainty and pale and smooth-skinned— hissing, "I hate them, I *hate* them, oh God *howIhatethem!*"

"Stop it, Sondra!" He tried to hold her but she was too strong and broke away—

—as voices neared them from ahead.

"The shot came from over there," a man said.

"Yeah," another replied, "maybe through that alley. Bill? That you?"

"Jesus, stand *up*, Sondra!" Roger had her by one arm and jerked her to her feet. "Be quiet," he hissed, looking around. He could see no one at either end of the alley but the voices were near and he knew they would be trapped in seconds. Holding tightly to Sondra, he searched frantically for an exit, a refuge.

He might be able to get over the fence, but he knew it would be impossible for Sondra.

"Over here," he whispered into her ear, dragging her to one of the gates that opened onto a backyard. He pushed and pulled on it, groping for a latch—

—and a flash of yellowed fangs and pink-black gums burst from the darkness, barking viciously, and Roger dove away from the gate as a doberman slammed itself against the mesh.

A porch light came on, illuminating the yard, and a woman shouted from inside the house: "Hush, Julius, shut *up* right *now*!"

From one end of the alley, Bill shouted, "Damn, now I've lost them! Where'd they go?"

From the other end: "Bill? Where are you?"

"John? That you?"

Sondra's knees buckled and she whimpered, "Kill me, please, before he finds me . . ."

Roger jerked her over to the nearest garbage bin, lifted the lid and leaned it silently against the wall. With a gush of breath, he lifted Sondra in his arms and dropped her into the bin, climbed in after her, and pulled down the lid.

The stench of rotten vegetables and cat shit and leftover foods and old cigarette butts and a dozen other odors stung Roger's eyes and nostrils and made him gag.

Sondra immediately tried to climb back out, hacking dryly, and Roger pulled her back down, slapping a palm over her mouth.

"Don't move, Sondra! Be very quiet!"

She mumbled into his hand and he pressed her head to his chest.

Footsteps clopped on the wet pavement outside.

"You get him?" John asked.

"He was hit," Bill replied, "but not bad. Not bad enough."

Roger closed his eyes and tried to calm his raspy breaths. Surely someone in the neighborhood had called the police about the gunshot; Roger didn't care to see them arrive either, but they were preferable to *this*.

"I thought they came down here," one of the voices said.

More footsteps, then Bill said, "Maybe they did."

There was a thunderous *gong* that bounced the length of the alley, lingering for several seconds.

Bill shouted, "You in there?" After several of Bill's limping steps, the gong sounded again. "Where *are* you, Roger? You can't hide from God, you know. He'll find you."

Gaaawwwnngg . . .

"And so will I."

Roger realized what Bill was doing: walking down the alley hitting each of the bins with his cane.

"Come on, Roger." *Gaaawwwnngg . . .* "Your probation is over. Judgement Day is here."

He's gonna find us before the cops get here, Roger thought with sickening dread.

Sondra's hands groped over his jacket and he grabbed her wrists, trying to make her stop. Her fingers were black with blood; he wondered if it was hers or his.

"Please," she said, her voice less than a whisper. "Please kill me." She pulled her hands loose and reached for his pockets. "Kill me, Roger. Please . . ."

She opened her mouth and vomited loudly, slapping her hands over her face, clawing at her eyes—

—which were filling with an evil, golden glow beneath eyebrows that were becoming sharp ridges.

"No-no, Sondra, don't let it—"

She joined her hands together in a doubled fist and swung upward, catching Roger under the chin and knocking his head against the wall of the garbage bin—

—and firecrackers went off in his skull and voices whispered in his ears.

The next echoing gong was not the sound of Bill's cane whacking one of the garbage bins but a footstep, a huge monolithic footstep followed by another, and another, accompanied by the roaring voice of an angry messiah that only Roger could hear:

Where's Carlton? Where is that little shit? Where—

"—*are* you, Roger?" Bill shouted.

"Look, Bill," one of the men said quietly. They were very

close now, just a few feet from the bin. "Maybe you should give this up, you know? I mean, there's—"

—*one over there!* a loud male voice echoed off the inner walls of Roger's skull.

The pop of a gunshot was followed by laughter.

Got him!

Running feet and panting lungs sounded all around Roger's hiding place.

There's another one! someone shouted enthusiastically. *It's a woman! Quick, get—*

"—off my back, Matt," Bill ordered. "I *have* to do this. It's my purpose. It's His will."

Roger squeezed his head between his hands as if trying to put it back together. He opened his throbbing eyes and, dark as it was, could see Sondra's claws tearing at her clothes as she gagged and tried to gulp air, growling, "Raaaaw-juuhhh! Kuuhhh maaayy! *Peeeeze!* Kuuhhh maaayy!"

She slammed her bulging knuckles into the wall of the bin and the metal made a thick wrinkling sound beneath the force of the blow.

"There!" Bill cried. "Hear that?"

Roger's hands began to fumble over his coat pocket, one holding the pocket open while the other clutched at the gun, getting a grip on the butt and pulling it out—

—but not before Sondra's arms flailed spastically in the dark, hitting Roger in the face, clawing his cheek, and knocking his head against the metal wall again—

—and he was on his back on the bloody carpet, naked, with Sondra sliding slowly up and down his cock.

Josh stood over them; he was healthy again, smiling, arm-in-arm with Mickey and Minnie. Mickey giggled as he scratched his back with one of Marjie's arms.

"What . . . what is it a-again?" Roger stuttered.

Josh said, "Five to seven years. Maybe sooner. Who knows? But think about it. Even if you've got seven years of health left, what kind of years will they be? I mean, *listen* to them!"

From somewhere in the distance, Roger could hear Bill shouting his name in a voice filled with hatred.

"And if it's not *them*," Josh said as he and the two big grinning mice slowly began to dissolve, "it'll be the cops, right? And they won't believe the truth. Nobody ever believes the truth."

Yeah, Roger thought, hearing the far-off wail of a siren steadily drawing nearer, *the cops . . .*

"And what kind of life will *she* have?" Josh muttered sadly, nodding toward Sondra, who bucked and writhed on top of him, her skin shriveling, breasts collapsing like large draining boils, fangs shredding her own lips. "Providing she lives at all, that is." Josh was a faint glow now, fading to a mist. "Remember, Roger . . . in the end, they always win . . ."

. . . they always win . . .

. . . always win . . .

The echo of his words dwindled as he became little more than a shadow . . .

Mickey waved goodbye with Marjie's arm as the three of them disappeared . . .

The gun.

It was in his hand.

Heavy.

Almost too heavy for his weakened fingers to grasp.

He lifted it—

I'm so sorry . . .

—and fired.

The sound was deafening in the small space and in the white flash of gunshot, Roger saw the small hole bloom like a flower in Sondra's left cheek and felt lumpy warmth splatter his face.

Sondra's body convulsed a few times, then grew still.

Through the ringing in his ears, Roger heard Bill cry, "Over here! In this one over here!"

The lid of the bin flew up and hit the wall with a loud *clang*.

A beam of light shined in Roger's eyes.

Bill screamed.

The siren grew louder.

In the light, Roger saw his hands: the claws sticking from his fingers, the patchy hair and mottled, crusty skin.

Has it happened again? he wondered. He hadn't noticed the pain or the sickness . . .

"Oh dear *Lord*!" Bill shrieked. "Oh, Father in heaven!"

The flashlight slipped from his hand and fell in Sondra's lap.

Beneath the blood that ran down her cheek like tears, her face was smooth and unblemished once again.

Lifeless . . . but beautiful.

The monster was gone.

Roger's eyes filled with tears, his heart with loss, and his gut with hatred and he shot to his feet in spite of the dizziness brought on by loss of blood. He slapped a hand aside Bill's head and closed his fist on a clump of hair, pulling Bill close to his face, pressing the barrel of his gun to Bill's throat.

Forming his words with effort, Roger screamed, "Look . . . what . . . you've . . . done!"

The other men stood around the bin like statues of ice.

Bill's pale face quivered like Jell-O, his eyes impossibly wide.

A deadly silence fell over the alley, broken only by the siren, which was just blocks away, and by the soft hissing trickle of Bill's urine spilling down his leg as he pissed his pants.

"Look . . . what . . . you've done . . . to uuuussss!"

Roger wasn't even sure if they could understand what he was saying; his words were garbled by the mouthful of needle-like shards that his teeth had become . . .

But it didn't matter.

In the end, nothing mattered because—

—*they always win.*

Roger stuffed the gun into his own mouth, bit down on the barrel, and leaned into Bill's face.

In the half-heartbeat before Roger squeezed the trigger, his mind screamed, *I only wish I could live long enough to see my blood splash all over your fucking head you goddamned worthless hypocritical son of—*

42

AUTHOR'S PAST REVEALS
SATANIC CULT CONNECTIONS

Napa

Police have been busy sorting through the past of best-selling author Roger Carlton who killed himself, 17 year old Sondra Nivens, and at least four other people over the last 18 months, including Nivens' parents, Paul Nivens, 49, and Georgia Nivens, 40, Sidney Nelson, a 44 year old bakery delivery man from Rutherford, and Napa resident Marjie Shore, 28.

According to Police reports and people close to the author, Carlton, who twice hit the best-seller lists with his novels of murder and sexual obsession, was an active member of a Satanic cult, although the specific cult still remains a mystery. Books on Satanism and the occult were found in his St. Helena home, along with keys belonging to one of Carlton's victims.

The FBI took up the case in a surprise turn two weeks ago when it was learned that Carlton ''just dropped completely out of sight for about 11 months last year, during which time Paul and Georgia Nivens were murdered in Berrian Springs, Michigan,'' according to FBI agent Garson Petrie.

Although some questions still remain unanswered, investigators believe Carlton met Sondra during those 11 months, while she was living with her parents, and involved her in his Satanic practices. After the death of her parents, Sondra moved in with her cousin Annie Dunning and her husband Bill in Manning, California. Investigators believe she participated in the murders that took place shortly after Carlton returned to St. Helena, a neighboring town, where he had lived six years earlier.

Bill Dunning, who attended college with Carlton, was the last to see the writer alive and witnessed his suicide.

Minutes later, he was found by police, running down an alley in St. Helena. According to attending officer Brian Spottaford, Dunning was screaming, ''Jesus help me! Jesus help me! I've seen the face of Satan!'' That night, he was admitted to the psychiatric ward of St. Helena Medical Center.

When asked what he meant by ''the face of Satan,'' Dunning said, ''Naturally I was upset. I'd just seen a man die. But he *was* evil. Roger was always evil. I've been saying that for years, but nobody's believed me. I guess they believe me now. . . .''

In the end, they always win . . .